Down to the Sea for Kicks

Samuel Fullerton

Published by Richter Publishing LLC www.richterpublishing.com

Book Cover Design: Richter Publishing

Editors: Erica Bouza & Jesse Olson

Book Typesetting: Kate Sabol

ISBN: 978-1-945812-81-1 Paperback

DISCLAIMER

This book is a fictional story based on life events of Sam Fullerton and is intended for entertainment purposes only. This information is provided and sold with the knowledge that the publisher and author do not offer any legal or medical advice. In the case of a need for any such expertise, consult with the appropriate professional. This book does not contain all information available on the subject. This book has not been created to be specific to any individual people or organization's situation or needs. Reasonable efforts have been made to make this book as accurate as possible. However, there may be typographical and or content errors. Therefore, this book should serve only as a general guide. This book contains information that might be dated or erroneous and is intended only to educate and entertain. The author and publisher shall have no liability or responsibility to any person or entity regarding any loss or damage incurred, or alleged to have incurred, directly or indirectly, by the information contained in this book or as a result of anyone acting or failing to act upon the information in this book. You hereby agree never to sue and to hold the author and publisher harmless from any and all claims arising out of the information contained in this book. You hereby agree to be bound by this disclaimer, covenant not to sue and release. All characters appearing in this work are fictitious. Any resemblance to other real persons, living or dead, is purely coincidental. The opinions and stories in this book are the views of the authors and not those of the publisher.

The happiest lot on earth is to be born a Scotsman.

You must pay for it in many ways...

You have to learn the Paraphrases and the Shorter Catechism;

you generally take to drink;

your youth... is a time of louder war against society,

of more outcry and tears and turmoil,

than if you had been born, for instance, in England.

But somehow life is warmer and closer;

the hearth burns redly;

the lights of home shine softer on the rainy street...

by Robert Louis Stevenson, 1883

CONTENTS

DEDICATION

I dedicate this book to my lovely wife, Shirley. She helped me type this story over 30 years ago in 1989 on a typewriter. After her death in 2003, I shelved the story away for good. It wasn't until 2019 I decided to pull it out of a box, dust it off, and finally have it published in her memory.

INTRODUCTION

This story is based on my life when I was a musician working on cruise ships back in the 60's and 70's. This was a pivotal time for the cruising industry. It used to be a much more exclusive affair, with only the wealthiest clientele choosing to cruise. None the less, they never had any idea what was going on within the lower decks with the shipmates. However, in the 70's emerged a more modern version like the ones we have today. Along with the ABC's TV series, *The Love Boat*, being released, everyday people now saw it as a vacation in which they could allow themselves to let loose. It was a fun time full of crazy shenanigans. This story is a glimpse into one cruise with my fellow band members back in the 70's. Come aboard with me as we embark on a journey back in time.

DAY 1

It was the first week in December. New York was experiencing a dry, cooling trend. It was freezing around the dock area at Pier 90. The huge liner, S.S. Nectar, was encased in rows of icicles, extending from the upper decks to the water line due to a snow storm the previous day. This situation was causing the captain to sweat blood at the thought of how the ship would look thirty-six hours from now when they reach the warmer weather on their way to St. Thomas. In the past, depending on the amount of ice, as it melts so goes the ship's paint. When this happens, instead of a beautiful luxury liner sailing onto the islands majestically, the shore people are greeted with a scarred, marred replica of the African Queen.

At the aft end of the ship, a gangway extended onto the lower level of the pier used by crew and shore workers. A slim built, middle aged man descends the gangway dressed in a black suburban coat with a fur collar. He is the drummer in the ship's orchestra. Reaching the dock, he is greeted by the cop on watch, who obviously knows him.

"Hi, Scotty; ready for a cold one?"

"Jesus Christ," came the reply. "How do you morons suffer this?" A cold shiver seized him after leaving the warm confines of the ship. "Just think, two days from now I will be lying on the beach basking in the warm tropical sun, while you are here keeping the welders busy!"

"Oh, get out of here ya bum!" the cop replied good naturedly as he beat his gloved hands together.

Scotty walked over to the dock edge and rested his elbows on the rail. He was waiting for his buddy who would disembark any minute now. Scotty looked up at the ship that had been his home for many trips. He thrilled as he felt the pulse emanating from her and the accompanying vibrations that were in tune with his own excitement of leaving harbor.

On the bridge, the officers were checking alarms and bells. Deck crews were getting everything ship-shape and battening down all moveable objects. The engine room staff were busy getting up steam. Dining room stewards were teasing each other as they laid the tables in anticipation of the monsters that would descend on them in a couple of hours to gorge on the first of many culinary delights.

Glancing upwards to the boat deck, his attention rested on a group of junior engineers leaning on the rail. They were known as seagoing studs and believed it to be their purpose to service all available females who boarded the ship. Dressed in nice white bib overalls, they looked and sounded like a flock of cooing doves as they passed judgement on the women ascending the upper level gangway.

"Look at the ass, on that one!" Coo! Coo!

"See the boobs on her!" Coo! Coo!

"Wonder if her old man's with her?" Coo! Coo!

These junior and warrant officers had, at certain times, permission to use the passenger facilities and bars; this enabled them to make contact with any and all desirable females. There are two phenomena that exist whenever people board a ship and sail away on the briny. One is their lack of morals and the other is an insatiable appetite for booze. All sexual inhibitions desert the females and the land lubber "sailors" try to drink the ocean dry. The younger engineers have their own wardroom which is used as a halfway house to lure the unsuspecting broads. They even have their own alcoholic concoction known as the "depth charge." Which is brewed in what can only be described as a witch's cauldron. After ingesting this love potion, the "ladies" will be spirited off to one of the love nests somewhere in the working alleyway to participate in the ultimate sacrifice. Of course, many a seduction has been ruined by the lamb's digestive system. Unable to cope with the poison consumed, she would empty her stomach by mouth all over the officer's nice white uniform. There is a God!

Scotty had a peaceful look on his face as his thoughts drifted back to younger days. As a little boy during the weekends, when there was not any school to worry about, his only pleasure was to dress in his best suit, collar, and tie and remove himself from the sordid side of the slums. He always headed for the Glasgow dockyards. Although they were not located in what could be described as any better part of town, just the presence of water and ships blotted out the surrounding environment.

Dressing up was another pleasure he enjoyed. That was one thing about Glasgow: anytime you left your own district, even if you were only going downtown or to visit relatives, you always looked your best. A tradition sadly lacking in the States. He learned early that the custom here seems to be the more prosperous, the more you endeavored to look like a bum.

Scotty's joy at that time was riding a tram car to Anderson and then taking the ferry across the River Clyde. This provided a little closer view of the cargo boats sitting at their mooring when the ferry passed under their bows. It could also cause the hairs on the back of his neck to rise with excitement. After this little trip, it was back on the tram car and to another dock to see which liners had just arrived. He was always envious of the suntanned crew that were either looking over the rail or disembarking for a little jaunt ashore. As he gazed at the big ship and watched the seamen, his thought of course was to be like them one day. Go to sea. Sail the tropics and return home all suntanned with a pocketful of money.

Scotty smiled, realizing that this early goal had indeed come true. He had a suntan and didn't do too bad with cash, but why did his dreams have to end? All the glamour and excitement of the little boy was gradually turning sour. The wonder of going to sea displayed at youth was being replaced by a cynical attitude as he grew older.

His thoughts drifted back to those days as a lad of ten and some of his more pleasurable moments. Twilight was his favorite time of day. They were long during the summer in Scotland. In the evening he could be found sitting on the sidewalk with his back against his tenement building listening to a loud bagpiper playing a Piobaireachd (pronounced: pea-broke). The piper was playing on the fifth floor of another building with the window open. This brought great delight to Scotty. There was also the sound of the bread carts with their iron clad wheels rumbling on the cobbled street. It was like a million marching men. The carts were returning after a hectic day of sales in the slums. The looms in the carpet factories were at last silent for an evening's rest. The drunken relics, whose only solace from their misery was the bottle, had ceased fighting with their wives. Each had at last crawled into his hole-in-the-wall bed in an effort to sleep the day's imbibing.

Scotty stood by the ship, but he was in his own gloaming listening again to the lament of the pipes in his thoughts. He was transformed to that feeling of peace and tranquility. He had heard people say that they could not stand the sound of bagpipes, but these morons only associate them with bands marching down the street. The magic was found in the Piobaireachd, the classic of the pipes. It is not something you hear, but something you feel deep inside. The melancholy strains of the grace notes wended their way through the deserted streets, between the tenement buildings, and finally to the very heart of one's being. 'Tis a pity this music had to share the environment with such poverty, degradation, and hopelessness felt by the inhabitants of those five story hovels. That little boy knew that he would escape one day and share his love for the pipes in more pleasant surroundings. The music was a blessing after all.

Hearing a familiar voice talking to the cop snapped Scotty's attention back to the present as he looked towards the source.

"Oh, there you are," said Scotty to his buddy who had just disembarked down the same gangway. "Ready to eat?"

The ship would sail at 2:30 p.m. The lads, having eaten such luxurious food day after day, found it very enjoyable to eat eggs, ham and home fries at the Market Diner opposite Pier 90.

Chuck Fisher was the keyboard man of the orchestra. Smaller in stature than Scotty with a mop of curly hair that made him appear younger than his thirty-eight years. He was quite the character and possessed some weird idiosyncrasies. Known as Dracula because of his habit of sleeping during the day and staying awake for hours into the night as long as he has a drinking partner. Chuck was an excellent musician. Chuck and Scotty especially enjoyed this group and signed on the ship for the cruise season every year. It was something of an alma mater. The same group had made these Caribbean trips together for the last five years. It was definitely their favorite gig.

Making their way through the crates and eighteen wheelers littering the dock, they headed for the exit.

"Jesus Christ," remarked Chuck, "I'm sure looking forward to that coffee across the street. My mouth's like the inside of a Japanese wrestler's jock strap!" Scotty winced at his friend's graphic description of the palate.

Leaving the dock, they had to wind their way through the hordes of passengers and all the autos that were conveying them on the first part of their trip. Crossing the street, the pair entered the Diner to be pleasantly greeted with the warmth inside. Their noses were treated to the delightful odors emanating from the typical New York grill. The restaurant was comparatively quiet. They rubbed their hand together in anticipation of the tasty morsels that would be forthcoming. Seated in a booth with coffee poured, their conversation turned to one of the musicians who would not be making the trip due to health reason.

"I wonder who the office will send to replace ol' Charlie," said Chuck, sipping his coffee.

"I sure hope that, apart from being a good player," answered Scotty laughingly, "this new man can hold his liquor. You know how Bob feels about that."

Bob Gibson, the leader, had been around a long time. An excellent violin player who at one time also played sax as a double; but having lost his lip, he now concentrated on the fiddle. He despised anyone who did not imbibe, but heaven help the musician who drank to where he could not do his job. That was an offence that could incur a penalty worse than walking the plank. He was, though, really a great guy. Bob believed in looking after his boys. Lord help anyone who interfered with any of the privileges afforded them by contractual agreement. The musicians in turn did their job well. They gave Bob little grief. The boys always pampered his cocktail hours and his little get togethers in his cabin. When Bob first started doing the cruises, he was in his mid-forties and on his third marriage. The wife at that time had given him that dreadful ultimatum, "the sea or me!" Bob thought about it for two whole seconds then decided to choose the lesser of two evils and went to sea, dumping the wife back to suburbia and her pinochle club.

A young man entered the diner. Spotting Scotty and Chuck sitting in the booth, he joined them. "Hi guys!"

"Hi, Tom," came their reply between mouthfuls of food. "What's happening?"

Tom was the steward in charge of the musicians. He waited their table in the dining room and looked after the cabins the boys occupied. Tom was always available to assist the lads in their needs. The most important one was keeping a constant supply of ice cubes always ready.

"Your substitute musician just came aboard. You guys must have left just as he arrived. He was asking where the musicians hung out, so he was directed to me. I took him aft and turned him over to Jimmy who is now taking care of him."

"What does he look like?" asked Chuck. "Is he young, old, or in between?"

"As a matter of fact," replied Tom, "he appears young. The type of guy that could be seventeen or twenty-five. He is short with horn rimmed glasses and seems kind of timorous. I don't know if he belongs on a ship like you buccaneers. And I wouldn't be surprised if he spends the cruise seasick."

Scotty and Chuck exchanged glances as the same thought occurred to them.

"That's all we need; a mama's boy that can't even keep coffee down!"

"Oh well," Scotty said resignedly. "We will just have to wait and see. How about some chow, Tom?"

Back aboard, the new arrival sat in Jimmy's cabin waiting while he shaved. Jimmy Brenner, one of the old school, knew the ropes like the other guys, but kept his conversation to a minimum. He was the type who could just sit and listen while everyone else made asses of themselves, and when finally forced to give his opinion, the result would usually be a classic. An example of this occurred when a group of passengers, after being on the sauce most of the day, were discussing the rights and wrongs of Vietnam. After much expounding, that did not add up to a bag of shit, someone asked Jimmy for his opinion.

Jimmy looked at them thoughtfully for a moment before remarking, "I think they should throw all the Vietnamese out of Vietnam!!" Then he took his leave. This little anecdote had the desired effect: leaving the others to realize how drunk and foolish they all were.

Jimmy Brenner really had a very profound sense of humor. There was another time that a couple of the musicians rented a car in one of the islands. They brought along a couple of the stewardesses from the ship and were heading for the beach. When they stopped for gas, one of the gals decided to visit the ladies' room. She was taking her time getting back to the car and guys were voicing their displeasure at the delay. All except Jimmy, who sat very quiet. On her return she ran into some heckling from the group and finally turned to the quiet man for some support.

Jimmy looked at her for a few hushed seconds and said, "Do you realize that man over there just poured twenty gallons of gas into this car faster than you pissed a pint?" The group roared with laughter.

Very early in their association, the lads had stumbled on Jimmy's one pleasure, his passion for visiting whorehouses. He must have visited every one of them in the entire Caribbean and never missed sampling the wares. This practice the guys ceded to him alone, as they all felt such a game too risky to indulge.

The new musician, Abe Rubin, was beginning to wonder what he had gotten himself into as he sat watching Jimmy shave. Abe knew that more experienced players had been approached about the job, but all turned it down on the grounds that they could not keep up the pace of alcohol consumption. The seagoing minstrels were referred to as a motley crew by the local N.Y. Union. They had an enormous capacity for booze and expected all newcomers to be the same way. Anyone lacking this qualification in the past was immediately made to feel that they did not belong. What a dilemma the boys were about to face with the advent of young Abe Rubin.

Abe had played gigs around New York for the past few years. He played alto sax, clarinet, and flute very well. He had not married yet. In fact, up until now he had always lived with a very protective mother who made sure he kept to the straight and narrow. The musicians were soon to learn that in their midst they had a twenty-four-year-old virgin who had never tasted liquor. Such a rare breed was difficult to find, especially in the musical profession. What strange turn of fate. Why, out of all the musicians in the world, would the gods inflict such a monstrosity on these poor, innocent, hard drinking, carousing, whore mongering jesters?

"Well kid," Jimmy turned towards his guest and finished toweling his hands. "Have you any idea what this trip is all about? Do you know where we are going and how long we'll be gone?"

"No. Just that it's a couple of weeks down to the Caribbean and back."

"Actually, this cruise is a ten-day jaunt with plenty of days at sea. Most trips are fourteen days with plenty of ports, but this one should be more restful. There will probably be more older people coming along for the sea air."

Abe pondered that statement for a few moments before asking, "Do you mean that one cruise could differ from another depending on the age of the passengers?"

"All the difference in the world, son," replied Jimmy, preparing to further Abe's education. "You see, a shipload of young passengers, such as we get inflicted with towards the end of the season, are a pain in the ass. They are not spenders. These amateur drunks are constantly staggering around being loud mouthed. They should have pacifiers stuck in their faces. Apart from that, their taste in music, if you can call it that, is a constant source of irritation. We, as professional musicians, have no interest in such garbage. Now, a complement of mostly older people makes the pendulum swing the other way. We very rarely play late at night because the old folks go to bed early. They like to be up bright and shiny so they won't miss any freebies. Depending on the situation, such as bad weather or a late arrival in port, the Captain may announce that the bar will be serving complimentary drinks for the next two hours. This will bring out all the heavy non-drinkers. You'll see them elbow to elbow knocking them back as fast as the bartender can set them up."

"Ha! Ha!" said Abe. "That's funny! I can just see them climbing over each other's wheelchair and throwing their canes over the side to get to the bar! Just like an old Charlie Chaplin movie I once saw. What a funny scene!"

"Now," continued Jimmy, pointing his finger in a most instructional manner and addressing his young charge, who was completely entranced with Jimmy's delivery. "The most ideal scene is the middle aged, successful business man who usually has a vivacious wife and likes to live it up. This is the type of passenger who will get involved in everything, right up to the wee hours in the night club. They like to show off and are not afraid to throw the cash around. Sometimes, in the larger cabins, they will have private parties and even book us to play. This, of course, is all extra money for the boys. There are also some private rooms available that the passengers can reserve and really throw a bash!"

Jimmy's demeanor changed along with the subject as he related to Abe how the scene on cruise ships was deteriorating.

"This is the last of the great liners, and she will soon be heading for the yards. The days of the great shipping lines are about over now. You see, most ships are being chartered by syndicates who are more interested in the bottom line on the ledger page – MONEY – rather than what service meant in the old days. In those days it was thought that service brought the money and profits. Maybe I'm just a snob, but I enjoyed the days when people dressed formally at every occasion. There was a certain dignity that went along with shipboard life. That's all gone. Sure, masses that could never afford to cruise are the mainstream passengers today, but what happened to class and sophistication? It's definitely all over. Why, I remember walking through the first-class lounges and enjoying the aroma of good cigars and the finest Scotch. Now," he added disdainfully, "the place stinks of old stogies and cheap white wine. But of course, this is the trend even ashore, Abe, my boy. I just played Vegas, where the motto is now mass for class. On the strip a few years ago, one had to dress to enter the showrooms. Shorts were never allowed in the casinos. Now it's cutoff jeans and cram them in. Casinos are more interested in selling hot dogs and five cent beer. That also goes along with the musical scene. They are about the same value. On that sad note, let's go topside and get you signed on."

Abe signed the necessary papers in the Purser's office on B deck. As they ascended the companion way to the Prom deck, Abe's eyes grew wider listening to Jimmy explain that most of the action occurred in this area.

"The first of the public rooms is forward and located under the bridge. It is, of course, the Observation Bar. This bar gives an excellent view of the forecastle head or sharp end. Let's walk aft. We have a small lounge here, where people like to relax. And on each side of the ship there are writing rooms equipped with paper and pens. Also, on the starboard side is a small library."

Continuing aft, they entered an elegant salon. This was Jimmy's favorite room and always had the same effect on him. Passing through the doors, Abe observed Jimmy's eyes light up as he envisioned the luxury and craftsmanship that this room held. Standing in the middle of the circular dance floor, Jimmy pointed out the highlights and Abe, too, stood in awe.

"This is the Grand Lounge. Most of the dances and functions take place here each night. As you can see, it is the nicest room on the ship. Notice the dome ceiling and the chandeliers."

"Whew!" exclaimed Abe. "I never knew a ship had such splendor!"

"Yes, she sure is a beauty," Jimmy said lovingly. "That's what I mean about a dying breed. Do you see those hand carved murals? All solid woods. That's mahogany there and teak over there. Great artisans used wood from all over the world on this ship. Go aboard the ships of today and all you will find is a floating, plastic monstrosity."

Abe noticed that Jimmy was not displaying anger in his tone, but was probably realizing that he himself, at fifty years of age, was also part of a dying breed. The type of music he played on the tenor sax was synonymous with the great sailing days. The dignity, the class, and the respect one earned for a job well done, from people with taste, no longer existed either. Leaving this beautiful room, they entered the Main Lounge.

"As you can see," Jimmy gestured with his hands, "this is also well laid out, but not as luxurious. It is here that such activities as horse racing, bingo, and other fun games for the passengers take place while we are playing the shows in the Grand Lounge. There is usually one show on the way down and one on the return journey. New acts come aboard each trip."

Still continuing aft, they passed another small lounge bar and descended some stairs onto A deck. Walking over to two plush doors, Jimmy invited Abe to enter, revealing a beautifully decorated cinema complete with sloping floor and curtains of thick velvet.

"Gee!" gasped Abe. "I never expected such a place! And it's a movie theater! It just never entered my head that people would want to go to the movies on a ship."

"Actually," replied Jimmy, enjoying Abe's amazement, "there is another cinema up forward. Not as elaborate, of course, but they change the movies so often that we can run from one theater to the other for a different flick."

This was probably the most talking Jimmy had done in years, but he was like a father taking his kid to Disneyland for the first time and enjoyed watching the wonder of his young friend's face. The duo went up and down a few more companionways. Poor Abe was so completely confused with his new surroundings that he had to ask how long it took to become familiar with the ship.

"Don't worry," smiled Jimmy, "you won't get lost; it's not so complicated. If you do lose your direction, just walk amidships until you come to an elevator and then take it from there."

"Where are we now?"

"E deck aft. This is the lounge," replied Jimmy.

Entering through the port side door, Abe could see that this huge lounge was shaped like the fantail of the ship. Straight ahead was a long bar on the port side, and to their left, between the port and starboard doors, was the bandstand. There even was a good-sized dance floor. The usual tables and chairs surrounded the dance space and extended throughout the room. Abe realized he was in a night club, the likes of which he'd never seen ashore. He was immediately amazed at how nice and clean it was and with no disagreeable odor. Go into any night club in the city on the morning after and your nose would be assailed with the mustiness of an upholstered sewer.

"Like it?" asked Jimmy, already having the answer from Abe's expression.

"This is where it all happens. You see, after we play topside, whether for a show or dance, we descend here to the King Neptune Room and it's jazz time until the wee hours. The heavy spenders and high rollers dig this room, and a good time is had by all. We also rehearse all the shows here, usually at 10 a.m. on the same day of the performance."

"I supposed you get some good acts to play for?" Abe inquired as they seated themselves in the empty room.

"Usually not too bad, but of course the type of entertainment is limited because of conditions. As you can imagine, tap dancers don't do too well on a stage that could be in continual motion with a heavy swell. We always have a comedian, and since a large number of passengers are Jewish, the funnyman is usually a graduate of the Catskills. I think this trip we have a singer, a magician, and the joke teller."

They sat silent for a few moments in the serene tranquility of the room, far removed from the noises of embarking passengers and the necessary stores coming aboard through the conveyor belts amidships. Abe felt himself relax enough that should he close his eyes sleep would overcome him. He had been up most of the night packing and was too wired up to lay down. Jimmy, observing Abe's state of subconscious relaxation, advised him that sleep on board was something of a valued commodity.

"Sleep is something you grab when the opportunity arises; like on the beach. Our drummer, Scotty, can be found during the afternoon in the aft library all snuggled up in one of those big leather arm chairs having his catnap. Unless you are an unconscious sleeper and can sleep through anything, forget it. Parties are constant on board, especially in our quarters. Doors are forever banging; that is one of the curses of life aboard ship. Also, anything left loose will create a constant noise, as the ship is always on the move. So, learn to live on catnaps if you want to survive."

Just then a head popped round the door. "Hi, Jimmy, what's happening?" asked Tom, their steward.

"Oh, Tom, this is Abe Rubin, who is replacing Charlie, so he will bunk with me."

"Yeah, Jimmy, we met when he came aboard. Hi, Abe." As they shook hands, Tom continued. "Scotty and Chuck are over in the diner. I just left them. The odd couple are zonked out in their cabin. Boy, they must have really tied one on last night. Bob should be aboard soon to shepherd his flocking flock of flocking musicians."

Abe's thoughts were occupied with Tom's previous statement. "Who are the odd couple?" he inquired glancing at each of them.

"They are the last of the great buccaneers," explained Jimmy. "Tex Farrow and Mike Henry. Tex plays trumpet and Mike is our bass man. Both are forty-year-old, swinging singles who obviously never married, and boy do they live it up. They were probably uptown all night in some jazz joint and got themselves good and fried."

"Anything I can get you guy?" queried Tom. "How about some coffee?"

"Great idea, Tom," replied Jimmy. "Abe is feeling his first effects of the sea air, and I think coffee should wake him up and get his heart started again."

As Tom took his leave, Abe turned to Jimmy. "Do they have gambling casinos on board? I hear this is the thing now."

"God forbid!" answered Jimmy with a look of horror. "As I mentioned earlier, this ship will go out in dignity. This is apt to be the last cruise season for the Nectar, and I would rather see it go untouched. Sure, one arm bandits and crap tables may increase profits, but it sure destroys that class I was telling you about. I know I am snobbish on the subject, but who needs Las Vegas shit kickers with their five-cent beer and rattling their tokens wandering around a ship as elegant as this? It bugs me that these morons enter the dining room in jeans and a tee shirt. Even the airlines are inflicted with this type of traveler, and they have a good name for them – BUSSSERS. You see,

15

when the airline fares dropped to equal bus fares, the sweaty set in their cutoff jeans with knapsacks on their backs invaded the terminals. The airline crews figured this new clientele earned the title. Why, I just took the red eye from the West Coast and was sitting beside a mother with a baby in her arms. When the kid squawked, she pulled out a big floppy tit and shoved it in the kid's yap. Some assholes call it no inhibitions. I call it no shame."

Abe was rescued from any further condemnation of low lifers by Tom who returned with a silver coffee pot and utensils. Placing the cups on the table, Tom poured a brew that spewed forth steam and a delightful aroma.

"Just leave the cups and pot. I will pick them up later."

"Thanks, Kid," came Jimmy's reply as Tom scuttled off.

A few minutes silence was observed only being interrupted by the clink of the cups and spoons on the saucers as the pair sampled the elixir of life. The hot stimulant served its purpose and jolted Jimmy into more instructional advice.

"The ship sails at two thirty. We will be on the Prom deck to play the ship out with all the silly tunes such as, "Anchors Aweigh" and the like. There is a music locker on that deck where we store the instruments, and there is a good supply of musical orchestrations for our needs. After we sail, we then adjourn to Bob's cabin to splice the main brace."

Seeing a look of puzzlement on Abe's face, Jimmy continued to explain. "You see, we start rehearsing with a case of Scotch to set us up for the trip. Bob likes these sessions, and they happen every day, so be prepared. At three thirty, it's boat drills back on the prom deck, starboard side and forward. Be sure to wear your life belt and head gear. At four thirty, it's a quick get together dance in the Grand Lounge so that the passengers can meet and greet the opening of the duty-free bars. This dance is always where the musicians sort out their chicks, if any, for the cruise. First night at sea formal attire is not worn, and we usually just play in this room for those not too tired. It's lunch time now; we usually just grab a sandwich from the pantry because the dining room serves a running sitting which is a bit hectic. Passengers are seated at their assigned tables at the first dinner tonight. Okay, Abe, I think that's enough instruction for you now. Let's grab that sandwich on the way down, and then you can unpack and stow your gear. Everyone should be up and about by now."

Walking down two decks to G deck, they turned left to the port side and through a door that would take them to the extreme end of the ship. Abe had already been in this area when he first came aboard, but hadn't really paid much attention. Passing through the door, they were now in a corridor that extended to the ass end of the ship.

"This," said Jimmy dramatically, "is the Inner Sanctum! It houses only the ship's musicians. Presence here is by invitation only. As you can see, there are four cabins; one to the left and three on the right. The one on the left is an inboard, meaning no porthole. It houses Scotty and Chuck. Chuck chose this cabin because he likes to sleep during the day. The first door on the right, here, is the home of our noble leader, Bob Gibson. By the way, never knock that door unless you are sure he is awake if you value your life. Here we are at our house," Jimmy said as he opened the door, "be it ever so humble. Oh, next door," he indicated with his thumb, "Tex and Mike." Abe already knew them as the odd couple.

The cabins, though not the most elaborate, contained two lower bunks with double drawers underneath, two lockers, and a wash basin. The three cabins were similar except Bob's, which had much more space, complete with a sofa and table and chairs.

"Toilet and showers are located aft at the blunt end," Jimmy advised his new roommate. "One room contains a bathtub and toilet, the other a shower. There are also a couple of showers forward, should ours be occupied."

"The musicians' quarters look a bit austere after the luxury topside. How come?" Abe inquired.

Jimmy smiled and replied, "There is an explanation for that. You see, no matter where you go as a musician, whether on land or sea, you will always find that those responsible for our welfare are either ignorant of our needs or a sworn enemy. This ship is no exception to the rule. Plus, the officers do not give a damn about us. When we first started these trips, the band was assigned cabins forward, close to the crew quarters. Can you imagine playing 'til all hours of the night, just putting you head down and the crew commence working outside your door? They would parade past at five a.m. in full voice. Then there was the added aggravation of rolling empty beer barrels down the corridor and bouncing them off the bunkbeds. So, we threatened to call it a day. We were offered very nice cabins amidships, but then we were surrounded by passengers whose presence would put a crimp in our activities. It was Tom, our steward, who suggested this area. At one time it was occupied by the leading hands, but they complained about the noise from the ship's crews located underneath. We decided to move in even with these engine noises. We figured it was worth the sacrifice of the luxury and putting up with the vibration to have our privacy. After a couple of nights, you will find the noise will actually put you to sleep. Anyway, you will either be so tired or so drunk that it won't matter. You may even have to put a vacuum cleaner under you bed at home to enable you to sleep!" Jimmy was laughing as he headed for the door. "You get on with the unpacking, and I will check on the others."

Abe began the process of stowing his gear. He had brought with him the standard black tuxedo and dark suit for the cool weather. A white tux jacket was supplied to him from the agency for the warmer climate. These items he hung in the locker. Pulling open the drawers, he began to feel the excitement as the reality of the situation hit him. "Oh boy," he thought, "I'm actually on a big ship going on a cruise. People pay a lot of money for such a vacation, and here I am being provided with room, board, and even getting paid. Hot dog! Man, this is the life. I wonder what the poor people are doing today! Whoopee!"

To be afforded such freedom, after so many years with strict parents, made Abe almost crazy enough to want to jump up and down on his bunk. All of a sudden, his thoughts were interrupted by a raucous voice from the next cabin. The bellowing appeared to be a song, a sort of sea shanty. He found himself amused at the impromptu concert. A look of consternation was on his face as the words finally sank home.

"Oh 'twas on the good ship, Venus,

By Christ you should have seen us!

The figurehead was a maiden head,

Two bollocks and a penis!

Singing, yo, heave, ho,

and we don't want any more beer!"

At first Abe was a little shocked. He began giggling as he realized the ditty was obviously emanating from one of the musicians referred to as the odd couple. As a matter of fact, Mike was the culprit responsible for the naughty song. Just as Abe finished unpacking, Jimmy appeared in the doorway and beckoned him to follow. They headed for the leader's cabin. Scotty and Chuck were seated on the divan against the bulkhead beneath the two portholes and looked content as a result of the delicious ham and eggs they had eaten at the Diner. Bob stood in the middle of the room with both hands in his coat pockets looking very much like a sea captain. All of a sudden, Abe felt like one of the crew of the Bounty facing Captain Bligh and anticipating ten lashes. His fears were soon dispelled and introductions were made. Abe thought that the two fellows seated on the divan appeared to be regular guys, and behind Bob's apparent sternness was really an old softy.

"I understand from the office that Abe here is a hell of a

musician," said Bob addressing the room. "Welcome aboard, son."

Abe was beginning to relax now.

"Yeah. Welcome aboard!" from the seated duo.

Bob then inquired from Jimmy if all the leg work had been done making Abe's position legal.

"Oh, sure," answered Jimmy. "He's all signed on and has had a cook's tour of the ship. He's unpacked and ready to roll."

Just then the door opened revealing a heavy-set male, garbed in only a bath towel around his waist; followed by a smaller, slightly bald figure. This was the infamous "odd couple," Mike Henry and Tex Farrow. Having been musicians all their lives, they just knocked around from town to town, ship to ship, or any place that offered them wine, women and song.

Mike's bulk indicated that he might be the gourmet of the group. He obviously enjoyed eating, and his appetite was surely sated on this ship. He never failed to sample all the culinary delights. Eaters of hamburgers and hot dogs were referred to as peasants by Mike.

Scotty would never forget the time he and Mike were having dinner at a posh New York restaurant. Before the main course, they had ordered a pasta dish as an entrée. Scotty was enjoying the meal and was certainly not prepared for the curve that Mike threw. Calling the waiter over, Mike asked to speak with the manager, who approached the table in his most charming manner.

"Yes, Sir," he addressed Mike. "What help may I be to you?"

Mike then placed his utensils on the plate and with outstretched arms placed his hands on the table edge. He looked straight into the manager's eyes and in a soft, charming, and relaxed manner replied, "would you kindly convey my compliments to the chef and tell him that the next time he cooks such a dish – stick it in his fucking ass!!!"

After recovering from the unexpected verbal acclamation, Scotty slid under the table, while choking on a mouthful of rigatoni, and made a bee line for the door leaving Mike alone to sort out whatever was about to take place. The manager had done three about faces and was cooling down enough to order the antagonist from the premises. Mike found Scotty sitting on the sidewalk bent over in hysterical laughter.

Scotty's reminiscing ended as Mike and Tex moved closer inward.

"What? Ho! Me hearties," exclaimed Mike in his best pirate imitation while surveying the scene. "What have we here?" Long John Silver, as played by Robert Newton, was Mike's favorite character. The fellows in the band received a constant performance from Mike that came complete with a half-closed right eye, especially when he had been drinking.

Introductions were made for the benefit of the pair; Tex squeezed around Mike and seated himself in one of the empty chairs. Tex, the trumpet player, was known as the band fixer. Any shore excursions or trips made by the gang were arranged by Tex. He claimed he could deal best with taxi drivers and rental companies. It usually turned out to be more expensive, but they let him have his fun. Another sideline handled by Tex was making sure the crew members had all the booze they desired from St. Thomas. He was their intermediary, and Tex kept them in good supply. Before reaching the island of John Barleycorn, as St. Thomas was called aboard ship, two of the crew would give him a list of crew members' names and what liquor was to be ordered. Tex would then proceed ashore to the local distributor, place the order, and have it delivered to the ship. The reward for his work came from the store owner and was ample. Each musician received a case of whatever his heart desired. So, party time never ended. As Tex put it, "we are just casting our bread upon the water."

Now that everyone had met Abe, Bob instructed his flock, "Remember, back here as soon as you stow your instruments for our little tete-a-tete."

"Sure, Bob."

"See ya later," came the replies, and they all left to go and prepare to play the ship out.

Scotty put on his coat and decided to take a little stroll through the ship, knowing he would finish up on the sun deck. As he walked along, he smiled at all the familiar sights and sounds of sailing day. Some old dears were looking for their luggage and were quite convinced it had been stolen. A frantic mother was looking for her twelve-year-old son who had all of a sudden made a hasty retreat from his nutty mother.

"I knew we shouldn't have come on this trip," she wailed at her poor dejected husband. "William has probably fallen overboard already and it's all your fault!"

The kid actually was having a ball exploring his great new world. At this very moment he was on the sun deck looking up at the gigantic funnel wondering if he could gain access through it to the engine room.

Passing the pantries, Scotty observed the bedroom stewards preparing for the assault of party goers. The last of the champagne glasses and ice cubes were held in abeyance hoping to reap a rich reward for their deliverance to the revelers, who by this time should be good and fried and feeing benevolent.

Passing the open cabin doors, he could hear the sendoff parties in full swing, while some of the drunks staggered along the passageways with bottles in hand. An old thought returned to Scotty: what is it about boats that compels usually upstanding people to become roaring drunks? Whether it's a sailboat, a power boat, a row boat or an ocean liner, the amateur sailor has to have a glass in his hand! And sometimes even a bottle!

Scotty found his way forward through the melee and climbed the enclosed companionway that brought him topside to the Sun deck. Stepping outside, he walked to the rail facing forward beneath the bridge wing. This was his favorite spot. He could survey his kingdom. Balmy nights at sea he would often stand here alone, enjoying the tranquility as the ship moved wondrously through the tropical waters.

At the moment it was anything but peaceful. He gazed across the forecastle head to Twelfth Avenue beyond and the overpass above the street. Cars were speeding to and fro frantically to get wherever the hell they were going. Taxi drivers could be heard using the extensive vocabulary of the noble breed, and jockeying for the favored positions outside Pier 90. Observing the scene from his ivory tower, a thought struck Scotty: that one day he may have to be a part of that rat race and find himself behaving just like those morons. Heaven forbid! There must be another way.

The P.A. system could now be heard throughout the ship sending forth its warning to potential stowaways.

"Will all visitors and those not sailing on the ship kindly proceed ashore now. The gangway is situated on B deck, forward. Thank you."

The decks were now assembling at the winches of the forecastle and were looking over the side. The remnants from the sendoff parties were beginning to descend the gangway with the usual shouts.

"Bon voyage!"

"Have a great time!"

"Wish we were going with you," shouted one poor drunk as he tripped onto the pier.

Well, thought Scotty leaving the rail, I suppose I had better get my drums up for casting off. Descending to the Prom deck, he opened the door to the musicians' locker. It was about eight feet long and appeared narrow. Tiered wooden shelves adorned each side of the room containing the musical selections and orchestrations. The shelves were also built to hold the instruments safely in place even in bad weather. The drums were sitting on deck at the rear of the locker. Apart from the rhythmic contribution to the ship's entertainment, the bass drum served a very special purpose. You see, the Customs officers do not allow the ship's bars to be open while in dock in New York. One does have to have an extra source of liquor to keep going during the lay over. So before storing the drums away at the end of each cruise, the lads remove the head from the bass drum and place a dozen or so bottles of Scotch inside and then replace the head. Now, on many occasions the diligent Customs Officer would enter the locker and check the instrument cases. It was a good job that the officer didn't try to pick up the bass drum or he might have sustained permanent injury. Not to mention the musicians.

Scotty started pulling out his drums and got a fit of the giggles. He recalled a situation that had occurred on a previous cruise. One old dear had taken a real shine to Bob, the leader, and he was constantly trying to avoid her. No matter what he did, she was forever tracking him down. Scotty had come across Bob in the locker one morning sorting out some music. While Scotty was standing in the open doorway with his foot resting on the high step over, Bob, who had feasted the previous evening on all sorts of heavy food and booze, released the most resounding and obnoxious fart to end all farts. The heat and stuffiness of the room only added to the odor that resulted from this impropriety. At that very instant the old broad spying Scotty at the door approached him.

"Good morning, Scotty. Where is Bob today?"

"Right in here," he answered, stepping back and indicating inside the locker.

Sticking her head in the gas chamber she said, "Hello, Bob." Her face took on an expression of horror as the toxic fumes assailed her nostrils.

"Ooh! Ooh!" She staggered back away from the door. "Dear! Dear!" she muttered, making a hasty retreat through the door leading into the lounge.

Bob was mortified as Scotty convulsed with laughter and staggered down the Prom deck. Bob was never to be bothered by the old broad again. His problem was solved. God works in mysterious ways.

The lads were all set up on the Prom deck wearing their dark suits, white shirts, and black ties, looking more like pall bearers than musicians, but that was what the company liked. Passengers were throwing streamers and confetti as the ship's lines were let go.

"Ok, guys," Bob turned to face them, "usual shit."

They broke into "Anchors Aweigh" and the ship gently moved away from the quayside. Then into reverse, swinging slowly around the end of the docks, the band played merrily. Once mid channel, the ship started to creep forward, indicating an end to the playing of the ship out. The boys packed up their gear and placed the instruments once again in the locker.

"Why do we play so loud?" Abe asked Jimmy.

"I thought you looked puzzled," replied jimmy. "The purpose is to blow the assholes off the deck so we can get down below. Some of these drunks are apt to think the party starts here and bother us with requests."

Abe took the answer with a shake of his head as he put his sax in the case and placed it in the locker.

Seated in Bob's cabin, the trip was now declared official. Observations were passed between them about the quality of passengers.

"Doesn't look too bad."

"Not as many oldies as expected."

"Quite a few chickies aboard!"

"What's the matter with your face?" Bob asked Chuck, noticing him deep in thought.

"It's that upright piano. We are always having problems with it. I keep asking them to take it inside after we play on the outside deck, away from the humidity, put the Purser just ignores me. The piano tuner was here this morning, and he says it's getting useless. Actually, we do need a new one, and then we should keep it in the lounge between the outside dances."

"For Christ's sake!" replied Bob. "For the amount of times we use that piano, I don't think it's such a big deal. So, don't let it get you down. Drink up and enjoy yourself."

Tom, the loyal steward, entered with an ice chest full of ice cubes, well aware of the ritual about to take place. Bob with bottle in hand approached the dresser where seven glasses complete with ice cubes were treated to a double shot of good Scotch. He poured the sauce and proceeded to hand each man what they had been awaiting.

"Here you go, Abe. Down the hatch," said Bob, turning to the newcomer and offering the glass.

Abe looked at his shoes and did a little embarrassed shuffle, scratched his nose and replied, "Not for me, thanks."

In the next instant all the things that Bob feared and dreaded came into focus as he stared at the little guy in front of him. Bob felt his heart drop into his lower bowel and expected it to expel right through his own asshole. Thoughts were racing through his head a mile a minute. Can't be! It's only a dream. This wouldn't happen to me. Bob's mood could be felt by all. A terrible silence descended in the chamber, followed by seven cases of paralysis. The steward, being the only one capable of mobility, sneaked past Bob out the door before the bomb burst. Bob, now regaining some of his joviality, took a shot in the dark even though he was expecting the worst.

"You mean it's too early for you, son. You only drink in the evening. That's it; right lad?"

Abe glanced around the room, uncomfortably looking for an ally and knowing his quest to be fruitless. Once again, he did a little shuffle, scratched his nose as he stammered for the words.

"I..I..I..don't drink at all, Bob."

The truth was out. He had said it. All in the room were aghast. Scotty took to giggling. Tex and Jimmy took large gulps from their glasses.

Mike knelt on the floor, making the sign of the cross in Abe's direction and began to mutter, " In nomine Patris, et Filii, et Spiritus Sancti"

Bob's demeanor once again changed as he assumed his familiar Captain Bligh roll.

"So, you don't drink at all, eh! Do me a favor. Take your teetotaling ass out of here. Go up and wave to the statue of Liberty because it may be the last time, you'll see it."

Abe once again looked at the others, raise his hands pathetically, then left the cabin. The room lapsed into silence for a full two minutes in sympathy for their leader. No one could think of anything that would ease the situation. Just then Scotty started to recite Robert Burns, the Scottish bard, a man held in great esteem by the ship's drummer.

"Wee, sleeket, courin tim'rous beastie,

O, what a panics in thy breastie!

Thou need not run awa sae hasty!

Wi' bickering brattle!

I would be loth to run an' chase thee,

We' murdering pattle."

Burns had written this when he unearthed a little field mouse while plowing. Scotty thought it appropriate to Abe's departure.

"Can you believe that?" Bob said turning to the group still in amazement. "Wait 'til I get my hands on that fucking agent!"

"Never mind, Bob, it's only ten days, so you may as well make the best of it and have another dram," comforted Jimmy, picking up the bottle and pouring a triple in Bob's glass.

Shrill blasts of the ship's whistle called the passengers and crew to boat drills complete with life jackets. This exercise was mandatory one hour after leaving harbor. The purpose was for everyone to know where their boat station was located should an emergency arise.

The usual pandemonium took place. It resembled a Chinese fire drill. Passengers bumped into each other with such dazed looks and confused expressions, and not knowing such nautical terms yet, as topside, portside, forward and aft, the stewards teasingly answered inquiries with this little retort.

"Go on up the stairs to the Prom deck and walk toward the sharp end. Now depending on your boat number it will either be on the left or right side."

The musicians were assigned to boat number two, starboard side. They usually took charge of the passengers and assembled them in some sort of order. This also gave the boys the opportunity to supply a little entertainment and keep the passengers amused during the drill. Mike, facing the bunch, adopted the stance of a real mariner and instructed them how to line up using his best pirate imitation.

"Har! Har! Ye land lubbers. Belay there! Old folk to the front and ye buxom wenches fall to the rear," he instructed three young gals obviously traveling together. The passengers relaxed and smiled as they realized they were being treated to some good-natured banter. Carrying on again as a pirate, Mike began to instruct the group on how to tie the life jacket tapes.

"Left over right. Right over left. That's it me hearties. Now you all face the front and hold your positions until the officers come by. Jim Hawkins there will check your life jackets and see that they are sound," he added, nodding to Chuck.

Chuck walked behind the passengers, pretending to be checking the rear tapes, until he reached the three gals standing with their backs to the bulkhead. Very deftly, Chuck took one tape from each of their jackets and tied it to the handrail running along the bulkhead. Chuck resumed his position in line. It was all the lads could do to keep from laughing at the anticipated result of Chuck's deviousness. Just then the Staff Captain and Chief Officer making their customary trip around the deck on their so-called inspection hurried by and made for the bridge.

Blasts from the ship's whistle and a message from the P.A. system brought the drill to a close; followed by an announcement that a get together dance would take place in the Grand Lounge at four thirty.

The passengers, more familiar with their environment now, took a more leisurely pace back to their cabins. They were full of smiles and salutations while strolling from the Prom deck.

Alas, our three young ladies, at number two boat, on attempting to step forward, found to their dismay that they had been the victims of a practical joke.

"What the hell," said the blonde to the others, unable to understand how it happened.

Until they heard Chuck's voice, "Bye girls!"

Looking in his direction the whole scene dawned on them as Chuck, walking backwards, waved bye bye.

They began to untie the knots and yelled after him, "We'll get you! Just you wait!"

Hell hath no fury like three broads tied to a rail, thought Chuck as he beat a hasty retreat to the Inner Sanctum. Drinks were already poured and waiting in Bob's cabin when he arrived to share the laugh.

The Grand Lounge was a hub of activity. The more energetic of the passengers were preparing for their first debauchery. The less lively were heading for the dining room where afternoon tea was being served. In the lounge, the customs seals were already removed from the bars; drinks and smokes were being purchased at a rapid pace. Bob made his usual announcement from the bandstand welcoming everyone aboard and told them how the orchestra would be busy keeping them happy with the usual jokes.

"If you have any requests, keep them to yourselves."

The merry minstrels had knocked back a few noggins before appearing and were now surveying the scene for the pickings before any studs among the passengers staked a claim.

"Look at the boobs on that one!"

"Yeah! She's for Bob!" Bob, looking in the direction of the lady in question, was smiling in agreement as his eyes feasted on a thirty-five-year-old looker. He had a passion for those gals overly endowed in that part of the female anatomy. There had been the odd occasion, when he anticipated the soft silky texture of a huge bosom, only to be devastated at the unveiling of two silicon filled rutabagas.

"There's one for Scotty, blonde with horn rimmed glassed." This type of conversation took place between the playing of instruments. Poor Abe felt like a fish out of water. Everyone appeared to be having a good time both on and off the bandstand. He felt like he had landed in the middle of a snake pit. "Well," he thought, "I am not one of these nuts, and it's only ten days, so fuck them!"

One old fellow walked towards the bandstand looking furtively behind him, then spoke to Bob, "My wife is in the ladies' room. It's our fortieth wedding anniversary. When she returns and I give you the signal, will you please play the Anniversary Waltz?"

"Sure thing, Pop, and congratulations from all of the boys."

"Thank you, gentlemen. I will have the waiter get your drink order."

"Cheers, Dad."

"All the best," came the replies from the bandstand.

Having gotten the happy couple's name and prearranged signal, Bob proceeded with the announcement.

"Ladies and gentlemen. We are honored today to have Mr. and Mrs. Edwards on board who are celebrating their fortieth wedding anniversary. Will the happy couple please take the floor."

The old couple walked to the center of the dance floor and were greeted with applause from all the bystanders. They prepared to dance and Bob continued his speech.

"Now Mr. Edwards, your husband, requested that we play this beautiful tune to celebrate this joyous occasion."

Turning to the band, they struck up as Scotty bellowed out in his best singing voice, "Please release me let me go."

The room, at first perplexed by the song, soon fell in on the gag and roared with laughter. The old fellow pointed to Bob and shouted, "I didn't request that!" Fully expecting his wife to punch him out right there on the dance floor.

After playing only a few bars, the band went into the Anniversary Waltz. Poor Abe, lacking a sense of humor, found it difficult to accept what was totally unreal to him. He knew that musicians, by nature, were fun lovers, but how do you explain this? Yet it was obvious to him that these jokers would have the passengers eating out of their hands in one day. Abe secretly wished to be a part of it but did not feel there was any way unless he lost his sanity, spent years on a job like this one, and drank half the ocean.

The three young maidens who had been subjected to the embarrassing incident at the boat drills were sitting at a table off to the side. They had their heads togethers and were surveying the bandstand. The gals noticed that between each selection played, Chuck would usually stand and sort out the music on top of the grand piano. He sat on a very nice upholstered piano stool which was about to become the focal point of the girl's plan.

After the conclusion of the next musical number, Chuck once again stood up as Bob called out the next tune. This time one of the gals had taken position just off the left of the band stand only a couple of feet from the stool. In her hand she carried a weapon that would prove deadly to Chuck. As he prepared to seat himself, she exposed a large glass of ice cubes and water which she dumped square in the middle of the stool just before he sat down. Taken totally by surprise, his eyebrows shot up. The soggy mess penetrated his pants, then through his jockey shorts, and then nearly froze his ass off on entering his rectum. The brain suddenly said, "jump" and he left the stool as though fired from a cannon followed by shrieks of laughter. His attention went straight to the gals who were wrapped around each other enjoying the result of their handiwork. The boys on the bandstand, now cognizant of the situation responsible for Chuck's yells, joined in the laughter. Chuck pulled at his pants in an attempt to extract his shorts from the anesthetized crevice to no avail. Bob called a short break in order that Chuck might change and regain his composure. He left the bandstand stiff legged and was assailed by Scott's rendition of – "Uh, uh, uh, uh, uh, uh! You shit your trousers!!"

Normally the band would play cocktails in the Grand Lounge from six until six forty-five every evening. The musicians were assigned to first sitting dinner at seven. Should it be a show night, the first seating passengers would attend the first performance at nine which would usually run about an hour and fifteen minutes. The second show started at ten-thirty until eleven forty-five. Midnight would bring the revelers to the King Neptune Club until whatever hour. Here the musicians let their hair down and played their kind of music. If it was a dance night, however, the fun would kick off at nine thirty and continue until midnight; then once again to the club.

Leaving the bandstand, the minstrels went a-mingling, seeking out the chosen few. Bob headed for the boobs, but found she had a husband along, so raised his antennas for a second available choice. Scotty, who had given his devastating wink of the eye to Miss Horn Rimmed Glasses, met her in the corridor accompanied by her companion; another good looker, though she appeared aloof.

"Hi," greeted Scotty as they were about to pass. "I love you." Directing his attention to the blonde, who acknowledged his remark with a wide grin that was accentuated by four glasses of champagne and a couple of gin and tonics.

Lorraine was a twenty-three-year-old secretary from Albany and about to have her first real vacation. For Scotty, this petite blonde doll's attractiveness was heightened by her horn-rimmed glasses, giving her a very intelligent, prim and proper appearance. Her buddy, Valerie, was a gorgeous, mysterious looking brunette; dark and sullen, but she did not appear to possess a sense of humor. Valerie was also of the secretarial profession.

They faced each other in the passageway. Valerie stood behind Lorraine giving Scotty the dead pan. Shit, thought Scotty, hope to Christ I haven't run into a dykey situation. The dark eyed one, if she is a butch, will probably beat the hell out of me.

Trying to keep the situation light, he followed up with, "Welcome aboard my Daddy's yacht. Hope you have a nice cruise."

"Thank you, kind sir," replied Lorraine continuing to smile. "Where is that accent from?"

"North Carolina," came Scotty's reply in a broad Scottish accent, causing her to go into a fit of laughter. The more she laughed, the more stern her friend appeared. This caused Scotty's attention to dart back and forth as though he expected the brunette to pull out a gun from her purse and shoot him.

"No, r-r-r-really," asked Lorraine, "is the accent Irish?"

"No, really," he replied, "it's Scottish."

"Oh, you were born in Scotland then!"

"I had to," he answered. "I wanted to be near my mother at the time." Scotty realized that the few belts he had consumed were responsible for his corny remarks, but he was only trying to soften up the companion who refused to be entertained.

"By the way, everyone calls me Scotty. What are your names?"

"I'm Lorraine and this is my friend Valerie."

"Are you gals enjoying yourselves so far?"

"Yes, of course, and I just love the way you talk," Lorraine added.

"Do you want to marry me?" he asked, as Lorraine continued with big smiles. Just then the silent companion decided to add her observation while directing her scathing tongue at Scotty.

"I think he's obnoxious," she spat out across her friend's shoulder.

"No! Presbyterian," he shot back in his best repartee at Valerie, "but don't worry, Honey, there's nothing wrong with you that a pre-frontal lobotomy can't handle."

Knowing that any further conversation would only cause a rift between the two, he took his leave in the direction of the Verandah Grill located aft on C deck. "Christ," he wondered, as he descended the companionway, "how the hell did I get into that? I feel like a real asshole." Like when you know you have used the wrong approach but continue getting in deeper and deeper. Realizing that Valerie was the cause of his discomfort, he decided to hell with the cold ass broad – who needs her!

Entering the Verandah Grill, his face lit up spotting Chuck engaged in telling jokes with the three broads who had revenged themselves with the wet pants treatment.

"So, you guys called a truce," said Scotty as they made room for him at the table.

"Sure thing," answered Chuck. "How could anyone stay upset with such a charmer as I? By the way girls, this is Scotty, our drummer, who claims to be the good looking one in the band. Scotty meet Peggy, Anne, and Muriel. All from Virginia and on their first cruise." How do's all around.

"Look out girls! You are in the company of a sex mechanic," informed Scotty.

"Not to worry," replied Peggy, "we're three sex mechanics against one."

"Whoopee," answered Chuck, "I'll drink to that!"

"I take it you guys have only one vice and that's your modesty," stated Muriel who was resting her elbow on the table and her chin on her fist looking a little glassy eyed. Drinking and carousing so early in the day, along with all the excitement, was beginning to show on these three young lasses thought Scotty.

"Are you gals on first sitting for dinner?" inquired Scotty, being very charming.

"Yeah, sure," from the trio.

"Great!" said Scotty. "Let's have one for the road, then we'll go off to dinner."

Drinks in hand, they toasted their meeting. Each of them smiling and secretly anticipating the excitement yet to come.

Having dispensed with the sumptuous meal, the band as usual assembled in Bob's cabin, this being part of a daily ritual. As Bob poured the drinks, they waited for whatever information he was about to bestow.

"We're just going to play dance music tonight from nine thirty in the night club so we should be all through by midnight."

Although it would be an easy night, no one was enthusiastic. Usually when performing in the Neptune Club, the guys had an opportunity to jam because Bob left them pretty much to themselves. Tonight, of course, he would participate; meaning a boring time. Being a violinist, Bob's preference was playing romantic ballads. The poor band would be inflicted with these all night, and should Bob be three sheets to the wind, they would all have to suffer the effects in silence. These capable players, with the ability to swing, could enjoy playing nice tunes, but a whole evening had the tendency to send them into orbit far removed from the business at hand. Scotty had a little snicker on his face because he was recalling the time he was playing in a society club in London and what happened as a result of such musical torture.

It was the custom, in these clubs, that drummers could only play with brushes so as not to be obtrusive on the elite patrons who were being jacked off under the table by their illustrious companions. He would always remember the tune, "The Tennessee Waltz." The left hand was swishing round the snare as the right hand played the monotonous one, two, three; one, two, three. Somewhere during the tune, he fell fast asleep leaving his body on complete automatic. The hands continued with the wearisome chore. The orchestra ceased playing. The dancers were dispersing, but the drums continued on.

Eventually opening his eyes, he looked at the bass player who laughingly retorted, "I didn't have the heart to wake you. It was the first time I'd ever seen a dead body play drums." That was it! He vowed never to submit himself to such musical grinding ever again.

Bob's voice jolted him back from his thoughts with more information for his flock.

"We have a rehearsal at ten a.m. in the club, gentlemen, for tomorrow night's little show." This statement created some confusion as the guys looked at each other and threw some queries at Bob.

"Tomorrow is not a show night."

"Are you sure, Bob?"

"Doesn't sound right."

"Hold on to your hats," Bob replied; raising his arms up and down as if conducting. "We are just going to play a selection of light music following the Captain's Cocktail Party."

"Why the rehearsal?"

"Okay, now listen up. We have a new member on the cruise staff this trip, and as you know, the cruise staff are usually a pain in the ass being frustrated amateur entertainers. We know they should stick to selling bingo cards and running the ship's tote, but now and then one comes along who thinks he is real hot shit. This one is an older broad who did some musical shows year ago, and now wants to be the star of this ship. The cruise director asked me if we would go along with the program and I said okay to it, but only on the condition that he puts us down for overtime, and you know he's good about that.

"Yeah, Bob!"

"Good show!"

"We need our extra money for the layover in New York."

Now that the mystery was cleared up, they were all smiles again especially at the thought of extra cash. Pouring another drink, Bob reminded Jimmy to inform Abe of the proceedings. He was not included in these social gatherings, and thus missed the instructions.

The Neptune room was half-empty as expected. Older people headed for bed, and most of the passengers were relaxing in the lounges after stuffing themselves in the dining room. The midnight buffet did not commence until the second night out, but would continue the rest of the cruise. A display of gourmet delights would be spread out on the Prom deck that seemed endless. It never ceased to amaze the musicians and the stewards how anyone could gorge on so much food at the eight o'clock dinner sitting, then stuff their faces again three hours later at the buffet. Oh well, they say it takes all kinds!

The lads were on their best behavior plodding through such selections as "La Mer," "Moonlight and Roses," and other such pretty ballads. Scotty was thinking about his income tax that would have to be straightened out someday. Chuck, the only member unfortunate enough to be married, was trying to dream up the perfect crime. Jimmy was anticipating the big black broad known as the best piece of ass in Haiti. Mike was drooling at the thought of a big Denver omelet later in the evening. Tex's attention was fixed on how much booze they would be able to acquire from their rum run in St. Thomas. Abe could feel what was going on as he looked around the bandstand and tried to sum up the situation. Actually, these guys each consisted of three parts, he decided. One part had enough liquor to render any normal drinker under the table. The second part could separate thoughts completely from the business at hand, while the third part could pour forth beautiful music, in time and with no wrong chords. "Amazing," he thought, putting his clarinet to his lips.

Amid all this, Bob continued on, eyes closed and just a hint of a smile. He fantasized that he was playing the aria from Tosca. Bob returned from his dreamland after recognizing the signals from the band indicating intermission. They would each start looking at their watches, bringing to his attention the fact that he was a minute over. Not a word was ever said, but the intention from each member was so strong that Bob would immediately make the necessary announcement.

"Thank you, ladies and gentlemen. The band will now pause for the cause. We shall return in a few minutes with some more of your favorites."

Leaving the stand, Chuck made for the table where his three lady friends already had a drink waiting for him. Scotty noticed Lorraine had sneaked in the starboard side door and was seated at a small table by herself. Approaching her table, he glanced nervously to the side expecting to see Valerie appear with a dagger in her hand, but she was not in sight. Coast clear, he sighed in relief.

"Hi, where's frozen face? Is she still having a good time?" he asked facetiously.

"Oh, come on now. Be nice," Lorraine answered matching his tone. "She sends her regrets but is looking forward to seeing you later."

"Ha! Ha! I'll bet! What's her problem anyway?' he asked, seating himself beside Lorraine.

"Well, maybe it's because you made such a fuss over me. She is the one who usually gets the guy. She is gorgeous."

"So that's it. Hell hath no fury and all that. Never mind. I'm so smart, I go for the inner beauty," playing his Don Juan role. "By the way, we usually party down below after wrapping up here. The booze is cheaper and the company's great, so if you are not too tired, go for it."

"Who else will be there?" she inquired, glancing at him sideways over her glasses. She had visions of being abducted into some sort of white slavery.

"Suspicious gal, huh? The rest of the guys with whatever ladies they choose to escort," he answered in his best English butler style voice. "As you can see over there, Chuck already has three candidates rarin' to go. Come on over and meet them before we go back to play. Then you won't have to sit alone. One more set and we should be through for the night." Leaving Lorraine with the three musketeers, Scotty joined the rest of group on the bandstand.

Two hours later, Abe entered the door leading into the Inner Sanctum to check out the situation. The party was in full swing with most of the bodies in Bob's cabin. Laughs and giggles could be heard from the females intermingled with a rendition of "Fever" being sung by Peggy Lee on the radio. All cabin doors were open just like a block party. The guys and their chicks stumbled from one room to the other. First night get togethers were more for warm ups than getting laid, so, nobody was concerned with scoring. Should the gals be on the shy side, this approach helped to reassure them that, although the booze was flowing, they were in the hands of "perfect gentlemen." Of course, being the experienced buccaneers they were, the boys knew that ignoring the female sensuality was a sure way of being attacked eventually.

Abe, witnessing this scene of debauchery, decided he would be better returning to one of the public rooms topside and continue reading his book. "May as well visit the toilet while I'm here," he thought. Walking past the open cabins, he turned left and opened the door to the bathroom to behold a wondrous sight. Unsure at first and not knowing the condition of the occupant, he then heard the sound of snoring. This caused Abe to fall against the door jam, convulsed in choking laughter. Abe closed the door and ran down to Bob's cabin. He entered waving his arms very excitedly.

"Hold it! Hold it, please," he shouted to get everyone's attention, yet at the same time howling with laughter. All attention was now on Abe as the group quieted down.

"What the hell's going on?" shouted Bob turning down the radio and looking quizzically at Abe.

Stifling his mirth for a moment, Abe addressed the revelers, "You have to see this! No kidding! Back in the toilet! Take a look!"

Piling out into the passageway, they followed Abe aft, picking up the stragglers from the adjacent cabins and feeling they were about to be the recipients of some kind of practical joke. They crowded outside the bathroom, Abe prepared for the unveiling; voiced a little fanfare – Da-Da-Da-Rah and threw open the door. What a spectacle! And a sight for all to behold!

Tex was in a very precarious position to the left of the toilet bowl. Having dropped his pants, he had intended to seat himself on the throne but the motion of the ship caused him to deflect his aim and he succeeded in jamming his ass over the pipes running from the bulkhead to the bowl. There he sat in all his glory; ass jammed, head resting on bent knees with lowered pants and snoring away. Being as drunk as he was, he was unable to extract himself so he just went to sleep. Hysterics caught the entire group, as the spectators took in the plight of poor Tex. While screaming with laughter, someone suggested getting a camera. Jimmy went to his cabin and returned with the deadly weapon. After several shots, they completed the foul deed and dismissed the broads. The guys untangled the human pretzel and carried him to his bunk.

The first night was ending. Eventually all headed for their bunks except Chuck, who, equipped with bottle, went seeking other playmates as the ship glided along peacefully into the night.

.

DAY 2
AT SEA

Stepping onto the after deck, Scotty welcomed the fresh sea air after leaving the stuffiness of his inboard cabin. Most of that stench was created by his roommate who lay dead to the world smelling like a bar towel and reeking of tobacco smoke. Smoking was Scotty's nemesis, and a complaint he voiced continually at Chuck, who agreed not to smoke when Scotty was in the cabin. Walking across the fantail, he rested his arms on the rail around the stern and gazed at the two large furrows dug deep into the ocean by the two gigantic screws underneath. It gave the impression of a huge plow pushing right through a shimmering green field leaving a frothy white track as far as one could see.

Joggers, plodding around the deck, were trying to sweat out the booze from the night before. The earlier joggers were already seated for first sitting breakfast. The freezing temperatures had abated. The old folks, curled up in the deck chairs, were wrapped in their woollies and scarves. A sure sign that there still was a nip in the air.

The lads never entered the dining room for breakfast. Tom had a deal with one of the chefs to fix egg and bacon sandwiches which he served them in their cabins. In return, the chef would be reimbursed with his choice of beverage each cruise. Tom always knew the musician's itinerary, such as today, a rehearsal day, sandwiches and coffee at nine a.m.

Returning to the Inner Sanctum after his walk around the deck, Scotty began the awesome task of trying to wake Chuck. It was always Scotty's responsibility to make sure Chuck was up and ready for all performances. He would usually let Chuck sleep until half an hour before playing, then kick his head if necessary. Usually Scotty would get himself dressed first, then shake Dracula at five-thirty giving him just enough time before the cocktail session at six o'clock. Chuck's routine was always the same. Crawling from his bunk, he would put a cigarette in his mouth, but he never lit it. Like something just arisen from the dead, Chuck would approach the mirror above the washbasin. Shaving soap was applied around the adult thumb sucker hanging from his lips to be followed with the process of removing the whiskers. Laying down the razor, he would invariably apply cold water to his face without removing the cigarette. This little action would render him half awake and cursing as he proceeded to remove what looked like pieces of shit from his proboscis. The cabin door would remain open during this performance, and the musicians would pass by on their way topside.

"Hurry up asshole!"

"You only have ten minutes."

"Did you get embalmed, Chuck?"

"See ya up there!"

Dressed at last, Chuck would then make the effort to reach the Grand Lounge. From the Inner Sanctum he had to climb two decks then walk amidships to the elevator that would take him to the Prom deck. Chuck would enter the lounge, climb on the bandstand, and await his elixir. Albee, the waiter, knew the routine and was always ready. He would place two double rums in front of the piano player. Chuck needed this to get his heart started. Downing the contents of both glasses immediately, Chuck would raise his head, smile, and wish everyone a good evening. Should it happen that Albee would have ever forgotten the heart primer, Chuck would probably remain in his catatonic state until the remedy was supplied.

The stench of the cabin as Scotty opened the door told him that Chuck was still dead. He began his chore by kicking him a few times. As soon as he saw Chuck's eyes open, which looked like pee holes in the snow, he reminded him that they had a rehearsal and, more importantly, that it was still morning and not cocktail hour. Assured his task was complete, Scotty headed for Jimmy's cabin where Tom was all ready with the food.

"Morning, Abe, Jimmy."

"Hi, Scotty," replied Jimmy and Abe.

"Tom, I'll have my goodies here," said Scotty as he sat on the edge of the bunk. "Smells like a pox doctor's office over there," nodding his head in the direction of his own quarters. Jimmy completed his ablutions and donned his white shirt and began tying his black necktie.

"Are you wearing a tie?" asked Abe expecting to be informed of a sea burial.

"Uh huh," answered Jimmy.

"To a rehearsal?" Abe was still confused.

"Son, on this ship, when you work for Bob Gibson you wear a tie when you go for a shit. The only time you are allowed to wear casual clothes around here is while playing those silly passenger games on the outside deck. Remember, Bob is a stickler for professionalism, and it helps us behave like perfect gentlemen to be so adorned."

"Perfect gentlemen? Ha! Ha! That's a giggle," laughed Abe. "Like last night when you carried Tex from the shitter and placed him in a short-sheeted bed. Tom says he looked like a forty-year-old fetus and was still in the same position this morning. He'll be lucky if he can walk today."

"Oh, you don't know the half of it," smiled Scotty. "Hey, Jimmy, should we tell him?"

"Yeah, sure, Abe's been around long enough to know that musicians have a nasty side to their nature."

"Yeah and you guys sure displayed this failing by posting that Polaroid picture of Tex's ordeal on the crew notice board," added Tom joining in the laughter.

"Tell Abe what happened, Tom. It's a great story, Abe, you'll get a right giggle."

"Well, after Tex awoke this morning, he went out for a little stroll. As he began passing through various parts of the ship, he was greeted with such invectives as, "Don't you know which end is up?" "You don't know your ass from your elbow?" "Hey are you potty trained?" He didn't know what was going on, so poor old Tex's only comeback was, "Any more shit and no booze for you." Someone finally showed him the picture and he just laughed."

"Couldn't happen to a nicer guy," added Jimmy as they left the cabin and headed topside.

Everyone was assembled in the club. Tom had already provided a coffee urn and some Danish pastries for anyone who felt so inclined. The musicians were introduced to the person responsible for this impromptu rehearsal, Miss Bonnie Long. The fellows sized her up in their own way. She was tall, but had a few miles on her. She was very patronizing and carried herself quite aloof. Probably not a bad looker twenty years ago, but obviously not dealing with a full deck now. This is the type of person who is desperately holding onto the Shirley Temple bag, complete with a flower in her hair.

"Okay lads," Bob addressed the group, "here's the set up. We'll open with the usual show warmer upper. You know," as he sang the first line of the song known to all as a circus gallop. "How do you do everyone. How do you do-do-doodley-do. Etcetera. Etcetera. The band will end off after the third chorus. Drum roll on the tom tom, Scotty. Lights will dim. Spotlight on the Port side door to the left of the bandstand. We will play a fanfare, then Miss Long will make her entrance, singing solo the first measure of "God Bless America." We will come in on the second measure and take it from there."

During the talk over, Bonnie was smiling at each of the musicians in turn like a mother hen about to pat each of them on the head and give them a cookie if they are good little boys. The mood on the bandstand had changed from mild interest to good natured joviality. The result of the coffee laced with a hefty dram from the Scotch bottle sitting to the left of the piano.

"After the opener, Bonnie will sing two show tunes. I already have the music here from the locker. This will be followed by a few light selections from us, and that should take us up to ten forty-five. Fifteen minutes break, then the ball will kick off at eleven. As you know, it's the Captain's Cocktail Party prior to this event, so all the passengers will be in formal dress. Musicians, of course, will wear dark tux and on your best behavior, gentlemen. Okay, let's do it."

All prepared, Bob gave the two taps leading them into the first chorus sung by all present in unison. Second time through was instrumental, and it prepared the onlookers for the biggie. Ending the tune, Scotty gave a powerful rally on the floor tom tom and struck the cymbal as the star of the show broke into "God Bless America." Completing the first run through, Bonnie made for the back of the room to fortify herself with another cuppa. It was obvious from the expression on musicians' faces that they were not about to be rewarded with a pat on the head or receive any cookies. It was taking every ounce of control to hold down the screaming laughter that posed every danger of surfacing. Bob, knowing his guys, was praying for good manners and breeding to prevail as he heard the muttering of dissent from the group.

"Is she fucking joking?"

"We'll have to tune the instruments to the ship's engines to play with her!"

"She has a nice voice, but she spoils it singing!"

"Her ears must be painted on!"

This banter could not be heard off the stage. Bob turned to face the group. His eyes looked like two organ stops and his complexion a ruddy blue as he suppressed the same desire to explode. With violin in his left hand and bow in his right, he shook his index finger, indicating that his crew should pipe down and cool it. This scene was embarrassing enough without their adding to it. Bonnie returned carrying her coffee cup. The band quickly recovered their composure and they continued with the rehearsal. The arduous task completed, they silently dispersed from the room and headed topside.

Instruments were once again stowed away. The stalwart seven made for the dining room and a hearty lunch. Most tables seated six people, but the musicians had a slightly larger table located on the portside near the galley doors. Always wearing dark jackets and ties at lunch time, they resembled remnants from an undertaker's convention seated at the table. It was agreed not to discuss this morning's work, and they all hoped the passengers would be too loaded tonight to notice.

The next item on the agenda, after second sitting, was a lecture in the Main Lounge given by a travel agent who was part of the ship's complement. The band just played a couple of tunes while the passengers were assembling. Then old James Wood took over and gave some interesting information on whatever island they would be visiting next. Questions about sightseeing, currency, bargains, and entertainment were answered at this time. After having completed their contribution by warming up the audience for the lecturer, the musicians left the bandstand and entered the pantry bar located aft of the Main Lounge. They usually had a shooter and listened to the latest shipboard gossip from Pete the barman.

"Okay, Pete, set 'em up," from Bob. As they all squeezed into the small area.

"What exclusive trivia do you have for us today, Pete?" asked Chuck.

"How come only six? Who's missing?" inquired Pete; checking out the band.

"The Devil done it!" Bob answered and related the infliction of being cursed with a teetotaler. This earned sympathy from his attentive fellow companions.

"Well, maybe you will all be on the wagon soon if what I hear is true," replied Pete.

"What do you mean?" Jimmy asked. "Are we going back to prohibition or something?"

"As far as this ship is concerned, that may be the case," continued Pete, pouring more drinks from the bottle. All the group's attention was now on the barman as he unfolded the latest turn of events.

"The Company has been concerned about what's going on among the crew because of the heavy boozing, and they are determined to put a stop to it. They don't like the fact that this vessel is now referred to as "The Rum Ship" and are taking steps to change the whole scene aboard." Silence fell over the group as they picked up the glasses, still waiting for Pete to impart the rest of the story.

"Have any of you ever heard of Staff Captain Breathwaite?" Looking at the bunch and not getting a reply except for a few shakes of the head, Pete continued his tale. "Breathwaite is a stickler for law and order. Especially where alcohol is concerned. He is a strict teetotaler, and any time the company has a ship that has such a problem Breathwaite is sent immediately to straighten it out. He is known to just wipe out a ship's entire complement. And make no bones about it, he can be tough!" A shudder ran through each of the guys in the pantry at the thought of prohibition.

"Well, we're not really crew, so screw him!" responded Bob. "And how 'bout another round for my boys?"

"Yeah!" agreed Tex.

"Cheers, Bob," added Chuck. They tried to joke it off, but knew deep down there was trouble ahead.

"Okay, Pete, we've had the bad news, so what's the good?" demanded Scotty raising his glass.

"So, you want to hear the newest shipboard tale," Pete replied laughing as he thought of the story he was about to unfold. "Well, gentlemen, here goes. A bedroom steward went in to clean a cabin this morning. In shock, he went back out into the cabin and asked the woman passenger what the hell happened? "Oh," she said to the steward, "my husband took some salts this morning." "Christ Missis," he replied "it must have been somersaults!"" The lads howled at the story.

"Cheers, Pete! That sure was a good one!" laughed Bob.

"Yeah! Thanks for keeping us so well informed," added Chuck.

The laughter was dispelling their fears about prohibition. They finished their drinks and took off down the passageway still chuckling over the somersaults.

They now had a couple of hours to kill before cocktail session, and each went their separate ways. Chuck went back to bunksies; Bob went to the music locker to get some orchestrations; Jimmy took Abe to the cinema; Mike went to the gym for a light workout and Tex went back to his cabin to finish his current mystery novel. Scotty picked up a copy of the day's news and made for a desk chair, aft of the Prom deck and out of the wind. He was so deeply engrossed in the contents of the bulletin that he was not aware of the gentleman who was occupying the chair to his right and slightly behind. Placing the paper in his lap, Scotty began to stare off into space; absorbing what he had read, there was a hint of sadness showing in his expression.

"Penny for your thoughts," the stranger addressed him. "You look very serious."

Turning his attention to the source, Scotty noticed the gentleman was well groomed, complete with a blue blazer and silk scarf worn like a cravat that set off his well-brushed grey hair.

"Yeah! I suppose I was," he replied. "I don't know why I bother to pick up this junk. All one is subjected to is how many deaths take place as a result of murder, plane crashes, terrorists, war, and all other types of mayhem. By the way," he interrupted himself and extended his hand, "the name is Scotty. Scotty MacFarlane."

"My pleasure." The gentleman shook his hand. "Walter Armstrong's my name."

Moving his chair further back to be in line, Scotty was impressed by Walter's calm expression and especially by the steady, shining blue eyes of his newfound companion. There seemed to be such a serenity not found in the usual passenger or in any of his musician buddies. It made Scotty feel good to be in his company. Almost as if he'd known Walter all his life.

"I take it from your clothes that you have something to do with the ship's management," Walter asked, indicating the dark suit and black tie.

"Heavens no!" laughed Scotty. "I'm one of the ship's musicians who venture forth on the sea of life to escape from all this garbage I've been reading about."

"How interesting," was the reply. "It is a fact that anyone involved in the arts is functioning on the aesthetic wave band and is indeed of a higher caliber than the common man."

"I like your thinking, but I don't think you would continue with such a thought if you witnessed some of the antics this band gets up to." Scotty was laughing.

"Maybe so, but on the whole, I have found musicians to be more profound and deeper thinkers than the usual proletariat."

Letting this sink in, Scotty was still reluctant to accept such praise.

"Maybe you are giving us more credit than we deserve. We act as crazy as a bunch of pirates on this ship; drinking too much and taking advantage of so many unsuspecting females. It's almost criminal," he added with a little smile to show he was not being too serious.

"Fine. At least that shows you have some feeling and no malicious intent. Intention is the key factor that separates you from the people you are reading about in the paper. Sure, you probably drink too much and take advantage of the weaker sex, but don't forget the female of the species is more deadly than the male and they are not entirely innocent. They also have to take responsibility for the part they're playing."

"Well," agreed Scotty, "I suppose that's about the extent of our mischievousness. But what bothers me is that one day this is going to be all over and I may have to be a part of all the craziness on shore. To tell you the truth, I don't have the same enthusiasm for this game anymore. All of a sudden, I'm beginning to react differently to the old fun and games. It's like there's no depth." Moving his hands to express himself, he continued, "For years I went along with the program, but now it's beginning to bore me. No real conversation, only drinking and partying because it's the thing to do. We just seem to live in one big fantasy as if this is all there is to it and there is no other world out there. It's like smoking or ignorance of politics. There is an excuse when you're fourteen years old, but if you still continue in your stupidity by the time you're twenty-one, then your head is up your ass."

Scotty sat back as his new friend studied him for a moment before speaking. "Could be, Scotty, that you are ready for a new game. You've played this one out and obviously the time has come to make the change."

"Like what?" asked Scotty, realizing that this person was having an effect on him. "Walter looked right at me when he spoke and really listened to me," he thought to himself.

"Let's look at it from a different perspective or a little hypothetical, okay?"

"Okay," replied Scotty all intent on listening.

"Let's assume we have two universes, a physical and a spiritual."

"Oh shit," thought Scotty, "I've got a holy roller. This mother is now going to convert me. Don't let him be a Jehovah's Witness who will pour on the fire and brimstone routine." Noticing Scotty's demeanor and perplexity Walter quietly asked him what was going on in his thoughts.

"Are you a preacher or some kind of man of the gospel?" Scotty asked with the sound of disappointment in his voice.

"No! No! Nothing like that," answered Walter raising his right hand as though he was taking an oath. The smile that accompanied his statement helped to quell Scotty's fears.

"By the way, it is not necessary that you believe everything I say, but let's have a little fun with our discussion. Okay?"

"Sure, Walter," replied Scotty appearing more interested now that he was assured that he was not at the mercy of some man of the cloth.

The newfound friend hesitated for a moment as though he was putting his own thoughts into perspective. He waited for Scotty's full attention and then continued with what sounded like a theory.

"Now as I was saying, imagine there are two universes in your environment, and each one has a part of its own to play. First, we have what could be described as the physical universe. In other words, all that we are able to see and touch in the world around us. Do you agree so far?"

"Okay," replied Scotty, nodding in agreement.

"Of course this group would include the body and all its parts, since it is something we can see and touch. Right?"

"Uh huh! Uh huh!" replied Scotty. "I'm still with you."

"Good," answered Walter preparing to continue. "Now the other universe would have to be the spiritual universe. It is the universe that is responsible for the physical."

Scotty felt that a reference to God was about to be made. Religion was not his bag, nor was it something that even involved the usual run of the mill musician. He placed his hands behind his head to rest more comfortable. Looking at Walter he presented his thoughts on the subject.

"I do not claim to be agnostic but I have never had much respect for the purveyors of the Lord's Holy Message. I find it difficult to take people such as clergymen, nuns, and the like very serious. They always appear to me to be in a state of hypnosis, playing a role calling for a pious attitude rather than being what they represent."

"I understand what you are saying, but there is much more to spirituality than merely handing your responsibility over to God. To add to what you just said, these people represent religious practices. This is a far cry from a religious philosophy."

Scotty looked at him quizzically, "You mean there is a difference?"

"Well let's take a look at it," Walter continued. "A religious practice is usually a compilation of morals; complete with certain rituals such as Baptism or Circumcision. People wearing crosses. The Hindus wear a red spot on their foreheads. The Orthodox Jew dresses in a fashion that dates back thousands of years. All are attempting what they consider to be the ultimate in divine communication as they parade to and fro from their churches and temples."

Now Scotty felt himself in the presence of a teacher who was about to unfold the secrets of the universe while at the same time hoping Walter was not a kook.

"You see," Walter continued. "The unfortunate part of this is that all the mores and ritual practices do nothing to improve the believer. These things actually place a barrier between him and what he is trying to achieve. It's like accepting the fact that this is all there is to it. Therefore, I don't have to look any further. I can hand all my responsibility to the benevolent Father up above. Then claim that anything that happens to me is His will. You see this all around you. The one quality that has deserted man can be summed up in one word – ETHICS. All sorts of transgressions are committed every day by the same people who run to their church and try to convince themselves that they are good in order to assure a ticket into heaven."

Silence reigned for a few moments. Scotty further contemplated the speaker and his words. He does not sound like a cynic because the anger that usually denotes such types is missing. He was not condescending either. He just speaks in a calm, serene, and matter of fact voice. He usually makes you want to hear more rather than feeling the boredom that usually followed an antagonistic conversation.

"What was it you said about religious philosophy?" asked Scotty awaiting the answer eagerly.

"Well, Gandhi said that religion is simply self-awareness, or know thyself. Actually, it's going to take more than Bibles or wearing a uniform to improve man and raise him to the heights of being truly ethical. What is required is a form of scientific technology that will enable man to reach into himself and rediscover the knowledge that has been lost to him. Only then will he know religion."

"I see," Scotty responded slowly while trying to put into words what he was thinking. "What about philosophical books like those written by Kahlil Gibran? I have read and enjoyed his books. What part do such teachings play in the role of things?"

"Kahlil Gibran's books, I agree, contain such beautiful thoughts. So does the Bible and other such idealistic books. You name any number of them I'm sure," answered Walter. "Gibran is more a pure philosophy. That's all it is. It is all very well to convey love and how one should treat his wife and children, but how can a man love his wife when he has a mental aberration to destroy women? In other words, we know the way it should be but have no cure. What we need is the key. This key would open the door and bring forth the cause and the cure thereby enabling the person to achieve the heights of what Kahlil Gibran describes in his books."

"I sure don't know anyone who is so inclined. Just imagine," said Scotty. "If everyone was like you describe, then we would have a sane society."

"Now you've said it," replied Walter. "If we can accept the fact that the spiritual universe was responsible for the creation of the physical universe, then something has gone wrong. Somewhere along the line, the spiritual became enmeshed in the physical. So instead of the spiritual universe in control of the physical, it is in reverse and now the physical impinges on the spiritual. Thus, creating what we have today, an insane society."

"I think I can agree with that! The world is nuts!" Scotty added.

"If I may add, Scotty, that is not a mere observation but a statement of fact. As you said, the world is nuts and insanity is not located in any one geographical area, but is everywhere. It may be dramatized a little heavier in certain countries such as the Middle East, Ireland, and wherever useless violence and killing is taking place. Unfortunately, it does exist, and it has many contributing factors within the society to make sure it continues. On that note, I think we should call it a day as time is moving on."

Scotty looking at his watch said, "I never even noticed the time pass. You sure got me interested. I suppose I better go change for the cocktail session."

Standing up, they looked into each other's eyes and shook hands. Scotty couldn't describe what he felt; he knew it was a good feeling. Like a mixture of admiration and compassion. Before leaving, Walter made one more comment.

"To complete what we have discussed so far about insanity. Remember, one does not realize how insane the society is until he realizes how much he contributes to that insanity."

Scotty knew, as Walter disappeared through the doorway, that he had been hit between the eyes with a double-barreled shotgun and that this would not be the end of his lessons. Walking to the aft companionway, Scotty could feel the pictures spinning around in his head as though seeking the answer to Walter's parting remark.

Entering his cabin, Scotty found Chuck already dressed and sitting back in a chair with his feet resting on his bunk reading a magazine.

"Where the hell have you been?" asked Chuck, raising his eyes from the pages. "I looked for you in the library where you usually hang out, but no sign of you."

"I met a passenger topside and found myself engaged in the most enlightening conversation. The time just flew by and it made for a pleasant afternoon."

Scotty's attention was still fixed on what had taken place as he began removing his clothes. He wrapped a towel around his waist and placed his sandals on his feet before heading for the showers located down the passageway. Chuck noticed his roommate had a faraway look in his eyes.

"You look as though you're off in the clouds somewhere. What the hell happened? Did you see a vision or something? Here, have a shot of this." Chuck pulled out a bottle of rum from the side of the bunk. "This will straighten you out."

"No thanks," Scotty replied laughingly. "Maybe that's the shit that causes visions." Then jokingly adding in his best Southern drawl before leaving the room, "Ahh's see-een de light!"

Christ, thought Chuck, that's all we need, another teetotaler.

Walking past the other cabins, Scotty could hear little squeals of delight coming from Bob's cabin. "Probably got some old broad in there giving her tits a massage," he thought. Music was blaring from the next cabin occupied by Jimmy and Abe; they were getting themselves dressed. Finally, Mike, in his best tenor voice, was serenading Tex, who was stretched out on his bunk fully dressed and sipping Bacardi rum and coke.

After passing the living quarters of his buddies, Scotty couldn't help but think it strange to have a different viewpoint all of a sudden. The environment hadn't changed. It was always the same scene and accepted by one and all as the normal condition. But that parting remark from Walter still sounded in his head.

"You do not realize how insane the society is until you realize how much you contribute towards that insanity."

"Sure, they all lived it up, but was it of any real consequence? Most of the time they were all half in the bag, laughing and joking around, but was it really fun or just the glee of insanity?" he wondered; similar to the junkie who gets spaced out and starts the giggles. Turning the taps in the shower stall, the cascading water felt refreshing and helped to return him to the job at hand.

The spirit of carnival was evident as one approached the lounges. All the male passengers were dressed in black tuxedos while the ladies were attired in their evening gowns. There was an air of gaiety, propriety, and bon ami as the passengers lined up outside the Main Lounge. Each couple was signaled to enter and shake hands with the Captain while the ship's photographer captured the memorable event with the highly desirable picture; at a price of course! After the introduction and picture taking, the passengers, equipped with complimentary drinks, would spill over into the Grand Lounge where the merry minstrels contributed to the festivities with a little background music. The boys would return here, after dinner, for the light music session which tonight would feature Miss Bonnie Long. A short break and then dance named, "The Ball De Fleur" would commence. For this occasion, the lounge had been completely decorated with all types of pretty flowers.

At that moment the lounge was a scene of splendor with everyone dressed so nice amidst the flowers. The passengers had consumed just enough bubbly to be happy and jolly; all intent on having a good time. Even the musicians shared the spirit and were contributing their artistic endeavor to the cause.

During the festivities one of the Junior Pursers appeared at the door. He stood watching the band as they played a number requested by one of the passengers. The scene was always the same. Husbands who never knew their wives existed on shore were all of a sudden transformed into dreamy-eyed school boys as a result of the liquor and romantic atmosphere. All stress and worries, from whatever useless occupation they committed themselves to at home, disappeared, and they became aware of the female they had married and yet had never even noticed for the past dozen years. With this newfound joy, each starry-eyed lover would request whatever silly song they recalled from that night long, long ago when the couple first met. The young officer strode through the throng and approached Bob just as the band finished the last request.

"Mr. Gibson."

Bob turned and stooped closer to listen to the young officer deliver his message.

"Mr. Russell sends his compliments and would appreciate your presence in his office after dinner at eight p.m."

This seemed to be a traditional courtesy aboard ships between officers. No matter how serious or trivial the communication, they would always start with Mr. So and So sends his compliments and wishes to inform you that you are to receive one hundred lashes at dawn. This custom must have started somewhere on British Naval ships and was typical of the stiff upper lip type.

"Very good, son, no problem." Bob expected the command to involve the usual "split a bottle" at the beginning of each cruise that he and the Purser have indulged in for years. Bob turned to the band, but the young officer called his attention again.

"Excuse me, sir, it's not just your presence that is requested, but all the musicians."

"All the musicians?" inquired Bob, looking perplexed and turning once again to the messenger.

"Yes, sir, after dinner then," the young officer responded and quickly made his retreat.

Walking across the dance floor, the Junior Purser was thinking to himself, "why do I always feel intimidated when conveying anything to those musicians? I can order all of the stewards, deckies, and even passengers with confidence, but always feel inferior when forced to deal with that lot."

"What's the matter, Bob?" asked Jimmy, noticing the leader's expression. "Anything wrong?"

"I'm not sure," replied Bob, "but we all have to be at the Purser's Office after dinner. Obviously, there's something brewing. Oh well, until then give us, "Body and Soul," Jimmy," Bob smiled halfhearted.

Dinner over, the group led by Bob made their way to B deck forward where the Purser's Office was located. Arriving at their destination, which did seem to take forever, they felt as though they were wearing iron boots, a result of the reluctance on their part to make the journey. Some sort of premonition was telling them to beware of what they were about to receive. Bob's knock was answered by Jim Russell, the Purser himself, who opened the door and invited all to enter. Filing into the spacious office containing a desk, four armchairs and a long divan against the bulkhead, they were confronted by a serious looking officer who had taken a position in front of the desk.

"Gentlemen," voiced the Purser, "may I introduce Staff Captain Breathwaite."

After the formal introductions, they were invited to be seated, which they did, except Bob. He wished to hold a position equal to that of the militaristic looking asshole in front of him. The Staffy, seeing the position taken by Bob, realized he was not dealing with some young school boy. However, he still felt superior in his little sailor suit and he did expect to win this war. Scrutinizing the group, the Staff Captain then proceeded to inform them of the reason for the summons.

"Gentlemen, I have been assigned to this ship for a very specific purpose, and that is to stamp out the abuse of alcohol." Seeing Bob was about to interrupt, the Staffy held up his hand, stifling Bob's attempt and continued. "Work has been grossly affected on this ship. Hours lost. Fighting among crew. Injuries and illnesses. All as a result of what can only be termed as criminal behavior."

Bob squared his shoulders as if for combat, looked straight at the Staffy, and said, "Are you implying that my musicians are neglecting their positions or are unable to perform because of liquor?"

"On the contrary, Mr. Gibson. It never ceases to amaze me how much liquor is consumed by a ship's musician and yet they are still capable of doing their job. I have witnessed this aboard other vessels. My main objective is directed at the crew. However, you and your subordinates are not so naïve to think that your behavior on board goes unnoticed by this ship's officers, and I can assure you that it is going to stop."

"Well," inquired Bob, taking a more relaxed position, "If your beef is with the crew, what the hell are we doing here?"

"Now, Mr. Gibson, let's not play games. Whenever a crew member signs ship's articles, he becomes a party of that agreement. One of the rules being that it is an infringement of the agreement to bring even one can of beer aboard ship. Although you have passenger status, which enables you and your musicians to purchase drinks at the bars, it does not alter the fact that you are still signatories on the ship's articles."

"Have I made myself understood, gentlemen?" He directed himself triumphantly at the crestfallen bunch around the room. The Purser, looking sympathetically at Bob, his old buddy, and wishing they were enjoying their usual dram and a tete-a-tete instead of feeling a party to this motherfucking robot who was threatening to destroy a way of life and end all the fun. The Staffy, knowing that he had them by the proverbials, added the piece de resistance as he drove home the final shaft.

"When we dock in St. Thomas, I will personally be at the gun port door all day to make sure no packages come aboard addressed to any crew member. All liquor will be confiscated, and the offending member dealt with harshly, and that, of course, includes your group, Mr. Gibson. As I have said, I have no authority over your drinking in the passenger lounges, but no alcohol will be brought aboard this ship ever again! With that, I will bid you gentlemen a good evening and expect your full cooperation."

The silence that pervaded a storm soon erupted into turmoil when the Staffy left the cabin.

The Purser, turning to them apologetically, said, "Sorry fellows. When I heard he was joining the ship, I knew we were headed for trouble. He is more the naval type, and should not be on pleasure cruises."

"Of course," replied Bob, "it's okay having a drink, but he is right; the crew do get out of hand and are inclined to be stupid. It's all down to experience and being able to handle it."

"He's sure on to us," stated Jimmy, now standing. "What the hell are we going to do tomorrow for our rations?"

Chuck got the attention of all and sermonized, "Do you realize what this could do to the economy of the West Indies? Starvation. Rioting in the streets. It could even finish up with war ending in a nuclear holocaust! And all for the want of a departed spirit."

The humor from Chuck helped to lighten the situation and encouraged a few smiles.

"Okay lads," said Bob, "let's head to my place and get our heads together. This calls for some serious strategy, and anyway, we are in need of fortification." Assuring the Purser that he was not to blame, they left the room and headed for the Inner Sanctum.

Seated once again in the safety of Bob's cabin with drinks in hand, the meeting of minds began. All sorts of suggestions were discussed including keel hauling the Staff Captain and then feeding him to the sharks. Scotty, who had been sitting in quiet repose sipping on his Scotch, suddenly jumped up and commanded the attention of the others.

"Hold the phone! I've got it! Boy are we dumb," he began, looking around at the faces eager for the solution. "How many broads and friends have each of us made since we sailed? You, Chuck, have at least those three broads of yours," pointing to his buddy. "Jimmy? Tex? Mike? You, Bob," turning in his direction, "apart from big boobs, you also have a few admirers. Get hold of shit for brains," indicating Abe, "and let's see how many bodies he can offer for the cause. What we will do is have all our liquor packages addressed to the passenger's name and cabin. Then, after we leave the island, we pick the booty up and bring it back here."

"Great, Scotty!"

"Good idea!"

"What ho, me hearties," added Mike. "Belay there! The plan John Barleycorn it is then! Ho! Ho!"

"That deserves another noggin," said Bob as he headed for the bottle.

The notorious six held up their glasses for refilling and settled down feeling victorious. Bob reminded them all that they still had the problem of how to supply the crew, who depended on them for the illegal contraband. Just then, Tom entered with a fresh supply of ice and was informed of the situation by Bob.

"When you go forward, Tom, tell Tiny and Jeff to come to my cabin after the dance. We may have a problem getting the booze aboard at St. Thomas."

Tiny and Jeff were two of the deckies who usually took care of the crew requirements by supplying Tex with the crew list before reaching port.

"Okay," answered Tom. "Will do. See you guys later."

The outlaws then returned to their respective cabins to freshen up before the concert. Scotty and Chuck were sitting back sipping on Bacardi rum and coke, in an effort to continue to support the economy of St. Thomas, when someone knocked on the door.

"Come in," called Chuck. The door opened to reveal Abe, looking as though his hemorrhoids were wrapped around the ship's screws and he was about to cry. Entering the cabin, Abe sat himself on the end of one of the bunks waiting for some sort of response.

"Bob is on my case and has forbid me to join in the jazz sessions in the club after hours. Just because I don't drink, I have to suffer," he said mournfully. "Bob told me to play the shows and formal dances, but to go to bed with the rest of the old fogies so I won't miss my beef tea in the morning."

Abe's doom and gloom received no sympathy. The lads just laughed at his misfortune. The kid excelled in jazz, so this was the worst form of punishment that Bob could inflict.

"Well, what the fuck do you expect?" said Chuck, turning on him harshly. "You're a grown man, a musician. You've hung around New York and you come on like some Mormon or a pussy afraid to live it up. What the hell's wrong with taking a drink? Somewhere along the line you're going to have to break down and be one of the guys. What better opportunity than among the most jovial and well-meaning chaps you are ever likely to meet?" Chuck gave Abe a hint of referring to himself and Scotty.

"You mean take a drink?" Abe asked wide eyed. Scotty looked a little mischievous, guessing what was about to take place.

"No, I mean kiss my ass! What the hell do you think I mean? It's just a little spirit laced with Coca Cola. You do drink Coca Cola I suppose."

"Well, yeah," replied Abe hesitatingly, "but I don't know about the other stuff."

"Look," as Chuck poured himself a shot of Bacardi. "It just looks like water. Now I add cola and you have a nice refreshing tropical drink." Smiling while mixing the two. "So why don't you join the two most pleasant people in the world and have a taste?"

Looking at Scotty for some kind of moral support, his plea was met with a shrug of the shoulders followed by, "Try it. You'll like it!"

"Okay," said Abe brightening up. "Let me try a little. It can't hurt."

Taking an eight-ounce glass, Chuck half filled it with rum. Scotty winced at the measure. Topping the glass with Coca Cola, Chuck handed it to Abe who stared at it for a few moments before taking it to his lips.

"Cheers fellows!" Abe gave a smiling toast. Of course, being an amateur, he proceeded to chug-a-lug the whole drink.

Scotty and Chuck looked at each other with amused expressions after witnessing the baptismal. They expected to see the booze rebound from Abe's chaste stomach and hit the wall. Abe, looking at the empty glass in disbelief that he hadn't dropped dead after all, realized he enjoyed the contents and requested another. This time Chuck poured more rum and less Coke, advising Abe not to be in such a rush, but to relish the flavor. His words fell on deaf ears. Abe again emptied the glass in two gulps, burped and hiccupped a couple of times. Putting down the glass, Abe looked at his newfound friends with a somewhat stupid glassy-eyed expression, then slowly started to giggle. The two conspirators waited with baited breath. The giggles gradually increased into raucous laughter, symptomatic of someone who had just blown his lid.

"Jesus Christ!" remarked Scotty, unable to control his own laughter. "We have a giggler on our hands."

The three musketeers were feeling no pain when they ventured forth to the Prom deck to play the light music session. Walking up two decks, they kept Abe between them in case he should go off course. He wasn't staggering, but now and again would burst out giggling when passing another passenger. Entering the elevator, they stood to the rear making room for two, not very attractive, old dears who entered just as the doors were about to close. One of the old matrons happened to mention to her companion that she had spent half the day in the beauty shop. A gift from her husband who offered to pay the bill.

Abe, hearing this, burst out laughing, tapped the old broad on the shoulder and asked, "What did you do with the money?"

Scotty and Chuck, now totally embarrassed, pushed Abe between the gals at the next deck and made a hasty exit leaving the ladies in a state of apoplexy.

Using the stairs again, they made it to the Prom deck and music locker to retrieve their instruments. Most of the passengers were already seated, and it looked like a first nightery at the La Scala with everyone dressed in their finery. The other musicians were on the bandstand awaiting Bob.

Before entering the lounge, Scotty, holding Abe's head between his hands, implored, "For Christ's sake, shut up and pull yourself together. We are going to play now, so cool it. Get on the stand and just play. Okay?"

"Sure guys. No Problem." He appeared as though the effects were starting to wear off, and he was returning to normal, much to the relief of his conspirators.

They seated themselves on the stage. Scotty's drums were not on a riser. He was seated just behind Abe and hoped that from this vantage point to be able to control him. Bob entered and joined them on the stand, not aware anything had taken place. He picked up his violin and bow from the top of the piano and prepared to play the overture.

"Okay gentlemen. All tuned up? Let's cut it." Bob beat off the introductory gallop.

Finishing the opener, the lights dimmed. Scotty played a crescendo roll on the floor tom-tom and a spotlight sent a beam to the port side door to the left of the bandstand. Completing the roll with a crash on the cymbal, Bob made the announcement.

"Ladies and Gentlemen. Miss Bonnie Long!"

The attention of the audience was directed towards the portside door encased in the huge spotlight. The band struck up and Bonnie came through the door like Lorretta Young. She was wearing a long flowing skirt and bellowing forth in her out of tune contralto voice, "God Bless America!"

She sounded like a banshee that had just been goosed. Abe went completely to pieces. He shrieked with hysterical laughter. He leaned back in his chair with both feet in the air and knocked the drums into Scotty, who landed on the floor on his ass. Jimmy and Tex were unable to sustain their instruments in their mouths. Their cheeks contained so much unexploded mirth that they were forced to eject the mouthpieces. The bandstand now sounded like a party of farts. Chuck buried his head in his elbow on top of the piano crying with laughter. Mike was hanging onto his bass, afraid he was about to piss his pants. While all this was taking place behind her, Bonnie, thinking only that the show must go on, continued singing. Bob, being the old pro, also continued to fiddle while Rome burned.

The audience came to the conclusion that this must be a comedy show, joined in the merriment, and the laughter proceeded around the room in waves. It finished up like the snake pit with everyone doubled over. Bonnie made her exit and the guys scampered off the bandstand through the door on the starboard side and continued in their hysteria. Scotty, grabbing Abe, advised him to make himself scarce before Bob came out, or he would probably start to die. As soon as he disappeared, Bob came charging onto the deck and approached the group.

"I'll kill that bastard! Where is he?" demanded Bob, glancing up and down the Prom deck fuming with anger.

"We advised him that it would be easier if he jumped over the side, so he's probably five miles astern by now," replied Mike who was still having a problem keeping a straight face. Seeing Bob's mood, they decided the levity was over and had better not aggravate the condition.

"What the hell happened?" Bob looked beseechingly at his men. "Has he gone nuts?"

"No, Bob. To tell you the truth he is drunk," answered Scotty.

"Drunk?! I thought the little shit didn't drink," replied Bob in disbelief.

"Well he didn't, until tonight. He came into our cabin all upset because you put restrictions on him. So, he decided that if you can't beat 'em – join 'em."

"You mean he actually drank? That's the reason he got so crazy tonight and somehow it's my fault?" He looked at them in disbelief.

"Okay, so we gave him the booze, which was our fault, but you caused him to want it, so that's your fault," explained Scotty.

Bob knew it was no use to continue this nonsensical diatribe. He decided to attempt a solution to what had just taken place on the bandstand.

"How are we going to explain this disaster, especially after what we got from the Staff Captain earlier? This has blown our whole credibility."

"Easy," stated Jimmy as all attention turned to him. "You saw the reaction of the audience, they all thought they were seeing a rehearsed comedy act. Bring back Bonnie and Abe and take a curtain call. I'm sure she'll go along with it, or she won't be able to show her face anywhere. The Senior Officers won't bother, and the Junior Officers are as thick in the head as shit in the neck of a bottle, so they won't know the difference."

So that was how the last scene was played, sounding too ridiculous to be true. Abe swore never to drink again, and Bob reinstated him to full status. The band then played a few selections from the most recent Broadway shows. The audience were attempting to be polite, but guffaws of laughter were heard around the room as some of the passengers were still stuck in the earlier performance. Abe had now achieved the distinction of one of the boys. He was also the source of amusement and the attention of everyone in the room as they eagerly anticipated another comedy sketch.

During the break before commencing the dance portion of the evening, Scotty bumped into Walter on the Prom deck and related the story of Abe's Baptism. Walter smiled at the outcome, then indicated Abe's presence further along the deck where some passengers were fussing over him and praising his talent for comedy.

"Isn't it amazing," Walter pointed out to Scotty, "that there was a little man of no significance screaming to be noticed, and he has now achieved that position? It just proves that the most important function on this planet is having the ability to create attention and here in his own little silly way he is now collecting admirers."

"Christ! You're right!" Scotty exclaimed. "Scratch a mouse and you produce a tiger! See ya later, Walter." Scotty made his way back to the lounge while still pondering Walter's statement.

Halfway through the ball, the musicians put into action the first phase of plan John Barleycorn. All unattached females and friendly males were drawn into the foul plot and really provided the minstrels with full names and cabin numbers. Each musician gave the unsuspecting passenger the same story about a birthday coming up and that they needed the alcohol for the party, but were not allowed to bring any aboard, because they were crew. Oh, how much their help would be appreciated as there were no restrictions on passengers. Abe had guessed right on his first night aboard, this group of pirates had these poor passengers eating out of their hands.

The ball was coming to a close and the usual scene unfolded. The seagoing jocks among the passengers had already sorted out their prey and were seen wandering off into the darkness of the after deck with their arms around their choice. The females were convinced that this was the man of their dreams, while the males were hoping that their choice would prove to be a good piece of ass. Forward in the small lounges, the gamblers were sorting out their pigeons for whatever card game they were about to indulge. The old folks headed for bye byes and the drunks made for the night club and party time.

Setting up the bandstand in the night club, the minstrels had the opportunity to observe the patrons. Chuck's three broads were on hand and as usual rarin' to go. Lorraine was seated in front of the stand with her companion, Valerie, who still had a weird effect on Scotty. However, they had declared a truce during the ball and Valerie agreed to accept the booze delivery, appearing almost friendly about the whole situation. She had a habit of just sitting back and staring as though she was making some kind of study. This was what unnerved Scotty. He would constantly find his attention drawn in her direction as if two laser beams were boring holes through his head. The rest of the room was filling with the high rollers ready to throw the bucks around and have a good time.

In the meantime, the two deck hands, Tiny and Jeff, joined Bob in his cabin as arranged. Complete with glasses in hand, they got down to the serious business of how to overcome the new rules being enforced by Staff Captain Breathwaite. Ideas were bandied around and then the solution was reached. Bob was elated at their creativity and couldn't wait to tell the others. They finished the gig and returned below. Tiny and Jeff had to be on duty early in the morning, so they left and returned to their quarters.

At about two a.m., the gang arrived at Bob's cabin complete with gals in tow. Chuck's three and Scotty's two. Mike had some married woman named Lorretta whose husband was an inveterate card player and neglected his wife, as gamblers are so inclined. The husband was already involved in a heavy poker game in the lounge and oblivious to his wife's whereabouts. So, while he was shuffling the cards, Mike was shuffling Lorretta between the bed sheets and thereby ensuring her of an enjoyable vacation.

Everyone was half in the bag by now and began relating different stories from various cruises. Rum and coke was the order of the evening. Even Abe was allowed to participate, but drinking his coke straight.

"Hey, Scotty," Tex shouted, seated on the divan with his arm around Muriel. "Tell the gals about the time in Cristobal when you guys got stoned."

"That's a good story," he replied, addressing the females around the room. "You'll enjoy it." He laughed as he recalled the event. Unwinding his arm from around Lorraine, he began to unfold the requested tale.

"Chuck, Mike, and I had stopped in one of the local bars for a beer. The type of place that also serves a little bag of pot as a chaser. Not being druggies, and knowing how Bob feels about that crap, we certainly knew better than to bring it back aboard ship. Anyway, we decided to turn on in the bar, which we did. Lo and behold, we got really crazy and couldn't stop laughing. We left the bar as high as kites, and of course got the munchies which, as you girls may not know, is a symptom of having smoked grass. We went into a Chinese restaurant and ordered all sorts of food. While we were eating, an old, mangy dog appeared at the door, pitifully smelling the cooking. The owner of the place threatened the dog with a meat cleaver, and we told him that if he touched that dog, we would do the same to him. He backed off and we made him cook more food, brought the dog in to join us, and fed the poor thing four plates of Chow Mein. That set us off. So, smoking another joint we headed for the Y.M.C.A., where we almost got ourselves killed."

The other guys in the room, being familiar with the story, were already giggling in anticipation. The girls sat most attentive as Scotty, between laughs, continued the tale.

"The men's room in the Y had half a dozen cubicles. Each cubicle contained a wooden seat with a hole that was above a trough of running water that ran through each compartment and flowed to God only knows where. By now we were totally nuts! Observing the situation, we thought it could provide us with some great sport." The girls had quizzical looks on their faces as they tried to guess in their minds what was coming next.

"Know what we did?" Leaning forward he commanded full attention and interest of all in the room. "We went into the end cubicle where the water seemed to begin. We took a newspaper with us and made little paper boats. When the other cubicles were occupied, we lit the boats with a match and sailed them down the trough."

The room was hysterical as they pictured the result of sitting there having the hairs on your ass singed. When the laughter abated,

Scotty described how lucky they were to have escaped in one piece because it was one tough town.

"But the funny thing about being stoned is that you have a feeling of false security."

Bob now took the floor informing everyone that it was time to call it a night. "But before you go, I have to fill you in on the game plan for tomorrow. As you know, Tiny and Jeff were here and came up with a great idea. The booze for the crew will be ordered as usual." He handed the list to Tex. "So, don't worry. The deckies have it handled. This is the way it will go down."

Whoops and cheers could be heard when Bob unfolded the plan and a final toast was had by all as the evening ended. The guys and gals took off, leaving Bob the opportunity of settling down with big boobs. Tex decided to take a stroll around the ship so Mike and his pinochle widow could benefit from the cabin. Chuck left with bottle in hand as usual, while Abe and Jimmy headed for their bunks. Scotty entered his cabin followed by Lorraine, who had no intention of leaving. Valerie had already left; well aware of what her friend had in mind.

Scotty removed his tux and laid down on his bunk as Lorraine stood in the middle of the room. She was a good looker with a nice petite figure and gorgeous skin. He really liked her and did not want this to be just another conquest. He always had mixed feelings about sex. It wasn't something he found easy to indulge in as he always felt some kind of guilt that could sometimes interfere with his performance. It was a combination of embarrassment and shyness. Even though he could be considered a man of the world, there was still that insecurity and unwillingness on his part. Somehow, he seemed unaffected with the vision of loveliness in front of him as she started to undress. Instead of the usual anxiety, he felt very calm and peaceful as she lay beside him. There seemed to be no urgency and he felt as though they had been together forever. Their love making was gentle and very natural, leaving them both serene as they slept away the night in each other's arms in the small space.

DAY 3
ST. THOMAS

At seven a.m. a shudder ran through the ship as the huge anchor was released and headed for the ocean bottom. The S.S. Nectar did not enter the harbor; she lay off the island. It would seem like slumming to include this beautiful vessel among the plastic, welded, stink pots that inhabited the dock area. The ship's life boats, equipped with engines, along with a private company, ferried the passengers back and forth during the course of the day.

Charlotte Amalia on St. Thomas is the capital of these islands. The harbor is pretty with pastel colored buildings and mountains galore. Passengers can take their choice of many planned tours arranged on the ship prior to docking or join with three or four couples and take a ride around the island in a club van. Usually passengers like to visit Blackbeard's Castle, a popular picture taking excursion. Then they go to a bar at the top of the hill for fresh banana daiquiris and donkey ride. The view is wonderful! You can see the distant islands and the beautiful beach below which forms a heart shaped bay known as Megan's Bay. Already passengers from other cruise ships can be seen running from store to store with all their heavy-laden shopping bags. They seemed to be afraid that they are going to miss something. It's amazing the passengers have any energy left after the frantic dashing about in search of the elusive bargain.

A companionway descended from the forward well deck where passengers, already in line, made their way down to the tenders and boats. Another short gangway, was located on the lower deck, aft, as a convenience to passengers whose cabins are located in that area of the ship. This entrance, known as a gun port, also serves as a loading dock. All deliveries, even passenger purchases, would be checked in before being conveyed to their final destination. It is here that Captain Breathwaite would take his stand and repel all ideas contrary to his own. Plan John Barleycorn was already in motion. Tex was heading for shore in a boat piloted by Tiny and Jeff. The other musicians were instructed to notify Bob the minute the Staff Captain took up his position at the gunport door. Abe, not having seen the island before, was told to go ashore and enjoy himself. It would take the passengers time to make their purchases and arrange for the goodies to be delivered to the ship. So, it would be a few hours before the action would start.

In the meantime, the musicians took advantage of the emptiness of the ship by relaxing in deck chairs on the Sun Deck. The top deck was quiet and very pleasant. The sun was warm, shimmering off the blue water, which constantly changed color as it lazily moved toward shore. The lack of sleep and over-indulgence added to their contentment. The musicians were flipping in and out of that relaxed state they called "the twilight zone." At eleven a.m., their steward, Tom, carried out his part of the plan. He made his way to the Sun Deck and relayed the message that the Staffy was in place, as threatened, at the gunport.

"Okay! Scotty, Chuck, down you go and don't forget to look concerned."

"Ten four, Commander!" The duo saluted Bob and made their

way for the after stairs. "See ya later."

Part of the scheme was for two of the musicians to join the Staffy when he arrived at his inspection station and just hang out. The purpose was to give him the idea that they were expecting a delivery. Thus, ensuring he would not move from that location. Arriving at the door, they found Captain Breathwaite had taken up watch accompanied by two Junior Pursers who were prepared to assist the Staffy in his mission of enforced prohibition.

Looking from the gunport door, Scotty and Chuck had a full view of the harbor that was playing host to all the other cruise ships. Scotty was thinking that it was a helluva lot better than staring at the filthy, smoke belching factories that he witnessed in Glasgow. He recalled there were actually five factories surrounding the room where he slept; creating a constant din with boilers blowing steam and the rattle of looms from the carpet factories. One had the feeling that the priorities were factories first and that the poor industrial prisoners, who inhabited the tenement buildings adjacent to these sordid hell holes, were regarded merely as a necessary evil.

At the age of fourteen he had started work in one of those huge engineering plants just a few blocks from home, but after one-year Scotty begged his father to let him leave. He felt he was being strangled by having to spend every day amidst such barbaric activity. His father reluctantly agreed to his wishes. Scotty then flipped from job to job seeking the ultimate in employment. At the same time, he began earning a little money from drumming. One day, he saw a movie about jazz musicians and decided, sitting in the theater – that's what I want to be! The next step was to find a good teacher and learn the academics of drumming, learn to read music, and really study the instrument. All of this he accomplished. By the age of seventeen he was a full-time professional drummer.

When he reached the age of eighteen, he left Glasgow and found himself playing full time in a ballroom located on the West Coast of Scotland. The town was called Gourock and the ballroom was the Cragburn Pavilion. After two years there, he moved down the coast to what became his utopia; the town of Largs.

Surrounded by beautiful green hills, Largs sits on the waterfront with the usual small hotels along the shore front. A Presbyterian Church, with old fashioned steeple, stood right in the center of the main street as it does in every "wee" Scottish town. Largs is mostly inhabited by retirees and well to do people who are very content with their environment. The Moorings, a three-story building of restaurants and shops, had a ballroom located on the third floor of the building. It faced directly on the ocean with a clear view from the huge glass windows. Scotty felt it in the cards that this was where he would finally hang his drumsticks.

He enjoyed two years in Largs before he was off to London and then to the ships. Another two years aboard various British vessels; then a miserable twelve years in London before heading for the U.S. Scotty had done it all in the states, including Vegas, Lake Tahoe, the Hollywood scene, D.C. and New York and as luck would have it, he was again on a ship.

"What do you think of that armada out there?" asked Chuck jerking Scotty back from his nostalgia.

"Funny you should ask. When I lived in Los Angeles, I was invited to go aboard one of those new ships down in the Wilmington docks. Walking around I was amazed at the décor or rather the lack of it. Climbing the companionways from deck to deck on this ship, you are greeted with the great workmanship of murals carved from exotic woods. All very pleasant indeed! On board that modern ship I saw nothing but huge, white, plastic panels and no carpet. What made it even worse was one of the public rooms. It had a very high deck head making the white plastic even more obtrusive. Well, when I was leaving the ship, two executives from the company had stationed themselves at the gangway soliciting opinions from all the visitors. These executive types were expecting, of course, nothing but praise for their new ship and most people are inclined to be polite, but untruthful. When asked the question, I just looked them in the eye and informed them that Cedars Sinai Hospital was a fucking sight more attractive than their floating bathtub."

"Ha! Ha!" laughed Chuck. "That must have shook 'em up!"

"As a matter of fact, it didn't. It took a minute or so for the penny to drop. Their smiles indicated that they did agree with me. But," added Scotty, "that's what happens when you take shipbuilding away from Scotland and farm it out to makers of plastic kitchen appliances and yogurt bashers."

"Yes," replied Chuck sympathetically.

"But it's all in the name of the cause," Scotty continued. "The rich must get richer and fuck the tradesman!"

A boat containing the first load of passenger purchases was just arriving. This prevented Scotty from getting on a soap box and attacking the evils of politics and the merits of those who follow in what he considers a dishonorable profession. The Staffy and his two deputies now engaged in seeking out contraband. They inspected all obvious liquor containers.

"Look at the assholes." Chuck nudged Scotty and speaking from the corner of his mouth. "That's about all they're good for – playing Customs Officials."

"Scotty!"

Hearing his name called, he turned around to see Jimmy giving him the thumbs up symbol indicating the main part of the plan was unfolding. The Staff Captain was gradually becoming annoyed at the presence of the two musicians and felt he had to address them in the hopes they would disperse.

"Are you gentlemen expecting something from shore?" he asked, implying an illicit delivery.

"No, sir," replied Scotty, appearing very innocent. "A friend of ours may be coming aboard who happens to be on the island and we were waiting to welcome him. We also have band members at the gangway in case he should embark there."

The Staffy turned his back, not really accepting their story, which sounded so plausible. He had no choice but to give them the benefit of the doubt and return his attention to the packages still arriving. Chuck winked at Scotty for his inventiveness.

Actually, it wasn't a complete untruth. They did have a friend they knew to be visiting St. Thomas, and in the past he had come aboard. His name was Alan Beasley and he used to be a member of the crew. He went ashore some years back, made it big as a rock star, and became quite a celebrity. Many of the people who worked with him were still on the ship including the band. He always liked to come aboard and visit whenever the opportunity arose. Unfortunately, and unknown to Alan, orders had come from the bridge that he was not to be allowed on the ship anymore. The order said he disrupted the crew and interfered with their work. The Officers were not concerned that he was a celebrity; to them he was nothing more than a nuisance. The musicians were aware of the situation but knew that the Staffy had no idea of the rule because this was his first trip.

Lookouts, on the stern of the ship, started to go into action as the source of their attention appeared in the distance. Tex had carried out his mission and instructed the storekeeper that changes were to be made regarding delivery. The tradesman was very happy to comply. Instead of dropping the booze at the harbor for the ship's tender to transport, the shop owner would have the supply trucked to a little cove just outside town off the main drag. A lifeboat was waiting with Tiny and Jeff ready to load the cargo. Now, it had to be gotten aboard the Nectar undetected. A very tricky part of the operation. Everything was going according to plan. A boozer, threatened with the fear of losing his precious stimulant, could prove to be more inventive and cunning than any dumb-shit officer. Truck delivery made and cargo loaded aboard the life boat, the pirates headed for their destination which was sitting peacefully at anchor.

Meanwhile, aboard the Nectar, the bosun's mate headed for the bridge and notified the officer of the day that he would be swinging out one of the after booms to bring aboard supplies in about ten minutes. To receive permission to use any of the ship's equipment was very important, because the electrical drainage would be observed by the officer on the bridge, and this could result in an investigation. The last thing the crew needed was any officer coming aft.

The lifeboat swung far out from the cove and well beyond where the S.S. Nectar was anchored before heading in her direction. These pirates showed their true skill by keeping astern and to the starboard side in order to avoid being sighted. Arriving alongside and holding their position, the boom was swiftly lowered with a huge net. A few hauls later, and at least one hundred cases had landed safely aboard. As soon as each load touched the deck, it was grabbed and hastily passed along what could only be described as an Indian file. Crew members had formed a living chain from one end of the ship to the other. Passing the treasure, hand to hand, up and down companionways and through the first-class passenger accommodations to the forecastle head. Should any of the officers appear on the scene, it would look like the crew were making the normal deliveries to passenger cabins.

Mission accomplished!

The lifeboat took off heading for shore to carry out the proper task of returning passengers to the now happy vessel. Scotty and Chuck were notified that the delivery was complete. They returned to the Sun Deck where the rest of the musicians were in a state of elation. They had all missed lunch, but they agreed — who gives a shit! The whole scenario was worth a hundred meals.

"Anyway," Jimmy piped up happily, "you can't eat on an empty stomach!"

Just then, Tom appeared with a tray full of sandwiches and beer for everyone.

"Tom, you're a gem," said Bob as he helped himself to a tasty morsel. "Remind me to increase your gratuity at the end of the cruise."

Washing down the roast beef sandwiches with Heinekens, the lads watched as boat after boat plowed back and forth to the harbor. They laughed heartily observing the behavior of those aboard the returning boats. They could discern who had taken the tour of the rum distilleries by the amount of heads hanging over the side puking into the blue waters of the Caribbean. The stomach of these holiday makers were not used to the potent, sweet concoction that was offered so generously in those gin mills. It would affect one or two on each lifeboat the same way.

At five p.m., Mr. Breathwaite and his two helpers felt that they had succeeded in keeping the ship's compliment on the road to sobriety and decided there was no need to remain at their station. Thanking the two young pursers, who were by this time well and truly pissed off, he headed for the bridge with the feeling of a job well done.

Tex and Abe, who teamed up in the harbor, came aboard full of joy and laughter to find the others already in Bob's cabin. Tex was greeted with handshakes and informed that all had gone according to plan. He accepted a glass of Scotch in preparation for Mike's toast.

"Here's to the success of John Barleycorn and up the Staffy's ass! You know they should never let the generals run armies, all they need are a few sharp musicians." Everyone raised his glass, even Abe, with coke of course.

"Remember you guys," cautioned Tex, adding some ice cubs to his glass, "after dinner we have to redeem all those cases from the passenger cabins. Tom is getting a couple of his buddies to help us so it shouldn't take long. Which reminds me." Tex's shoulders shook with laughter. "You know, Chuck, I bumped into those three gals of yours after we came aboard, and they are going to strangle you. They said they couldn't get into their cabin for cases of booze stacked all over the place. It was their impression that only a couple of boxes would be delivered. They are worried that their steward will think they are alcoholics." Everyone enjoyed the story and agreed to empty that cabin first.

"By the way guys, you have to hear what took place on the harbor this morning," Abe began as he looked around the room.

"Yeah? What happened?" some of them chorused.

"There was a guy on the quayside. I did not recognize him at first but Tex told me who he was. You know the rock star, Alan Beasley."

"Yeah sure," they agreed nodding their heads.

"Well, he wanted to come out to the ship. Tex told me that this was his usual custom, but the officer wouldn't let him on the tender."

"Mathews, the Second Officer," Tex piped in. "He was the officer in charge of conducting the passengers safely on and off the tenders today and looking like the fourteen-carat asshole that he is, dressed in his white suit, white hat, white gloves and being very officious when Alan appeared. You go ahead with the story, Abe. You saw more of it than I did."

"Anyway, Alan started to argue with the officer after an empty tender left the dock. Then Matthews just told him his presence was not desired aboard because he was a disturbing influence to the rest of the crew. Matthews turned his back on Alan and walked over to the dock edge." Tex and Abe started to giggle and the guys in the room began to anticipate the punch line hopefully.

"He didn't?" asked Bob wide eyed.

"He sure as hell did," answered Abe. "He walked over, put his foot on the officer's ass and pushed him off the dock."

"You should have seen Matthews climb out looking like a drowned rat," added Tex gleefully. The room exploded with laughter and cheers.

"Alan never expected what happened next, but Matthews walked over and threw a big wet soggy punch that landed on the side of his face. It was just like being hit with a wet flounder."

"Really?" they all chimed together.

"What then?" they asked in a more serious note.

"Alan jumped back a couple of steps in surprise and probably afraid he was going to be attacked. Then he held up his arms and shouted, "Remember you are an officer and a gentleman!" Well that stopped the show, and when I left, someone was taking pictures of the two of them arm and arm like old buddies."

"Christ," remarked Bob, "if I didn't know Matthews better, I'd swear it was a publicity stunt." They completed their glasses of the mighty spirit and made haste to change clothes in preparation for the cocktail session.

The dance tonight was on the after end of the ship, beyond the Prom deck. Gaily decorated lights surrounded the dance area and, combined with the twinkling lights from shore, made for a very romantic setting as the passengers danced or smooched in the moonlight. Passengers who had acquaintances on St. Thomas could invite them aboard for the dance because the ship was sailing until midnight. Although the setup was pleasant for the passengers, it was not the ideal scene for the musicians. Should the weather be very warm or humid, they found it most uncomfortable to perform. Dressed in white dinner jackets and black pants, they would grind and sweat through the evening. They always preferred to play in the comfort of the air-conditioned lounges. Chuck's bone of contention was the piano. He was always begging the officers to take it inside; in order to protect it from the dampness which constantly played havoc with the tuning. Chuck was not permitted to untie the fastening and move it himself. Only the deckies were allowed to touch these metal eyelets on the deck that held the piano fast. Of course, the deckies were in bed by the time the musicians finished, so the poor piano remained exposed to the elements all night. Chuck, on an earlier cruise, had actually taken the felts that had become detached from the mechanism to the Chief Officer and told him that the piano was not playable.

The officer's only reply was, "Man, when we are in battle and run out of bullets, we don't give up the fight!"

Chuck just looked at him; realizing what he was dealing with and replied, "How odious to compare bullets to music," and walked away.

The dance was in full swing on the after deck with the spirit of carnival prevailing. Those who had over indulged ashore knew the only cure was to keep going; thus, the booze was flowing. The Verandah Grill was doing a roaring business with waiters hopping from table to table trying to keep the mob happy. The band strummed merrily on while Chuck sat cursing the out of tune piano.

On the bridge wing, Staff Captain Breathwaite stood contemplating his day's work and relaxing in the balmy tropical air. He had been at sea for a long time. Ten years with this company, but when was he going to command his own ship? Moving him from ship to ship as a trouble shooter was okay but was not fulfilling his desire to be top dog. Sure, everyone knows that the Captain on a big ship is more or less a figurehead and the Staffy actually runs the vessel. His position is the ultimate in training. He has to be familiar and involved with all aspects of running each department. Being the Staff Captain was not what Breathwaite wanted and it never entered his head that maybe he had an attitude problem. He was not the type who would be willing to sit back and be Captain. The company was aware of this and were just holding him off. Breathwaite, of course, did not realize what an oddity he was either. Having been at sea so long, spending so much of his life with hard drinking mariners and yet never touching the stuff himself. One could only admire such a man who could abstain amidst such peer pressure, but abstain he did, causing him to live a lonely existence.

His thoughts were interrupted when he detected the sound of voices singing somewhere in the distance. Listening more intently, Breathwaite realized the source to be in the crew quarters located on the forecastle head.

"What the hell?" he muttered. All sorts of terrible pictures flashed in front of his face. Leaving the bridge, he made his way down to the well deck and walked over to the hatch entrance that led down to the crew quarters where the singing was more audible. Descending the stairs, he continued along the passageway as the voices increased in volume. Empty liquor cases were outside some of the cabin doors waiting to be dumped later. It was obvious that drinking parties were in full swing. The voices now resembled a bunch of radio stations all mixed together. A look of disbelief crossed his face as he continued through the den of iniquity. Reaching a bend in the passageway, he stopped outside a large cabin. Considering the amount of voices emanating from it, half the crew must be inside, he thought. They were now bellowing forth the second verse of their famous sea shanty.

"The Captain had a cabin boy,

He was a little nipper.

He stuffed his ass with broken glass

and circumcised the Skipper.

Singing, Yo – Heave – Ho

and we don't want any more beer!"

All of a sudden, the door opened by one of the occupants. He was intending to leave with his bottle of St. Croix Rum, when he was confronted by the Staffy.

"Oh shit!" he exclaimed drunkenly, realizing who was standing in front of him.

Looking over the shoulder of the inebriated reveler, the Staffy observed a dozen or so bodies. A mixture of deckies and stewards all engaged in the process of splicing the main brace. The room was thick with cigarette smoke and stunk of rum which caused the Staffy to screw up his nose when he pushed the drunk aside and slipped into the foul atmosphere. All the guys felt like little schoolchildren caught in the act by the teacher. Some dropped their heads. Others, unable to comprehend the seriousness of the situation, started to giggle. This only added to the anger and humiliation that was boiling inside the interloper. Pointing his finger at each crew member around the room, he demanded to know how the liquor was brought aboard. One of the imbibers, not conscious of who was before him or what was happening or maybe he just didn't care, raised his bleary eyes and answered the Staffy.

"My fairy godmother came tonight. Hiccup! Hiccup! And she told me I had three wishes. Hiccup! So, I wished for three cases of rum! She waved her magic wand and lo and behold there they were. Hiccup!"

The Staffy, regaining his composure, turned to the door where some onlookers from adjacent cabins were enjoying the spectacle. Picking out one man who appeared sober he addressed him.

"Your name."

"Jack Nelson, sir."

"Jack, go to the bridge and have the Master-at-arms here at once."

"Yes sir." And he took off.

Turning again to the debauched scene, he informed them that they would all be logged and probably demoted.

After the Staffy left, the forecastle head was a hub of activity as word spread. Cut up liquor boxes and empty rum bottles could be seen flying out portholes. Hiding places that deserved praise for ingeniousness were created. Vent covers were removed in crew washrooms and bottles were stashed inside. Half a dozen cases of rum were uplifted to the crow's nest. To reach the lookout's position, one had to climb a ladder inside the forward mast. More than halfway up was a compartment containing two astronaut chairs which provided comfort for those on watch. A case of booze was then attached to a line lowered from the nest and hauled up. No one knew that a hundred feet above the water, six cases of booze were safely stowed away for future use.

The Staffy was too enraged to sleep, so he made his way to the night club where he would confront the band. He had no idea what he would say to them, only that he was suppressing a strong desire to murder the whole lot. He continued his journey aft muttering like a bumbling idiot.

"They done it to me! They got the bloody booze aboard. I'll get them! I'll get them! I will!"

The band had just completed a favorite number when the Staffy entered the club. He headed directly to the bandstand. All eyes were on him as he approached. The lads looked cool as they sampled their shooters, and were not in the least perturbed with his presence. Bob, seeing the apoplectic expression heading toward him, was quick on the draw as he greeted the Staffy.

"Good evening, Mr. Breathwaite. Do you have a tune you would like us to play?"

"The only request I want is your demise!" Before he could continue, the musicians all looked at each other as if the response was planned.

"Sorry, sir, we don't know that one. How about another, sir?"

Aware that they would just make him look ridiculous, he turned his heel and stormed off while the band played, "Popeye the Sailor." Scotty, of course, supplied the beep-beeps by blowing through his hands.

After the Staffy's exit, Bob turned to the motley bunch, who were having a good giggle at their repartee.

"Now the shit has hit the fan," said Bob, signaling them to pipe down. "We are now in the middle of a cold war. So, you better all tread softly. Breathwaite is going to do his damnedest to shoot us down. We'll call it an evening gentlemen."

"Okay, Bob."

"We'll be good Lord!"

"Sure thing."

DAY 4
AT SEA

This morning, the rummage raid took place as expected. It did not bare too much fruit, not only because of the good planning, but because those employed in the task were sympathetic to the crew. At least twenty crew members were placed on report for drunkenness. This meant a loss of pay, a demotion, and in some instances being fired. Two stewards were demoted and sentenced to spend the rest of the cruise taking care of the crew washrooms. They started a running crap game and became wealthy by the end of the cruise. The Staff Captain realized he had been outwitted by a force stronger than he had imagined and vowed to keep an eye on those "damn" musicians. He suspected them of playing a key role in his downfall.

Mid-morning, the ship plowed lazily along in no particular hurry. There really was no distance between the islands. This was exactly what was needed to ease and relax the passengers. The sky was wondrously blue, making the ocean more translucent and adding to its color. There was a gentle swell causing the ship to sway as though her movements were musically inspired. Members of the crew, who were off watch, were lying on their towels on the forecastle head. This area of the ship was reserved for the crew. They could enjoy the tropical sun and sweat out the rum consumed the night before. Passengers, enjoying the tranquility of the day, were scattered around the ship in deck chairs. The aroma of coconut oil tanning lotion was prevalent everywhere.

The musicians were assembled in the night club rehearsing the show that would be presented this evening. The rehearsal was scheduled to go until lunch time. After lunch they would return to the after deck where they had played the dance last night. Today they would have to play some silly tunes while the passengers engaged in games inspired by the cruise director, Vic Lehman. A few hours off before cocktails, then two shows after dinner. The first show was for the first sitting passengers and the second for the convenience of those on the second sitting. It would be a busy day for them.

Tom had the coffee on hand as usual, and the lads were nice and neat in white shirts and black ties. Today they were rehearsing the singer, Jan Kelly. Everything went pretty smooth. Her arrangements were straight forward and really no effort at all for the guys. The comedian was just on and off; which meant they played him on with whatever tune he chose then the same again at the end of his act. The only problem was the magician. He was an American who posed as a Chinaman. He had special arrangements for a big band. The musicians had a laugh when Bob showed them the lead score. Some witty musician from a previous orchestra had written across the top, "Arranged by Chang Kai Check." They soon realized why when they started having trouble with the music. Whoever wrote the parts was trying to capture the sound of Oriental music, which is played in quarter tones. Apart from the music having no form, it sounded worse being played by only a small band. There were just too many holes from the missing instruments. Bob explained this to the magician, Bill Belan. He was not in the least put out and left it the band to come up with whatever solution would suffice. So, they agreed to play the old "Japanese Sandman" and "Limehouse Blues" as background music during his act.

During breaks and discussions, Scotty's thoughts would drift back to funny experiences he'd had with various acts. When he was twenty-four years old, he played in what had become the American Air Force Officer's Club. This comedian was a fat, roly-poly type guy and a very funny man, but he committed the cardinal sin as far as Scotty was concerned. Scotty did not mind being pulled into the act so long as the person doing the performance got his agreement. He resented being taken for granted and used the source of amusement to enhance any performer's act.

As it happened the fat comedian turned to Scotty, who was seated at the drums, and said, "Drummer, stand up."

On hearing the command, Scotty muttered under his breath, "Fuck off!"

The bandleader, fearing an unpleasant situation, moved over to the drummer's side and whispered, "Please, for my sake, do as he asks."

Scotty reluctantly got to his feet. The comedian began taking advantage of Scotty's thinness, pinched appearance and bow tie.

The roly-poly comedian pointed to the victim and announced to the audience, "Ladies and Gentlemen! Britain's answer to Frank Sinatra."

Scotty being a master of the ad lib himself, pointed back at the comedian and in full voice fired back, "Ladies and Gentlemen! America's answer to Sophie Tucker." Scotty's line won the day and the audience showed their approval by laughing heartily at the comeback.

Meeting in the men's room after the show, the comedian remarked to Scotty, "You sure got me, didn't you?" He was good natured about the whole thing, unlike so many people in the business who would go bananas at anyone daring to upstage.

Another time in the same club, a well-known American movie star came onto the stage and gave an impromptu performance that was enjoyed by all. The club offered to book him to entertain the Sunday night audience, but it did not turn out too well.

A rehearsal was arranged away from the club and the star, known for his ability to consume large amounts of Scotch, proceeded to uphold his image. The booze flowed all day and by the time they reached the club they were all shit faced. The celebrity was scheduled to go on at nine p.m. and had taken up residence in the club bar adjacent to the showroom, where he continued with the sauce. Problems arose with the P.A. system causing a delay, so he was not able to hit the stage until nine twenty. He had to be admired for holding his liquor. He did not look drunk, nor staggered in any way, but the booze sure did have its effect.

After the introduction, the movie star reached the microphone and attempted the difficult task of being a stand-up comic, but there was one problem: he couldn't remember any of the punch lines. He would jump from one story to another with the same result. The audience started to squiggle in their seats. Realizing he was unsuccessful in the comedy department, he tried one of his funny songs but with no more success.

He turned to the drummer and in full voice shouted, "Hey, Scotty! I forgot the fucking words!"

That did it! He was escorted off the stage by the club manager. Of course, the band were delighted at the comment and thought it was extremely funny. The best part of the show!

At intermission Scotty, left the stage, and headed for the actor.

"What the hell happened?" Scotty asked.

"I was twenty minutes too drunk!" was the proud answer.

The ship's rehearsal declared over, they all headed for the dining room and tied on the lunchtime nose bag. Playing so early in the day helped to increase their appetites. The food in turn helped to fortify the stomach for the elixir that no doubt would be consumed later. Bob addressed the guys round the table, reminding them of the fiasco that had taken place as a result of the rummage raid in the crew quarters.

"Remember, the Staff Captain realizes he was outwitted and will be like a crazy man for the rest of the cruise. He will have to vindicate himself somehow, and after such a big loss he will be grabbing at straws. The Purser advised me that the Staffy suspects we had a hand in all this. So be on your toes. Although we have the right, keep out of the swimming pools if they are busy. If you have to swim, use the indoor pool, it's always quiet. Same with the Observation bar. Don't give that asshole any reason to come down on us."

The musicians did not like the idea of having to be on their best behavior, but understood it would be for their own benefit.

"I have a feeling Breathwaite won't be with us after this cruise. You know how vindictive the crew can be," Bob continued. "By the way, don't have any drinking sessions in the after-barber shop. That would really fix it for us if he got wind of something like that!"

George, the hair dresser, was another member of the boozy set who was always ready to party. The guys would go there with the intention of making appointments for haircuts. This would usually finish with George closing the salon in the middle of the afternoon for a boozer. If there should be any broads around, the sessions really got going. Passengers knocking on the door intending to use George's services were told that ship was rolling too much down that end today and were advised to use the forward shop. George was a real character and considered himself one of the boys. While the ship was in port one trip, a crowd of them were having a party in one of the forward cabins that had a lower and upper berth. His usual performance, after heavy drinking, was to pass out wherever he was, as he did that night. There was just one unfortunate result. George's own cabin had just a lower bunk. When he awoke, in the middle of the night for a pee, he thought he was in his own cabin. Swinging his legs over the edge he dropped out of bed expecting to touch the deck immediately. Instead he felt himself engaged in a free fall, then bounced off the floor nearly breaking every bone in his body. His screams were heard all over the ship, followed by a stream of obscenities before he realized what had happened. That story kept the crew laughing for days.

After lunch the energetic passengers assembled on the after-dance deck. This was the day that all the judges, lawyers, and business tycoons lost all sense of reason and let their hair down. These so-called pillars of society could be seen engaged in the egg and spoon race, potato sack race, musical chairs, or rolling a grapefruit from chin to chin. The band tried to look serious while suppressing the desire to throw hand grenades at the mob and hang the cruise director from the highest yardarm. Vic Lehman, who presided over these infantile activities, took it all very seriously and blew his little whistle like a drill sergeant in a kindergarten. Usually he wore the precious whistle around his neck, but on a previous cruise he made the terrible mistake of laying down his whistle on the edge of the bandstand. That was just a little too near the musicians. Chuck leaned over and picked it up while Vic was issuing commands to his group of passengers. Chuck promptly threw it over the side. Vic, turning to retrieve his instrument of torture, was devastated to find his only means of communication gone! His questions to the band were met with shrugs and shakes of the head. Scotty offered a solution that some kids were running to and fro in front of the bandstand and possibly pinched it. Everything came to a halt. Participants had to freeze wherever they were while Vic returned to his cabin for a new whistle. How large was his supply?

Scattered today around the perimeter of the games deck were the remnants of the night before. Some of these seagoing studs were not physically able to join in the fun. They had made their play last evening and thought they were ready to score, but, unable to get it up, they resorted to the bottle. Now they sunk to the deepest of depressions and suffered great humiliation aggravated by a huge hang over.

Deck games over, and another well-earned dollar safely in the coffers, the lads headed for the locker to stow their instruments. Scotty, Jimmy, and Chuck returned aft. Hearing Scotty's name called, their attention was drawn to the gentleman that Scotty had the conversation with a couple of days ago.

"Oh, hi, Walter!" Scotty greeted his friend seated in the deck chair.

"Gentlemen," he answered them with a nod of the head.

"Jimmy. Chuck. This is Mr. Walter Armstrong, whom I was telling you about." After handshakes they accepted Walter's invitation to be seated.

"Will you gentlemen join me in a refreshment?" Walter signaled Albee, the deck steward, who was always close at hand.

"Thank you," the guys replied and requested beer all 'round. Walter gave Albee an order for three Heinekens and a glass of orange juice for himself.

"You know, Walter," Scotty began, looking at his benefactor. "You got me going on that statement you left me with the other day about one doesn't know how insane the society is until he realizes how much he contributes to that insanity."

"Well, wouldn't it follow that a person who became that aware would also realize that he needs help?" replied Walter. A lull took place as Albee returned handing each of them the drink of his choice. Sipping from the glasses, they settled back to enjoy whatever was about to unfold and knowing that it would be a treat after playing those nonsensical deck games.

"So, what you're saying," Jimmy took up the conversation, "is that there is a specific reason for this condition and it is unknown to all of us."

"Something like that, Jimmy, but I don't want to sound like some sort of guru. It's really more simple than people realize, but a condition they find a bit difficult to confront. Let's take a look at what we refer to as the mind." The lads were now all ears.

"As medical and mental practitioners are aware, it's composed of two parts. They consider the good mind to be the nice one and the nasty mind has been given the title of the subconscious. That's about the extent of their knowledge regarding the subconscious. Other beliefs refer to the mind as being controlled by God or the Devil. And credit all sorts of human behavior to one of those other entities. By the way, I want to point out that you do not have to believe anything I say, but I'm sure we can have some fun with this discussion and remain interested in each other's point of view."

"Great," answered Scotty. "Well how would you describe the mind or minds as you put it?"

Chuck and Jimmy were sitting back experiencing the same feelings Scotty had felt on his first meeting with Walter but were ready to give him the benefit of the doubt. The man seemed personable and very eloquent and after all, Scotty said he was cool. Eyes glued to the speaker, they awaited his reply.

"Let's look at it this way. First of all, you have what could be referred to as the analytical mind or the good guy. What is it?" Walter looked at each of his audience. "It's nothing more than a compilation of pictures. For example, if I asked each of you where you were on your last vacation, you would inform me by looking into that portion of the mind for the answer. In other words, you are constantly manufacturing pictures to store away; filed for future use. Like a computer."

Pictures were now flashing through each of the fellow's heads as though in obeisance to what he was saying. All understood as Walter looked around the group.

"Yeah!"

"Okay," they chorused, allowing him to continue.

"Now on the other hand, that part of the mind called the subconscious is really the villain. It also contains pictures that are beyond the ability of the analytical mind to retrieve. So now we have a problem."

"What is the difference between the pictures in the analytical portion and those in the lower or subconscious?" asked Chuck.

"The experience associated with their inception, Chuck. You see, all the pictures in the analytical mind were accepted when you were fully awake and you knew what was going on. On the other hand, the bad or unwanted experiences were installed, or establish themselves in what is known as the subconscious, because it's beneath your ability to see them. That's why the word sub was used. To give you an example," he continued. "Imagine what happens when a person is rendered unconscious by a blow to the head or anesthesia in an operation or even being hypnotized. This trauma has closed down the analytical mind. Leaving the other mind open to absorb all data in the immediate vicinity. When the poor fellow recovers consciousness or becomes analytical again, he has no knowledge of what took place simply because the analytical mind was closed down. This mechanism is to protect him from all these bad experiences." Walter paused to let the fellows absorb what he was saying.

"Now don't go looking into your own past experiences. Just remain interested in what is taking place now." He was right on the money and knew that each of them was thinking back to some bad experience.

"Do I have your attention?" he asked, snapping them back from the past.

"Sure! Fire away!" Walter smiled at their response.

"So, here's the major difference. Analytical pictures you can see. The pictures contained in the subconscious you are unable to view, but you can feel their effects. Should any of these pictures be brought into lay by some means they can cause all sorts of problems to the body such as headaches or just an ill feeling. Not knowing how or why this is happening, the average person resorts to pills or whatever remedies will suffice to quell the unpleasant feeling. Even alcohol," he smiled and gained the expected result from this statement.

"Now you're treading on dangerous ground," the lads jokingly teased Walter.

"My apologies, gentlemen. I will retract that last statement — for the moment," he added; telling them that this was not the last they would hear on the subject. "Let's try an illustration of what I have been talking about. Assume a man is walking across the street and is struck by a vehicle. He is knocked unconscious when his head strikes the pavement near a pile of manure. There is also the sound of running water from a storm drain. A witness to the accident runs over to the driver of the car and begins yelling, "Are you blind?" The person responsible for the accident is now, possibly, as non-analytical as the poor victim lying on the ground." The boys were all very intent as Walter continued.

"What is the result of all this chaos? Okay, here is the scenario. The accident victim is taken away in an ambulance with sirens screeching and eventually awakes in a hospital, is discharged and returns to his everyday life. Maybe days, weeks, or months later this fellow is out having a pleasant drive in the country with his family and not feeling too great. A little tired from a heavy week at the office. He is now all set for the subconscious and the next act. A fire truck goes by which starts the first in a chain reaction. The siren recalls the incident and all events thereof without his permission of agreement. His head, where it struck the pavement, starts to hurt a little. Driving past a farm, the smell of horse manure assails his nostrils and the pain increased. Now you can imagine what happens when he passes a little country waterfall, which can only simulate another aspect of that terrible day? He is now desperate for the aspirin bottle. What is taking place is that he is feeling the effect of all these pictures but unable to see them or control them. The next day adds to his problem. The trauma is in top gear. His vision is even affected because of the remark made by the witness. So, he goes to the eye doctor thinking it's time for glasses and hoping his headache will go away."

Walter sat back and allowed all that he had said to sink into the boys. Each one of them was silently examining the logic of what they had just heard and putting it into perspective.

"That makes sense," piped up Scotty. "When you think of all those who preach that the mind controls everything and that we can cure the body with its power."

"But only when the person can bring to view the pictures contained in the subconscious mind. Remember, they are brought to life unwarranted by outside stimuli. Now you can see why there is so much insanity. That part of the mind contains tons of unwanted incidents such as sex related pictures, murder, and numerous more things that you would rather not remember. In other words, everything that is degrading to you originates in that area of the mind. You know all those uncontrolled emotions of anger, fear, and grief. The debilitating conditions that are constantly impinging themselves on a person making it difficult for him to function. Simply, the more analytical the person, the more sane. The more he is in effect of the subconscious, the more he's insane. To sum up this topic, I'm afraid we are living in a society that is stuck in the negative part of the mind which results in what I describe as mass insanity."

"Whew! This sure is heavy stuff," remarked Jimmy. "I feel like my thoughts are racing a mile a minute."

"Yeah," said Chuck, "I'm working hard to comprehend what you are saying, Walter. But I feel a conflict taking place somewhere inside my head."

"Like some kind of machine that had lain dormant for centuries and was now being put into motion," interjected Scotty.

"That's a good explanation of what is happening to you," responded Walter, who was sympathetic to what he was creating in the three disciples.

"Yeah, Scotty's so smart," kidded Jimmy.

"Okay, fellows, let me describe what part the theory of good and bad and God and Satan play in all of this. You see, if you have one faction representing good and the other bad, then it is obvious that both these factions have appetites that have to be constantly sated. The moment any truth appears, the bad obviously rebels and repels what would mean survival for you and the analytical mind. As I stated, most of the people are stuck in the subconscious portion and are satisfying the bad by the games they elect to play in the world. That's because they don't know or understand what is happening. A term they use in the computer world fits perfectly – GIGO. Meaning garbage in – garbage out! The more garbage given to the subconscious, the more overwhelming it is to the analytical mind. Putting the analytical out of commission; the subconscious simply takes over."

Chuck held up his hand. He wished to say something, but was still searching for the words. Looking at Walter, he posed a question, "How can we distinguish the hunger of the good mind from the hunger of the other?"

"Good question, Chuck," Walter acknowledged and proceeded with the answer. "You could say that the good part is ethical and only interested in creating what would be described as beauty, culture, good music, artistry, actually functioning on the aesthetic wave band and tending towards survival for itself and all others. The most important of these is ethics; a commodity that has all but vanished and something that cannot be taught."

"What do you mean can't be taught?" asked Scotty displaying his confusion with a slight frown.

"Let me explain it another way. There is a difference between ethics and morals. Morals are what you are asked to observe when you join an organization. Those certain rules you agree to abide by. I'm sure you have certain rules and regulations here aboard ship that you have agreed to obey."

The three little devils looked at each other with sly little grins. How did Walter know? They each thought. He must be so wise.

"Everything okay boys?"

"Oh yeah."

"Sure, Walter."

"Yeah, please continue."

"If you are ethical, of course, you would observe the rules and play the game as expected anyway. Does that happen in real life?" Walter looked at his audience as they all shook their heads no.

"Here is an example. A person belongs to a church which has a code of rules demanding that his behavior be moral. What happens? The person violates the rules and leaves the church, condemning it and all its followers as something distasteful. This same person now changes his beliefs and joins some other church or religious outlet and is once again asked to observe the morals of that group. This can go on and on all through his life. He will not know or want to face the fact that his decision to leave these so-called righteous institutions was a result of his own transgressions and refusal to obey the rules. He will always blame "them" and never himself. This is the type of person one can see later in life walking around carrying a sign that reads, "Beware, your sins will find you out!" Remember he is referring to your sins; not his own."

Walter obviously threw in that last part to lighten the situation because it had become a very serious conversation.

"Okay," Jimmy said as he took the floor. "Now you explained how the analytical mind survives, but what about the fuel for the subconscious?"

"Well put," began Walter. "Fuel is a very appropriate word and shows that you probably have the answer already. Today we are inflicted with all sorts of stimuli used to aggravate and supply fuel to this entity. Two of the worst are television and drugs. Society is being destroyed by the exploitation of our youth, who are the main recipient of these evils. If you can imagine that this portion of the mind contains all sorts of horror, then what better way to refuel it then by the ingestion of more of the same. There are plenty of sponsors out there who, being so degraded themselves, are permitted to create and supply all sorts of trauma in the quest of money. They know that something is stimulated when a Homo Sapiens is subjected to blood and thunder or pornography or any other theatrical garbage, because it guarantees immediate riches and success, which proves a lack of ethics in that area. It's obvious that these merchants of degrading behavior do not understand how it works, but they know that their victims are constantly attracted by their offerings."

At that point Albee appeared and was given another order of the same while Chuck and Jimmy headed for the rest room leaving Scotty and Walter to take delivery of the drinks.

"What do you think of this conversation?" Chuck asked Jimmy as they faced the urinals. "The guy is something else, huh?"

"Actually, I'm enjoying it, Chuck. It's like a breath of fresh air after an existence of booze and nonsensical chatter. You notice how steady his eyes are? Like he's got it all together and he makes you feel important."

"Yeah," said Chuck. "A couple of times I got those chills up the back of the neck. You know, the kind you get when you hear good music or play in a good group that's really swingin'."

"That's it," replied Jimmy, drying his hands. "But you know what I think those feelings are? Simply a reaction to hearing the truth."

"You got it man. Simple truth."

They left the rest room and headed for their seats. Drink glasses once again replenished, the three focused their attention on Walter, who was sipping the hot tea that he had requested.

"Are you getting bored yet?" Walter asked.

"On the contrary, we're having a ball and want to hear more," replied Chuck while smiling at Scotty.

Jimmy opened the proceedings by asking, "How come institutions like churches, who preach the so-called commandments, and the government, who claims to be so concerned, are unable to stem this flow into hell that is taking place all around us?"

"They are also victims of that part of the mind just as any other member of society. They are playing the game too. Not that it's right, but they view it as being right. Just because a person wears the collar or enters the arena of politics does not exempt him from the insanity that engulfs everyone else. These are subjects I will take up with you at a later date but will just point out something in the meantime. First of all, you have to realize that most people, whether they be clergymen or otherwise, are guilty of trying to conceal their true feelings. They are not even conscious of what they are doing. Have you ever walked down the street and noticed a person unaware that you were approaching? Maybe he had a look of apathy or anger. He was probably in the depths of that portion of the mind that we've been talking about this afternoon. He might suddenly look up and smile at your greeting. If you sneaked back and took another look you would no doubt find that the expression that person was wearing before you met returned. The big smile was only the social face and the angry or whatever face was probably more truthful as far as his real feelings are concerned."

"Sure," they chorused. "Seen that a hundred times!"

"Yeah," said Scotty. "The old broads sitting in the foyer of the apartments where I once lived were like that every day. They were only concerned with how bad they felt each day. Their operations and visits to the doctors and, of course, how terrible all the neighbors were. I would enter the lobby with an overwhelming, "Hi Gals!" They always gave me big smiles, but when I stood in the elevator waiting for the doors to close, they each had resumed their real display of emotion – bitterness.

"You see," Walter added, "the identity a person is wearing is not necessarily that which he represents but is only what is apparent. It's unfortunate, but I'm afraid everyone has skeletons in the closet. Even though they are experiencing guilty feelings, they cannot explain why. So, they acquire this other mode or identity to enable them to face the world and be socially acceptable."

"That makes sense." The attention went to Scotty as they sipped on the cold beer. "What you were talking about before – you know – the rules you are supposed to observe when joining a group. How about the example of the Catholic Church? They always denounce what they consider degrading practices. Now they have priests demanding that a homosexual life style be accepted. Boy is that a contradiction!"

"Correct, Scotty. Good example!" replied Walter with a smile; pleased that he was getting through to them. "That subject we must talk about one afternoon too. There is another important factor to be revealed that can help you to understand more fully why the world is, as you put it, nuts and heading for disaster."

"Is that why we prefer to live this life?" queried Chuck. "Even though we are guilty of our own form of insanity, it's not as bad as what is happening ashore."

"Could be Chuck," answered Walter. "On board here most of these people are able to separate themselves from all the stupidities ashore and are intent on having a good time. After all," he added jokingly, "they paid for it in cash! Not being exposed to whatever ails them during the normal day at work or at home, they have a chance to suppress the desire of the subconscious. Temporarily, and consequently feel better."

"Unless," laughed Scotty, "the wife they bring along is the cause of all their woes, then they have no chance. Poor Bastards!"

"Ah-hah!" remarked Walter, pointing his finger at Scotty. "That statement would indicate how you feel about women and marriage!" Scolding Scotty with a little humor.

"He hates it," verified Chuck.

"Yeah, like the plague," confirmed Jimmy.

Scotty just smiled at the good-natured teasing. He knew they were right!

Everyone settled down again. Walter knew there was a feeling of harmony within the little group. The musicians were willing to accept Walter as their mentor and were looking forward to whatever he had to offer. This afternoon had proved more enjoyable then discussing broads and boozing.

"All right then." Walter observed them to be relaxed and at ease and ready to continue. "Let's move on that important factor that I mentioned. It has to do with what we've been discussing. What people do not seem to comprehend is that the physical universe they have been involved with so long is one big lie factory. It has become such a part of life that they don't even know the lies and beliefs are all tied together making it difficult for you to find yourself."

"You've got me there," inquired Jimmy.

"I'm not sure what you're getting at either," added Chuck.

"Okay, let's play a little game. As I said before, you do not have to believe what I say, but go along for the fun of it. Right?" Walter surveyed the interested three. Then indicating Jimmy, he asked if he might pose a question for him.

"Sure, Walter. Fire away."

Looking steadily at Jimmy he asked, "What do you consider you are?"

Jimmy looked a little bewildered stumbling for the answer, "Well, uh, I could say I am a body made up of skin and bones, and as we have established, I have a mind or several minds."

"Good show." Walter mentally made note of his reply. "Now, Chuck," looking in his direction. "What do you consider you are?"

"I suppose, like Jimmy, I am a body with the mind and a brain."

"Very good, Chuck."

Scotty realized the same question was about to be directed at him and he was more prepared when Walter asked him.

"Well, I, of course, have to go along with the guys, but I feel that there is something else involved. Something like the existence of a soul or whatever name you put on it. Maybe it is Life Force or prana or karma or something like that."

"Okay, Scotty." Walter studied Scotty approving of his reply. "Let's take a look at what we have. First of all, we came up with three different answers. Correct?" Walter was taking his little class step by step. He wanted them to comprehend what he was explaining.

"Now I could have asked a dozen people that question and received possibly a dozen different answers." All attention was riveted on Walter in preparation for some revelation as he continued.

"There can only be one truth. If one of you is right, then the others must be wrong. This would indicate that lies had unwittingly entered your thoughts somewhere along the line, thus making you susceptible to such erroneous beliefs."

Walter now sat back watching the effect of his statement. The lads needed a minute for all this to sink in. Walter wanted each of them to sort it out in his own mind, which is, after all, where these ideas originate. Pictures were now whirling away in their heads. Each searching for the source of his own beliefs. Gradually, their attention returned to Walter, who was wearing a kindly smile and already seemed to understand what was taking place. Walter had also anticipated the next question, which came from Jimmy.

"Okay, Walter. Now it's your turn to answer the same question. What's it all about?"

"Very well, gentlemen, let me put it this way. My answers may or may not meet with your approval, but I will do my best to make them acceptable. First, the body, is part of the physical universe. This also applies to the brain or anything else you can see or touch. In other words, the ship, the chairs and all solid objects belong in the physical universe. We talked about this already. Now what is the difference between all these things and your body? Simply that another force has to exist to introduce life. If there is no life force, then we have what is called a dead body."

"So, what you're getting at," asked Scotty, "is the existence of a soul or spirit?"

"Before we get into that, let's take a look at what considerations people have on this subject. Certain religions will say you have a soul. Depending how good a Catholic you happen to be or how much respect you have for the priest, most people seem to accept the belief. But remember, anytime you use the word belief, you introduce an element of doubt and this interferes with the credibility of the subject. Now I can state you do not have a soul, but that you actually are a soul or spirit inhabiting that body and are responsible for the life endowed to that body. The same criteria apply to me. If you consider me to be a nut, then you will discard what I have said. On the other hand, if I seem sane and earn your respect, you will accept this theory I have presented. But that puts us back to square one. You can either agree or disagree, but if you agree with what I have said, then you are once again open, possibly, to more lies and false beliefs from an outside source."

"It all appears like a vicious cycle," remarked Chuck in response to what he had just heard. "How are we to know what the truth is?"

"That's the sixty four-thousand-dollar question," Walter once again grabbed their attention. "You can read Bridie Murphy. You can read the tabloids which contain countless stories of life after death experiences. You will either accept or not accept the existence of spirits. The truth is you will never know for sure until you experience being a spirit. At that time it will no longer be a mystery."

"How the hell do we manage that?" asked Jimmy jokingly.

"Well you know what the book says, "Seek and ye shall find." But one sure way to find out is to jump over the side. I'm sure you will become aware soon enough."

"No thanks," laughed Jimmy. "I'm not that inquisitive yet."

"So, if we are spiritual entities, then this must have something to do with reincarnation," asked Scotty, looking seriously at Walter.

"Before I answer that, let me give you an illustration of how the spirit is tied in with the body. Imagine your body to be an automobile. Your eyes are the windshield. We can even refer to the brain as the motor. Now, before the motor can start, there has to be an operator to turn the key. That's where you come in. You are actually the driver looking through the windshield, turning the key and putting the body in motion. You are responsible for whatever direction you take and in keeping that automobile in good shape. Should you be crazy enough to run it into a wall and render it useless, then you would simply find another car or body. That way you can stay involved with the game of living. Now for the question of reincarnation, the operator or spirit cannot be injured or killed as it is not physical. In other words, it just carries on, either learning from the past, or being more stupid than before. So, for reincarnation to apply, something has to die. The body has died, and obviously it does not return, so it does not reincarnate."

"So," implied Jimmy, "when the layman talks about reincarnation, he is really referring to the continuation of life."

"Exactly," answered Walter. "Of course, as I stated, you cannot shoot a spirit, but it can be rendered into a state of deterioration by the advent of bad experiences such as your own transgressions, drugs or other inflicted trauma."

Walter, noticing Chuck deep in thought, directed his attention to him. Chuck felt this and made his own summation of what had been discussed thus far.

"What you're saying then is that there is no death. That we just go from lifetime to lifetime playing this dumb scene. What the hell's the purpose in that?"

"Well, there are many schools of thought on the subject. Such as returning to handle those you had problems with in past lives or attaining much higher altitudes of awareness. But the important part is that you become aware of who you are and remedy your own universe. Maybe you will find that you have many more abilities and there is much more joy to be obtained as you approach optimal survival."

"Well, I hope the next one is better than this," added Chuck. "This world sucks!"

"That will be up to you," Walter answered Chuck's cynicism. "Jimmy, will you be kind enough to take part in a little experiment? I think it will give just an inkling of what I'm talking about."

"Okay," replied Jimmy. "I'm ready for anything."

"Good! Just close your eyes, okay?" Jimmy complied. "Now, in your mind, make a picture of your father.

"Do you have the picture?"

"Yes."

"Describe what he's wearing."

"Dark blue jeans and a plaid flannel shirt."

"Good! Now open your eyes. Okay. Who was looking at that picture?"

"I was," replied Jimmy confidently.

"Excellent! And did you notice you said, "I was," and not my brain or anything else?"

"You mean, I, as a spirit, was looking at it?"

"That's how it works. You made the picture and put it in the mind, and have it filed along with all the others. Like a computer. So now you can perceive that you are composed of a body, a mind and you, the operator, without whom none of this would work. Remember you were not looking through the body's eyes as they were closed. But you still were able to see the picture of your father."

Looking around at the observers and the reaction to the little test, Walter then added, "This was not meant to convince you that you are a spirit, but just to give you something to think about. Sometimes the simplest approach to the metaphysical can open many doors and arouse curiosity."

Scotty, getting Walter's attention, presented his thoughts. "We have established that man is really a spiritual being and he is totally responsible for all things created in the physical universe including bodies. Then he got lost in the degrading part of the mind, and now that controls him instead of the other way round. This produces insanity."

"Correct," answered Walter.

"That means," continued Scotty, "this situation applies to everyone and we are all victims."

"Continue," encouraged Walter, noticing Scotty had more to offer on the subject.

"Then what we consider to be analytical is not true. We are really functioning on a false premise that is secretly destroying us and preventing the victim from seeing what is real."

"Well put," acknowledged Walter. "As you stated, this applies to all of us regardless of any position in life. Be the King, President, or man on the street, they all suffer in one way or another." The group now focused on Chuck who held up his hand to address Walter.

"What I was thinking was, if we are spiritual beings, then this, of course, would introduce the existence of other planets. Wouldn't that make it feasible for people more advanced and more intelligent than us to exist?"

"To answer that, Chuck, it would be very narrow minded not to consider that there are other inhabited planets in this very galaxy; who are many years ahead and much more capable than us."

"If that's the case," interjected Jimmy, "why don't they help to straighten us out instead of letting us sink in our own shit?"

"Can't help being vulgar," Walter teased Jimmy. "Okay, we'll look on this as just a theory, but it may help to guide you in forming your own thoughts." They all agreed, and Walter continued. "If these beings are so far advanced to us, what factor would you assume to be absent from their mode of living that prevails here?"

"Well," started Scotty. "I guess maybe violence and drugs."

"Very good," responded Walter. "To put it simply, it is the absence of the most insane game in which we indulge. The one called war. Having put such stupidity behind them, they are able to concentrate on the more practical areas for survival. They put an end to war. We, on the other hand, put an end to peace and continue to involve ourselves in nothing but destruction. Jimmy, you want to know why they don't help us? Consider for a moment, what would they achieve? What do we do when we condemn criminals or unwanted elements of society? We incarcerate them in prisons built for that purpose. A few years ago, we sent them off to penal colonies to separate them from the decent citizens. As distance narrowed, we just locked them in jails. Get the idea?" Walter looked at each interested face.

"Now if we accept the theory that the beings on other planets are so far advanced and have the know-how, what do you think they would do with undesirables in their midst? Simply banish them forever, to what they would regard as a penal colony. Then they would be completely rid of them."

"You mean here," stated Scotty wide eyed. "In other words, all of us are rejects from somewhere else?"

"Wouldn't that be the most practical thing to do?" Walter answered Scotty. "Not just criminals, but the non-conformist who refuses to obey and is constantly in a state of rebellion. He is a bigger nuisance then the criminal, and don't forget, as is in our society, certain people realized that the quickest way to make a man insane is to place him in an insane environment."

"Boy, do we have one here!" added Scotty.

"Yes, Jimmy," Walter said noticing him to be deep in thought.

"If the other planets are so far ahead and denounced war, how come they have criminals or non-conformists?"

"Good question. But remember, you are referring to conditions as they are today. Maybe the expelling of such individuals took place a long time ago. If we buy the concept of lifetime to lifetime, then what we have is a continuation of life cycles here on Earth. To keep this individual on such a merry-go-round, there would have to be some sort of game to attract him and keep him locked up here in the first place. What do you suppose is that attraction?" Walter paused only for a second. He did not wait for their comments but uttered one word. "SEX! The most aberrated form of behavior we have in this society. That is the basis for much insanity."

Each of them went into his own limbo as the message sank in. Looking at all types of pictures relating to their own nuttiness on the subject. Scotty's anxiety as a young man being scared of catching a disease or causing pregnancy. Chuck's inability to complete the act with his wife had causes the couple much grief. Jimmy's habit to screw everything in the West Indies was really only a change of habitat. They each realized that the compulsions were enforced by the idea of being macho. This is what made you a man and all the clichés that encouraged the act. Then Walter snatched them from their thoughts.

"Why would anyone sitting in an ivory tower want to help such a bunch of misfits like we have on this planet. Although they may be ahead of us in some ways, technically speaking, they may still lack certain advancements in the humanities. We have the knowledge of splitting the atom and are probably two hundred years ahead in such activities but are thousands of years behind in spiritual concepts. Meaning, the only use we have for our technical efforts is destruction. We lack the desire to put our knowledge to more humanitarian purposes."

"On that note, we better get ready for the cocktail hour," reminded Jimmy, standing up to leave.

"Thanks, Walter, for an interesting chat," said Chuck.

"Yeah," added Scotty, "I hope we will be able to continue this conversation our next day at sea."

"That will be find, gentlemen. I also enjoy the company and will look forward to our next time together."

Chuck and Jimmy headed for their own cabins, but Scotty headed for his favorite place, the aft library. He wanted some time by himself before starting work. He procured a cold glass of beer from the Verandah Grill and settled back in one of those huge leather chairs he found so comfortable. The room was empty so Scotty did not have to be concerned with any distractions while he contemplated on the recent enlightening conversation.

His thoughts drifted to the subject of war and how he felt about it. As a young boy he would walk home from the docks and pass the windows of the Independent Labor Party offices. In 1936 these windows displayed actual pictures of dead and mangled Spanish children that had been dragged from the bombed ruins. Looking at these pictures, he had only felt outrage and boiling anger as he viewed the results of man's sickness. These incidents, he realized, were to cause his rejection of all authority and distaste for the military. How can grown men be responsible for such horrible acts as the destruction of helpless, little children. Sitting in the silence of the library, he could once again feel the indignation and hatred that assailed him at that time many years ago. It hit, all at once! This is the type of situation Walter was talking about. The bad part of the mind is brought into play by old trauma and impinges itself in the form of thoughts that represent non-survival. Seeing this situation in its proper perspective, he found himself adopting a more calm attitude and now dismissed these unwanted pictures. He closed his eyes and crept into that little twilight zone he enjoyed so much.

It would only be a handful of years after seeing those pictures in the shop window that Scotty would actually see, first hand, the result of bombing raids in his native Glasgow during World War II. This would solidify his contempt for war. Conscription was still in force three years after hostilities ceased in Europe. So, Scotty ignored the call to register until finally authorities caught up with him. He was taken to the registration office and ordered to register for either Army, Navy, or Air Force. The documents were placed before him with the instruction to take your choice.

His reply, "Go to hell! I refuse to sign any of these."

"You cannot leave here until you sign," he was told. "Your only other alternative is to register as a conscientious objector."

"Well I am not a Conchie," he replied, "but if it will satisfy your desire for my signature, then so be it." The documents signed, he felt hatred from the officials around him.

One of the morons made the remark, "What they should do with guys like you is to drop you over Germany in a parachute."

"Do you know something?" Scotty replied, "I'd probably land among nicer people than you."

The result of his signing the conscientious objector papers now required his presence at a C.O. Tribunal. He appeared before five judges. One was, of course, a theologian to outwit the defendant, should he try to be too smart on quoting the "good book." Actually, the only grounds for seeking immunity were religious. No statement or defense was permitted on political views. To introduce such evidence would probably reveal the real culprits.

Although he was not an atheist, he decided to play a game with the five over-age, red nosed pillars of society confronting him on his day in court. There was no way he was going to escape the vengeance of these shitheads on the bench, so he had nothing to lose. He entered the dock and proceeded with their game. He was approached by an official, complete with Bible. Instructed to place his right hand on the book and recite the oath.

"I refuse to take the oath, but wish to affirm," was his reply, much to the indignation of those present. Good, thought Scotty, as this action had knocked out the need for the theologian. One down and four to go.

The holy roller had to get one in as he asked Scotty, "Don't you believe in the Supreme Deity?"

"I don't consider that relevant. It is I who is being forced to join your army, not God."

"Why do you refuse to go to the army?"

"I refuse to be trained to kill."

"Why do you refuse non-combatant duty?"

"I refuse to assist a killer or administer to his needs."

Scotty was dying to introduce political factors into the discussion but knew it was a waste of time. He would love to have gone after these assholes with The Treaty of Versailles that imposed such horror on Germany with its reparation clause or the Ottawa agreements when the French marched through the Ruhr looting and pillaging. These were the preludes to a vindictive peace policy that had created a man like Hitler and the advent of World War II. Not to mention the fact that the war lords had to be fattened. Scotty questioned the sanity of the person sent to judge him as the interrogation continued.

"You are a drummer?"

"That is correct."

"You earn your living on the hide of an animal?"

"That is correct."

"You don't seem to object to the animal being killed to provide you with your livelihood."

Scotty was so taken aback by this insane observation that he had to suppress the desire to leap on the bench and destroy his own credibility by choking the living shit out of the whiskey sodden gasbag.

Scotty was dismissed from the tribunal with "request denied."

"You will go to the army or go to jail."

That evening's newspaper carried a short story on the finding outlining the judge's remarks entitled, "Drum Beats Drummer." The next day a rebuttal letter appeared in the same paper written by someone with far more intelligence than the old farts on the bench. It stated, "Nothing is so consistent in life that a young man should stop drinking water in case a few germs are killed in the process!"

As it happened, Scotty beat the system. He did not go to the army nor jail. When the warrant came out for his arrest he took off for London; found his way to Tilbury Dock and through a little devious cunning managed to sign aboard a liner bound for Australia as a steward. Now he was a member of the British Merchant Marine and in the clear. The Merchant Navy was not a branch of the service one could register for, so it took a little planning to make it all work. At least he knew where he was going, when he would be home, and how much money he would have in his pocket.

On his return to England, he received a letter from the authorities recognizing his Merchant Navy stint and acknowledging that it would constitute national service after two years. His sea book and the I.D. card were the same for any position on board ship, so Scotty simply left that ship after three months and joined another. On this ship he was a musician instead of a steward, and he had a ball for the next two years.

His face lit up with a smile recalling how he fucked them in those days gone by. Finishing his beer, he headed for the cabin feeling pleased with himself. Boy, he thought, descending the stairs, I want to hear more from Walter. He makes me think and feel good too!

All were seated at the dinner table after having played the forty-five-minute cocktail session. They were discussing the latest gossip and other stories that were doing the rounds on the ship. They were all ears as Bob unfolded the tasty morsel about the two old broads on A Deck who were inviting all comers to engage in a sexual marathon.

"It seems the old dears keep their cabin loaded with booze and started on the bedroom steward. After getting him half in the bag they began playing doctors. Pretty soon they were playing house. They told him to bring a friend next time and they'd have some more fun together. In no time these sixty-year-old gals were running a halfway house. Guys were trooping in and out all day and keeping the old darlings happy. By the way, they never seemed to tire either. The place soon resembled a barber's shop. They were practically lining up to service the aged sponsors who would get the sex mechanics loaded with booze before emptying the bags."

The fellows were amazed, but Bob swore the story to be true.

"I actually went there out of curiosity, of course, and witnessed the debauchery."

"Oh yeah," Chuck teased.

"Now, you know I'm not inclined to play that kind of game."

"Sure, Bob," said Scotty, "you'd bang a snake if someone held its head!" They really milked Bob's story.

"By the way, Bob, I don't recall seeing Joe around this trip. He certainly is not here in the dining room. Is he on vacation?" Tex asked. Joe was the waiter that took over for Tom whenever Tom was on leave.

"Oh, he got into a little scrape on one of his second sitting tables; that's why you fellows missed it," replied Bob.

"Joe?" asked Scotty. "He's one of the nicest and best waiters, what could he possibly do to upset anyone?"

"Well," began Bob, "according to the scuttlebutt, he received a very meager pittance from his table of six passengers on the second sitting as I said. Joe changed the paper money into quarters, took up a position at the top of the dining room and in full voice shouted, "Hey! Table forty-five!" There was dead silence and everyone in the dining room looked up to observe the source of the shout. An irate Joe now having everyone's attention, rolled all the coins in the direction of that table shouting, "Stick it in your ass! You cheap mothers!" It had served the purpose of humiliating the donors, but it cost Joe his job."

"What a bad break, but he's a good lad and will probably do better," assured Scotty.

"He already has," said Bob. "Joe is now the captain in one of the top restaurants in New York. I called him just before we left port and he said that he only wishes he had done this years ago. Why, he is even happy to be home with his wife!"

"Hell! I can't believe that!" added a cynical Chuck. "The wife part that is!"

"Seems one of the other stewards, on the last trip, was assigned six Rabbis at his station," Mike began. "He promptly complained to the head waiter. "Come on, for Christ's sake," the steward had moaned, "tips are what we depend on. What the hell am I going to get from six Rabbis?" The head waiter just replied, "that's the way the chips fall, and you just have to go along with the program." The steward was not happy to say the least. As it happened the six came aboard and apart from just requiring the usual service, they requested everything Kosher from the gallery. This took more of the steward's time trying to please them and his other tables too."

"At the last dinner when the gratuities are usually paid to the table waiter, the Rabbis simply thanked the waiter as they did each evening and departed. The crestfallen waiter went into a deep depression and complained all night to the sympathetic ears of his buddies."

"What happened to the waiter?" Scotty asked.

"Well, the poor fellow never expected to see the stiffers at breakfast the next day as the ship docked in New York early. But there they were all ready to dig in one final time. At first, he thought that maybe it was just an oversight. He went out of his way to please, expecting the money would be forthcoming. He was, however, disappointed once again. The Holy Six thanked him and took off."

"Bastards!" chorused the musicians in complete sympathy.

"Never fear, this steward was not one to give up so easily."

"What did he do?" Jimmy inquired.

"Well," continued Mike, "it seems he stood by the gangway while the passengers were disembarking, hoping for a miracle. Just then the holy men approached ready to leave. Seeing him standing there, they once again thanked him for his excellent service and descended the plank. The waiter was just about to send them on their way with an obscene epithet when the last Rabbi made an about face on the gangway and returned to the deck where the waiter was standing. "Oh," he said. "We nearly forgot." The Rabbi handed the dumb struck seaman six one hundred-dollar bills. Looking at the money unbelievingly the waiter addressed the bearer of the gift. "You know, you guys never crucified Christ. You fucking well worried him to death!"

"Hooray!" shouted Jimmy and Chuck.

"Up the rebels!" added Scotty.

Everyone around the table was tickled pink with the tale. The musicians always looked forward to the next episode of the continuing saga of "Life Aboard Ship" while enjoying their splendid food.

After the meal, the gang, as usual, headed for Bob's cabin to splice the main brace. Scotty excused himself by saying he had something to do. Although willing to partake in most of the festivities, he felt changes were taking place. His desire for the raucous living was beginning to subside.

Complete with after dinner drink, Scotty headed to his favorite sanctuary once again, the after library. He knew that at this time of the evening, the room was nice and peaceful. He selected his favorite armchair and got lost in his own thoughts. Knowing the way he felt now about this crazy scene, he realized the day was not far off when he would have to make some sort of decision about his future. Working ashore, in the usual type of job, such as selling automobiles, was, for the musician or entertainer, a drag! When you consider the kind of people one comes in contact with in those jobs, it can only be equal to the worst type of madness. He had already tried his hand as a sales rep. It wasn't too bad being out on your own and only having to contend with the customers. The problem was always the ones stuck in the office handling the administration side. These were the sleaze bags of the world.

His thoughts wandered back to London when he was thirty years old and had been playing full time for the last twelve years. England was not overly generous with wages paid to musicians. So, he decided to find a day job and supplement it with a few nights playing. Making the rounds in his quest, he soon discovered that the typical employer, in that red taped bureaucratic asshole of creation, frowned on anyone who would spend so much time thumping a drum, instead of contributing to the slave bearing industrial network of peons. Failure to achieve a position in the workaday world prompted him to scribble a little verse one night as he contemplated the course of his unsuccessful endeavors.

"Woe is me a hapless case, who would disgrace the human race.

For these twelve years, winter and summer;

I earned my living as a dance hand drummer.

123

A lad of thirty, that was me; well groomed, smart and strict T T.

Had industrial thoughts, whilst in my prime;

The reason for this cynical rhyme.

The applications, I did write; interviews from morn' til night.

Interrogated by the same industrial tool;

An over-age office boy, no more than a fool.

How come he reigns supreme, think I;

Hard work, free mason, or the old school tie.

So harken, ye young drummer lads, with the innermost intention;

Who dare to drum in yon dance band and ridicule convention?

Your judgement day will surely come; not when you're dead and gone.

But when you seek some other work; you'll find that you're not on."

Just like this morning in the Library, his thoughts drifted back to the circumstances in 1948 when the threat of going to the army or jail forced him to be inventive and at the same time, answer the call to go down to the sea. The various hotels he had played in gave him the opportunity to furnish himself with letterheads on which he wrote himself a nice reference letter and signed it with some phony name. On the day he arrived in Tilbury Docks there was an old Orient liner just arriving from Australia, so he headed for the offices that were located just a few yards from the bow of the ship. Presenting his documents and references, he applied for a position with the shipping company. During a brief interrogation he was asked the dreaded question.

"How come you have not served in the army?"

"I was involved in essential occupation, sir," he replied. "Making rum jars for the Royal Navy."

His answer, he knew, was taking a chance. Should the official be alert and nail him, but as luck would have it, the gods were on his side. He actually had done this job for a short time during the war, but had been fired for being a rabble rouser at the age of fifteen and calling the workers out on strike. Had this official really been on his guard, he would have realized the war was over before Scotty was old enough to be conscripted. So, there was no essential occupation at that time. Anyway, he got the job and was given a letter to join the Seaman's Federation. One had to have a position with a shipping company before being eligible to join the Union. One week later he had a medical exam and was accepted. Returning to the Orient Line office with his new sea book and I.D. card, he was assigned to the same ship he had watched docking a week ago, the S.S. Orontes.

The hairs on the back of his neck had that tingling sensation as he climbed the gangway. I'm really going to sea, he thought. An ambition fulfilled. I can't believe it. He felt like he had achieved a new identity that was making him a man. Drums had been pushed aside at the thought of visiting strange and exotic countries. It would open his eyes to what he now termed a load of bullshit.

Reporting to the chief steward, he was assigned cabin number one hundred and advised his position would be posted the day before sailing. Being a first timer, he expected to be washing dishes in the galley. Such stewards were called pearl divers. Boy, if he only knew then what was in store for him, he would have taken off and headed back to the hills of Bonnie Scotland. Leaving the chief steward, he found himself on one of the upper decks looking for cabin number hundred which he soon found. This is nice, he thought, examining the quarters, but he noticed the beds had no sheets nor pillow cases. Walking along the passageway he located some bedroom stewards in one of the pantries where he sought advice on obtaining the necessary linens for his cabin.

"Are you a passenger, sir?" Scotty was asked by one of the groups.

"Me? No," he replied. "I'm a steward. Just joined the ship."

The stewards looked at each other in bewilderment before breaking into laughter and realizing they had a cowboy on their hands.

"You just joined the ship, did you?" taking advantage of poor Scotty's naivety. "Well get your ass down below to cabin one hundred in the Glory Hole where you belong. This is the First-Class area you're in."

Receiving the directions, Scotty, totally humiliated, headed for the crew quarters referred to as the Glory Hole. He soon found his cabin with four rows of bunks in a narrow room with one drawer and locker to each bunk. Staking his claim to a lower bunk at the far end of the cabin, he unpacked and stowed his gear. The crew were on leave according to Port or Starboard watch; leaving those on board to act in store parties carrying all merchandise from the trucks on the quay to wherever. The worse job was carrying sides of meat to the huge freezers aboard ship. You had to wear your duffle coat and mittens and the men looked like a bunch of refugees from Alaska. The experienced waiters were exempt from this duty because they served the ship's officers and shore officials in the dining room the usual meals while in port.

Everyday Scotty expected someone to come aboard, seek him out, and pull him off the ship accusing him of being there under false pretenses. The hours worked while in port were eight to five. The crew then took off for the pubs and a night of boozing. The eve of sailing day, the names of the newcomers were posted on the bulletin board with their post assignments. Scotty nearly shit a brick as he read that he was now a waiter in the First-Class dining room. His references were so good that the chief steward had no other choice in the matter.

"Holy Christ," he voiced in the cabin. "What the hell am I going to do? I don't even know the difference between a soup spoon and a fish fork!"

"Don't worry," his new found buddies advised. "We'll get you through."

He should have known this would happen as his cabin contained only first-class waiters.

Sailing day, the passengers would not board until the afternoon, so Scotty started his stint as waiter serving the Customs officials lunch. All food was served from silver platters and required dexterity in using the proper utensils to transport the food from platter to plate. Scotty, lacking the technique necessary, would make sure the head waiter was not in sight, then just push the fish or steak onto the diner's plate. Living in Scotland all his life, he was not familiar with baked potatoes. He decided they were too large for just one person so he cut them and served half portions to each diner. No wonder the Customs officials were nodding their heads as they left the dining room.

Later, the other waiters bailed him out by helping him practice using the spoons to pick up food. Being a drummer, it did not take long before he became adept and earned the title of a good winger. Winger is the name attributed to waiters on board English ships and green peas are called cowboys. When a waiter goofed in some way he would be assailed with the song:

> "You're a real humdinger,
>
> But you'll never make a winger.
>
> You're a cowboy!"

Scotty's education was about to begin. He would learn the meaning of slave labor on his first cruise. When he was fourteen, he worked from nine to five-thirty in an engineering factory in Glasgow for $1.50 a week. To work in such an establishment was considered an honor and one should appreciate the privilege of being taught a trade and disregard the meager pittance. At that time, he also had to fire watch either on Saturday or Sunday in the event the Germans dropped incendiary bombs on the building. He was equipped with a tin hat, a bucket of water, a stirrup pump and a couple of sandbags around his nick. For this ten hour shift he was rewarded with another $1.50. What it boiled down to was that the preservation of the factory was far more valuable than his survival. That was nothing compared to what awaited him now.

Now he had achieved the status of Mercantile Mariner, a title worn with pride by the stalwart British who were always singing about, "Britons never, never shall be slaves." They had never been anything else but slaves; as he soon found out on board the illustrious S.S. Orontes.

"Wakey! Wakey! Rise and shine, me lucky lads. Show a leg." This daily greeting from the Glory Hole steward was screamed at the top of his lungs as he punched holes in the cabin doors at 5:30 a.m.

Scotty had to turn to at six a.m. Complete with bucket, soap, scrubber, and wash cloths. He would scrub, on his hands and knees, the whole port side of the dining room. No mops were permitted, only the old-fashioned method like mother did at home. Another steward had the center of the room and another the starboard side. Completing this chore, he then set up the tables for breakfast. He had one table of six and half of another table, totaling nine people. He served two sittings of each meal; this was called a double nine. Your partner, who shared your split table, stood guard over the tables while you ran down for your own breakfast. There always seemed to be shortage of silver resulting in other waiters pinching from your table. Scotty would return and guard the precious utensils while his partner grabbed some food.

After serving two settings, each steward had another cleaning station. Scotty had to scrub the huge buffet and polish the mirrors in the dining room. Then they started all over again by setting up for lunch; racing down to grab a bite to eat; guard the silver while your mate ate; then serve two sittings of lunch. As soon as lunch was over, the tables were prepared for afternoon tea. After this English tradition was over, the tables were once again set for dinner. Should the waiters be lucky, they might grab an hour to do their own ablutions. Fifteen hours a day. Seven days a week. In tropical heat, no air conditioning, all for $40.00 a month. What was that shit about Britons never shall be slaves?

The first port of call was Port Said, Egypt in eight days. Scotty had planned to jump ship, wait until it left, then give himself up to the British Consul. They would have to return him to England as a British Seaman in distress. Most British ships have accommodations set aside for this purpose, and Scotty intended to use them. But by the time the Orontes arrived in Egypt, he was getting used to the routine and was actually feeling pretty well. His body was beginning to toughen, and he realized that going back would only mean the hassle with the courts would start again. So, he decided to make the best of the next three months.

Arriving at Port Said, a half of the crew had shore leave and, as usual, headed for the source of booze. Landing in some bar, they proceeded in sampling a powerful rum while being entertained by the belly dancers doing their thing. Other patrons included some British army guys who considered this bar part of their private domain. Crew members from other ships were also in attendance, and when you put these varied groups together it always smells trouble.

The boys from the Orontes were known as a wild bunch and were famous for creating some kind of disturbance. Scotty was alert and able to perceive the scene. He realized what was to take place when one of his bunch climbed onto the stage and accompanied the dancers in their belly routine. The army guys removed their belts and wrapped them around their knuckles. This presented the ultimate challenge. World War Three broke out right in front of his eyes. Scotty managed to get behind the bar taking refuge from the milieu. He had seen plenty of this growing up in Glasgow. All of a sudden, a couple of dozen Arab police descended upon the room kicking any head that came into view with their huge hobnail boots. Rounding up the participants, they were all taken by van to a station further up the town and incarcerated.

Scotty found himself in a huge room with some of the other others who required medical attention, but which was not forthcoming. The door opened and a policeman, pointing to Scotty, directed him into another office. There officials, garbling in their own language, were making reference to him. As it turned out he was exonerated and pushed out into the street alone. It was dark and well past midnight. He didn't have a clue where the hell he was. So, he made his way in the direction of the water and started walking towards the center of town. The ship was to sail at eleven p.m. So, it was probably already gone. Plus, when a ship enters the Suez Canal, a pontoon bridge is swung out provide access to and from shore. It was long past sailing time and Scotty feared the worse. Just then he heard some English voices approaching. He realized it was some officers from the ship heading for the jail to retrieve the crew. So many crews were involved in the scuffle, the ship could not sail without them. Scotty darted into a doorway as the three officers passed. They were sharing ideas on the penalties and punishments to be inflicted on the unfortunate combatants when they got them back aboard ship.

After the officers passed, Scotty took off down the road in the direction of the ship. Arriving at the dock, he was dismayed to find the pontoon bridge had been removed in preparation for sailing. Oh shit! He thought. The officers must have come ashore in a small boat. Noticing an Arab nearby sitting in a small dinghy, Scotty offered him a pound and some smokes to row him to the ship, which he was willing to do. Scotty was then able to sneak through the gunport door and escape being seen by anyone who would report him. Once again, he had managed to sneak under the wire. The bridge, however, was active the next morning. Those who had participated in last night's fun were fined and received demerits in their sea books. This was called a D.R.'s or declined to report. A double D.R. usually ends your career in the Merchant Navy.

The next two weeks passed uneventfully as the ship left the Suez

Canal, crossed the Red Sea, and stopped at Aden. Followed by a brief stop at Ceylon and on to Australia where once again the fun begins.

Fremantle was the first port where the seamen received a pay packet and proceeded ashore to enjoy it. Usually at muster the night before docking, the head waiter explained the dangers of sampling what is offered in the wine houses and warns all green peas not to partake. Those entitled to shore leave would head for the "plonk" shops and go at it. "Plonk" was the name given to cheap Aussie wine that could be bought for a nickel a glass.

Scotty decided not to get involved. He wanted to witness the "Battle of Fremantle." It started in the afternoon as the local constabulary rounded up drunken crew members and transported them to the dock where they were dumped unceremoniously at shipside. Drunks could be seen staggering across the bridge clutching wine bottles. Those still standing would attempt to raise the fallen. This action would finish up in what could only be described as a heap of arms, legs and bottles shrieking with insane laughter. It was a sight to behold. Bodies were placed in nets and lifted onto the forecastle of the ship, close to the crew quarters.

Scotty decided, after the events in Port Said, that for the rest of the trip he would only venture ashore by himself. Being the curious type, it was far more pleasant to find what was happening and make new friends rather than spend all his spare time in boozers. In Sydney, he was exploring the bridge when he met one of the supervisors who gave him a tour and explained about the maintenance bridge. This was what he liked about travel.

By the time the ship neared England, Scotty was recognized as a good worker and a capable waiter. Taken aside, he was asked if he would consider remaining aboard with a promotion to center man. Center man meant looking after salt and pepper cruets, a little more money and NO SCRUB OUTS! Scotty looked at the Head Waiter who he never really liked anyway and gave him his answer.

"As far as I'm concerned, you can take this piece of shit with all who sail aboard her and use it for torpedo practice. The only thing missing on here are the oars, chains, and a guy beating a drum to keep up the image."

Leaving the gangway in Talibury, Scotty put down his suitcase, walked to the bow of the ship, and spat at it.

A couple of months later, he joined a P.O. liner, the Corfu, as a musician and headed for Hong Kong. Another mistake! They were leaving England at the beginning of the monsoon season. May, June, and July east of the Suez Canal is the pits with rainy humid weather. Clothes in the lockers actually turn green with mold. As if this wasn't enough, it was the worst band Scotty had ever played with, and he was stuck with it for the next three months.

Arriving in Hong Kong, Scotty experienced the hottest place on earth during those summer months. Most of the day he spent sitting in the pool at the Y.M.C.A. in Kowloon in an attempt to escape the torrid weather. He had met many people who raved about the exotic East, but as far as he was concerned, they were all nuts! The poverty and degradation he witnessed in Bombay, Malaya, Singapore, and now this stink hole held no beauty for him. Scotty had been reared in the slums in the East end of Glasgow, but that was paradise compared to what he witnessed in the Orient. The only delight he found there was a little gal in Pinang who took him to the movies then back to a hotel where he was introduced to the mystique of the far East.

The return trip was plagued with even worse weather. The ship bounced for five days across the Indian Ocean. Even the Mediterranean was rough, and many passengers received injuries that required ambulances to meet the ship in London. So, once again cursing the ship, Scotty left.

Now he landed aboard what was to be his favorite ship, the S.S. Stratheden, where he remained for the next fifteen months. The ship's run was Australia. Then she was also chartered by the Cunard line to carry overflow to and from New York. The band was good. The crew were a great bunch, and the ship had the feeling of a large private yacht. He probably would have been content to stay on her forever, but as they say, all good things come to an end. It was off to London for the next ten years.

London provided him with work and an abundance of pubs, but as he looked back, it never was a happy time. The beauty of Scotland wasn't there. The open space that even the ships afforded wasn't there either. Living in an apartment, to the pub, to the dance hall or club was such an unproductive existence and unfortunately you don't see it until it's all behind you.

Awaking from his trip down memory lane, Scotty headed back to his cabin, changed, and entered Bob's quarters where everyone was already in fine fettle.

"Where the hell have you been?"

"Don't you like us anymore?" The guys in the room teased him.

Chuck's three gals, Lorraine, and even Valerie, who seemed to have an interest in Mike now, were all there. Becky, with the boobs, was seated on Bob's bunk, with drink in hand, surveying the scene a little glassy eyed.

"Oh," said Bob, "I'm glad you came in. We got a cable from Curacao. The guys are picking us up in the morning as soon as we dock. So, get ready for a big day!"

The guys Bob was referring to were involved in the oil business in Curacao and had made a couple of trips on the Nectar. Half a dozen of them were sons of oil rich parents and they just loved to party. They fitted in perfectly with the minstrels who had shown them a good time with the booze and the broads. It had become a ritual when the ship arrived that they return the hospitality in a big way. Cars were always waiting dock side to pick them up get it on. Shit, thought Scotty, there goes my good intentions. Knowing full well what to expect from their friends ashore.

"Have you notified the gals yet?" Scotty asked Bob.

"No, but we will later. If you see them tell them to get down here after the second show."

The gals were three of the shop girls and three stewardesses who had been involved with the oil barons when they were on board and who also loved to party.

"Ok! Will do!" Scotty now accepted a glass of Scotch from Bob.

The Grand Lounge was filled to capacity with the passengers from the first sitting waiting to be entertained. The musicians were seated on the Starboard side looking on to the left of the stage. The acts would enter from the Port side door, climb a few steps, and approach center stage. Everything went okay, and the passengers had a good time. After the first show, Scotty and Chuck took a stroll round the Prom deck while the others headed for the pantry and more sauce.

"Are you going to make it tomorrow, Chuck?" he asked as they rounded the forward part of the deck.

"Sure thing! These guys are always good for a high time." Chuck's usual routine was to sleep while the ship was in port, but Curacao was the exception.

"You don't seem too enthusiastic yourself. Are you going?"

"Oh sure," Scotty replied. "What else is there to do? But I think we should go easy on the booze. Don't forget, we still have to get back and play cocktails and the dance. Remember the last time we came back from Curacao? Mike was crawling along the working alleyway on his hands and knees unable to stand up while Tex was trying to ride him piggyback."

"Ha! Ha!" laughed Chuck, recalling the scene. "It sure was funny, and we did get away with it."

"Yeah, but Bob was sure pissed. Mike had to miss the first session, and you know that's criminal as far as Bob's concerned."

Passengers from the first show were now in the Main Lounge getting involved with the horse racing. Six wooden horses were moved according to the throw of the dice while bets were placed. Other rooms had bingo games that usually attracted the older folks and allowed the cruise staff to justify their existence by selling bingo cards, calling the numbers and paying out the winnings after they pocketed their cut.

Once again, the Grand Lounge was packed as they prepared for the second show. The band in position, they struck up the overture to bring on Jan Kelly the singer. Everything was going along okay except for Tex, who seemed to be having a slight problem from over indulgence and was hitting a few clinkers on the trumpet. Noticing Tex's dilemma reminded Scotty of the one time in his life he had tried to play a show after smoking a joint on another ship.

Pot was something Scotty discovered he did not handle too well and never did again when playing drums. Taking a few puffs of the weed while out on deck, he returned to the room and seated himself behind the drums. Opening his music, it seemed to be moving in circles on the stand. He picked up his drumsticks, which appeared to be six feet away, while trying to focus on the leader. The overture was the usual fast circus gallop, and as the band took off, Scotty very slowly hit the cymbal and never got past the first measure. Some of the members glanced back in Scotty's direction and soon realized the source of his predicament. They had a hard time keeping a straight face.

The very perplexed leader addressed the front line, "What the hell's wrong with Scotty?"

"He's bombed out his fucking head!" came the reply. "Don't worry about it. He'll be okay."

Each of his cohorts attempted to protect him, while Scotty in the meantime looked like a two-year-old delinquent who had just strangled the family cat and couldn't understand why everyone was so upset. His head was nodding like the little dog seen in the rear window of many cars in L.A., complete with stupid expression. All around him everything seemed to be in slow motion. His head felt upside down. This caused him to wave the drumsticks back and forward looking for something to hit. But he was unsuccessful in his quest. It took half of the show to pull himself together and get going. Playing jazz may be okay while under the influence, but trying to read music and play a show, forget it! Tex also appeared to have the same stupid grin on his face.

The singer left the stage, preparing the way for Bill Behan, the magician. The band began to play "Japanese Sandman" while Bill made his entrance in Mandarin costume, droopy mustache, Phillip Morris hat, and the usual paraphernalia. As the Oriental music continued, Bill lifted a huge silver salver complete with dome cover and went into his act. Tapping the dome with the magic wand he then lifted the cover to reveal a pigeon. Replacing the cover he gave a few more taps, raised the cover to find the pigeon had disappeared.

Replacing the cover once again, he gave a few more taps announcing, "And now radies and gentermen, I make plidgeon reappear."

Lifting the cover, to find an empty salver, he stated with a surprised look. "Radies and gentermen, where has plidgeon gone?"

Tex looking up at the stage answered, "It flucked off ya' clunt."

The band and even Bill went into contortions at the retort. The first couple of rows who had overheard the remark passed it on to those who missed it. Bill went through the rest of his act choking with suppressed laughter. He was received warmly from an understanding audience.

DAY 5
CURACAO

Seven a.m. The ship was alongside the quay, and lines were being thrown to the stevedores ashore as the musicians trooped out onto the deck. Looking around at the motley bunch of passengers, Scotty snickered to himself. The typical American tourist dressed in his finery always provided entertainment for the locals. Instead of covering whatever deformities they may be inflicted with, the tourist seems to emphasize and display their yucky appearance in the name of comfort. In hot countries, like India or the Middle East, people cover their bodies from the sun. But this is America's finest! The fat women in the brightly colored shorts, looking like the little man in the Michelin tire ad with grids of cellulitis resembling tires needing retreading. The men, with their white buckskin shoes and black ankle socks, always show their misshapen legs which are engaged in the task of supporting a heavy overhang resembling disgusting fifteen-month pregnancy. These wondrous sights caused Scotty to think once again of the quote from the famous Scottish bard, Robert Burns:

"Oh would some power, the gift tae gie us.

Tae see ourselves as others see us!"

Oh well, he thought, never mind being so bloody critical. They should be pitied, not scorned. Anyway, they're probably off to have a good time.

Taxis lined the quay waiting for passengers who could share the short ride through the oil plants into Williamstad. The town was so pretty. The houses were all painted in different pastel colors. They resembled the little village in Disneyland. It was a pleasant place to shop, with well-kept little malls containing nice stores where duty free perfumes and jewelry could be purchased. The bay, known as Santa Anna, cuts through the town center and has a pontoon bridge, called the Queen Emma, built in 1888. At that time, it was used as a toll bridge. As ships prepared to enter the harbor, the bridge swung out, causing a delay. If you enjoyed watching the movement of big ships that close, as Scotty did, it was a great experience. He had pictures of himself taken standing on the center of the bridge while on previous trips for posterity. The novelty of visiting the town had worn off for him and his buddies. Fort Amsterdam, the water front, and other interesting places provided good sightseeing for the tourist without having to travel too far. The hotels were nice and the casino usually opened early when cruise ships were visiting.

The gangways were now in position for the exodus of the fat brigade. The passengers rolled onto the dock and commandeered the taxis. The behavior of the average tourist is embarrassing, to say the least. He always acts as if there is no tomorrow. Whether it's getting into the dining room, only to sit in their assigned seat, elbowing each other as they charge into the showroom, or just going down the gangway. Everybody has to be a "firster." The musicians were accustomed to the panic-stricken neurotics. So, they just stood back and cooled their heels until the charge had subsided.

Six musicians, minus Bob, accompanied by the three shop gals, three stewardesses, Chuck's gals, and Lorraine and Valerie, piled into the four awaiting station wagons that had been sent to transport the gang to where they would spend a pleasant day of eating, drinking, and being merry. After a twenty-minute drive, they arrived at a large beach house complete with indoor slip where a couple of boats were docked. Introductions were made hastily before they got down to the business at hand. They entered the largest room that served as a bar. The boys, being thoughtful, had provided some bottles of their own, though this wasn't really necessary as the house was obviously well stocked with everything. Changing into swimsuits, they cavorted on and off the beach. Taking a little cooling dip then proceeding to tie one on. Their hosts informed them that the food was being prepared on another private beach where they would sail to later, using the boats in the enclosed dock. One was a fast ski boat. The other was a thirty-six-foot, flat bottomed boat with a blunt nose. It was a relic from World War II used for landing right on the beach to unload equipment. Christened the "Sea Toy," she had been completely refurbished. A superstructure had been added containing a new wheelhouse and, overall, she was a very comfortable vessel.

The gang was half in the bag as they all piled onto the Sea Toy and headed across the bay to spend the rest of the day on the other beach. Scotty and Chuck were lying on their stomachs right on the bow. The boat skimmed across the glistening blue water. The effects of the rum punch, aided by the hot sun, tempered by a nice balmy breeze, engulfed them with a euphoria only experienced by the content.

"Oh, man, this is heaven," Scotty remarked to Chuck.

"What can't everyday be like this?"

"Not a care in the world," added Scotty.

"What cares do you have? You asshole, you're not even married! All the money you make is yours. You can go where the hell you please at any time. So, what the hell are you concerned about?"

"I'm not talking about marital or work problems or any of that shit. I just mean this feeling I have at the moment, where you don't even care that you have a body. How can I explain it? It's like you're floating on air instead of feeling the weight or the attachment to the lump of skin and bones."

"So," answered Chuck looking at his friend, "how long do you think that crap would last before you found yourself bored to tears?"

"That's the point I'm trying to make," he said, turning on his side and addressing Chuck. "When you feel like this, there is no time because, as Walter was pointing out, a spirit is not involved with those kinds of considerations. When you are stuck to a body then you have the concept of time only because you agree that that's how it should be."

"You know, Scotty, you're getting more full of shit every day!" Chuck stood up while laughing. They were too fond of one another to say or do anything that would cause any kind of friction.

Scotty and Chuck were both standing when the boat approached the beach. They entered a narrow inlet and the boat was heading for the sand bow first. The helmsman advised the guys and gals to walk forward to the bow and make their assault onto the beach just like marines. Chuck and Scotty made the jump first. They assisted the ladies, who were following the direct orders. Tex was impatient. Dressed in white shorts, a new T-shirt, and his beach towel tucked under his arm, he decided to jump over the side amidships expecting to land in shallow water. Before he could be stopped, over the side he went, disappearing from sight. The whole gang laughed as his glasses and beach towel hit the surface first followed by a bald head. Why me God, was Tex's thought as he failed to touch bottom as expected. He felt there was no end to his descent through the sea. Panic set in, causing him to kick and flail his way to the top after he consumed half of the water in the bay.

"Thar she blows!" shouted Mike, the ever-ready pirate, as water spouted from the poor guy's mouth on striking the surface. Those on board managed to retrieve his glasses and towel. Thus, the reason for the orders to exit via the bow became clear to other doubters. The channel had been dredged out and there was a sheer drop from the edge of the sand that immediately went to a depth of about twelve feet. The girls were hysterical watching poor Tex attempt to paddle his way ashore. Between being totally confused and just being Tex, he started off in the wrong direction. The ski boat piloted by one of the hosts used a boat hook to guide Tex toward the beach. After the invaders were safely landed, the boat backed out into the bay and dropped an anchor.

Their hosts had a chuck wagon all set up complete with cooks who were serving up hamburgers and the greatest tasting chicken legs cooked in a garlic sauce. Everyone was having a ball. Booze was flowing. Chicken legs were being gobbled up, and there was lots of swimming. None of the guys had ever tried their hands at water skiing, but by now they were game for anything, thanks to the sauce. Mike had a go first, but as soon as his big fat ass left the water, he nose-dived back again. Some of the others managed to get up after a few attempts, but the effort was short lived. Scotty was the only one who actually succeeded. His strong arms and a good sense of balance made him a natural. Tex, on the other hand, after the third try, managed to achieve the desired position. Giving the thumbs up sign for more speed, he decided to show off by lifting one ski out of the water. That did it! The water caught the ski, slamming the point of the ski into his forehead and nearly knocking his brains out. When the boat picked him up, there was blood from the cut floating all around him in the water. Tex was singing "Somewhere Over the Rainbow" at the top of his lungs and asking for a drink. Obviously not too seriously hurt, he was patched up and given another snort for all his efforts, and the party went on.

Abe, sitting with Scotty, was the only one not drinking. He shook his head as he looked towards Tex.

"Is he always goofing up and getting into trouble, or is he just having a bad day?"

Scotty smiled at Abe's question and attempted to answer him between bites of succulent morsels.

"No, that's just Tex. You can always depend on him to do the unexpected, and he always seems to make it. Last cruise we were in Haiti and were in a taxi heading for Ibo Beach. That's about twenty miles from town. The drive takes you through some wild areas. Tex always needs a bathroom at the worse possible moments. Have you ever noticed the combinations of food he eats? Like rum followed by souffle or ice cream; he is forever suffering from the boiling bowels. Anyway, there we were, taxi full of guys and gals halfway to the beach when Tex yells the inevitable, "I have to go!" Stopping the taxi, he ran across the street and dived through a bush. All of a sudden, we heard a splash and a call for help. We dashed to where Tex had disappeared. He had jumped right into some kind of swamp and was up to his waist in crap. We broke off a branch and got him out, minus his shorts and drawers. They had gone down without him. So, we just wrapped a towel round him and traveled on to the beach. We refused to let him buy anything ashore. So, he looked quite cute going back aboard the ship. He was a Gandhi look alike."

Abe enjoyed the story. While sitting there, he secretly wished he was able to join in the fun like the others. He was accepted by the guys now, but always felt sort of out of it. They kept him around as a "go for." Hey, Abe, fetch us a drink. Abe, get us some food. He was always ready to oblige just to be with them. How he wished he had the charm that swept the chicks off their feet or just to be able to join in and be one of the boys.

Abe, however, wasn't too gullible. He noticed people disappearing behind the sand dunes in pairs. One of the hosts, with one of the shop girls, went off arm in arm laughing and giggling in expectation. Even a dingbat knew they hadn't gone looking for sea shells.

Scotty and Lorraine decided to walk along the beach just to get a break from the festivities. They felt very comfortable in each other's company, strolling hand in hand in silence. Looking at Scotty, she voiced her thought.

"How do you guys take it? Do you ever let up?"

"Well," Scotty smiled at her, "it does take the stomach of an ostrich, and nerves of steel. You also have to be totally nuts. That's why you never take all of this seriously." Scotty knew that Lorraine was manifesting the female notion of falling in love. This seems to inflict all women who expose themselves to expeditions such as cruise vacations.

"You have heard the story, Lorraine, about sailors who have a girl in every port," he teased her. "Well musicians usually have twenty!"

Lorraine was a big girl and wise enough to accept the cliché about passing ships in the night. She realized that she was being let down lightly.

"It's bad enough," he continued, "to team up with anyone who earns a living by going to sea, but musicians? Yuk!" He shook his head.

"Anyway, I'm glad to have met you and have no intention of putting a ring through your nose," she said while playfully running into the water.

"Good," thought Scotty, "I'm glad that's over with. Lorraine is really a nice gal and I did not want her to feel that she had been used and abused."

"Okay," he shouted after chasing her in the water. "You're still my pal."

By the afternoon the gang were really cooking. When the boat once again nosed up to shore to take them back to the beach house, everyone was in a good mood. They were harmonizing "Moonlight Bay," "The Whiffenpoof Song" and all the old favorites. Chuck and Scotty with Lorraine and the other three girls were on the bow of the boat. In all there were twenty-three of them scattered around the old World War II vessel. Some were on top of the wheelhouse listening to Mike strum his guitar. Some were below in the cabin still eating and drinking, while others sat on the aft deck. No one seemed to mind Tex donning one of the host's captain's cap and declaring himself captain of the ship. He took over the wheel and offered to perform any desired shipboard weddings. The gang just laughed at him.

Everything was going along okay with Tex at the helm, when all of a sudden there was a series of crunches and the sound of splitting wood. The boat felt as it had gone over some bumps in the road. The boat owners quickly regained their sense and rushed to the wheelhouse. Those below confirmed what happened. Tex, not knowing the bay, had drifted into the area of an old sunken pier. The bumps they felt were the boat striking the submerged pilings three times and knocking six holes in the boat aft of the bow. The water was rushing into the cabin at a great speed.

"Head for that shore over there," the owner shouted as one of the locals turned the wheel hard and fast. "At least we can make contact and save time. There's nothing on this side."

The boat continued to make way, but was taking on water very fast. The lads below tried to stem the flood by using their sea drills. They were busy stuffing mattresses and whatever else they found into the holes.

"It's no use. She's going down! Prepare to abandon ship!" came the cry from below.

Life jackets were brought forth for everyone. Scotty found himself wearing a child's preserver, which caused much humor. It looked like a huge collar around his neck. No one was in any condition to take the situation too seriously. They all climbed up onto the roof of the wheelhouse. Mike continued to pluck his guitar as they stood together and sang, "Nearer my God to Thee," emulating the Titanic. The boat slowly sank. They couldn't have been more than fifty yards from the shore when she touched bottom with about one inch to spare. Some of the heroes started to swim ashore. Tex and Chuck, swearing to purify the ocean, peed after the survivors. Taking a line, they attached it to the roof of the wheelhouse while one fellow swam to where he could stand above the water. He held the line from the boat to the shallows so that the girls could pass along hand over hand to safety. The boat had sunk in about fourteen feet of water, which was the exact height from the keel to the top of the wheelhouse. The ski boat soon came to rescue them in groups of six and return them to the shore.

Entering the beach house once again, they had another few drinks, got dressed, and prepared for the trip back to the ship. The girls were very excited about the experience of sinking a boat and being rescued. Our stalwart lads acted as if nothing out of the ordinary had occurred today. The owners of the sunken boat were not too concerned. They actually thought the whole thing very funny. They assured their visitors that they would have the boat pumped out and floating tomorrow. Money was no problem for them, so it would be hauled and repaired before their return and the next party. The boys cheered and toasted their good friends.

Back aboard the Nectar once more, they all split and headed for their respective cabins. The lads changed for the cocktail set and converged on Bob's cabin to splice the main brace and discuss the events of the day. They were seeing it in a different light now. The more they talked about the incident, the funnier it became. Relating the story to Bob, who did not share their amusement, only brought a reproach. He lectured them like a father scolding a bunch of unruly children.

"You realize, don't you, that had you been in deeper water it might not have turned out so funny. I don't suppose the boat carried twenty-three life preservers. That could have been catastrophic for the non-swimmers, and we may have had a very serious situation on our hands."

"Oh, come on, Bob," Mike said, attempting to make light of the leader's remarks. "You know God protects fools and drunks, so we had nothing to worry about. Give us another dram," he tendered his glass to Bob, who was holding the bottle of Scotch.

"Talking about preservers," Chuck joined in, "you should have seen Scotty with a tiny tot's jacket around his neck. It looked like he was wearing a flea collar and would have served about as much purpose in the water as it would have helped a dog get rid of fleas."

"You little shit," Scotty shouted at Chuck. "I didn't see you below trying to save the boat. Your concern was the case of rum you were sitting on."

"Ha! Ha!" Chuck laughed. "You think I'm fucking crazy. It's a question of priorities, and what's more valuable than a case of rum? Anyway, you should have seen your face as you looked up from below with water up to your neck making the fateful announcement in your best British accent, "I think we better abandon ship!" Boy did you look and sound like an asshole." Everyone in the room laughed as Scotty playfully lunged at Chuck pretending to attack.

"What happened to the case of rum you were so valiantly protecting?" Bob asked, trying to get Chuck's attention, who was fending off Scotty's pretended attack.

"Do you know what he did?" interrupted Abe. "He placed it in one of those hard life belts and towed it to shore. Can you imagine that?" The group recalling the picture, had another giggle.

"He really didn't have to," continued Abe, "the ski boat would have picked it up anyway, but Chuck seems to have a flair for the dramatic and has to upstage everybody."

"What is this other part about certain guys pissing in the water as others left to swim ashore? You mean you actually did this in front of those ladies?" inquired Bob, appearing shocked.

"Christ! Don't get your dander up about those ladies," piped in Tex. "As far as I'm concerned, seeing cocks was nothing new to any of them after what went on behind the bushes and sand dunes today."

"So, it wasn't just a party, but you immoral fiends were also engaged in and participated in a sex orgy."

"Belay there!" Mike responded in his familiar Long John Silver voice. "We was just a bunch o' pirates enticed by them thar buxom wenches who was only interested in our silver and our rum. Har! Har! Correct lads?"

They all showed their approval by holding their drinks above their heads and yelling in reply, "Har! Har! Long John!"

What a bunch of idiots, thought Bob, accepting the fact there was nothing to be gained by trying to be serious. Secretly he was sorry to have missed such an adventurous outing. He realized long ago that he had to keep some distance from them in the hope of providing some sort of stability. Although a little crazy, they were a decent sort and only behaved as expected by the normal red-blooded musician. After all, exposure to such temptations was just a part of the profession.

The cocktail session was in full swing. The passengers availed themselves of the caviar and sipped the concoctions of their choice. The men were sporting new watches bought ashore today. The whole room stunk of all types of perfumes purchased by the ladies in the duty-free shops. Scotty, sitting at the drums, was glad the ships no longer stopped at Cuba. After stopping there for a day, you would have to suffer the stink of cigar smoke from the people who never had an adult pacifier stuck in their faces before.

Leaving the Grand Hall, it was once again time for dinner. One dozen oysters, followed by a nice steak, a souffle, and coffee. Not bad for a wee boy from the slums of Glasgow, thought Scotty. Dancing would be on the aft deck again tonight, much to the consternation of the musicians. Chuck would once again face that lousy upright piano which spent its days and nights on the open deck. He had to play it tonight and one more time tomorrow for the afternoon kiddy games for the grownups, and that would be it for this cruise.

The sumptuous meal over, the gang headed for the usual tete a tete in Bob's cabin. Scotty settled himself down in his own sanctuary, the aft library. He was reading the ship's newspaper when his attention was drawn to the approaching person.

"Hi, Lorraine. Have you recovered from your uneventful trip ashore?"

Raising her eyes, she replied laughing, "When I took this cruise, I didn't realize that it would involve a shipwreck as part of the entertainment, but it seems to be all in a day's work for you guys. Do you mind if I invade your privacy?"

"No of course not, sit down. Actually, your company is always welcome." Sitting back restfully in the adjacent leather chair, she was silent for a moment.

"Now I know why you like it in here. It's so peaceful with just the murmur of the engines. God, if I stay in this chair, I think I would just fall asleep."

"That's why I spend so much time in this room. Most of my sleeping is done here, usually in the afternoon when the ship is in port. As you know, trying to rest below can be a problem."

As they sat in the restful room, their thoughts were on the same track. They enjoyed each other's company but were sensible enough to know it was just a vacation and not to expect any future commitments from such an association. Not wanting to be mistaken for the pursuing female, Lorraine posed a question in general terms, "Don't you musicians ever think about settling down with a nice home and family instead of this will of the wisp type of existence you lead?"

Scotty was resting his head on the back of the chair. He turned to face her and replied, "That would be okay if this profession offered a town when one could make enough money to live such a life, but it's difficult to find. Most jobs are temporary, so you can never have that stability to make the mortgage and car payments. Try to get a loan when you're a musician and see what happens. It's really the life of a nomad, always on the move. I did okay in Washington D.C. for a few years, but the continual grind of playing cocktail parties or conventions becomes a bore, and so one has to move on. Apart from that, music has changed. The only ones making money in this business are the nonentities who blast forth with rock and heavy metal."

"I suppose that could be a source of irritation," she picked up on his mood. "So, where do you go from here?"

"When I was a young player, you had to improve to achieve a better job. As your ability increased, so did your status and income, but it's not that way anymore. The Dictators in tin pan alley dictate to a gullible public what kind of music they should like and so it goes. Encouraged by this scourge, these scumbags now exploit the kids. With only their three chords, they are forced on the music scene with all sorts of neurotic gimmicks used to enrich themselves. Gimmicks are nothing more than a substitute for talent, and should the particular group make it, they, of course, can now do the demanding. Should they fail to create the demand desired by the dictator, they will be dropped so fast and replaced with another bunch of little boys who seek stardom without really earning it. Being unsophisticated and inexperienced as these kids usually are can pose all sorts of problems for their own sanity, as has been evidenced in the past. What you have is a professionally trained musician who is always seeking the ideal scene, which is to play the kind of music he wants to play, but he can never do that and make a living too."

"So, what you're saying is that the days of jazz are over?"

"Not entirely. There are towns, like Los Angeles, that may offer the opportunity to play with some great guys with big names, but they do it for starvation wages. At one time that town employed plenty of musicians in the studios to accompany the film industry, but even that is disappearing too. Most television, movies, and shows are going to the electronic systems where one man can emulate sixty musicians using a computer. He programs whatever sound is desired and once again the public don't know or don't care whether it's played by an orchestra or sounds like trash cans being accompanied by pile drivers."

"I suppose that could make you cynical and bitter, especially if one has poured his heart into the study of an instrument."

"Well," continued Scotty, "I suppose there are always two sides to every story. In the old days, when you only had jazz and big swinging bands, the musician also adopted an aloofness from the public and treated them with disdain. Musicians in those days even created their own language and slang to keep communication limited to the "hep cats." So maybe what we're seeing today is a revolt against those who were always a world apart from the industrial prisoners."

"Are you saying the musician is partly to blame for his own demise?"

"Yeah, something like that. But it doesn't alter the fact that the ears of the general public are only painted on, otherwise how could they put up with the racket that passes for music today?" Becoming more intense as he looked at Lorraine, he added, "You know when I lived in London, the B.B.C. would not permit jazz to be aired? That music was only heard by those who ventured to the appropriate places. When I came to America, F.M. stations would not play rock and roll. Now what do you have? A constant barrage of this garbage all day long from every form of media. You can hardly find a radio station that plays good music. You can't even enjoy a T.V. show without the stuff blaring in the background. It is psychotic music for the brainless and is producing more nuts every day by encouraging the morons who attend rock concerts in the name of entertainment."

"Boy, you sure are bitter on this subject. I think you need a drink." She beckoned the steward who had stuck his nose in the door. After the steward took the order and left, Scotty was once again on his soapbox.

"Getting back to the subject of marriage, I don't think it's for a musician who is young and still ambitious. It may be okay for the guy who has done it all and is ready to settle down. Usually by then he's prepared for it and probably has changed his profession. What woman is going to accept the constant travel or late hours, if he should work near home? I've seen too many marriages go down the drain. Personally, I always advise drummers not to marry before the age of forty."

"How good of you," laughed Lorraine. "Considering how you guys live, what could a woman expect marrying a musician over the age of forty? A decrepit, burnt out, old juice head would be my guess."

"Now be nice," Scotty shared her humorous mood. "Any more of that and I'll cut you off!"

"Oh no sir! Not that! Please don't be so cruel," she teased.

They both shared the good-natured fun. Drink in hand, Scotty thought for a moment, then looking again at his companion, he took up the conversation once more.

"You know we poor musicians have other problems. The biggest gripe is trying to find a peaceful place to sleep after work. When I lived in London, it was dogs. Everyone in England has a dog. That's why Englishmen always seem to look down when they walk. They are watching out for dog shit. It's all over the place. To avoid stepping in it you either have to wear galoshes or learn the tango!" Lorraine enjoyed Scotty when he got in this type of humor. He could be so funny and graphic in his descriptions of various happenings.

"Go on," she giggled. "Tell me more."

"Well, where I used to live the workers, as usual, arise around six a.m. and throw their little beasties out in the backyard to water the flowers and dump their load. Then the barking starts. It's amazing that people who rise early never consider someone else may be trying to sleep. They usually don't give a damn. Anyway, this one dog in the opposite backyard used to commence his stupid noise every morning, arousing me. I had retired at about four a.m. after a hard night's work. I couldn't take it anymore. So, I acquired a pellet gun. It was Lincoln, all steel, powerful beauty that fired double headed bee-bees. It was a very accurate pistol, and I was hot shit with it too. At that distance the pellets would not penetrate the dog's skin, but it did give him a helluva sting on contact." Giggling like a little boy as he recalled the scene, he unfolded the scenario. "I used to wait until the dog barked, aim at its ass then peel one off. That mangy cus would let out with a yelp and jump six feet in the air. It only took a couple of days. Just like the dog in Pavlov's experiment, he soon realized; bark means sore ass, jump in air and more sore ass."

"Oh, how cruel you are, doing that to the poor dog," Lorraine admonished him, but not too seriously.

"Well it was either me with no sleep or a dumb dog with a sore ass. So, screw it!"

"Have you lived in many cities in the states?" she asked.

"Los Angeles was my residence for a while. When I first went there it was enjoyable, but to make any money you had to play the resorts, like Vegas and Lake Tahoe. Now as far as I'm concerned, L.A. would be the ideal place to test the Hydrogen Bomb. But I suppose it's like any other big city today with the craziness and noise. When I arrived there, I found a nice apartment building where I rented a two-bedroom apartment. What attracted me to this particular building was a sign saying, "No Pets. No Children." Ideal I thought. There should be very little in the way of disturbance for the poor musician. Boy was I wrong," he said, emphasizing the word for Lorraine. "The local lawmakers, in their infantile wisdom, introduced laws in the name of discrimination. In their quest for greed, they created congestion by flooding the city with all types, mostly illegals and not just from south of the border but from all over the world. At the same time, building of new apartments and houses ceased under the pretense that rent control made it a poor financial investment. Before rent control, my apartment was $240.00 a month. That same abode is now $1200.00 and climbing. That's with rent control. But now back to discrimination. This nice peaceful apartment building became infested with noisy rug rats. The kids have no play area because the complex was never designed to accommodate children. So, they invade the hallways with their insane shrieking, play in the street and in the lobby, and ride up and down in the elevators just for fun. They even skateboard in the garage. Cute!"

"Well, I suppose the kids have to live too." Lorraine put in her two cents worth. "Don't you like kids?"

"It's not a question of whether or not I like kids. As a matter of fact, I'm fond of them. You might even have seen me amusing the kids on board the ship here. But it is a question of rights. The kids have the choice of living with adults or children, I don't. Some of the older people, who lived in that complex, even suffered from heart and other illnesses because of the noise. They were forced to move out and head for Senior Citizen complexes far away from family and friends to get peace and quiet. As the old move out, the rents go up again. So, who really gains? Not the tenants."

"I suppose that's why you musicians prefer to be here with your own Inner Sanctum; no rent or payments of any kind."

"You got it, Baby. We play dances, shows, and jazz. We have our food and booze. So, to hell with it!"

He sat back contemplating, while Lorraine formed her own conclusions. Sure, they were a rowdy bunch who liked a good time, but they were harmless. They bore no malice against anyone except, maybe the odd ship's officer. The only fault she could find was their lack of responsibility. Compared to the little people in the business of living ashore, they sure knew their way around and were obviously more interesting to be with, she thought. How can I go back to the work-a-day types with their three-piece suits sporting little name tags clipped to their breast pockets? Are these labels really I.D.'s or is it to remind the yuppie who he really is should he forget his name? One thing she noticed about musicians, although they could get into the booze pretty heavy, there was never was any evidence of drugs. She couldn't say the same for her office boys or girls back home.

The same scene can be witnessed in any town. Office buildings spew their refuse straight into the cocktail bars around five p.m, where the children now try to play grownups. Drinks in hand, they attempt to give their own impression of sophistication while discussing the latest software and expounding their vast knowledge of the latest computer. Credit cards, which are packed to the limit, pass to and fro in an effort to impress the ladies with really only one thought in mind. Hoping to score. Of course, the type of broad who frequents these overpriced pick up joints is just as bad as their male counterpart. She sports her unisex garb complete with collar and tie. She wouldn't be seen dead without her Gucci briefcase. All this is an attempt to be equal. It's amazing, they scream about being liberated when there is really no difference. They are just as stupid as the men they secretly hate. You can tell when the cocktail hour is over by the number of autos being driven erratically as they head for their respective opium dens. If they arrive safely, they can prove what men of the world they are by indulging in the new opiate of the masses, smoking or snorting their way to hell. Lorraine realized that as far as these musicians were concerned, they did not play the games of seduction with or without drugs. If it happens, it just happens. Their openness and approach could be very diverse. Valerie, her friend, found this out to her own surprise last night.

Valerie was playing a coy game with Mike. Leading him on proved to be a mistake. Instead of letting her complete her teasing strategy, he just looked her straight in the eye and asked, "Do you want to fuck?"

Valerie, of course, not being accustomed to such brashness, stood still for a moment in total disbelief of what she had heard. She turned heel and took off, appearing outraged and insulted. She only got about

154

fifty yards when she realized her ploy was silly. Turning back, she entered Bob's cabin. Sorting out Mike; she shouted across the room, "Yes!" The gang had a good laugh, and Valerie and Mike were pals again.

"Boy, you appear to be miles away. What were you thinking about, Lorraine?"

"Sorry," she replied apologetically. "I was just running over in my mind some of the things you mentioned about all this coming to an end. If the music scene has changed so much, what will you do if you have to resort to menial tasks like the rest of us?"

"Don't get the idea that I am completely incapable of facing the business world. I have contributed my superfluous energy to the cause of enriching the employer. I have sold automobiles. I have been a sales rep. And if I may say so was pretty good at it. The jobs are not too bad and can sometimes be more profitable than music. It's the people one has to associate with that are the problem. You see, I can do what they do, but they can't do what I do. And that can cause resentment. The biggest deterrent to working ashore is the back stabbing that goes on. I'm sure you have experienced this in your own job. But let's take musicians for example. Sure, there may be a few bad apples, but on the whole, they respect each other. Should one excel in playing something good, he will receive accolades from his peers. When musicians know that a top-quality player is appearing in town, they will flock to hear that particular instrumentalist or band. They applaud each other. Now how often do you find that among your workers? Although I'm speaking in general terms and do not wish the demean the whole population, but it's a fact of life that those conditions do exist out there. Do you know what I've noticed? A group will get together to oust somebody and really work at it. When the poor guy gets the axe, the people responsible for him getting dumped will now lend a sympathetic ear and tell him how bad they feel. They even say that they are going to quit too! But never do. Sometimes they will even run a benefit for the victim or take him to dinner to convince themselves what good people they really are. Two faced bastards! All wacky! Anyway, so much for today's lecture. Let's go below and grab a shooter before I'm excommunicated from the club."

Leaving the library, they made their way to Bob's cabin where all appeared calm and mellow. The mood would probably stay that way after such a hectic day. The drinks were acting in reverse, providing the feeling of reverie. The body's fuel had been exhausted during the course of the day. Each shared the same thought. Thankful that they only had to play dance music tonight and not a show. Even if it was somewhat of a discomfort out on deck, it could be played without too much effort on their part. The numbness in their bones would help to disguise the effects of the weather.

"By the way," Bob addressed. "Watch out for the Staff Captain and Chief Officer. They are out to hang us, so take no chances. Don't give them any excuses like being in passenger cabins. They have spies all over the place."

"Yeah, I know." Scotty began. "That happened to me. I popped into Lorraine's cabin the other night after dinner and it was obvious, I was being watched. A knock came to the door and it was one of the stewards with the excuse that he had to check the portholes since the cabin is on a lower deck. You know what these guys are up to. So, Lorraine stuck me in the locker where I nearly suffocated among the fur coats while the asshole hung around for quite some time telling her that a heavy swell was expected, and the dead lights had to be shut down good and tight. Consequently, I stayed in there until the coast was clear. I escaped without being nailed."

"For Christ's sake," Bob started again, "keep it cool. Apart from the rum running episode, you know how officers feel about musicians. It breaks their hearts that we have the privileges we have and would like nothing better than to reduce us to the rank of able-bodied seamen!"

"Reminds me when I was on the Far East run," interrupted Scotty.

"Boat drills were called for the crew and I was standing in line at my particular station when the First Officer saw a chance to pick on me. He knew, of course, I was one of those impossible musicians. By the way, on that ship, we were all separated and assigned different boats, not like here where we are all together. Anyway, the tapes on my life jacket were not tied properly, so he started on me. Pointing to the jacket he asked, "Do you know what would happen if you jumped over the side?" "Sure," I replied without batting an eyelid, "I would get wet!"

The room full of eager listeners giggled, and Scotty continued his story. "Musicians, of course, were the only crew members who do not wear uniforms, and therefore, have no funny hats to wear either. The officer's face turned purple because I had made an ass of him in front of the crew. He was not about to give up on me. "Where is your head covering?" he demanded. "Never cover my head and do not own such a thing as a hat," I replied. "Well, you will go below and return with a cover on your head. This is necessary should we have to take to the boats in tropical waters." "Aye, aye, sir," I replied, mocking him in my best seaman's salute, and I took off below. I found some of the stewards who were excused from drills and they offered me any number of hats. Instead I took a plastic cover with elastic that fits over the hat for bad weather. I placed it on my head, pulling it down over my ears. Returning to the boat deck, I looked like a real jerk sporting this new look in head gear. Seeing me, most of the crew cracked up, especially when I rejoined the line, saluted the officer, and in my most nautical voice announced, "reporting for duty, sir! In headgear as instructed.""

"Ha! Ha!" the guys chorused. "Boy, you must have pissed him off."

"Sure did," laughed Scotty, "but I knew I was in trouble, and this guy was sure to have it in for me now."

"Did he get revenge?" asked Lorraine.

"Sure did! On the way back from Hong Kong, we had helluva bad weather with no respite until we hit Aden. It also happened to be my twenty second birthday. So, I went ashore with some of the crew and got into what they call their Balanaki Rum. The stuff's lethal! Anyway, we had a great time celebrating my birthday, and I returned aboard three sheets to the wind. The next morning the steward advised me to report to the bridge and be logged. Following instructions, I was escorted with the Purser on one side and the Chief Steward on the other, just like in the movies. They were carrying their caps under their arms like regular military. I thought the whole scene funny and asked them if I would have a choice of walking the plank or a firing squad. Lacking any sense of humor, I was told to be quiet and refrain from any conversation. Some passengers were waiting for the elevator with us and were told to stand aside as this elevator was reserved for the prisoner. This really cracked me up. I shouted to the passengers, "Tell my mother I love her," as the elevator door closed." The group in Bob's cabin were all smiles and happily waited for the next installment of Scotty's story.

"I walked into the bridge cabin, and there he was, the First Officer, presiding over the investigation with a couple of junior assholes on either side. I could see his look of triumph as he addressed me. "Do you know why you are here?" he asked me in his best Captain Blight imitation. "I suppose it has something to do with yesterday's performance, but I'm sure you'll come up with something." "I will not have any impertinence, and advise you to have more respect for this office." "Okay, I'll be good," I answered. "Tell me why I'm here?" He began looking at his notes, then he addressed me. "I have here a series of charges relating to your behavior yesterday afternoon aboard this vessel." I looked at my companions on either side with amusement, but they just stared straight ahead trying their best to be serious as he continued. "That you came aboard in an intoxicated state, entered the tourist lounge, whereupon you donned a funny cap, tap danced on a table, sang Scottish songs, and kissed lady passengers. How do you plead?"

The gang in Bob's cabin was rolling on the floor with laughter. Lorraine always knew Scotty was funny and a bit of an imp, but she could not have imagined this in her wildest dreams. Scotty, being the clown that he was, could never resist the opportunity to take advantage of a situation for comedy. His defiance and desire to turn this whole debacle into a farce was, of course, fostered by his hatred for anything broaching the militaristic attitude that this moron was displaying.

"What happened then?" they pleaded.

"All was silent, and the officers awaited my reply. Then all of a sudden, when I had their full attention, I broke into a tap dance and began singing, "Make my bed and light the gas, I'll be home for a piece of ass. Blackbird Bye! Bye!"

Bob and the other musicians were howling now. They could easily picture Scotty doing this on the bridge. A break was called, and more drinks were poured.

"Boy," said Jimmy looking admiringly at Scotty, "you must have been in deep shit then!"

Scotty was still laughing in his impish way as he continued. "You should have seen the effect. It was so funny. The mate was about to have a coronary. The other officers were restraining the urge to piss their pants and I now assumed a very serious demeanor. But that wasn't the only thing that had pissed the officer off. We had a ballet dancer on board who agreed to a little impromptu concert for the passengers involving me. She came out dressed in her tutu and danced "Swan Lake." At the end, when she folds over in death, two guys came out with a large screen concealing me dressed like her. As they left the floor, she moved off stage, leaving me in her final position. The illusion was that she was still there. You can imagine the surprise to the audience when I rose wearing a tutu, large hob nailed boots and carrying a feather duster. The band played part of "Swan Lake" again and I went into my interpretation of the ballet. It brought the house down! Although our little vaudeville act was great success, it was frowned on by the officers who look for any excuse to put us poor musicians down and prevent a little fun."

"What were the results of all your monkeyshines?" asked Bob with merriment in his voice and shaking his head in disbelief.

"Well, after things settled down on the bridge, the officer fined me the huge sum of one guinea or about two bucks and advised me that I would no longer be required to perform aboard the ship and to keep out of the forward bar. "Is that an order?" I asked. "No, it's advice," he replied. "See ya in the bar," I said as I took off waving bye-bye. When I got to the bar, all the passengers greeted me by telling me what a wonderful time they had yesterday. They were astounded when I informed them that I was fired for this little bit of fun. So, they immediately gathered a petition and presented it to the bridge. It stated that they intended to complain to the company on arrival in England. Such support prompted my reinstatement, but I knew that as soon as the passengers left the ship, my ass would be booted down the gangway, which it was."

The laughter subsided, and Bob reminded them that they had better get their instruments and head for the after deck to commence playing the dance.

The evening again was very romantic. The ship was gaily lit, and the passengers were dressed for the ball. The weather was warm, but not too humid, making for less discomfort. The six friends of the musicians from ashore were aboard ship and continued to tie one on in celebration of their now famous shipwreck. Teaming up with the gals from earlier, they kept popping below. The musicians would join them during intermissions. A steady supply of booze, of course, was available.

"Don't forget," the musicians kept reminding them, "we sail at midnight so make sure to get ashore in time."

Their friends, as instructed, managed to exit the ship and waved bye-bye drunkenly from the dockside. All the good intentions for an easy night had been ruined by their presence. The guys were feeling no pain by the time they all left Bob's cabin in the wee hours. Tex and Mike, being non-smokers, were dismayed to find the odor of stale cigarette smoke in their cabin left behind by whoever had occupied it during the evening.

"Oh shit," said Mike. "Let's open the portholes and clear this awful air out. I can't stand the smell."

"Okay," answered Tex, "but make sure to close them before we go to sleep."

It was never advisable to open these ports if you were on a lower deck, in the event that any kind of bad weather should occur. One heavy list of the ship could result in a catastrophe. The open port permitted the flow of fresh air into the room while the lads lay on their bunks enjoying the ozone. The effects of tiredness and a heavy day's boozing soon sent them into a pleasant slumber.

A half hour later a heavy swell lifted the ship a dozen feet, causing a sharp dip to port. The portholes, left open by our stalwart pair, served as an entrance for one hundred tons of water. Thrashing its way around the cabin, the water whisked both of them clear out of their bunks and deposited them on the deck. They awoke to find themselves sitting on the floor with salt water up to their necks.

"Christ," hollered Tex, "that's the biggest wet dream I've ever had!"

The commotion, along with water beginning to seep under the other cabin doors, brought the others racing to the scene. Thanks to the high step-over into each cabin, the water was somewhat contained but was running down the corridor. Scotty, wading through the flood, managed to enter Mike's cabin where Mike was already closing down the portholes. The beds and linen were ruined, and personal belongings were floating all over the cabin. Scotty, turning to Chuck in the hallway, instructed him to go forward and wake Tom and have him round up some of his buddies to help. Empty bottles and glasses were used to bail out the area. They rushed to and from the cabins pouring their private little sea into the sinks. Tom, with three stewards, appeared, complete with proper gear. The boys soon had the situation handled. Tom was able to acquire new mattresses and linen without anyone knowing about the mishap, and he promised to sort out their clothing in the morning. The gang were all sober now. Their desire for sleep had long since gone. Retiring to Bob's cabin, they decided that they might as well get started on the sauce. After all, it was a new day. Bob ranted and raved at the two culprits.

"You must be out of your bloody minds to have opened those ports while at sea. Not only did you endanger the ship, but that is a capital offense."

Tex and Mike sat with pursed lips knowing that Bob had to chastise them and that he was right. They also knew that it would soon be another one of their tales to unfold and laugh at later.

"It's lucky we only had one wave. What if the portholes had remained under water? You would probably have drowned!"

"I don't think so," Tex said stupidly looking at Bob. "There was never any fear of us drowning. Shit floats!"

"Oh, you dumb bastards," he said, realizing the heavy hand was useless. "Have a drink. By the way," Bob continued while extending them the bottle, "the stewards who helped us were promised a case of booze apiece. So that's coming from your rations."

"Fair enough," they replied, thankful that their stupidity had been covered up and no reprisals would be forthcoming from the bridge.

DAY 6
AT SEA

Mid-morning found the Nectar gliding lazily through the blue water, gently rocking to and fro as it was being pushed by the long rolling waves. The swell, accompanied by the warm sun, should have provided the expected euphoria while lying in the deck chair. Few seemed to experience that beautiful, healthy, tired sensation, and they wondered why. Instead, most of the travelers were feeling edgy and nervous. Their bodies felt like ton weights when attempting to climb from the prone position. It never entered their heads that the diet of the past week could have something to do with this awful feeling. What the passengers ate back home was bad enough, but now it was reinforced tenfold. Eight meals a day with heavy intakes of sugar and all this fortified by large amounts of alcohol and caffeine. Sure, the brochures describe the wonderful fresh air and restful atmosphere, but that alone does not create the relaxation and peace of mind one seeks by taking a cruise. Temptation to over indulge the free goodies can never be ignored. The gluttons wait for the gong to sound, sending them rushing to the eating temple. Even people who were on diets before sailing went nuts and made up for lost meals. Passengers return home claiming to have sun or sweat rashes, which may or may not be true. What they probably were suffering from was a sugar rash caused by swilling too much of the local rum available in the West Indies.

Another phenomenon that became obvious as the trip progressed was the gradual appearance of joggers on the deck each morning. First couple of mornings out, they can be seen in their nice new athletic clothes. They always look like large tots in romper suits plodding around the boat deck. Now they were either sleeping it off or nursing their swollen bellies in deck chairs. Certainly not running. It was a shame that ship workers become cynics, but they have every reason. People who deal directly with the consumers ashore always complain how tiresome a chore it can be having to condescend to their every whim, but can you imagine doing it under these circumstances?

The two old gals from A deck who were providing such wild entertainment for the crew were sitting playing gin on the starboard side of the Prom deck. Their faces had a glow that could only be found on those who have seen the light and then shared this joyful awareness with the less fortunate. The more energetic passengers were found on the upper decks taking part in various ship board tournaments. Deck quoits, a form of tennis played with a hand ring, was in full swing. The hustlers from St. Petersburg could be seen and heard playing the favorite sport of Florida, shuffleboard. One has to be careful when walking through St. Pete because some ninety-year-old fanatic is apt to attack you with the cry, "Wanna play shuffleboard?"

On the forecastle, the crew had rigged a canvas swimming pool and filled it with salt water via the ship's hoses. The crew were attempting to impress some young gals standing at the rail above. The more the females taunted them, the more ungraceful their water sports became. The lethargic passengers were already seated in the movie theatre. Here too were the musicians, still recovering from the night before.

The lights would remain on until the movie started at 10 a.m. This would prove to be a source of embarrassment for poor ol' Tex. The lads seated themselves near the front of the theatre in two separate rows. Tex sat between Mike and Jimmy in one row and immediately behind sat Scotty between Chuck and Abe. Most of the passengers had already taken positions beyond the minstrels. During a lull in the conversation, Tex let go with a whore of a fart that resounded off the wall, pulling everyone's attention to the suspected source. Tex, being quick of wit and attempting to shun responsibility for such a crude performance, immediately turned to the guys behind and in a loud voice remarked, "Abe, that was terrible! You should be ashamed!"

Tex thought he had succeeded in passing the buck. He was dismayed to learn that during his admonishment of Abe, his buddies were pointing their fingers down on him from above his head. The passengers had no doubt where the obnoxious explosion had originated. Realizing the betrayal by his mates, he slid down in his seat with a loud groan. The patrons now punished him with their laughter.

After the movie, it was lunchtime followed by another round of kiddy games for the grownups on the after deck. They were seated in the dining room discussing the subject of having to play for musical chairs and pass the grapefruit. They considered this task a joke.

"We shouldn't complain too much about this little stint," Bob told them. "After all, we are paid overtime. Look at what's happening on other ships that we have visited in various ports. The professionals have gradually been replaced by kids with their rock and roll trios. Everywhere you go now, it's two guitars, drums, and a lot of amplifiers. The unfortunate thing is that the officers have the power to call the shots. They know they are dealing with inexperience and take full advantage. Now look at our situation. We have the run of the ship. The accommodations of our choice. We could in the cabin class section, but we prefer our Inner Sanctum where no one will bother us. The young musicians of today are just put in crew quarters and have to eat in a separate mess. Look at us sitting here in the First-Class dining room complete with our own waiter. We know of at least one ship where musicians are not allowed to even talk to the passengers. Can you imagine? The most important public representative on board instructed not to fraternize! Although we have some problems with certain officers, I have never found a bad captain. Whatever it is they may be going through at a particular moment, they always seem to have more understanding and go out of their way to be friendly towards musicians."

"That's true," piped in Scotty. "I remember on the Stratheden we used to play forty-five minutes of light music each morning on the dance deck as the passengers sipped the hot bullion. One morning a real dingbat of a women set up a typewriter and proceeded to pound away while we were playing. Protests came from the other passengers, but she just ignored the requests to be quiet and continued the annoying racket. All of a sudden, the Captain appeared and stood in the doorway obviously enjoying the music. His attention was drawn to the clackity clack of the typewriter and the moron behind it. You could see the expression on his face change to total resentment at such an imposition. Walking over to the woman he wasted no time being courteous, "Madam," he said, "you have one minute to remove that infernal machine before I personally throw you over the side." Boy! She put up no protest but gathered up her junk and took off!"

"Good for him," was the general agreement.

"Could you imagine that being handled by a junior officer?" asked Jimmy. "He would have just told the band that she was a paying passenger and gone against the musician."

"So really," continued Bob, "we can't complain. You all realize that this stint will soon be over, and this ship will be heading for the yards. So, we may as well enjoy it while it lasts as I can't see us ever sailing or being booked aboard one of these new floating tin cans."

"You have to realize also," they turned to Chuck for his words of wisdom. "That music is not the predominant factor aboard these vessels. Gambling is the big thing now since the introduction of casinos. Music has now taken a back seat, except for playing the so-called productions that are inflicted upon the passengers."

"Yeah," Scotty interjected. "I took a couple of quick jaunts on two cruise ships, and what a joke. The so-called cruise staff, who are really rejects from Broadway, think they are stars. They attempt what is supposed to be a Las Vegas type extravaganza. What a load of crap and a mockery of what were once great musicals."

"Don't be too hard on them," Jimmy said in complete defense. He could never think anything bad of a group of good-looking broads. "They're just trying to find their way. This situation gives them the chance to dream."

"Living under a pretense is one thing, but it's being done at the expense of big-name acts who have lost that source of income because of these amateurs," responded Scotty.

"Well isn't that the name of the game everywhere?" Jimmy continued. "Look at Vegas and any other media. They have all gone the same route, cheap, cheap, cheap!"

"Okay!" Bob help up his hands. "What we are conducting here is our own memorial service. Times are changing. We have had our shot. We saw it all happen, and we are part of the reason it's taking place. There is no sense harping about it now. We will just do our thing. As they say, it's the age of mediocrity. This is evident all around. Who knows, the way people think nowadays, maybe entertainment will eventually take the form of throwing able people to the lions? Considering it is the non-entities who run everything!"

Coffee over, they made haste to Bob's cabin and a little sauce to fortify them before being called upon to contribute their many years of musical study in accompanying the egg and spoon race. The spirit of carnival prevailed on the after deck. The passengers were in swim suits and shorts. The casually dressed pranksters gather for the games. Vic, the cruise director, was in attendance and as usual complete with blue ribbon holding his new whistle around his neck. This was the only time the musicians were allowed to wear open neck shirts and chino pants. Turning to Scotty, Vic gave him the signal to roll the drums, ending with a cymbal crash. It was as though they were in Medieval England. Then the cruise director made his dramatic announcement.

"Ladies and Gentlemen. Let the games begin."

The dreaded chore was finally over. Scotty, Chuck, and Jimmy seated themselves at the after end of the Prom deck with copies of the ship's newspaper. The main topic in the paper was what was happening all over the states, especially California with the growing homosexual community.

"What is it with these guys?" Jimmy said, indicating the subject in the newspaper article. "They're demanding all sorts of rights! Want to have Gay Parades. Voices in every form of government. Join the police force and be denied nothing. They should have all this because of what they call a "life style." Their life style is repugnant. If they could be spotted at birth it would have been more beneficial to put them down!"

They were all chuckling in agreement and voicing various opinions when Walter appeared.

"Good afternoon, gentlemen. Seems like I'm interrupting a very heated dispute." He seated himself in one of the deck chairs just as Chuck was holding up the paper and slapping it to emphasize the general source of annoyance.

"It's these fags!" Chuck blurted. "The paper is full of not only what they are, but the demands they are making because of what they are! They now have a Homosexual Lobby with so much power that it is overriding all common sense!"

All attention was now on Walter, hoping he would solve their discomfort on what they considered to be distasteful. Surveying the group, he seemed to be dispelling the prevailing anger before ever making any comments. Walter achieved some calmness before he began.

"From our previous discussion you are all aware how I view this planet and those on it. What you lads are describing are opinions that you claim to be entitled. What you consider to be good or bad is just that. No more than an opinion. As far as I'm concerned, the question of homosexuality is nothing more than another manifestation of the insanity that is prevalent in today's society." The group, accepting this statement, showed their agreement by nodding to each other, feeling they had won the day.

Getting their attention once again Walter continued, "My objection to homosexuality is not meant to be critical. It is based on understanding and a little knowledge of where they are coming from."

The lads realized they were being slightly rebuked, but made no effort to argue the point as they looked back on times when they encountered homosexuals. Jimmy was recalling a piano player who would blow the guys on the bus while traveling across country. He could never bring himself to partake of the sport with the others and found fags repulsive. Chuck's thoughts returned to a time when he was eighteen years old. A producer friend got him drunk and lured him to his bed. When he awoke, he found the guy playing with his joint. Scotty recalled how a group of musicians on the Stratheden, unknown to him, had promised him to a middle-aged fag as long as the guy kept the booze flowing. That night, as Scotty slept, he was aroused by the old homo sitting on his bunk attempting to get his hand under his blankets. Scotty jumped up and beat the shit out of the intruder, calling him all sorts of names as he tossed him from the cabin. During all this, the homo kept shouting "Just let me touch it! Just let me touch it!"

Another time on the China run, Scotty had a drink with a big macho looking guy who was going to be a prison warden in Hong Kong. Scotty left the bar for the men's room only to be followed by Mr. Macho begging the same "let me touch it."

"For my money," Scotty interrupted the conversation having just returned from his unsavory past, "they are fucking sickies, but as you say the whole world is nuts!"

"Exactly!" Walter again cast that calming spell. "As you say, they are sickies and anyone who would encourage them is just as sick and is perpetuating this form of insanity."

The group was now all ears knowing that if anyone could make sense of this it was Walter.

"If you recall, we discussed the component parts of man. First of all, the being and then the mind which is in two parts. That which is sane is described as the analytical mind and the mind that contains the hidden material is the course of all that is degrading to us."

"In other words," asked Jimmy, "homosexuality is a result of the incidents contained in the part of the mind that impose on him to create the condition?"

"Exactly!" Walter smiled. "The homosexual is so overwhelmed by these effects that he has lost all track of who he is. He is just as much a victim of this overwhelm as the criminal, murderer, or rapist. He, of course, can't see this. Just as any other person involved in irrational or aberrated behavior can't see the obvious."

"But how does this take place?" asked Chuck looking puzzled. "That some of us are and some ain't?"

"Getting back to the true person. If you agree that you are a spiritual being, then you would also have to realize that you have existed for a long time. That being the case, you would have lived a lot of life times. Understand?" Walter looked at each of them and they nodded in agreement.

"Now during those life times you must have been exposed to many traumatic incidents that you have carried with you in the form of pictures. You can imagine that death itself could be very traumatic. So, to protect yourself, you, the being, stored those pictures where you thought they would pose no threat. Unfortunately, that is not the case. Circumstances in your present life have stirred up these pictures. These undesirable incidents are brought to the surface that now impinge on you, but you still cannot see them. What you feel is the effect of these pictures and a desire to follow the dictates and compulsions thus putting you in a secondary position. Now let me go a step further. As you look at the condition of the inhabitants of this group, you can understand how far man has fallen by all this obvious insanity. What is the purpose of sex?"

"Procreation," replied Jimmy.

"To produce babies," answered Scotty.

"Correct," Walter acknowledged both replies. "That's all it is! A body game. Just to provide more bodies. Even animals know that and make no pretense about it. We on the other hand have lost all sense of reason even though that it is the one thing that separates us from our dumb animal friends. So, what happened? If you can imagine the being, that is, you, at some time along the line, fell from grace and became involved with sex. What he felt as a sensation that was most enjoyable became a trap for his further deterioration. Then emotion got involved in the sex game and that gave vent to love, romantic novels, and all the other mistaken attitudes; believing they were somehow enjoined. Falling further down the tube we now find that man is unable to perform in what we will describe as a natural function and enters the realm of perversion. Having gone this far, the only way is down even further, until he reaches the depth of degradation. So, what do we have? Sensation, emotion, perversion, and degradation. Prostitutes and homos are people who, first of all, lost their self-respect and are pretty much degraded beings. What they are seeking is not sex. It is self-degradation. The practice of promiscuity it gives them the opportunity to degrade others."

"How come," asked Scotty, "that many of them can be so able and hold important stations in life?"

"There's no doubt about that! Many of these people function very well, but just consider how much better and more able they would be if they could actually be themselves and free of all that other stuff?"

"I was reading somewhere that certain situations imposed were responsible for the condition," said Jimmy. "It was observed that men isolated from women, such as in prison, resorted to homosexuality. Experiments with rodents proved that rats did the same thing when isolated."

"So, what you are saying," Walter continued with Jimmy's statement, "is that man has sunk to the level of a rodent?"

"Yeah, I see your point," Jimmy agreed. "It's unfortunate that we have such abnormalities in our midst, and there seems to be no simple explanation."

"Many facets are involved," continued Walter, "and some of the most simplistic situations can throw a person off kilter. I will give some examples, but I do not wish you to dwell on this stuff. For a man to be a murderer, he must have been murdered. For a man to be rapist, he must have been raped. This applies to all aberrations. Now without intending to make you feel guilt, just consider for a moment how many young men are introduced to sex, not by the female, but have the first encounter with his male peers. Should there be any inclination toward homosexuality, this could be enough to start the ball rolling."

"Sex is sure a fuck up!" Chuck made light of the situation. "Excuse the pun."

"Being more serious," Jimmy directed his question at Walter. "What you were saying a moment ago would apply to degradation too. That a man to degrade, must have been degraded?"

"Yes," he replied. "And if you consider that you have existed for many life times, then just imagine how often all these things could have been experienced."

"So," added Scotty, "what we are is just a walking mass of junk. If all these things have been going on for millions of years no wonder we are all nuts!"

Walter smiled and, leaning forward in the chair, made another statement. "Now, I have used the word insanity many times but would now like to clarify this point. Until you really absorb the data about mental pictures, I refer to that word. Really there is no such thing as insanity, but just some of your pictures out of whack. When these pictures, from down in the depth of your subconscious, get misplaced or misfiled, and hit you, you manifest what society calls insanity or what mental practitioners refer to as psychotic."

Questions were now forthcoming from the trio as they sought further information.

"So, are these pictures always in a state of agitation causing these conditions?"

"Well, not always, as a change in the environment can cause them to settle down. You've heard the expression; a change is as good as a rest."

"But what about the ones that never settle down? Those people so inflicted must be having a hard time."

"Exactly. When the condition becomes that acute, it causes man to see all life through that aberration, which is pretty sick. A person in good shape can see and experience all aspects of life, but to have his attention rooted to one desire that is enforced and not of his choice causes the problem. In other words, the homosexual is seeing life through aberrated sex. The same is true for the prostitute or child molester or anyone else so afflicted."

"What about the theory that homosexuals are like that because of a dominant mother or living in a family with all sisters? How does that fit into the picture?"

"Let's extend this a little with some more data on the subject. If the example you gave me about the dominant mother or an all-female household were the real reason a person became a homosexual, then the condition would cease when he recognized the cause. The nature of his family may play a part in triggering or kicking up whatever trauma was responsible for snapping him from male to female; but the fact is, it is not what you know that causes aberration. It is what you don't know. Here's another little analogy. You may have heard someone say, "I have had a sick stomach since my grandmother died." If that was the truth then the stomach condition would be over. Since the statement is not the truth, the condition persists. The sick stomach originated in a time and place beyond the ability of the person to reach. Do you remember what we said about overwhelm? The victim is so overcome by the demands of the sordid mind that he actually believes it's really him and will stand to the death to assert that rightness. This is the same as the paper you are reading. Everyone is making claims in the name of humanity and decency. What they fail to realize is that they are living a big lie. Talking about newspapers, they also play a heavy part in feeding those hungry sordid pictures. Everything contained in them is entirely negative, and yet look at their enormous circulation. The citizen is so stuck in the bad part of the mind that it needs constant refueling. If everyone threw away his television and newspaper it would be a change for the better. I pointed out some time ago that it was a dangerous practice to fall asleep with the T.V. still running because the material from the show is being played straight into the subconscious. This could result in the person suffering all sorts of ill feelings the next day and of course he does not know why. So, what does he do? Resorts to the aspirin bottle."

Scotty was eager to explain a similar type experience. "One night I feel asleep on the couch and my girlfriend was seated in a chair behind my head. All of a sudden, I was jolted from sleep by a woman screaming. Not realizing it was coming from the T.V., I took my body off the couch and completely over the coffee table before touching the floor. I know I was not fully awake. I ran down the hallway believing my girlfriend was being attacked in the bedroom. It was her anxious voice shouting from behind me, "What's wrong?" that brought me to my senses. It was a weird experience, and I really had the shakes for a while."

"Very good, Scotty. Now that proved you have an understanding of what I'm talking about. Although we should not delve further into your trauma, it does give an example of how those deep hidden skeletons are brought into play. Something on your mind Jimmy?" Walter had noticed that his friend looked as though he was reaching inside his head for something.

"Yes, Walter, I was wondering if this applies to dreams. When you talk about pictures, it seems to me that dreams are pictures."

"Right. Let's examine that subject. As you have no doubt experienced when dreaming, they seem to be a mish mash and jumble of nonsensical pictures and vocabulary. When they get really out of hand, we call them hallucinations. But what are the average dreams? Nothing more than you, the spiritual being, attempting to sort out whatever is bothering you. Should you have problems during the day and fail to solve them, you seek the solution as you sleep. Not having solved the problems analytically, you delve into the subconscious area for help. But what happens? This portion of the mind now says, "If you are too stupid to handle and solve whatever ails you, then to hell with you." And throws all sorts of garbage at you just like a computer. Garbage in – garbage out. Now let's take a very common example. A person loses a loved one. Someone very close goes away or dies, causing grief or what is known as heartache. To solve this problem, the grieving person substitutes what is not available during the waking hours by putting a picture of the departed person during sleep. Thus, a dream. During the dream he might fondle or caress the facsimile as though it were real. Usually on awakening the person will once again experience grief and cry some more. This condition can exist for a very long time as the person continues to grieve, but can be halted very simply and without drugs. Just by realizing that you are putting a picture of the person to replace his absence while you sleep and that it is only a game and not real. The whole thing will turn off and permit you not only to sleep better but get on with your life."

Each one of the lads was silent once again as they recalled similar episodes. Everyone has had losses in the past, and this example had hit home. They also understood that Walter was not just referring to relatives and friends, but also to pets and anything regarded as precious.

"Now," Walter once again addressed them. "There is another factor involved that can cause this condition to persist longer than necessary. Simply, what did the deceased person leave you hung with? Let me explain. During your association you may have committed acts of transgression or overt acts, or sins if you prefer, that have caused you to feel guilt. Follow me so far?" Walter noticed the boys drift in and out as each one viewed his own pictures while trying to soak it all in.

"Let's imagine a wife has been unfaithful to her husband but this is unknown to him. She doesn't feel good about it and before she can unload her subconscious, the guy ups and dies on her. What happens? He has left her stuck with all that garbage before she was able to seek forgiveness and has now condemned herself to purgatory. This poor woman will forever suffer for her indiscretions and usually seek solace in some other degrading form of behavior like liquor, or prescription drugs is a favorite. That's the meaning of that old cliché, 'Oh, what a tangled web we weave when at first we do deceive.'"

"Shit," spoke Chuck, "I think we better all head for confession!"

"I doubt that would do much good," responded Walter while he eyed Chuck slyly.

"Well, wouldn't telling somebody about it get it off your chest?"

"Getting it off your chest may give you some relief, but getting it off of YOU would certainly be more beneficial."

"I don't follow." Chuck appeared even more puzzled than before.

"Well look at it," Walter began. "You go to confession and hand your responsibility to somebody called God, then walk out with your head high, only to commit the same acts again. There can be no permanent relief until you take responsibility for whatever sins you committed."

"Oh shit!" replied Chuck as he squirmed in his seat. "I feel I'm going to get it here!"

Walter had actually stirred the conversation in Chuck's direction, feeling something was bothering him, and it would be an act of kindness to help.

"Is there something you'd like to unload while we are on this subject, Chuck?" Chuck's head had fallen to his chest as he sat very quiet.

"There is something I would like to discuss," he said raising his head and looking a little awkward as he spoke. "But not in front of the guys."

"Oh, come on!" they teased. "Let's hear your dirty little secrets." Walter kept his attention on Chuck.

"Okay, fellows. Take five." Walter had even learned their lingo. "Why don't you gents go to the bar and have a beer while I listen to Chuck."

"Spoil sport! Liar, liar pants on fire!" They always had to have a good-natured tease with one another. After Jimmy and Scotty exited,

Walter once again put his attention on Chuck.

"What's on your mind?" he asked in his clear, understanding yet firm manner.

"Funny, I feel I can talk to you. You know how the guys are. They never take anything serious. Everything is always a big joke to them."

Walter waited patiently as his troubled friend struggled to volunteer further information.

"It's like this," Chuck began. "I have a wife and we have been very distant for some time. Every time I return home we are at each other's throat, and I can't wait to take off again."

"What are your feelings towards your wife? Do you care for her?"

"Oh, yes! I do very much, and I know she loves me but this situation is driving me crazy."

"Okay." Walter began speaking in a slow and gentle manner. "Describe to me what takes place when you are at home."

"Well, the first couple of days are mild enough, then I find myself wanting to escape. So, I head for the bar and usually get sloshed. She starts to get on my nerves."

"Okay, now one question, and answer me truthfully." Walter then fired the one-word question at Chuck. "Sex?"

Chuck looked bashfully at Walter, and without hesitation replied, "There is none!"

"Okay. Now is it because you are incapable of the act, or just that you cannot seem to make it with your wife?"

"Christ! I'm not incapable! I've been screwing the ass off those three broads this whole trip and I've never had any problems during the other cruises either."

"I see," answered Walter, continuing to be very patronizing. "Let's investigate what is going on here. You have a wife who is a nice person, correct?"

"Uh huh," replied Chuck.

"You admire and are fond of her, and as I take it you do not want to end the association, but wish to salvage the marriage."

"For sure," answered Chuck with confidence.

"Let's take a look now at agreements. When two people enter into any form of contractual association, it is expected to be binding and observed by both parties. Now one thing that will kill a person eventually is breaking his own agreements, especially if it is done in secret. Such covert behavior can fill hospital wards and cause much unhappiness because of ignorance."

"You mean I am guilty of these acts?" Chuck now appeared like a little boy lost. Walter studied him for a moment before posing the next question.

"Do you remember your wedding day, Chuck?" Walter was snappy and curt with his question.

"Of course, I do." Chuck responded in a similar manner.

"Then you should be able to tell me what agreements you made that very day."

Chuck looking at Walter searchingly muttered, "You mean the wedding ceremony?"

"Does the wedding ceremony refer to agreements?" asked Walter.

Chuck hesitated for a moment before replying in a quiet voice.

"To love, honor, and obey, forsaking all others." A minute of silence passed as Chuck examined the meaning behind what he had just said. "That's what you're driving at, Walter. In other words, I broke those agreements. Christ, I sure did!"

"All right then. Let's examine the outcome of all this deceit. You have a wife at home waiting. When you go home all the transgressions committed by you have formed a shield making it impossible for you to communicate. The feeling of guilt has prevented you from carrying out the sexual act, which of course upsets your wife, making her feel unworthy. Now to make yourself feel good, you fabricate all sorts of stupidities such as not having a clean shirt, or her cooking is no good, just to make her wrong. The next step is that you escape to the bar or sail off to avoid the unpleasant scene. Do you know what's really going on? Your wife is too nice a person and you, in your crazy way, are running away so as not to hurt her."

Chuck's face turned crimson for a moment. Then he took on a healthy pallor as everything fell into place. His eyes had a new brightness.

"I have been a real fuck up! All this shit is really my doing. What a dumb bastard I've been."

Walter sat back and let Chuck relish the moment. He was enjoying the scene of life once again being restored to this poor lost soul.

"What do I do now?" Chuck asked quizzically. "Do I go home and confess to my wife what has been going on?"

"Hum," began Walter. "How do you think she would take that, Chuck?"

"To tell you the truth, I don't think she would take it too well. She would probably throw my ass out, complete with baggage."

"Well," Walter leaned forward solicitously, "this is what I was referring to earlier when we were talking about the confessional and responsibility. As long as you are willing to be responsible for your own acts and realize where the blame belongs, then there is no need to inflict the iniquities on your wife. This also means you have decided to reform and not repeat past mistakes. Just respect your own agreements and personal ethics, and I can assure you of a happy life."

Chuck's eyes had tears as he took Walter's hand. A feeling of tremendous compassion shared by two beings in complete harmony.

"Thank you, Walter. All of a sudden, my desire to see my wife is all I want. I love her even more now. It's amazing how simple life can be, but us assholes have to complicate it and destroy what's good."

"You're welcome!" Walter wrapped both hands around Chuck's. "Just to finish this, you can now understand what causes unions, such as marriages, to fall apart. Two people are in love and marry. Later if they end the marriage, it's obvious something happened to change their feelings toward each other. Actually, there are only two reasons to cause a separation and the hatred that usually follows. One being cruelties inflicted on one of the partners by the other, leaving no choice but to escape. But the most common reason is the fact that one of the partners does something to feel guilty about. Piling all these indiscretions together will result in the guilty party constantly trying to make the other wrong. Should this continue, then the other spouse will find it necessary to commit breaches of the marriage. When it gets this involved, it has to end in a calamity. I believe your association has not reached this critical point and indeed has been salvaged."

"Right on, Walter!" Chuck accepted his mentor's observation willingly. "I'd die at the thought of my wife ever hating me."

"The only consolation I could add to that is that one person only hates another to the degree that he loved him in the first place."

Chuck's reaction to that piece of wisdom was to scan past the times when he had observed such highly charged emotional behavior among various married acquaintances who had considered themselves betrayed. Just then Scotty and Jimmy appeared, complete with a round of drinks.

"There you are, Walter, orange juice for you, and Chuck, how about a nice bottle of beer?"

"Great!" The beverages were accepted.

"Did we time it right or did we return too soon?" asked Scotty looking from Walter to Chuck.

"Right on the money!" replied Chuck, looking like the cat after eating the canary. He settled back to enjoy his Heinekens. "One thing I'll say about getting things off your mind, it sure gives you a helluva thirst! Cheers!" Chuck and the other lifted their glasses.

A few more pleasantries were exchanged before Walter and Jimmy took their leave. Scotty and Chuck were the type of friends that could enjoy each other's company in silence. It wasn't necessary for them to engage in a constant babble of small talk just to convince each other of their presence.

Sipping the beer, some time passed before Chuck, turning to his friend said, "You know, Scotty, I think this is going to be my swan song. It looks like permanent shore leave for me. One way or another, it's going to come to an end, but I think I'm more prepared for it now."

Scotty realized that Chuck had made some decisions and began to share some of the same feelings.

"I feel the same way, but do you have any plans other than playing gigs?"

"No, but somehow I feel it doesn't matter. That things will come out right. I may get involved in some sort of social program. I think we have always been aware of the wrongs in society, but elected to be apathetic towards it by choosing this type of life. Along comes a guy like Walter who is cunningly making us look at the part we're playing."

"That's for sure," answered Scotty, "but don't forget, joining groups is not the answer either. As Walter pointed out, rehabilitation starts with the individual. Not just the blind leading the blind."

"Yeah, but Scotty, there must be some way to get through to people that the life that they are leading is really nuts. All we see in society is reward for insanity. Whether it's being a fag or a soldier or even an exploited member of the working class, it's a constant perpetuation of stupidity."

"I understand what you're saying and wish I could give a simple answer, but you have to accept the fact that you cannot be responsible for all that happens nor for every individual. As Walter told us, the masses have lost the spiritual concept or the awareness that a person is something other than a body. Holy men and purveyors of religions talk about it, but obviously have had no results for their effort. Maybe it's because they are part of the big lie too, and are just as much in apathy as we are!"

Another few minutes of silence was observed before Chuck once again struck up the conversation.

"We are discussing the conditions of all these people out there in the world and regarding them as insane. Does that mean we are sane or are we just kidding ourselves?"

"The fact that we are discussing the subject indicates a change has taken place. No, I would not say we are sane, but at least we have come to realize we need help and are reaching like hell for it. That's a million light years ahead of the rest of the population. Since talking to Walter, I have come to realize that, as my mother used to say, "everything is sent to try you." Whenever you are involved in a trauma, such as illness or accident, obviously you are supposed to sit up and question what the hell am I doing wrong and correct it so you don't repeat the same thing again. When two people disagree, such as a husband and wife, the parties should then take a look at what the hell they are doing and learn from that lesson. What usually happens is the guy gets a divorce after twenty years of marriage and runs out and buys a sports car to replace the wife. That's about how valuable she was to him! The price of a car! So, all he is doing is proving that he is just as big an asshole as he was twenty years ago!"

"Ha, ha, ha, ha!" laughed Chuck. "That's what I like! You get on your soapbox and you always make it sound funny."

"But it's a fact! Whatever way you look at it." Scotty acknowledged his friend's remark but wanted to continue. "If nothing is gained from the mistakes, then they just continue on in ignorance. Take a look at people who get a scare. They always look for the solution in the body. All of a sudden, they start to jog or diet or have elective surgery. The body. The body. The body. Never a chance to examine themselves. Everything in society is directed at the body. Whether you are a body builder creating huge muscles or a beauty queen contestant displaying this piece of shit, it's all body, body, body!"

"After all," interjected Chuck, "there's nothing wrong with exercise or eating right, is there?"

"Of course not, but the point is some of these people have lost the sight of what's really important. They are not giving themselves a chance to grow as a being. Let's get into this spirit and body shit a little more." Scotty appeared more intent on getting his point across. "Walter was explaining to us that we are beauty, truth, and creativeness. The body is nothing but an I.D. label that we have elected to take over. The purpose of you, the being, is to survive. The body, if you can imagine it as having a mind of its own, is bent on suicidal behavior. That is what I mean when I say the likes of weightlifters, beauty queens, fags, people who jump out of airplanes, and soldiers are all being bodies. Look at the movie stars. They pump silicon into their breast or have ribs removed to make their waistline appear smaller. They are bent on destruction, and that's sick! From the moment this lump of meat makes its exit from the womb, its only purpose seems to be to destroy, and it finds plenty of allies in its quest."

"I see what you're saying, Scotty. It is like an analogy. Like the two parts of the mind. The good can be described as representing you and the bad is the body."

"Suicide seems to be the goal of the body. That's why we have such things as armies and the like," replied Scotty. "There is nothing wrong with having a nice healthy attractive body, but not at the expense of losing yourself. So now that we have once again straightened out the world, let's go below and prepare for the cocktail session."

As they left their chairs, they did not notice Walter hiding outside the lounge window where he had obviously been eavesdropping. Walter's face was beaming. "Yes," he thought turning away, "Scotty is on the way."

Meanwhile all sorts of anger and frustration ran rampant in the crew quarters caused by the Staff Captain's continual interference. Rummage raids were conducted at all hours resulting in the confiscation of booze and loggings for drunkenness. And in some cases, more crew members were being fired. The Staffy was determined to succeed in his mission, but he was only making things worse. Fights were breaking out in the forecastle, brought on by this attempted prohibition. This area before the mast was becoming an unhappy place. On a ship, there is always four or five crew members regarded as the leaders. These men were putting their heads together and coming up with all sorts of ideas for stopping the monster that had invaded their happy little kingdom. The Staffy was succeeding in restricting what had become to them "a way of life." Prohibition on board ship had no more chance of being observed than the same law did during the Twenty's. To the Staffy, drink was the root of all evil, while the crew members regarded it as the nectar of the Gods. The odds were against the Captain a thousand to one. His position was in jeopardy to say the least. Passengers had no knowledge of the conflict that was taking place below decks, mostly because they were also half stewed during the cruise themselves. It's ironic to inflict such an environment upon the poor holy Staffy. A man, so opposed to John Barleycorn, having to live among and face the cursed alcohol every day in his job.

According Walter's philosophy, when a person is so fixated and protests constantly on the evils of drinking, then the first question he should be asked is, "When were you a drunk?" Like the man who rants and raves about hanging all rapists of ten-year-old girls, the question would be, "What ten-year-old girl did you rape?" Scotty recalled meeting one old broad who was campaigning against lesbianism and was really psychotic on the subject. He later found out that she had been a lesbian and had committed many overt acts as a result of her past involvement. She now had flipped. In her attempt to be right, she opposed such activity; thus, hoping for her pass into heaven. So, here was the poor old Staff Captain Breathwaite trying to play God and not realizing that he was only getting in deeper. The old saying "when in Rome" sure did apply here. The Romans aboard the S.S. Nectar certainly had plans for making sure this plague was removed from their midst. Even the ship's Captain enjoyed his sauce, as did the other officers. Very seldom did you find a mariner who was not partial to a little noggin, and thus, included it in his daily routine. From the bowels of the Engine Room to the upper decks, booze was enjoyed as much as Girl Scout cookies at the school carnival.

Chuck and Scotty changed and entered Bob's cabin to find the gang, including Lorraine, in attendance. Glasses in hand, a toast was made to the Staff Captain by Scotty, "May the hairs on his ass turn to drumsticks and rise to batter his brains out!" All cheered and giggled at Scotty's inventiveness.

"I suppose you will all be heading ashore tomorrow in Haiti," stated Bob as he looked around the room, addressing no one in particular.

"Not me," answered Chuck. "I have to catch up on my beauty sleep!"

"What about the rest of you? Are you going to Ibo Beach?"

This was a private beach the lads sometimes visited where they could dine on wonderful chicken and lobster to their hearts content. The beach was small and pretty, adorned with cabanas with roll up sides that provided the most restful and serene feeling. A meal, a few jugs, and just lying in a hut provided the desired serenity. The warm sultry breeze embracing your body as it passed through the open side of the cabana was certainly heaven itself. But it seemed that on this trip no one had eyes for the twenty-mile, high speed taxi ride over the zigzagging pot-hole road. They agreed to stay local.

"Actually, Bob," said Tex looking up, "we have a little plan prepared for Abe." He was absent from the cabin.

"Oh, no! What kind of crap are you guys going to get into now? For Christ's sake don't give me any more grief! Wasn't your shipwreck enough for one cruise?"

"Nothing too heavy," continued Tex. The others in the room began to smile. "You know his situation regarding broads. All we're going to do is help him crack his cherry."

Scotty had a frown on his face. He had not yet been informed of the plan and sought to be let in on the secret. After unloading the highly confidential material to Scotty, he laughed like hell. Lorraine just lowered her forehead and refrained from sharing the glee. She felt that such an outburst would imply her approval of the little conspiracy.

Whatever beauty was to be found in Haiti was never visited by the musicians. Like any other port, it was just another excuse for a booze up ashore. If it was Ibo Beach, one could see life in the raw during the twenty-mile trip. African-like villages were in abundance. Women washed clothes on the river bank using rocks to beat out the dirt.

Travelers on the road, though, had to pass through military check points. The boys had one occasion that after passing, a rifle shot was fired at their cab. Coming to a halt and inquiring what the hell was going on they were informed that the cab had a missing tail light. How fucking cheap can life be? This was the thought they all had as they continued their trip in silence. Their only source of amusement were the bars on the steamy side of town. These places were not considered respectable enough to take a lady. All these islands had the same iniquities in common. In the past these islands had served as a refuge for pirates who robbed, raped, and plundered. Traders would dump slaves by the boatload for transfer to the respective benefactors in the various so called civilized countries. Today, the pirates of the modern world still milk these islands to death by sending cruise ships to appease the inhabitants. Cruise ships are very similar to the pirate's vessels of old. You still have hordes invading the island. They screw the female population and sail off with the loot. Thank God that they at least no longer cut the throats of the locals. The ships do provide some slight relief to the poverty-stricken inhabitants. They sell their wares. It is much like unemployment benefits serve to keep riot and rebellion off the streets back home.

Scotty would often argue with himself, who had the better deal? The natives of the islands, although not living in splendor, had the perfect weather, plenty of fresh fruit, and sea food in abundance. The natives do have a short life span. This is evidenced from their diseases and lack of medical care. This must subject them to some kind of stress though.

How do the natives compare to the hustler living in the big city? The average city dweller has already conceded to being a victim. He fights the freeways in his dumb automobile every day. Striving to outsmart his peers. This adds to his own heart disease and other debilitating ailments. If all this effort resulted in health, wealth, and happiness maybe there would be some merit to it, but unfortunately all it does is knock you down. The more successful one becomes, a price ultimately is paid with the deterioration of the body in spite of the best medical advances, health food, and work out gyms. Even marriages collapse with all this successful living. There is, of course, the other argument that wealthy people who have never worked a day in their life are more prone to illnesses than the industrial prisoner.

The common denominator was becoming more clear to Scotty. The body and everything else was under the dominance of that sordid side of the mind and was actually controlling the being or spiritual entity and not allowing him to experience what could be considered "the good life."

Scotty liked the more laid-back feeling of places like Trinidad, Granada, and Martinique, but the more the islands became infected with civilization, the more the neurosis crept in too. People from the big cities who claim to be suffering from stress rush to the islands to try and live like the natives. Then the natives, infected by the lure of money, head for the cities to degrade themselves like the big city boys. That's one of the jokes on living. The grass is always greener on the other side. This explains the compulsion to keep moving. Sure, it's fun to have something different to look forward to everyday and enjoy the spirit of adventure, but this is a condition reserved for the young and inexperienced. What happens eventually is the grass gradually loses its emerald hue and starts to take on a brown color that resembles a dung heap. One day, if you are lucky, you wake up and realize it's all shit.

Scotty thought about Scotland's famous bard, Robert Burns. He was the greatest man that ever graced the earth to Scotty. Burns had all this knowledge and intellect far beyond the contemporaries of his day and even today. He achieved no fame until his death. All Burns got for his efforts were a bunch of drinking pals with whom he constantly shared his talents. Robert Burns lived in poverty all his life and knew nothing but hard labor, and then he succumbed at the early age of thirty-eight. Who knows? Maybe he also became interesting while having to constantly look down on the morons he served. At least he left a legacy more valuable than all the treasures put together. The one thing that remained with Scotty throughout his life was Robert Burns' own creed:

"Whatever mitigates the woes or increases the happiness of others,

this is my criterion of goodness;

and whatever injures society at large or any individual in it,

this is my measure of iniquity."

The group left Bob's cabin and made their way to the Grand Lounge for the cocktail set. Everyone was already dressed for the evening. There was going to be a ball held in this room after dinner. The band was setting up when Scotty, looking through the window, saw Walter standing by the rail outside on the Prom deck. Leaving the stand, he joined Walter outside.

"Hi, Walter. Don't usually see you hanging around this time of day. Having your constitutional?"

"Something like that," he replied. "Something on your mind?"

"Funny you should ask." Scotty then related to Walter how he was finding it more difficult to be involved in the small talk with his buddies.

"I just spent a half hour in Bob's cabin and wasn't listening to a bloody word. I found myself absorbed with my own thoughts. I've been thinking about your theory of being interesting instead of interested. Am I beginning to think I'm something special and that the world owes me living?"

Walter chuckled as he listened to his friend before replying, "I can assure you that is not the case. The simple fact that you are questioning yourself tells me that you are not. You see, a person with that much awareness never has to be concerned of becoming effect of that condition. The person who does adopt that type of sick behavior is too immersed in his own importance to be that sharp." A smile appeared on Scotty's face as the reality of what Walter said sank in.

"Once again I feel reassured. It's nice to know I'm really a sharp ass."

Scotty extended his hand to Walter. "Thanks a lot!" Leaving his friend at the rail, Scotty entered the Grand Lounge with his head high, ready to beat the hell out of his drums.

Meanwhile down in the dining room, the head waiter was presiding over a muster of the staff, explaining the menu for the evening, and chastising whichever waiter warranted such abuse. Indicating one of the waiters, he reprimanded him for his conduct at lunch. One of the passengers, an old broad at his table, had thrown up on the deck and he had been instructed by the head waiter to clean it up. His reply had upset the head waiter who was now giving him twenty tongue lashes.

"When I give you an order you will carry it out!"

"Bullshit! I'm not in the habit of cleaning up some old fart's puke while serving food to other passengers. Anyway, she wasn't seasick as she claimed, she was drunk, as always. Every meal, even breakfast, she comes in sozzled. It would be to everyone's benefit, especially the other diners, if you would advise her not to enter the dining room anymore in that state. I know her table partners have already voiced their complaints, but you have ignored them. This old juice head has already cost me one good passenger who demanded another table."

The head waiter let it all pass now. He knew the waiter was right, but felt deep down resentment at the impertinence of this hash slinger. Somewhere in the future he would get revenge. Turning his attention to another waiter, he prepared to launch an all-out attack and vent his anger on this poor soul.

"You, Thompson, how many times have I told you? Trays are never carried on or above the shoulder. Trays are always to be flat on the arm and held with both hands. This is not a New York steak house but a ship that is always in motion. The slightest off balance can cause all sorts of embarrassment just like today." What had happened was, while waltzing through the dining room with tray held high, a slight movement of the ship had resulted in a bowl of ice cream leaving the end of the tray and landing smack in the middle of a passenger's bald head, where it sat.

"As if the ice cream caper wasn't bad enough," the head waiter continued, "you had to add insult to injury by placing a linen napkin over his head."

The rest of the assembled, unable by now to suppress their feelings, howled with laughter as the incident was replayed. Mixed retorts were now forthcoming, with the head waiter even joining in the laughter.

"The old guy didn't even like vanilla!"

"And he was looking up at the ceiling for the pigeon that shit on him."

Order once again restored, the head waiter took charge with his usual command, "Gentlemen, to your stations."

"To the ramparts, he should announce," one of the waiters said as they spread across the room. The opening of the doors signaled the first onslaught of locusts as they descended on the dining room. Usually they were the eaters who just pointed at the menu and muttered, "Everything!" The more moderate diners strolled in a little later at their ease allowing the waiters time to stoke up the grab alls.

Passengers on ships are unaware how tough the job can be for the stewards. These men usually work long hours with very little sleep owing to the nature of ships. Unless one can achieve complete unconsciousness, it is difficult to obtain the sufficient rest to do the required work. Not like ashore, where you may be lucky enough to have a nice quiet bedroom. Crew members are on the move at all hours around the clock. This makes it very difficult for those off duty to sleep. For some unknown reason, ships are equipped with the worst doors ever invented. It seems impossible for them to be closed quietly. Thus, a constant staccato of banging can be heard. This is not just a problem in crew quarters but also in the passenger accommodations. Most of the offensive portals are usually loose and, even while closed, they create s definite din as the ship rolls. So up and down the corridors can be heard the continual "rat-a-tat-tat" of those loose fixtures. It has always amazed Scotty how the passengers are able to sleep at night and why they never seem to complain. Maybe they are all deaf!

The sex game had evolved into a three-ring circus where the musicians were concerned. Valerie, who had created this impression of being "Miss Aloof," had suddenly revealed her hidden talent. It was obvious that she had set her sights on Mike and made no bones about it. It started one afternoon while Mike lay on his bunk relaxing and enjoying a book. All of a sudden in walked Valerie, looking gorgeous dressed in a very brief bikini. Mike was naked except for a small towel covering his private parts. The look on his face was one of complete disbelief but it soon turned to a lecherous leer as he began to visualize what was in store. His only greeting to this vision of loveliness was a gulp. Valerie seated herself on the edge of his bunk and proceeded to rub her hand up and down his leg.

"Hi, Mike. I thought you might enjoy a little company."

The book in his hand was now upside down as he unsuccessfully tried to make conversation. The seductive siren just kept her eyes affixed to his while continuing her tactile administrations. All of a sudden, the towel took the appearance of a little tent. It was being supported from underneath. Valerie, observing the new structure and being a circus lover, made haste in enjoying the show. Removing the towel, she gave her own rendition of "Trumpet Blues in Cantabile" on his organ. At the same time, Mike mockingly blessed himself and asked the Lord make him truly thankful for those gifts that he was about to receive.

When Valerie left, she passed Tex in the corridor who was making his way to the cabin.

"Hi, Val!"

"Hi, Tex," she replied as if nothing out of the ordinary had transpired.

Tex entered the cabin to find his buddy looking as though he had just finished smoking an opium pipe.

"Was it a good book?" asked Tex facetiously while looking sideways at his mate.

"Marvelous!" he replied, extending both arms skyward and adding, "Never judge a book by its cover."

Chuck, on the other hand, had been experiencing a completely different situation. Trying to keep three horny broads serviced was not an easy task. His journeys into the night, complete with bottle, had turned into a regular orgy. He felt like the village idiot being attacked behind the barn by the farmer's three daughters. Never had so much been owed by so many to so few, he thought one night, limping back to his quarters in the early hours. The gals were becoming possessive as they vied for top banana. Thank Christ it wasn't a long cruise, Chuck thought. He was concerned about this continual drain on his stamina.

Tex had been having a little tete-a-tete on the after deck with the gambler's wife during intermission. Their little affair was being conducted in a paint locker behind the mast where she lured Tex at every chance while her husband was involved with his card playing. Her idea of extramarital sex was just to play, but don't go all the way. Thus, she considered herself a very faithful wife. Tex, after leaving the love nest, was never sure if the giddiness he felt was caused by frustration or from paint fumes.

Bob was handling two ladies. He had to schedule the damsels to prevent the off chance of an embarrassing situation arising. The musicians were warned never to knock the door. It would be locked as a preventive measure while Bob was engaged in any sort of Bible study. Otherwise the door remained unlocked. Jimmy, of course, never paid any attention to what he considered these "sick broads" aboard but saved himself for the dusky maidens ashore.

Abe spent his days wandering around the decks staring at the bikini clad chicks feeling like a total outsider. The sea air and the constant exposure to temptation was playing hell with his libido. He shuddered at the thought of how his mother would feel if she knew what he was thinking. Actually, he was becoming desperate as the desire engulfed for the ultimate experience caused him to imagine all sorts of situations. There was always the two old broads on A deck, but after what they've been through, or rather what's been through them, he would have to put his name and address on the soles of his shoes.

Scotty and Lorraine continued their association in a very contented manner. It could be said that theirs was the only relationship with any feeling. Scotty never considered himself a stud and always had to have that romantic tie to arouse his interest.

The evening passed uneventfully. The Grande Ball was enjoyed by all. Passengers were formally dressed and none too drunk. During the intermission, Bob sneaked off into the service bar for his usual shooter. Chuck, hoping to be alone, went aft to the Verandah Grill expecting to have a nice relaxed drink, but no such luck. The same three damsels he hoped to escape took no time locating him. They were each determined to stake a claim. These are the penalties one has to pay for being God's gift to women!

Mike and Valerie were strolling round the Prom deck looking

like a honeymoon couple, while Tex was being dragged off to the chamber of horrors. Meanwhile, Scotty took Lorraine to his favorite spot on the Sun Deck. They looked over the forecastle. The night was perfect with a warm balmy breeze and the sea so calm it looked as though the ship was sliding along a huge lake of ice.

"Isn't this lovely?" inquired Lorraine, looking toward the starry sky. "Just like you see in the movies. If only life could always be like this."

"Dream on, Honey, that's the problem," answered Scotty, leaning on the rail and staring straight ahead. "Movies, remember, are not for real. This only makes you fall in love with the idea of love and is responsible for all those romantic notions."

Scotty was forever on the defensive, as though the worst thing that could happen to him would be marriage. He had dreamt of tying the knot but always remembered the feeling of dread at the thought of not being able to sail again. What relief was felt on awakening! It was always a cause for celebration. So, the nuptial scene to him was a fate worse than death. Just like that famous quote; "Love is blind. And marriage is an institution. Who wants to finish up in a blind institution?"

"Don't worry," laughed Lorraine. "I don't expect this scene to be more beautiful by hearing a proposal of marriage. But please allow me to feel a little romantic tonight. Guys like you are too spoiled!"

"And as it should be," joked Scotty, matching her mood. "Can you imagine us, after all this, being married and living in some apartment in your small town? You working in your little office job and me as a car salesman. We come home at night with a pizza, sit in the kitchen and look across at another apartment building or try to watch television while some moron fixes his motor cycle or does body work on his car outside our window. These are the things I dread, and I guess they keep me at sea. Believe me, those assholes called, "week-end grease monkey," are even worse than their stupid barking dogs!"

"On the contrary," he fired back being a little more serious. "Could be that I have too much soul. Could be that I have too much consideration and respect for others, a commodity that is scarce out there. It appears to me that people with feelings are the ones who suffer in this world. As they always say, "the good die young." What I have observed is the hard-nosed, greedy, avid robot, totally devoid of any soul is the type who makes it in that world out there. Sure, maybe I'm escaping, but I'd rather be a prisoner on this ship than be one in your jungle. Anyway, shut up and give us a kiss. There's no sense in letting this romantic setting go to waste."

Raising her head, she offered her lips and they embraced warmly. However, Lorraine couldn't help wondering, "How can a guy have such notions and at the same time be so loving?" This spot would be theirs. They would return here. This evening for them ended in complete serenity locked in each other's arms.

DAY 7
HAITI

The rattling of the anchor chains sent shudders through the ship, indicating arrival in Haiti. The morning sun behind the mountains gave this side of the island a dark and mysterious appearance as the ship lay off Port-au-Prince. Huge glass encased launches, like water taxis, were resting nearby. The passengers were ready to spend a happy day ashore on yet another spending spree. Wooden carvings were the hot items in Haiti. The poverty could easily be seen everywhere. During carnival time it was fun to join the locals in their celebrations. Gorgeous colored dresses were worn by the native gals. Everyone would play some sort of percussion instrument while dancing through the streets. There were hundreds of people all merry and acting as if they hadn't a care in the world. It was really the only time the musicians from the ship enjoyed staying in town. They would be half in the bag, of course, and could acquire an assortment of claviers, maracas, banjos and the like to contribute to the carnival, and would parade off with the rest of the noisemakers. Otherwise, unless they were heading for Ibo Beach, they would not even bother to go ashore.

Today was special! They had plans for Abe, and he had no idea what was in store. They were in no hurry to rise and shine, in fact they were all still in bed. If not sleeping, they were waiting for Tom to appear with the proverbial egg and bacon sandwiches. He soon arrived, but minus the lifesaving sustenance. Poor Tom appeared somewhat in a panic. Rushing into the cabin occupied by Scotty and Chuck, he found Scotty awake, reading in his bed, but Chuck was zonked as usual.

"What the hell's the matter, Tom? Is the fucking ship sinking?"

"Worse than that, Scotty. We've got a problem. Get up!" Tom sputtered.

Scotty scrambled out of his bunk and made a grab for his pants, "What's up?"

Tom, pointing his finger to the forward part of the ship, took a few gulps and blurted, "Some old guy died during the night and they're bringing him to the mortuary right now! That means the doctor, Staff Captain, and whoever else decides to tag along, but they will be coming this way!"

The mortuary had an entrance in the rear of the Inner Sanctum where the bodies were stored and prepared for embalming.

"So?" asked Scotty frowning. "What's the big deal?"

Tom looked at him aghast and in total disbelief. He thought Scotty must still be asleep because he would never say such a thing. Tom, still in a bit of a panic, began pointing aft in the direction of the mortuary. Suddenly, Scotty was restored to his senses.

"The BOOZE!" Scotty shouted.

"That's right! There's about twenty cases of fucking booze belonging to you guys and the deckies in there!" Tom quickly reminded him.

"Oh shit! Get the other guys in there fast and throw those cases in the nearest cabin. Don't bother Bob or this shithead," indicating

Chuck. "He's out of it."

Once again, the wheels of contrivance went into motion. Tom literally dragged the resting bodies from their bunks and herded them in the direction of the mortuary. Luckily, both the musicians and Tom had keys to what they referred to as the pickle factory. Entering the ghostly tomb, they wasted no time in extracting the contraband and dividing it between the three cabins. Mission accomplished! Tom provided the long awaited and greatly deserved breakfast, which was certainly much appreciated this morning.

"Nothing like a little larceny to whet the appetite, me lads," stated Mike as he took a pirate's chomp out of his bread.

Half an hour later, two deckies appeared carrying a stretcher with the covered remains of the dead passenger. They were accompanied by the ship's doctor, Chief Steward, and Purser. They made their way through the musician's quarters to deposit the cadaver in the fridge. Arrangements were being made for the unfortunate passenger to be removed later that day and flown home. Scotty realized that every ship he had ever sailed on had lost a passenger. On the long trips, they were buried at sea. He learned early in his sea career that it was true about sharks following ships at sea. He had actually witnessed the scene of the deadly fins astern waiting while the ship did what it would have to in preparation for the burial.

Everything back to normal, the lads prepared to go ashore. Jimmy wasted no time and was already aboard the launch heading for shore. He was eager to seek out the best piece of ass in the West Indies at the going rate somewhere between two and five dollars. This was his treat of the cruise. Launches were picking up those going ashore at the gunport door today near the musician's quarters. So, they did not have to walk far this morning. Scotty, Tex, and Mike, with Abe in tow, boarded one of the boats and took off. This area of the Caribbean Sea could, all of a sudden, produce some heavy seas which made for an uncomfortable ride. Many a passenger's vacation could be ruined during this short ferry trip. After making the cruise down the Atlantic coast with no ill effects, some passengers would experience sea sickness on this ride just to and from the ship. Today was very pleasant with a gentle swell and a following sea giving the impression that the launch was surfing.

The landing was mobbed with local vendors trying to entice buyers with the assurances that their prices were much less than those in the stores. What the passengers did not realize was that on the way back the bargains would be more abundant. The vendors knew it was their last shot and would discount everything. The musicians were never interested in anything that could not be carried in a bottle, so no time was wasted in bartering.

Abe was astounded at the hordes of people and the shouting that was taking place. Walking away from the business district towards an area that seemed to consist of mostly bars and restaurants, they passed the shops filled with passengers already buying all sorts of carved elephants, voodoo dolls, baskets, and local jewelry. The buildings were wooden structures and painted white. There was an array of characters hanging around each building. Abe felt a little trepidation as the group made their way into what could only be described as a ghetto type area.

"Don't worry, Abe," assured Scotty, noticing the little guy's concern. "Nobody here will bother you. They know they have to depend on people like us to make a living, so it would be to their disadvantage to drive us away. This is the red-light district you are in now. Like a lot of the islands, because of the poverty, many of the men are employed as taxi drivers, pimps, or a combination of both by the various establishments you see here." Indicating a rather sorry looking lot of fellows and shacks. "Many of the females know nothing but prostitution and grow up with it and in it. It's sad to visit such places, I think. Why, even in Hong Kong kids solicit their ten-year-old sisters for a couple of dollars!"

The conversation and the feeling all around him of depraved sex was wreaking havoc on poor Abe. He knew there was something dirty in it, but could not suppress the excitement and the sensation felt in his groin. Gals were hailing them from doorways, as they passed, trying to entice them into the houses of ill repute and using all sorts of devices. Raising their skirts to show no panties was the most common used technique along with an assortment of obscene gestures. All this was ignored by the four musketeers. The boys knew exactly where they were heading even if Abe didn't.

Soon they reached their destination and entered one of the houses. It was similar to all the rest, containing a bar and a number of cubicles around the walls of the room. It was in these cubicles that the customer received his money's worth from any one of the bevy of dusky gals. They were now seated, and the drinks were ordered, when they were literally attacked by the surrounding females. The girls would each select a victim and proceed to use every trick in the book to sell sex. Abe was bug eyed when his gal grabbed him by the groin and started to slowly stroke his joint.

Looking at each of his buddies, he mumbled, "Is this for real?"

The gal had him at a gallop as her friends worked on the other lads. Brushing the hookers away, Scotty, Mike, and Tex ordered more drinks. They were reveling in Abe's predicament. The poor guy's peter looked like it was waving as it bounced up and down inside his pants. Not since he played doctors as a boy with little Becky next door had Abe felt such a mixture of guilt and elation. This was exactly what the motley bunch had in mind for the poor guy when they brought him ashore. The plan was to tantalize the hell out of him and see how long it took to drive him nuts. At what point would Abe give up his virginity? After their second drink, they left the establishment and entered another further down the street. This performance was repeated several times, leaving Abe a sweating, shivering wreck of humanity.

They headed for the next bar, and this time, Scotty had the

broads line up for his inspection. He was looking them all over and could hear Abe's voice in the background.

"Oh, look at the one in the green! Look at that one in the yellow! Oh my! Oh my!"

Scotty shook his head and winked at his deviate partners, "No, nothing here. Let's go!"

By this time they had visited a half of dozen hostelries. They were feeling no pain from the booze except poor Abe, who would just limp down the street behind them, like a poor, sad, little puppy, yet still muttering, "The one in the green! The one in the yellow!"

Abe still had no idea that his buddies had him on a trip and were playing with his head. They were again in yet another bar. Scotty had once again dismissed the hookers and was preparing to leave when Abe broke at last and came to his own.

He had reached the end of his frustration and yelled, "You can't leave without buying something!"

Everyone roared! In their drunken state the laughter bordered on hysteria. Abe looked so beseeching, standing in the middle of the room and finally realizing he was the source of amusement. The lads were hanging round each other's necks and knee slapping while wrenching in belly laughs. Mike was the first to recover. He sat Abe down with another coke and advised him that they had a place in mind for him and were going there after they finished their drinks.

A few doors away was another club very familiar to the lads. The place was larger than the others with a bigger circular bar and more cubicles. They entered and Scotty spotted Jimmy seated at the bar like a contented cat. Tex and Mike took Abe over to a little corner table so he could observe the stock. Scotty seated himself next to Jimmy and ordered a round of drinks for his buddies. He began to inform Jimmy, in his drunken gleeful accent, the story thus far of Abe's baptismal.

"You should have seen it, man. The best gag we've pulled in a long time. The poor guy was ready to rape anything, male or female." He then gave Jimmy the punch line of Abe protesting their leaving. Another drink in hand and Jimmy had a suggestion.

"Here's what we'll do. See that tall broad over there?" Indicating a tall good-looking gal who took no part in the sexual assaults round the room. "She's the number one mama here and a little expensive, but she's clean and knows her stuff."

"Good. Okay," Scotty agreed to his choice. "Call her over."

Responding to Jimmy's signal, the broad approached her favorite customer, thinking that Scotty was to be her trick. Jimmy explained the situation and, while pointing out Abe, he advised her to give him the works.

"We'll all chip in some more money to cover the extra time and fun you're going to give him. Okay?"

"Yeh! Ya got it honey. Ahs sho nuff gonna look afta that boy fo ya. Ahs like dis one too." She was still hopeful for Scotty, but that was not his bag. Together they walked over to the table where Scotty introduced Abe to Belle. The introductions were hardly complete when Abe started to drool. She took him by the hand. Abe stood and she led him to one of the cubicles. As he was being led away, he could hear his buddies singing to him.

"Give me some men. Give me stout hearted men who will fight for the right to be free."

Belle passed through the door first. Abe had a look of complete innocence on his face while being pulled in the cubicle behind her and looking a little embarrassed too. The door closed finally, and Scotty once again joined Jimmy at the bar.

"Yeah, I thought you'd be here. You horny old fart. I suppose you've already done your thing."

"Sure," Jimmy answered with a big smile. "Big Belle there is sure some kind of woman."

"You amaze me," Scotty began, half-heartedly rebuking his friend. "Aren't you ever afraid of catching something from all these expeditions of yours?" They were typical of the kind of guys seen in any neighborhood bar having a drunken conversation.

Jimmy looked at his friend before replying, "Shit no! You know, the only time I ever caught clap was from a nice little respectable librarian in one of your hick towns. Oh, so decent. Bullshit! I've screwed in every brothel from the Pacific to the Atlantic and have never had a problem."

"Well, maybe I'm just jealous." Scotty raised his glass to his lips. "I never seem able to perform under these circumstances. Something in my make-up makes me afraid. I even attempted to try one of these broads, but as soon as I'm put to the test, my cock just disappears." They both laughed at Scotty's plight. They had always enjoyed each other's camaraderie.

"Maybe it's just as well," Scotty continued while looking at his friend. "If I had been like you, I'd probably have screwed myself to death!"

"What a way to go!" added Jimmy.

"Cheers!" They toasted each other laughingly. Scotty thought for a moment before once again demanding Jimmy's attention.

"I think I know what it is that makes you guys want to impregnate every female on the planet. I've got it all worked out!"

Jimmy looked up at Scotty and asked, "Tell me asshole. I can't wait for this one."

"No. Serious, Jimmy, it's that you guys are just as fucked up about screwing as I am. You're sick in one way and I'm sick in another."

"What ya mean I'm sick?"

"Well, somewhere deep in your subconscious there's a terrible fear that there will be no body for you to occupy."

"What do you mean no body?" asked Jimmy, frowning drunkenly.

"Well what if something happened to cause bodies to disappear, then what would you do? Maybe that's all you're doing by your acts of promiscuous intercourse." Scotty was using his best aristocratic accent to make his point. "This will then ensure that you will have a body to pick up in the future."

"Good God, old boy!" Fresh drinks in hand only prepared Scotty for his next oration.

"Just imagine a nuclear war that would wipe out all material things. That would include bodies, right?"

"Right," replied Jimmy nodding and very glassy eyed by now.

"Okay, then what would happen to all us little ghosties without these I.D. cards and no automobile to carry us around? What would we do?"

"I don't know!" Jimmy shook his head.

"Well I'll tell you what would happen. We would all be floating around unable to drink cause we have no mouth. Hiccup! Unable to screw because we have no peters. Hiccup! Unable to have a pizza oven. As a matter of fact, we would be in a helluva state of anxiety, and awful unhappy." Jimmy looked at Scotty and pretended to be deep in thought before responding.

"So, you reckon I've been in a nuclear holocaust that causes my psychosis to screw all broads in an attempt to keep enough bodies in supply?"

"Correct," answered Scotty standing up straight and slapping the bar. "Ya got it!" Scotty looked as confident as a scholar and almost sober.

Jimmy took his glass in hand, raised it to his friend, and answered, "Scotty you've helped me to make a decision."

"What's that?"

"In case there should be another nuclear holocaust, I'm going to screw all the more. I don't want to have spent all that time being unhappy and anxious."

"Oh, you asshole," replied Scotty as they both laughed at Jimmy's announcement.

"Hey, Scotty," called Tex from the table. "What's happened to the little shit?"

"You mean he hasn't come out yet? It's been twenty minutes," Scotty observed, looking at his watch. "Jesus, I never expected him to last this long!"

All of a sudden, the cubicle door opened revealing Abe who shouted to the barman, "Could I have a condom please?"

The room broke into laughter at the realization that he hadn't even started yet. Jimmy took the rubber from the bartender and reached into his glass for an ice cube. He walked over to Abe and handed him the packet and the ice.

"What's the ice cube for?" Abe asked quizzically.

"Put it in the condom. It will help keep the swelling down."

The merry group were once again hysterical as Abe threw the ice cube at Jimmy before closing the door. Two minutes later the cubicle door opened and out walked Abe with flushed face and looking as proud as a peacock. Standing in front of the gang he made his proclamation.

"Today I am a man!"

His friends applauded and cheered wildly. They knew that if you scratch a pussy you only reveal a tiger.

"Okay guys," said Tex, rising to his feet. "Let's have that old favorite, the California theme song. Ready now? And one – two – three." They all joined in, "A tisket, a tasket. A condom or a casket!"

Staggering out onto the street the gang hailed a cab to take them back to the dock. They were all drinking from beer bottles and had an extra six pack for the journey.

"Hey!" Tex shouted. "Give the driver a beer."

"That's not a good idea," pleaded Jimmy.

"And why the fuck not?"

"It's not good to drink while driving. He might spill some!"

"One up for Jimmy," they all chorused.

"Hey," suggested Scotty between hiccups. "Let's sing the driver our famous sea shanty."

"Yeah let's."

The driver shook his head at this bunch. They began to belt out a very nasty song that they insisted to be the theme song of the S.S. Nectar.

"Twas' on the good ship Venus; by Christ you should have

seen us.

The figure head was a maiden head, two bollocks and a penis.

Singing yo – heave – ho, and we don't want any more beer!

The Captain had a Cabin boy, he was a little nipper.

He stuffed his ass with broken glass and circumcised the Skipper.

Singing yo – heave – ho, and we don't want any more beer!

The Captain's daughter, Mabel, she did what she was able.

She gave the crew, their favorite crew upon the charten' table.

Singing yo – heave – ho, and we don't want any more beer!"

Arriving at the landing they all piled from the taxi.

"Here buddy." Tex handed the driver what was left of the beer. "Cheers! See ya' next trip." Taking the beer and the taxi fare, the driver was probably hoping that he would not.

They made their way through the throng of vendors and passengers, boarded one of the launches, and headed back to the ship. Back aboard they checked Bob's cabin door to find it unlocked. The signal that he was not entertaining a lady. They entered the cabin in high spirits and still singing their song. Bob was reading the paper and having a quiet little noggin. He had spent a lonely day on an empty ship.

"C'mon Bob," stated Tex, checking out the ice chest. "Get out the bottle! We've got some heavy celebratin' to do here!"

"You guys look as though you've had your share today. Remember we play the cocktail set in two hours."

"Never fear, Bob, the strong one is here," asserted Scotty while pointing to Abe who was still relishing his glory. "We have to tell you what happened ashore." As drinks were poured, Scotty related the events of the day to Bob between fits of laughter from everyone. Bob, who was not pleased nor amused by their tale, looked at Abe expecting some sort of denial.

"Is all this true, son?"

"Sure," Abe spoke up, displaying more confidence than had ever been seen before, "and furthermore, I want a fucking drink!" They all broke into cheers hearing the demand from the little squirt.

"Bow, Abe," Mike began, trying to hush the room, "from this day forth your new name shall be, Tiger."

"Yeah!" they yelled. "Three cheers for Tiger. Hip, hip, hooray!"

Bob poured a very mild Bacardi and coke. Offering it to Tiger, he cautioned, "No giggles now. No repetition of last week. Okay?"

"No problem!" spouted the hero of the hour, raising his glass.

Scotty, the master of parodies, broke into, "A-be, A-be. No longer a Goy. What will he tell his mom now?!"

"The name's Tiger, asshole!" responded Abe sharply to Scotty.

"Yeah!" they all roared once again. "Three cheers for Tiger!"

At five o'clock they left Bob's cabin to dress and prepare for playing the cocktail set. Weird thing about these guys, thought Bob, they had the capacity to be drunk when it's fun time, drink some more, and then sober up when called upon to be serious. Musicians are a rare breed!

Scotty entered his cabin and wrinkled his nose. Chuck was dead to the world and the stink of stale booze and cigarette smoke hung in the air. Scotty switched on the lights, opened the door as wide as possible and turned on the cold air louvers before going through the chore of arousing Dracula. Scotty was showered and changed in fifteen minutes, leaving the wash stand and room for Chuck who would remain as always unconscious until he downed the famous two double rums on the bandstand. Scotty cautiously approached the body laying there, slapped him hard on his ass and prepared to duck the fist that was forthcoming.

"Wakey! Wakey! Up and at em! Show me a leg lucky lad!"

Groans from under the blanket indicated Chuck to be still alive. Pushing down the blankets, he crawled out and groped for the usual weed. Stuck it in his mouth, lit it, and stood up. As the fellows passed the open door, Chuck was assailed with usual patter.

"Hey guys – Chuck is still alive!"

"I don't know," said someone, "the stiff in the mortuary looks more alive to me!"

"Oh, piss off," Chuck mumbled incoherently, continuing to shave.

Somehow Chuck always made it to the bandstand where loyal Albee had already placed the two glasses of rum. Every night it was the same. Chuck would down both glasses, straighten his bow tie, smile and greet the band.

"Good evening, gentlemen. Play ball." This was the signal for the music to begin. Season after season the pattern never changes.

The cocktail hour over, it was time for their dinner. Tonight their conversation centered on Abe. The story had to be told to Chuck, who missed their little escapade. They each had a little something to add to the story. Chuck could not help noticing how Abe had already assumed the role of being one of the boys.

"Well," Chuck began to address his buddies. "You gentlemen

have to be commended for the conversion of our young friend here." Looking at the source of honor, Chuck added, "Welcome to the club, Abe. But you and the others failed to tell me what took place the first twenty minutes you were in bed with red hot mama."

Abe help up his finger and, laughing, addressed Chuck, "First of all, the name is Tiger!" This caused Chuck to sit back in his chair while appearing somewhat startled at the admonition. "Secondly," Abe continued and laughed some more, "I ain't gonna tell you! Except this." Abe was now choking as he tried to speak through his merriment. "If my mother could have seen me today, I wonder what her reaction would have been when you consider she used to rebuke me for picking my fucking nose!"

All the lads had to stifle their feelings by laughing into their hands. After all, the dining room was not the place for such an outrageous display.

Abe added the clincher to the meal by ordering coffee for the first time during the cruise.

"How would you like it, Abe?" asked Tom before serving.

"Like my women," he shot back pretending to be tough. "Hot and strong!"

Tom never batted an eye when he burst Abe's bubble, "Black or white, sir?"

"Okay! So, I still have a way to go," he said, punching himself in the forehead. The others just laughed at their little prodigy.

After once again enjoying another sumptuous meal, they headed for Bob's cabin for the usual after dinner drinks and talk through of the evening's music.

It was an early sailing tonight at about eight o'clock. The passengers were all aboard. The dance tonight would be held on the after deck, as usual, but without visitors. It was all downhill for the musicians now. Two more days at sea then back to New York. The last night would be a show, so there would be a brief rehearsal that morning. After the franticness of Haiti, things always settled down. Passengers were grooved into the routine now. The joggers would start to appear again in a last-ditch effort to discard unwanted pounds. The small gymnasium and saunas always became popular around this part of the trip as passengers tried to sweat it out. Even the Staff Captain had eased off on his commando tactics, much to the relief of his assistants and the crew. At least forty crew members were expected to be fired, unless a change of heart and some Divine providence intervened. It broke the Staffy's heart that he was unable to nail the minstrels. He still suspected they were the ones responsible for the rum running scam in St. Thomas. Maybe next trip the gods will be more kind and assist him in bringing the scalawags to justice.

Seated in the privacy of their own council chambers, Bob poured forth the desired beverages. He noticed a lack of exuberance from his previously merry men.

"I have a feeling that we may not all be returning after this cruise. Chuck has already mentioned to me that this will probably be his last. I, more or less, feel the same way," continued Bob, "but the problem is, where do we go from here?"

"I don't think we are dissatisfied with the ship," interjected Jimmy. "I know that I'm not. I am concerned about the state of the music business ashore."

"Yeah," said Tex, "take Vegas for example. The days of live music in the big showrooms are nearly over. Electronics are used more and more. It only needs one man to run the program. Cheaper than all of us. A computer supplies all the music for shows. Even the music for the dancers and showgirls on stage. The public doesn't notice any difference. They wouldn't know a half note from a bank note anyway. The lounges are all the same: two guitars, drums, and a chickie singer.

They all play the same music and sing the same songs. I think that if the cocktail waitresses and keno girls didn't wear different costumes in the various casinos, you wouldn't know where you were 'cause you sure as Christ couldn't tell by the acts in the house."

Tex and Jimmy both seemed to join Bob in his look of despair and this brought the floor of conversation to Scotty.

"It's the same in L.A. The studio musicians once earned a good living. They are also being replaced with electronics. Movies and especially television are mostly all backed by that crap, totally displacing the live musicians. That's not all! Back in the day when the cool cats worked for the studios, it was okay for them to accept small salaries to play in the clubs and just blow their jazz in their off time. They still had their studio gigs to pay the bills. Now that mere pittance has become the order of the day for these clubs. Jazz musicians are basically starving in that town. I was talking to a player who was rehearsing with a big band one day and asked him if they had some gigs coming up and the guys said, "Yeah we're rehearsing for three this weekend, two Saturday and one Sunday. I should make about fifty dollars this weekend.""

"Jesus Christ!" said Jimmy. "It's worse than I thought!"

"We sure do belong to a redundant profession," added Tex.

They were all shaking their heads in amazement while Bob poured some more fortification, before Scotty continued.

"Of course, that's not the worst of it. These kids with their rock shit have really destroyed the whole game. There are actually clubs where the musicians themselves have to sell as much as $900.00 worth of tickets before the kids receive any pay. In other words, they have to make sure the room is full!" The boys were listening in total disbelief as Scotty told more. "Some of these kids have fathers with more money than brains, so they just sponsor the brats to get them out of the house and give them their little showcase. There are other clubs where you play for free as a showcase, but you have to rent the club's P.A. system.

Can you fathom that shit?"

"Of course," piped up Mike, "music is a dying art anyway. What we have now is some rock star singing, or trying to sing, the so-called popular songs and making a fortune in the name of entertainment – not music! At the same you have all these three chord morons trying to emulate them. This has destroyed our profession."

"Yeah!" chipped in Scotty, "but it couldn't have happened without the support of the public, like Tex was saying. Back when I played in Washington D.C. in the early sixties, we had society dances in abundance, and we were never short of decent gigs around town. Then all of a sudden, the so-called elite adopted the craze of the day. They appeared just as stupid as their own fourteen-year-old brats, cavorting round the ballroom in their formal evening wear doing the twist, the pony, mashing their potatoes, and doing whatever else it was called."

Scotty, as always, managed to bring a smile to his buddies with his vivid description of D.C.'s socialites. They had each seen such behavior, but he described it so well.

"Now instead of hiring musicians," he continued, "we were replaced by the weirdies in funny clothes and even funnier hairdos. These same types would not have been allowed in these country clubs a few years before even if their parents were members! Now they had our jobs."

"One for the road," Bob interrupted, feeling the topic was exhausted. "We'll head for the dance deck soon. Remember lads, whatever will be will be. So, let's just take one day at a time and enjoy the moment. Cheers lads!"

"Cheers, Bob!"

"Yeah! Good old Bob!"

"Watch that old stuff now. I can still take on any one of you."

The last dance to be held on the open deck for this cruise was now over. The musicians made their way to the night club where the entertainment continued in the nice air conditioning. On their way to the club, they stopped off at Bob's for a shooter. Chuck was already moaning and groaning about the piano that he had been forced to play all evening.

"It's alright for you guys. You have your own instruments. You don't have to perform on that piece of junk."

"Well, it's over now," Jimmy consoled.

"Yeah," assisted Tex, "one more day of kiddy games and you won't have to worry about it anymore."

"Come on, Chuck. Have a drink and cheer up for your Uncle Scotty!" Chuck was handed a water glass full of rum with just a splash of cola for coloring from Scotty, who was smiling broadly.

"Okay," responded Chuck reluctantly as he took the glass. "I suppose you're right."

"Belay thar me hearties. Be thee drinking up or we'll be late. Har! Har!" reminded Mike. They all quickly finished their drinks and continued on their journey.

The night club wasn't very busy and the group soon dwindled down to a trio. Chuck, Scotty, and Mike enjoyed playing rhythm section as it offered them more freedom to improvise. Chuck's gals had already joined the rest of the gang in Bob's cabin. They were eagerly awaiting their lover boy, but he had other plans. Lorraine and Valerie were on hand in the club to enjoy the company of Mike and Scotty while they were on their breaks. Chuck, at each opportunity, was belting back the booze that was forthcoming from passengers in payment for requested songs. Scotty, who was watching his friend, noticed that Chuck was into the sauce pretty heavy tonight as though he didn't give a damn. Well, thought Scotty, when he goes home he will have plenty of time to sober up.

At two a.m. they called it a night and vacated the bandstand. The two couples took a stroll on deck. Chuck headed for his cabin, grabbed a couple of bottles, and made for the forecastle. He was sure to find some of his drinking cronies. Making his way as far forward as possible, he knocked, then entered a cabin after receiving the answer to come in. Inside was a large room with two bunks on each side of the cabin, one above the other. Six huge bodies were seated on a couple of chairs and boxes around a card table that held the remnants of whatever they had been drinking. By their appearance they must have been going at it pretty good in the course of the evening and were obviously glad to see the visitor. Chuck had spent many an evening in their company and never came empty handed.

"Hey, Chuck, baby! Where ya been? Draw up a pew, ya little shit!" They attempted to make some room for their guest.

Chuck was feeling no pain and managed to climb onto the offered box. The place was clean enough, but it did smell like the bosun's locker with the odor of paint and turpentine emulating from their work clothes that were hanging on pegs. The deckie to Chuck's right was the ever popular Tiny, famous for his ingenuity in the great rum run. Tiny pretended to reprimand Chuck for his sins.

"These broads must be keeping you pretty busy, neglecting your old chums! We haven't seen too much of you this trip. What have you got to say for yourself?"

Chuck opened one of the bottles and poured a good healthy portion of Scotch into each glass on the table before replying, "I've been raped, plundered, and sexually assaulted for the past week, but NO MORE! I've decided to take the pledge and become celibate," he added with a giggle.

"Oh, you little bullshitter." They all joined in with the teasing. This type of conversation was to be expected from a bunch of drunks.

"Probably that dick of yours has got you in trouble."

"No! No!" he insisted, holding up his hand in the act of taking an oath. "I've seen the light. I am heading ashore for good. Giving up drinking as a New Year's resolution, abstaining from religion for lent, and preserving that special gift that I have been endowed with, for my beloved wife."

The fellows roared at the mere thought of such lunacy. One of the boys pretended to play the fiddle and they all began to sing, "I saw a horse climb up a tree and you're a fucking liar."

The booze continued to pour, and more bottles were magically produced so that the fun would never end. Eventually Chuck passed out and lay on the deck. His cronies discussed the merits of their little pal and what a wonderful giver he had been all these years. During the course of the evening, Chuck had blasted them with his usual sufferings of the bloody piano on the after deck and what he thought should be done with it. Tiny, looking down at Chuck in his sweet repose, turned his attention to the others.

"Harry, you have a spare bunk next door. Let's put good old Chuck in there. Okay?"

"Sure thing, Tiny. Let's get him to bed."

Lifting Chuck like a baby, they soon had him tucked in and returned to their booze den. Harry, rubbing his nose, looked around at the others in the cabin. They were all in a drunken stupor and were either pouring drinks or belching.

"Hey, fellas! I have an idea!"

"What's that?" asked Tiny.

"Chuck's a good guy, right?" asked Harry.

"Right!" They chorused in agreement while trying to keep Harry in focus.

"Well," he stammered. "It's not fair. Him havin' to play that shitty piano all night. So why don't we scuttle it?"

Looking at each other as best they could, they nodded in agreement and proceeded to put, what Tiny dubbed, Plan Nasty Upright Organ into effect.

Leaving the forecastle, the commandoes crept their way through the passenger accommodation and up to the sun deck. They descended to where the bone of contention sat covered by a tarpaulin that had been placed upon it by the bar steward in an attempt to protect the now destroyed mechanism. It was amazing how stealthily the group moved, considering they were far from sober. They uncovered the piano and then untied the ropes from the eyelets. Each man took his proper position almost as if this was a regular sea drill. Lifting the instrument, they placed it on their shoulders like a casket. At first, they were startled by the tinkling of keys. Was it an angel reprimanding them for their foul deed? They were not deterred. Placing the doomed piano in a position to prevent any further musical protests, they walked aft across the fantail. Reaching the rail, Tiny looked down at the wake. It was glistening like millions of fireflies from the phosphorous caused by the agitation of the ship's screws.

"Okay fellas," he whispered, "after three. One. Two. And away we go."

Without as much as a prayer, the stringed casket flew off over the rail and landed with nary a sound except for a twangy discord as it floated off into the night atop the ship's wake. Feeling they had indeed done the right thing, they congratulated each other with slaps on the back. They shook hands for a job well done. All this for their little buddy. When they arrived back at the cabin, they swore each other to secrecy.

"Not even Chuck has to know what happened this night. It would only incriminate him," advised Tiny. "So, remember, mums the word."

DAY 8
AT SEA

The ship passed from darkness into the light of dawn totally unaffected by the abortion that had taken place. Chuck, aroused by the strain of a boiling bladder and the feeling that he must have had a tongue transplant, realized he was not in his own bed when the light filtered in the cabin through the porthole. Finding the lavatories down the passageway, he relieved himself and wound his way aft to his own tomb and the comfort of darkness.

On the decks above there was once again a hub activity. The passengers rallied to be first to play the deck games. Finalists were competing in both shuffleboard and deck tennis. Ping pong was going full steam on the Prom deck. It had drawn quite a crowd of onlookers to watch the enthusiasts rush to and fro smashing the little ball within an inch of its life. One could not help but wonder what imaginary target was in the thoughts of the great white hunters, the trap shooters. It was the general consensus that more so the successful shooters were probably aiming at a mother-in-law, and that is why they seldom missed.

It was a different world below decks. The Inner Sanctum was

silent except for the noise the from the ship's screws. Creaks and groans only added to the eeriness. There was no doubt that the hosts of old mariners haunted this area. The minstrels had just retired for some much needed shut-eye when they were rudely aroused by Chuck, who wanted to continue partying. He entered each cabin with bottle in hand, but found no takers on his return from the forecastle. Each of his buddies ejected him with the threat of murder if he didn't shut up and go to bed. That was the last thing Chuck remembered until Scotty woke him for lunch.

"Get up you drunken sot and get some food. You have to play the games today." Once again Chuck crawled from his bunk. Gaping through blood shot eyes, he finally brought Scotty into vision. Chuck started to giggle, and Scotty knew that he was not completely sober yet.

"Can you imagine the assholes on those T.V. commercials who set up in bed and greet the day with outstretched arms and a song? I wonder what the hell they smoke to feel so good in the morning. I'm sure some broad must be under the covers blowing the guy. Why else would he look so cheerful?"

"What happened to you last night?" inquired Scotty after Chuck had finished his philosophy lesson. "Those three broads of yours were ready to put out a man overboard alarm on you! You never even said, good night, ya little shit!"

"Well, you should just have explained to them, the Lord giveth and the Lord taketh away!" Chuck looked very profound while attempting to pull on his sock for the third time.

"Ah you're hopeless!"

"That's not what those three broads think," he threw back at Scotty. "They think I'm super stud!!"

"You make any more racket like you did this morning and I'll have you spayed and confined to a sandbox where you belong. Watch you don't drop that sock, it's apt to break."

Chuck still giggled away to himself then started to sing. "Was all over my jealousy. My crime was my blind jealously."

"I'll give you jealousy," laughed Scotty, picking up the jug of cream that Tom had brought with the morning coffee. He very calmly walked over to Chuck and poured the contents over his head then beat a hasty retreat from the cabin to the sound of Chuck's extensive vocabulary.

"Ya lousy no good Scottish bastard. I'll get you!"

After lunch, the musicians headed for the after deck where they found a very concerned cruise director. Vic and his staff were engaged in some serious head scratching and seemed to be looking for something. Vic came rushing toward Bob like a mother hen who had just lost her chick.

"Bob," he called excitedly, "I hope you can shed some light on this situation."

"What situation?" inquired Bob, looking very confused.

"It's the piano!"

"What's wrong with the piano?" Bob did not like guessing games.

"We can't find it!"

Bob and the other musicians looked at the empty spot and then at each other in total disbelief. Suddenly they all had the same thought, could Chuck have been crazy enough to have caused it to disappear? After all, he was pretty drunk last night and did not return to his cabin until early this morning. Each one in turn began to look around for Chuck, who had stopped off at the service bar for a little wake up shooter. Bob began to walk toward Chuck as he arrived on deck.

"Do you know anything about the piano?" Bob asked in his authoritative manner.

"Yeah, it's a piece of shit!" The shooter had only served to stir the alcoholic content still in his system from last night and return his nice little buzz.

"I mean do you know where it is?" Bob was losing his patience now.

Chuck's attention drifted to the empty parking place and his expression resembled that of somebody who had just had his car stolen. Chuck now realized that the situation was serious.

"Was it taken into the lounge or the Verandah grill?" Chuck asked.

"No," replied Bob, feeling that asking Chuck anything was fruitless in his present state.

"We have searched everywhere and are unable to find it," wailed Vic. The Chief Steward is going to check all the nearby cabins in the off chance that some prankster among the passengers hauled it away."

"You mean there is no sign of the piano at all?" Chuck asked starting to appear a little elated.

"That's right," answered Vic, "and if it's not found there is going to be hell to pay. I can assure you!"

Deep down Chuck felt he had something to do with the present dilemma but was not ready to make light of the problem.

"I know," Chuck said excitedly. "It's the Bermuda Triangle! The Martians must have stolen it during the night which proves one thing: they don't have ears for music if that's the best they can do!"

The lads decided not to encourage Chuck by laughing, for they knew that frivolity was not what Bob needed right now. Vic was growing more aggravated each minute; he never could understand musicians.

"Vic's right," Bob began addressing all his men. "There's going to be hell to pay. Chuck you better go down and fetch your accordion to play the games. We will sort out this mess later."

Chuck walked across the deck then suddenly stopped and looked back at the solemn bunch and shouted, "You mean it's really gone?" He did not wait for an answer but instead let out with a wild yell, jumped in the air, clicked his heels together and took off at a fast pace to his cabin.

Chuck soon returned with his accordion. He only used it when playing in the smaller party rooms that didn't have a piano or in passenger cabins. As penance, Chuck had to stand and pump on his accordion during the deck games. Bob noticed the Purser, Chief Steward, First Officer, and Staffy pacing at regular interval around the perimeter of the games deck. During the band's first break, Bob took Chuck aside and tried to piece together what must have happened.

"Where did you do your boozing last night?" Bob asked, intent on sorting out this mess.

"I was up in the deckies' quarters with Tiny and some of the lads."

"Did you, in your drunken state, talk about the piano?"

"Yeah, I suppose so," he answered Bob. Then the penny dropped. Looking up at Bob he gasped, "Jesus Christ! Do you think they may have thrown the thing overboard just as a favor to me?"

"It certainly looks that way," Bob replied. "So, here's what you'll have to do. Don't mention any of this to a soul. Not Scotty, the deckies – NO ONE!! Understand?"

"Yeah, sure, Bob. Not a word."

"Now Chuck, there is probably going to be some kind of investigation, after they have exhausted all efforts to unravel the mystery, so you had better lay off the sauce in case you're called up. Okay?"

Chuck was willing to be reprimanded by Bob, but was having a difficulty keeping a straight face at the thought of what must have happened. Bob was sure that he had managed to curtail Chuck's glee and that he finally had grasped the seriousness of the situation.

"You know," said Chuck looking at Bob very piously, "it brings tears to my eyes when I think of those deckies and their loyalty to a friend. Greater love hath no man." Before Chuck could finish his quote, Bob grabbed him by the collar and rushed him towards the bandstand. Chuck continued to giggle and squirm as if he just fallen drunk again.

"You little shit! You mention one word of what we've discussed to anyone and I will personally throw you over the side!" Bob was very serious, and Chuck finally got the message and came to his senses.

The games ended, and Scotty, Chuck, and Jimmy went to the Verandah Grill bar to pick up their beer before heading for the after end of the Prom deck. Once there, they found Walter already seated and waiting for them.

"Gentlemen," greeted Walter as the trio seated themselves in his company. "I trust you had a pleasant visit in Haiti yesterday."

Nearly choking on their beers, the musicians shared glances and snickers. Finally, Jimmy said, "Walter if I didn't know you better, I'd swear you were trying to make us feel guilty!"

"Oh, I see," Walter replied. "You must have been up to some mischief to have such misgivings. Guilt always follows the deed." Scotty admired the way Walter could point the finger and at the same time keep it all airy and light. He had the feeling that this man could look into your very soul and know all.

"Talk about feeling guilty," Chuck said to Walter. "Just wait 'til you hear the one about the phantom piano." Chuck began to unfold his story to Walter. "Those four officers kept parading round and round the deck. It sort of looked like musical chairs without the chairs. They would stop to look over the side of the ship and then look at me as though they expected the piano to pop out of the water like a flying fish and land back on the deck!"

"My! My!" exclaimed Walter looking coyly at Chuck. "You have no idea what happened to the instrument?"

"None at all. I was just as surprised as the rest of the fellows to find it gone this afternoon when we came on deck."

"Well, I would surmise the intentions of the officers were to make you feel guilty, and you must have given them reason to be suspect."

"I guess I did constantly moan about the condition of the piano to the officers, but they just ignored any suggestion I gave about its care."

"I must say," Walter said to Chuck, "that's a good trick and pretty clever of you too! You have a real ability here, my boy. Just to complain about something in your environment until it eventually disappears."

"Gee, if that's true," interrupted Jimmy, "why don't my taxes go away?"

"Yeah, or rock and roll," added Scotty. The levity continued for a few minutes and they all had a good laugh.

"You see," Walter began, "the officers were using a very old technique. They probably don't even know how it works, but it does; I'll explain. First of all, the game is to impose guilt. They put you in a position of being uncertain whether or not they know that you are the perpetrator. In other words, you are stuck with a mystery. Even if you had nothing at all to do with the situation, you still wonder, do they know it was me?"

"I'm trying to follow you, Walter, but if I had nothing at all to do with the piano mystery, why would I worry about it?"

"Okay, I'll expound on this subject with a couple of analogies. Imagine you are in a room. Let's say a classroom, and everyone just left but you. A pack of cigarettes is laying on top of one of the desks and you decide to take them. Just as you are putting them in your pocket, one of the students happened to be walking by and glanced through the door. Now you don't feel very good about what you did. You leave the room and walk down the corridor only to find that same student having a conversation with a group of students from your class. One of the students that he is talking with owns the cigarettes in your pocket. As you approach, they stop talking and seem to have difficulty looking in your direction. Get the picture?"

"Yeah," replied Chuck.

"Good," continued Walter. Now how do you think you'd feel in that situation?" The looks on the three faces made it fairly obvious that each of them had been placed in a similar predicament many times in the past. "Another common example that we have all experienced is walking into a room where the conversation comes to an abrupt halt when we enter. You probably were convinced that the former conversation was about you and, like Chuck here, you feel guilty."

"In other words, what you're saying," Scotty began, "is that we all have skeletons in the closet, and we carry that guilt with us always."

"I'm afraid so. After all, it would be very difficult to go through life completely pure. Don't you agree? Remember that if you buy the concept that you, a spiritual being, have existed for a long time, then I think you will agree that there are plenty of reasons for feeling guilty."

"That would explain," continued Jimmy, "what happens after a major crime. I read somewhere that police stations receive numerous calls from people who want to confess."

"Exactly! It's just that people feel they have done something, but they don't know what."

"No wonder we're all stupid. Probably," continued Chuck, "all of our troubles stem from just who you say. Therefore, it's our own unethical action that is really doing each of us in!"

"Good point, Chuck. Now here's another example of how guilty feelings can affect someone." They were all ears awaiting Walter to once again share his wisdom. "Let's talk about Mr. Macho with the nice wife and family. We all know someone like this fellow. Well, one day he meets his old flame. He hasn't seen her in about ten years. She makes a big fuss over him and really boosts his ego. He invites her to lunch. This may cause him to stray a little or maybe not. Anyway, he decides that it would not be a good idea to tell his wife. As the couple are sitting in the restaurant, possibly holding hands, Mr. Macho looks up to see Mary, a friend of his wife, walk past. Mary leaves, but not before she glances back in his direction. Now the drama unfolds. Did she notice us? He wonders a little what will happen but pushes it from his mind for now. A few nights later he comes home from work, and everything is peaches and cream. He is reading the newspaper when all of a sudden, his wife says, "Guess who I talked to today?" "No idea." "Oh, you know, my old friend Mary." After that his wife leaves the room. Can you imagine how this man feels right now?"

"I bet he feels like disappearing up his own asshole!" said Scotty.

"Serves the bastard right for cheating on his wife," added Jimmy.

"Ha, ha, but there's the rub," Walter continued with their complete attention. "Maybe he did nothing. It is all that prior guilt that has been kicked up and brought into play just because of one stupid mistake. Now his heart is pounding. His blood pressure is elevating, and he is stuck, like you Chuck, in a big mystery. Does she know? His wife does not offer any further information about her conversation with Mary and, of course, he can't ask her. Now for the next episode of this silly game. As I said before, first is the guilt, followed by the mystery, and then comes the hysterics. Mr. Macho starts screaming at his wife over all sorts of trivia. This serves no purpose except to destroy the marriage."

Chuck now realized that this conversation was meant not only to assist him with the phantom piano, but also to complete his education and enhance his marital situation. Recalling how on one occasion ashore he and his wife had teamed up with another couple, one of the barmen from the ship and his wife. The friend had constantly made reference of how the ship's musicians always sweep the female passengers off their feet and into their cabins to take unfair advantage of these poor young things. Chuck realized that this had been thrown at him by his wife during regular spats when he came home. Being guilty and then getting hit with the rest of it, he had only one recourse after the hysterics – head for a bar.

"What are you thinking about?" asked Walter directing his attention again to Chuck.

"As far as the piano is concerned, I honestly don't know what has happened to it, therefore I shouldn't feel guilty."

"No guilt at all?" Walter, looking at him with one of his all-knowing expressions, questioned Chuck.

"Well other than I did constantly moan about it."

"Well is it possible your lamentation in some small way led to its demise?"

"You are a crafty bugger, Walter, I must say. Okay a little guilty."

"So now that you understand how the plan is laid out. You can easily take responsibility for your part in the disappearance of the piano and prevent phase two and three by not becoming intimidated by the officers nor anyone else who may try to blame you." Just then Albee made a welcomed appearance.

"Hey, old Buddy," yelled Chuck. "Let's have a noggin over here, please."

"Sure. What will it be, Gents? Albee hastened to the service bar to fill the requests.

"Och, aye!" came a very thick Scottish accent directed to no one in particular. "Problems. Problems. Problems. Everyone has problems," continued Scotty as he sat back in his deck chair.

"What's wrong with problems?" Walter asked, "Life would certainly be dull without them. Show me a man with no problems and I'll show you an apathetic creature. That's one of the curses of the idle rich. A lack of problems. This type usually gets into all sorts of unethical and kinky games because of a lack of problems."

"Well," laughed Jimmy, "I have a few problems I could do without, so if you want them you can have them."

"Now what we have here," said Walter turning to Jimmy. "Could there be a wimp among us?"

"Oh, c'mon, don't be like that. I'm only joking."

"No really," the orator addressed the group. "The only problem with problems is allowing them to remain unsolved. People are walking around all day with these loose ends unable to function and they don't know why. Don't forget, everything that happens to you, whether it be a solved or unsolved situation, is your creation; even an unhappy environment. Whether you have a good or bad marriage, it's your creation. In other words, everything that happens to you – you created. If you have a problem and you attempt to point the finger at another, claiming he is responsible, then you are being a wimp."

This statement really hit home. The three of them, with bowed heads, realized the truth in what Walter was saying. Allowing the boys time to recover, he softened the blow by explaining that most people do not understand how the problems came about in the first place, so are unable to take the necessary steps to solve them.

"Let's take a simple situation," Walter continued, with their full attention. "You decide to leave the ship and work ashore. Next day you change your mind. You have just created a problem. Okay?"

"Okay," they chorused in eager anticipation.

"Of course, all one would have to do is lay it out in front and weigh the pros and cons, then make a decision. Right?"

"Sure!"

"That's easy enough, but let's take another example. A person is working in a job, but feels unhappy or even ill most of the time. The first thing the victim has to do is examine who in his environment is causing him to feel this way. He is a wimp! The poor fellow is unaware that the intimidation is from another source. Maybe he does know the cause, but permits the problem to continue. Let's assume it's the owner of the company. Every time the owner makes an appearance, our poor fellow feels uncomfortable. Maybe the victim has committed some foul deed detrimental to the company and is suffering the pangs of guilt each time the owner comes around. Follow me so far?" Walter looked around to find that the lads were all ears and literally hanging on his every word.

"On the other hand, the owner is not a very nice person and often verbally abuses his employees. This, by the way, is a sign of his own insecurity and an attempt to control others. Now let's assume the person has done nothing wrong, but finds it difficult to face the boss anyway. He will try to avoid any confrontation by physically avoiding him. He might take off in another direction when he sees the boss approaching. Why would he do this? Simply so that the boss and anyone else would not find out what a coward he really is should he receive a reprimand or even an undeserved tongue lashing. This poor person goes through day after day leaving the problem unsolved until he becomes so miserable and ultimately ill."

"Okay!" Chuck interrupted. "How does this add up to pointing the finger and blame at somebody else? The poor guy has no idea what's wrong."

"Look at it," answered Walter. "Who is really to blame? It's not a problem for the boss, but the person who is being totally affected and doing nothing about it."

"I see," replied Chuck, "but what's the next step?"

"All right," acknowledged Walter. He now put his attention on the oldest member of the group. "Jimmy, how would you handle such a situation?"

"Simple! I'd break his fucking jaw!"

The other two musicians looked at Walter expecting some sort of rebuttal. They all felt Walter was sort of peace loving, aesthetic person and definitely opposed to violence. His response surprised them to say the least.

"Good idea, Jimmy, but if one has to resort to such measures you'd better make sure the violence does not create a new problem. Many people, such as the employer type we are discussing, attempt to control by using force, and these people are really screaming to be handled. Often these individuals have no respect for anyone until they are looking up from the ground. So, you see you would actually be doing this employer a favor as long as you can be responsible for your actions. In other words, make sure he goes home with the headache and not you! Should you have an aberration about violence, you would feel its effect when you strike out. Do you understand, Jimmy?"

"Sure."

"Okay, now make sure when you strike the blow that it's not in anger but in cold blood, and that it is what is needed to solve your problem. Of course, in that case I could not call you a wimp, and probably the boss, seeing this strength, would not be willing to pick on you anymore."

"So, what about the wimp?" asked Scotty. "He still has his problem."

"Very well, let's assume he is aware the boss is his problem. He must either withdraw from the place or improve the situation by walking into the boss' office, closing the door and laying it all on the line. Most of the time we are afraid to make waves because of economics and we realize how bad we need the job. Don't forget, bosses know this too! If that is the case for our poor wimp, he will continue to suffer. If not, he will throw all caution aside and do what has to be done. If the boss is any kind of a man, he will respect our hero. If he should get fired, all he will lose is a little money, but he will have restored his soul by creating a manly image and will walk out of that place leaving his frustrations behind. This usually leads to better doors opening in the future. There are times in life when your integrity means more than a job." A brief respite was called as Albee approached to check their glasses.

"Yeah, bring us another round, Albee." Chuck placed the empty glasses on his tray. "This is thirsty work!"

Albee returned quickly and handed out the welcomed iced glasses of beer for the lads and pot of hot tea for Walter. Each of them cherished that first long swallow.

"Now," began Walter, once more observing his class had come

to order. "Another very important and vicious method of creating problems is the existence of a third person. Not only is this person a walking problem himself, but he plays a game of inciting problems among others. To let you understand this a little more, just remember that no quarrel can exist between two people without the advent of a third person. A simple example is the sneak who runs to the boss and informs on his fellow workers. This is usually a wimpy weak excuse for a man who does not have the courage to face the people he is complaining about."

"Yeah!" Scotty interjected, "I was on a ship where we actually had a musician who continually ran to the purser's office and told him what we were doing. Whether it was being in some broad's cabin or how much booze we were drinking. It took us some time to catch on, but we did find out."

"How did you handle that situation?"

"Oh boy did we fix his ass! Of course, it was dirty politics on our part. He had to sit at our dining table, meal after meal, and be totally ignored. I told him if we were fired, I would see to it that he never sailed again. At that time, I had no idea how to accomplish such a statement, but do you know what happened? We were terminated at the end of the trip and three weeks later, when the ship was ready to sail again, that asshole was carried off the ship ill and sent to hospital!" There were some sighs among the listeners.

"Served the bastard right!"

"Oh, you're an evil mother!"

"We'll have to watch you!"

Walter was studying Scotty as the others made their evaluations then asked, "Have you made such threats before? Threats that actually turned out to the detriment of your target?"

"Sure. Whenever I find anyone who is threatening my survival, I just put the whammy on them and get them out of my way. My mother used to call me a warlock!" Scotty smiled at his past victories. "I could tell you about some real nasty ones, but I don't think you'd enjoy hearing about them." Scotty fell back in his chair and looked very smug after warning his pals of his hidden power.

"Remember fellows," began Walter, "that if Scotty is capable of exerting such abilities, this too could be a problem."

"Yeah, for us!" pleaded Chuck.

"What do you mean?" asked Scotty knowing that Walter was not just kidding around.

"Let's assume you are upset with someone and decide somehow to be rid of that person. You put your power into effect and it does not work. The result is that the intention you put out will back fire on you and result in a reverse effect." The boys were hanging on Walter's every word. "Have you ever had the desire to withdraw from a situation that made you unhappy?"

By the look on Scotty's face it was obvious that Walter had struck a chord. Scotty's eyes now narrowed as he looked seriously at Walter.

"That's been the story of my life! Running away! Even as a little kid I was always running away. My parents used to constantly pick me up at the police station after one of my little adventures. Later in life if I didn't like something or was faced with a problem, I just left. Even being at sea, I'm still running." Walter waited a few moments because he knew that Scotty was seeing all those past experiences in his head right now.

"That could be one reason why you found it necessary to run away. First of all, the person or situation is not to your liking. Then you intend it to go away. That's fine, but if it doesn't, there's a backfire! The result – you have to leave. It can also work another way. If you desire that someone be fired from a job and there's a backfire, the result is you get fired! Sound familiar?" Walter looked at his pupils who were all nodding in agreement. "Now take a look at all the sickness around you, people you know, relatives and such. You can chalk most of it up to the failures these people have experienced using evil thoughts. Now, as far as you are concerned, Scotty, things have been working pretty well for you in the past because you are a strong person. But beware of how you use your power! My suggestion is to flow good thoughts and weaken that curse upon that poor man. You will destroy yourself with resentment. And that goes for the rest of you lot."

"That's right!" Jimmy agreed to add to the conversation. "Look at the situation the Staff Captain is in on board this ship. Everyone resents the Staffy and wants to get rid of him. Now forty or more of the crew will be dumped in New York and the rest are at each other's throats!"

"Exactly my point, Jimmy, and a very good observation. The Staff Captain has created so much resentment that the ship will probably have six like him on the next trip."

"God help us!"

"There goes the rum running!" Solemnly, they all looked with reverence at the glasses of beer.

"Okay now." Walter wanted their attention again. "Later we will take a complete look at the subject of resentment, but let's return to what we were discussing, before we got off on that subject. The third person and how this evil person affects your everyday life. As I was explaining to you, no quarrel can exist between two people without one of them being poisoned by another person. Here's an example of what I mean. Chuck comes to me and says, "Scotty thinks you're a kook and says you are a real nut case." Get the picture?" Walter paused for a moment awaiting their nods. "Now the first thought I should entertain is that Chuck is the one who resent me and is too big a coward to take responsibility for his own evaluation of me so he has to hand the dirty work to poor Scotty who is unaware of the whole conversation. Whether or not Scotty feels this way about me is not important at this point. The fact is that I have a covert, nasty, little man here in front of me. Knowing what's going on, I would immediately point out his failings and inform him that it was Scotty's place to denounce me if he wished and not his. This applies in all walks of life. Whether it be a worker pitting worker against worker or housewives listening to the gossip of their so-called friends advising them that so and so does not like them. It's all part of a stupid game to create unhappiness and share the misery of the person who is running around doing this."

They took a breather while the message sank in, thus permitting a few more gulps of beer to pass down their throats. Chuck, being the only married one of the gang, was thinking about divorce and the third person connection.

"I see how that could interfere in marriage where the third person would be the correspondent," stated Chuck.

"Exactly," answered Walter. "Such a person is very weak. Who else but a weak person, seeing a man or woman already stressed by an unhappy situation, would take advantage of these pitiful creatures? It may be unfair to lump them generally as weak, but you will find that they do not have the fortitude to seek out a strong able partner. They find it easier to control what is now a victim. Divorce has now been made easier. In most states it doesn't even involve a correspondent. Why, in the old days the correspondent would have hit the trail when the heat was turned on. It's unfortunate, but everything around us is based on control. Whether it's a spouse controlling the mate, a man controlling his dog, a boss controlling his workers, or a kid bullying another kid. It's all control, control, control."

Chuck was still stuck in the subject of divorce and asked Walter, "You speak about the third person in the marriage scene, but does there have to be another man involved with your wife before a couple will break up?"

"Well, as you understand the part you played from our previous conversation, let's look at another angle. You and your wife are back on track and obeying the nuptial agreements, but still there is a problem. Got it so far, Chuck?"

"Yeah! Sure!"

"Okay. Now let's take a look at your wife's associates. Who possibly resents you or the close relation you have with your wife?"

"Her mother," responded Chuck without hesitation. "The old bastard! She is always harping at her about marrying a dumb piano player when she could have had a nice stable bricklayer or plumber." Chuck was experiencing all the pent in anger of those past years as he continued to denounce his mother-in-law. "Why the old shit. I should go home and kick her ass out the door. The interfering old bat." Chuck rambled on for a few more seconds. The entire gang waited for him to run out of steam. Eventually he looked at his pals and smiled. He had unloaded his emotions and felt like an ass when he added, "Yeah, I see what you mean, Walter. These people can't help being nasty. The dumb bastards!"

"Here is a perfect situation of resentment. You resent your mother-in-law. She resents you. So, the more you resent each other, the more you are stuck together. Even though you are now thousands of miles apart. There is no distance with hatred."

"And," added Jimmy, "it doesn't matter how much money one has, everyone is affected. Christ, the movie stars continually marry, divorce, and marry again. What the hell's their problem?"

"Well," continued Walter, "there is another factor involved. They each think that they are something special." Attention was now back on Walter as they each anticipated his wisdom.

"Apart from the third person or resentment felt towards each other, there is the question of carrying the previous association into the next one. In other words, what may be good in the previous marriage is now missing in the new one. All that was bad in the old marriage is inadvertently brought forth and vice versa. This only causes discontent. What is happening is that the parties involved, instead of putting a complete end to the previous relationship, are still stuck with whatever trauma was present and are still mentally hanging on. When a person decides to end such an association, everything that was involved in it has to be eliminated knowingly so it is not used as a comparison." Walter could detect a little confusion among his flock as he continued to explain. "Have you ever seen the person who starts a new job and constantly compares it to the one he just left last week? He often complains that he didn't do it this way in his last job and usually drives his new co-worker nuts in a few days. If he continues to carry on this way, he will find that he has no job. It's the same in a marriage, especially with movie stars. They simply jump from marriage to marriage, never really ending the previous one. I'm sure you can imagine how nutty this would make a person by the time he gets to the sixth partner. Pity the poor partner. So, remember now, if you ever marry more than once, the golden rule is not to compare, and make sure you have ended the last one. This works with jobs too. When starting a new job, you must be willing to do it their way until you are in a position to effect change. These changes should be improvements and not because it is the way you used to do it before."

"Albee," Jimmy shouted, spotting their favorite waiter making his rounds. "More sauce for the boys, please." Albee collected the glasses and double checked the orders before heading for the bar.

"Christ, I feel that you are treating us to some form of psychoanalysis, Walter," commented Scotty readjusting himself on his chair. "It's like getting a head job."

"Not really," answered Walter. "It's nothing more than a lecture on human behavior. This may be all there is to mental therapy as far as their technology is concerned, but I'm afraid it goes much deeper. I've often said, it's not what you know that causes mental pain but what you don't know. All we have done here is align some of the confusion that exists in your everyday living and reassure you that it can be handled simply."

"Correct me if I'm wrong," said Jimmy, "but I gather from your conversation that you don't hold much to so-called mental practitioners?"

"It's not whether I consider their methods valuable, but how do they feel about themselves. You see, they also have to go through what they have to go through to achieve what can only be described as ethical behavior."

"Here you are fellas," interrupted Albee, passing around the awaited bottles of beer to eager hands. After a few gulps and some lip smacking with an occasional belch from Jimmy, they were ready to continue.

"If I may be so bold," began Scotty, "I think the so-called medical profession is not applying what is needed in the field of mental sickness?"

"No, on the contrary," Walter proceeded to clarify his previous statement. "You will find it's becoming more apparent to the general practitioner that there is more to sickness than just treating the body. Dealing with case after case, they are beginning to recognize the existence of a common denominator. And that is, that more illnesses are of a psychosomatic origin. And don't forget the psychiatrist is hoping to find the solution to his own problems by listening to those of his patients."

"Yeah," interjected Chuck. "You have to be nuts to see a psychiatrist! No pun intended."

"Maybe you're not far wrong, Chuck, when you consider some

of the methods used. There is less of it now, but any doctor who could even think of prescribing a frontal lobotomy, electric shock, hypnosis, or mind controlling drugs is not a sane man." They lapsed into silence for a moment.

"I see your point," Jimmy spoke again. "If it turned out that most body problems were psychosomatic, then it would be nothing short of criminal to cut pieces out of it."

"Yes," answered Walter, "but as you can see, a doctor is necessary should you fall and break bones or get yourself shot or stabbed. Addressing the spirit would not compensate for the medical attention needed now. After he is mended it may be wise to address the spirit and try to establish why he got himself shot in the first place. That would help to prevent a recurrence of such incidents."

Just then Tom, the steward, made an appearance and approached the group.

"Chuck. Bob asked me to find you. He wants to see you in his cabin pronto. Okay?"

"Sure, Tom. No bother. I'll head there now." Tom returned to his duties.

"Here we go," said Chuck turning to Scotty, "I guess this is the start of the shit hitting the fan over the piano. The only regret I have is that Bob is taking the brunt of all this. He doesn't deserve it."

"Oh, Bob has been through the wars before, and I'm sure he'll come out on top again," answered Scotty. "Actually, I think the old fart secretly enjoys these conflicts. It helps to break the monotony."

"Okay then." Chuck got up. "I'll see you guys later. I venture forth into the valley of death." They smiled at his parting remark, feeling he was being outwardly brave to cover up his natural nervousness.

Instead of Chuck taking the elevator, he made his way aft,

descending each companionway, in an attempt to delay whatever evil awaited. He entered the Inner Sanctum and knocked Bob's door hoping the occupant was absent.

"Come in!" came the reply, dashing all hopes. Entering the room, he found Bob alone and looking serious.

"Yes, Chuck. Come in, please sit down and make yourself comfortable." Bob picked up a bottle of Scotch from the dresser and poured two hefty drinks before seating himself in one of the armchairs.

"Well Chuck," Bob opened the conversation, "it appears we have a serious situation on our hands and your presence is required in the Purser's Office between cocktails and dinner tonight. Do you know what to expect?"

"Yeah, Bob. I'm only sorry to have caused you so much grief. You certainly do not need this mess."

"Of course, I'm not entirely innocent," Bob said in an attempt to take the heat off Chuck, who had been his friend for so long. "I should have done more to correct the bad piano situation. You did protest often enough, and I just turned a deaf ear. Anyway, what's done is done and we will just have to deal with this present problem, which is your confrontation tonight with the Staffy. Now between you and me, did you have a hand in the piano disappearance?"

"Honest, Bob, what I told you is the truth. I passed out with the deckies and they put me to bed. I think, as we suspect, they dumped it. A sort of favor to me I guess, but I would never mention that to anyone, only you. As far as being present at the burial, if that's where it went, I honestly don't know."

"All right. You know, I asked to be present in the hope of giving you some back up, but the Staffy refused to have me in the room. He's obviously going to attempt to overwhelm you. There will be other officers present in their little uniforms. Do you think you will be able to handle the Staffy when he gets on your case tonight?"

"I'll just have to wait until the time comes," replied Chuck. "Actually, I'm not too concerned about that asshole, because I don't feel I have anything to lose. This will probably be my swan song, and they can't throw me in jail. So what? My only concern is the trouble it has caused you."

"Don't worry about that," answered Bob pouring another noggin. "I have already spoken to the Purser and some of the other officers. They have no more respect for the Staffy than anyone else aboard ship. It's even in the wind that the crew have plans of their own to deal with Breathwaite in New York. If it happens, we may not have to worry about any of his old reports. He will probably trash himself. In other words, should it go our way, the Purser's Office has agreed to just write a requisition for a new piano in order to replace the "worn out" one."

"Oh great, Bob!" Chuck's eyes brightened and he raised his glass in salute. "So, the world hasn't come to an end after all!"

"Cheers!" Bob acknowledge, touching glasses. "Please try to stay cool tonight, and for God's sake, don't go there smashed!"

"Oh, don't worry about that, Bob. I have no intention of being that wimpy. I'll just have my usual lot and face the music."

"I have your word on that, Chuck. You won't be drunk?"

"You got it, Bob!" They shook hands. Just then, a knock on the door was followed by the others filing into Bob's cabin.

"Curiosity was killing us," said Jimmy.

"Yeah we couldn't wait to hear what evil was afoot," remarked Scotty.

"Settle down boys. Here, fill your glasses," ordered Bob, "and I'll inform you what will take place tonight."

"Har! Har! Thee are about to be keel hauled me lad," said Mike. "Maybe walk the plank or one hundred lashes be thy choice. If thee kicks the bucket I, Long John, will volunteer to sew thee up in a sailcloth sack. For this I receive a bottle o' rum and ten dollars! Belay there me hearties!"

"Shut up, fat ass, or we may use you for shark bait," replied Scotty laughingly. "No, on second thought, that would be cruelty to the poor fish."

The door opened and in walked Abe strutting like a little turkey.

"Hi guys! Am I in time for a shooter?"

"What a change in one week." Bob smiled as he picked up the bottle. "This little shit is behaving more like a seasoned buccaneer every day."

Abe accepted the glass from Bob, but sensed a note of tension in the room.

"Is everything okay?" asked Abe. "Did I come in at the wrong time?"

"Oh, you're fine," assured Bob with a wave of his hand. "It's just that we are concerned about Chuck. He is going to get the third degree from the Staffy. He is to be in the Purser's Office after cocktails."

"No shit!" responded Abe approaching Chuck who was seated on the bunk. Placing his hand on Chuck's shoulder, he looked into his friend's eyes in a very serious and consoling manner. "Well old friend, I have only one thing to say before you go to the hot seat and I hope it will carry you through this trauma."

"What's that?" asked Chuck expecting some helpful advice.

"Do you know who had turned gay?"

The question snapped everyone's attention to the little shit as he waited for Chuck's reply. Abe looked around the room to see the fellows' stare in wonderment while shaking their heads.

"No. Who?" replied Chuck.

"Give me a kiss and I'll tell you!" answered Abe, who burst into laughter. The group cracked up. Chuck slapped Abe around the head and then tossed him onto the deck where he lay kicking his heels at his own joke. Their little convert was just trying to ease the situation a bit.

The cocktail session about to start, Albee approached the bandstand intending to service Chuck with his usual noggin.

"Not tonight, Albee, but thanks anyway. Just fix me one at the end of the session to fortify me for my date with the devil."

Albee looked astonished at the refusal of the spirits, so Chuck briefly explained what was about to take place.

"Christ," laughed Albee, "I thought you had gone on the wagon, Chuck. That could be fatal you know. The Staffy would be a piece of cake compared to that."

That's one thing about being aboard ship, thought Chuck as his attention returned to the piano. Nothing is ever taken seriously. Just one big fucking laugh a minute.

The session over, Albee returned and gave Chuck his shooter. Chuck downed it in one, smacked his lips, and took his leave.

"See you guys at dinner. I'm sure this won't take long."

Chuck made his way to the Purser's Office, as instructed, aware that he was about to face an inquisition. He suspected, of course, the fate of the infernal instrument and realized that the wrath of the officers was about to rain on his head. No matter what the threat, he would just have to play dumb and keep his cool. His heart was pounding and palms damp. He stood in front of the door of the enforced place of confessional. He was glad to have fortified himself with that double noggin. It was just starting to take effect, thus causing his fear to subside. Chuck knocked the door. It was opened by Mr. Russell, the purser.

"Good evening, Mr. Fisher," greeted the Purser, who tried to convey a sympathetic smile unseen by those behind him in the cabin.

"Mr. Russell," replied Chuck. Normally it would have been "hi" and first names, but under these circumstances, formality was being observed. Only a tiny win for those officers present.

Entering the room, Chuck was confronted by the Staff Captain seated behind the Purser's desk, and on either side of room sat the Chief Steward and the Chief Officer from the bridge. Chuck took his position before Staff Captain Breathwaite and the Purser sat near the door behind him.

Circling the wagons, thought Chuck, realizing this technique was intended to break down his own fortifications and reduce him to the desired nervous wreck. Somehow, he felt within himself that wasn't going to happen. An inner strength was appearing on the surface, caused by his newfound ability to stand back and look at the whole scene objectively. Thanks to Walter's guidance, it was as though he was a spectator instead of being a part of the picture. He even felt that Walter was in the cabin with him as he recalled those little pieces of wisdom.

"Remember, no one can hurt you unless you agree to be hurt. No one can upset or make you angry without your agreement to be angry."

Chuck's thoughts were so preoccupied that he showed no sign of the fear expected by those in the room. A little smile creased the corners of the musician's mouth. He realized that this might turn out to be a fun game and not so threatening after all. Chuck threw a scant glance at the two cohorts to the Staffy's left and right before returning his attention to the presiding judge. The Staff Captain was attempting to conceal a desire to explode. He knew his intimidating tactics were not having the desired effect. Breathwaite continued to display an apparent calmness that was required of officers. Chuck was well aware of the Staffy's state of mind. This helped him to grow stronger, realizing that he was now in control of the situation. He thought he would love to pull out the pack of cigarettes from his pocket and light one right in front of the Staffy. But he figured, why resort to cheap tactics to merely aggravate the poor fool? Chuck's response to the Staffy's eyeball treatment proved to be unsuccessful. The Staffy hoped to recover from his round one loss by using his superior position. The silence in the room was deafening and encouraged the usual nervous coughing used to fill a void. The two officers fidgeted in their chairs, probably wishing they were someplace else. It was unusual for them to be seated in the Purser's Offices without a drink in hand. As this was not a trial but an investigation, the Purser's Office had been enlisted instead of the Bridge. No notes were being taken nor were any records kept of the conversation. The proceedings were formally opened.

"Mr. Fisher," the Staff Captain addressed Chuck. "I expect you know why you have been called here?"

"Yes, Mr. Breathwaite. I suppose it has to do with the missing piano."

The veins stood out on the Staffy's temples as the musician fired back his answer using the cordial surname treatment and voice.

"Do you not have enough respect for an officer to address them properly as, sir?"

"On the contrary, I always refer to the Captain as sir, because I do respect his position. He is an officer and a gentleman. In this situation I feel it would be dishonest to bestow such title on you unless you are a knight of the realm and, somehow, I do not think that's possible."

More leg crossing from the spectators was in order as the Staffy attempted to regain his composure. Chuck was on a roll and was actually looking forward to the next pitch as much as the other officers.

"If this was a naval ship, I would know how to deal with you. You insolent pup." The Staffy played right into his opponent's hands.

"Ah, if we were on a naval ship, there wouldn't be a case of a missing piano, and we wouldn't be here enjoying each other's company." Chuck responded. He heard the shuffle from their audience as they noticed the Staffy's face only getting redder. Chuck could have sworn he heard a chuckle slip from his right. Chuck wasn't done yet.

"Seeing as there is no evidence that this was me, I don't see why I even need to be sitting here. And with that, I hope you have a great day." Chuck almost couldn't hold back his laughter as he made his way out of the office.

Chuck strolled to dinner with a grin on his face. After picking up a beer from the bar, he found his buddies and sat down across Walter.

There was a pause in the conversation as Chuck not only took a sip of his beer, but did some reflecting on his past life. He had often acquiesced to the wishes of others. Whether it was an artist questioning his ability or someone putting him down, he always tried to be the nice guy. But no more!

"You know, Walter, as I walked back from the Purser's Office, I was actually observing people for the very first time. That is something I have never done before. I could sort of feel their misery and unhappiness, but I was not a part of it. Right now, I am looking around this room and I feel that I can spot where these people are coming from. Sort of see into each of them. Does that make any sense at all?"

"Yes. Please go on, Chuck." Walter knew that he was right on the edge of a breakthrough.

"Probably the reason I avoided really looking at people before was because I was seeing my own misery and did not want to be reminded of it."

Walter leaned forward in his chair. Chuck found himself sharing a strong compassion for this man. Walter's eyes settled softly on his enlightened friend as he posed a question.

"How do you feel about all these people now?"

"I realize," Chuck began without hesitation, "that you can't tolerate anyone else until you can tolerate yourself."

"Very good, Chuck. Now get yourself below if you intend to make dinner tonight," Walter added with a smile.

"To tell you the truth, I do not feel too much like food. It's as though this good feeling has overcome the desire to eat. Who knows? Maybe we don't really need food. Maybe we only eat because we feel shitty most of the time and try to replace the happiness by stuffing ourselves full of garbage."

"Good thought, Chuck," replied Walter as he stood up to take his leave. "My advice is try and combine both sensibly. Starvation does not work."

"Well, Walter, I must confess. I intend to really tie one on tonight, and with any luck at all I'll stay drunk 'til New York!" Walter shook his head as they said good-bye.

Chuck headed for Bob's cabin where he found his buddies already involved in the usual after dinner nuptials and eagerly awaiting his return from destiny. He settled down with them and, while knocking back a few drinks, related the story of the Purser's Office. Little was said by the group who sat absolutely enthralled and enjoying every last morsel."

"Well," laughed Bob at the conclusion of Chuck's tale, "I must say this has been one helluva cruise. Between your antics and having that Staffy aboard, there has been no lack of excitement. Now tonight we have the craziest of the crazies – the fancy-dress ball!"

"Oh!" exclaimed Abe. "That's what all the fuss is about. People are running to and fro with loads of clothes and I was wondering what the hell was going on."

"Yes, Abe," Bob explained. "Every cruise we have this dumb night where the passengers act out their fantasies. The ship has lockers full of costumes available to the passengers who are not inventive enough to create their own."

"Everyone aboard," Chuck interjected, seeing the perfect opportunity to play with poor Abe's head, "has to be in fancy dress tonight. People tend to manifest what they would love to be by what they wear. So, what in the way of fancy dress do you have in mind, Abe?" The lads realized Chuck was playing a game with poor Abe as the band never, nor would they, dress in costumes like children.

"I, ah," Abe stammered as he looked sort of lost. "No one told me about this event, so I don't have any clothes. I don't have any idea what to wear. What am I going to do?" he implored.

"Well," answered Chuck, "as I said, you have to wear what suits your personality the most. So, there's no problem. Just stick a stick up your ass and go as a toffee apple!" The musicians howled while poor Abe fell back on the bunk smacking his forehead realizing they had done it to him again.

"By the way, fellows," Bob called them to order again and poured one last round, "the Purser asked that we not play the "Bridge on the River Kwai" song during the grand parade tonight. You know where you guys start singing the English lyrics, "Bollocks and the same to you Cobblers?" It seems that although we think it's funny, some of the passengers are familiar with these words and know we're poking fun at them. So, we better cool it!"

"Okay, Bob, we'll be good," said Scotty, and they all agreed.

"Wait a minute," interrupted Mike, "I have an idea! Why don't we just have a rap session for the parade instead of playing marches? Something we could rap together."

"Like what?" inquired Bob, frowning at the thought of his merry men creating a rap fit for passenger ears.

"Oh, let me think a minute," Mike responded looking deep in thought. "I know! I know! Like this:

>   Now, here we are one and all
>
>   At the S.S. Nectar's fancy dress ball
>
>   With good queen Bess the three musketeers
>
>   Roger the rabbit with great big ears
>
>   Now the musketeers want to bang queen Bess
>
>   And Roger the rabbit will handle with ease.
>
>   So, let's get together and have a ball
>
>   Have a great big orgy, have a great big orgy with
>
>   No holds at all.

If everyone there gets in his licks we will know why they call it "Down to the Sea for Kicks.""

"Get the hell out of here you dirty lot," yelled Bob, the leader, but with a soft spot for his gang. Bob closed the door behind them. When he turned, Abe was still sitting on Bob's bunk. "What do you want?" he asked Abe. "I thought you left with the rest of them."

Poor Abe was still trying to get on Bob's good side so he decided to offer a joke. "Bob, do you know who turned queer?" he asked, very secretive like a spy.

"No, I don't," replied Bob.

Now Abe was all alert with the punch line, "Give me a kiss and I'll tell you."

Bob could not suppress a giggle as he grabbed Abe and threw him out of the cabin.

"Yes, Bob, I would rather switch than fight." He was smiling as he strolled down the passageway. Abe then changed his thoughts. he remembered he had received an invitation for drinks in a certain lady's cabin. During his afternoon wanderings around the ship, he struck an acquaintance with a middle-aged matron. She was about forty-five and hot to trot. Madeline had confided in Abe that her husband was much older than she and confined to a wheelchair. Her loving husband had sent her on this holiday in appreciation for all her help and administration. Even Abe knew that her husband must have been very naïve in sending her off on a ship where celibacy was the last thought on any woman's mind.

Abe was ready. He had tasted the forbidden fruit and was now having a problem keeping his mind off his joint. He felt the invitation for drinks was really an invitation to be seduced. He had guessed from their conversation that she had not been serviced for some time. His own thoughts were causing him difficulty as he tried to suppress his overwhelming desire to screw the ship's mast or any other crevice that came into view. Madeline was a nicely built woman, and respectable looking. She was not gorgeous by any means, but possessed a sensuality that was driving Abe crazy. Abe was sure that she could have been laid from stem to stern by any of the free-floating studs who roamed the ship in constant lookout for new conquests. He also knew that was not what she wanted, because of her respectability. Abe was eagerly anticipating all sorts of sexual fantasies.

Abe was trembling slightly as he made his way through the First-Class section towards her cabin. He thought to himself that he really posed no real threat. Her slight flirtation with a seemingly innocent youth would lesson any breach of promise to her husband, John. As Abe approached her cabin, he remembered the warning from Bob about any spies looking for musicians entering passenger cabins. He was looking up and down the passageway, but before he could knock, the door opened suddenly as if she had been standing behind the portal listening and waiting. Madeline was wrapped in a beautiful silk bedroom gown. Abe walked through the door and realized that was all she was wearing.

"So, you decided to visit me," she said. "I thought maybe you had forgotten, you naughty little boy."

"Oh. Ah. No," Abe stammered. He was caught off guard a little. She must like little boys he thought. "I just had to be briefed for the program tonight. You know the Grand Ball. It changes our normal schedule."

"Sit down," she invited indicating the end of the bed. "What would you like to drink, Abe?"

"Scotch and water," he replied. He had learned from his friends that scotch was a more sophisticated drink and certainly more civilized than rum and coke.

Madeline walked across the large room to the bar. Her cabin seemed more like a good-sized hotel room. The bed was in the center of the room instead of against the bulkhead like the lesser priced cabins. As she returned with the two drinks, he could easily view the length and shape of her leg protruding the opening of her gown. He was trying to control himself. Madeline joined Abe on the end of the bed. They clinked glasses and attempted to make small talk. Abe tried to quell the shaking in his body. He could smell her tantalizing perfume. The shapely thighs under the silk robe in such close proximity were driving him nuts. She started running her hand through his hair, then she kissed him lightly on the lips. She knew he was ready to burst. She took his hand and placed it inside her gown on top of her breast. This time her kiss only preceded her tongue going down his throat.

Abe was visibly shaken. Should he rape her or shout for his Mama? This was far more than even he had fantasized. Mama was not needed. Abe felt his seducer slip to the floor between his legs. She quickly tore at the zipper on his fly, and Abe simply looked down at the top of her head in wonder. She had his fully erect self in her hand and was fondling the top. It looked like an English Bobby's helmet! Abe gurgled in delight as the more experienced Madeline went into her deep throat act, but not before she piously looked to the ceiling and proclaimed, "Forgive me, John."

A few minutes later they were laying together on the bed. Her gown was fully open revealing her naked body.

"Kiss my darling," she moaned. Abe leaned toward her lips ready to oblige.

"Not here. Down there," she rebuked pushing his head between her legs.

Abe's first instinct was to run for his life. He had heard of such things happening, but had always thought that he could never solicit that kind of act. Yet he was under her command and with the state he was in there were no holds barred.

After his wild experience, he returned to the Inner Sanctum. He felt totally spent and weak at the knees. He entered Scotty's and Chuck's cabin to find them dressed and enjoying a little shooter.

"What the hell happened to you?" asked Chuck seeing the expression on Abe's face. "You look worse than you did in Haiti after that big black ass!"

"I need a drink," said Abe as he collapsed on the bunk, still in a dreamlike state.

"Here," Scotty offered as he silently studied the little guy and wondered if someone had turned him on to some smokes or something.

"You know," Abe stopped to take a gulp from the glass, "all those descriptions of sex you guys use?" he took another gulp as his listeners eagerly awaited his story. "I have experienced them all tonight!"

"Yeah!" Chuck's interest peaked. "Like what?"

"Well," began Abe in a more excited voice and keen on relating his latest exploits. "There was muff diving. Yodeling up the canyon. Sucky, sucky. My ass feels so puckered it's like it's been sown shut!"

"Who is she?" interrupted Scotty in shock. "Someone we know?"

"Ha! Ha!" replied Abe pointing his finger at them. "That you will never know! So, don't waste your time asking again. She's a lady!"

"After what you just told us. She ain't no lady," laughed Chuck.

"That's right," agreed Scotty.

Abe thought a moment, then joined in the merriment. The three left the cabin singing together, "She's a lady – She's a lady – She's as quiet as a mouse!"

The fancy dress ball went off without a hitch. The usual prizes were given for the various categories of costume. The hit of the evening was the most inventive costumer. A nondescript little man dressed in a raincoat complete with umbrella, derby hat and briefcase. The surprise came during the grand parade. He appeared to be wearing a suit under the raincoat, but this was an illusion. His trousers only went to his knees and were held in place with garters. His collar and tie were just that! No shirt at all! Indeed, the flasher was the most inventive costume. The musicians were disappointed to see that he was wearing a special pair of jockey shorts. However, they did laugh when they read the inscription, "Where's the beef?"

The dance finished at 1:00 a.m. and it was not necessary for them to play in the night club that night. They were all pretty beat from the evening, so they headed back to the Inner Sanctum. Chuck was feeling no pain. He had been drinking very heavy all night, so instead of roaming the ship looking for drinking pals, he just crashed in his own bunk. His buddies were quite surprised, but understood that he had been through a lot today. None of the groupies were invited below tonight, even though the boys were gathered in Bob's cabin. They were settled down for a rather peaceful evening, including Abe. There were laughs to be shared over Abe's love making expedition and deep philosophical discussions that were accompanied with the usual libation.

By 2:30 a.m. the lads were nice and shit-faced. A mischievous mood, commonly shared by musicians, was setting in, and the subject of their practical joke would be their own sleeping beauty, Chuck. He won this auspicious honor as payment for this misguided desire to wake them the day before after returning from his drunken booze orgy. Now it was their chance for revenge.

"Here's the plan," began Tex, culprit and ringleader of the event. "You, Scotty! Wake him up just as you normally do and let him think it's time for us to play the cocktail session."

"Okay," replied Scotty, eager to partake in a little larceny.

"The rest of us will dress and walk past the open door, you know, as though we were on our way to the dance deck," continued Tex to his partners in crime.

"I'll bet he goes through his whole routine and falls for the gag," added Scotty. They were all still giggling as Scotty stood up and prepared for his command performance.

"Wakey! Wakey! Show a leg me luck lad. Up and at 'em Chuck, ol' boy," greeted Scotty as he shook his poor buddy trying to arouse him. "Come on it's time to get up!"

Chuck's bleary, blood shot eyes made every effort to open. He tried several times before he was successful in sitting upright on his bunk. Chuck began to mutter something totally unintelligible as he finally vacated the bed. In the meantime, Scotty was dressing himself. He put on his bow tie and white tux jacket.

"See ya top side," said Scotty to Chuck as he left the cabin.

Chuck stood at the washstand trying to prepare himself. He applied the shaving soap around the inlet that held the cigarette.

"Aren't you ready yet?" shouted Abe as he passed the cabin.

"Oh! Dracula's awake," barked Jimmy.

"Delay thar," said Tex, "the be after puttin' a move on. Har! Har!"

It was fifteen minutes later before Chuck was dressed and ready to commence his journey to the Prom deck. He was still staggering slightly, but he just figured it was the motion of the ship. He climbed two decks, then walked amidships to the elevator in order to ride the rest of the trip. It did not seem to bother him that everywhere he had been seemed deserted. The elevator didn't stop on any deck during his trip. He left the elevator, walked down the corridor, past the pantry, and into the ballroom. The mischief makers had taken their positions outside the windows of the Grand Lounge. Bob was trying to keep them quiet as they eagerly awaited their prey. His buddies stood watching breathlessly. Chuck climbed onto the bandstand and sat down at the piano. The lads never guessed that their gag would go this far. All of a sudden, a figure appeared in the empty room. It was the night watchman doing his clock run. He was not expecting to see Chuck sitting alone on the bandstand at this hour.

"Hi Chuck," he greeted the lonesome figure. "Having some late-night practice?"

"Late night practice?" queried Chuck looking down at the master-at-arms. "What do you mean, late night practice? What time is it?" Chuck looked as if he might have just landed here from another planet.

"Why it's about three thirty," answered the obliging watchman. "Three thirty a.m."

"Three thirty?" Chuck sat for a moment struggling with this battle in his head. His friends were still waiting outside with baited breath. "Wait a minute. Wait just a damn minute here!" The penny had dropped. Raising his hand above his head he began to roar, "I'll kill em! I'll kill em! Those rotten bastards done this to me! I'll kill the lot of them!"

Just as he stood up from the piano, he heard a little rap rap rap on the window. He looked in that direction to see his laughing buddies waving bye-bye just before they began to run down the deck. Chuck took off too in hot pursuit. He looked like an enraged bull intent on committing murder. The villains had a good head start on him, though. Finally, Chuck burst into the Inner Sanctum very tired and out of breath, only to find the cabins empty. Not a soul in sight. He figured they must be with their gals or hiding out somewhere else on board, so he just crawled back into bed. It was about five a.m., and Chuck passed out almost immediately. The devilish lads were glad that he was out for the count and returned to their bunks from their hiding place, the mortuary!

DAY 9
AT SEA

The Nectar proceeded north along the American coastline. The passengers and crew were aroused at about seven a.m. by a squall. This was common and could happen at any time in the Atlantic. Passengers who had previously considered themselves seasoned sailors after only a week of sailing on a virtual mill pond, were now subjected to the real sea. Unfortunately, very few of them realized what it was to experience such rough weather. It was a shame that the vacationers should conclude an otherwise pleasant vacation under these circumstances, but that is the nature of the elements. Many were confined to their bunks. This, of course, was the worst place to be. The brave traveled the decks only to be seen either hanging over the rail or walking around looking the color of most of the Irish on St. Patrick's Day.

Down in the musicians' quarters the tossing of the ship was much worse because they were at the very end of the ship. Not only was she rolling, but the Nectar was engaged in a fore and aft pitch. This created a thrill as the screws completely cleared the water permitting them to run free at a much higher than normal speed. Each time this happened the lads felt as though they had little propellers attached to their asses and were about to be shot from a canon. The stern would then drop about thirty feet back to the water. This would leave the musicians in midair as if they were totally levitated. Their bodies would crash back onto their mattresses much like an astronaut experiencing a force of ten G's. Sleep was practically impossible, and so they each just lay in their bunks enjoying the ride in a very nonchalant manner. All except Abe. He was the only one who was not feeling very well. In fact, he felt green around the gills, which went with his white knuckles as he held onto the rail around his bunk. For a while he was sure the ship was sinking and he was about to face his maker. The deadlight was closed over the porthole so Abe could not see the water, but he could hear it as the ship dunked up and down.

"Christ," said Abe to Jimmy, "I feel like we're in a fucking submarine with that water out there. Will the port hold up against those waves?"

"Yeah, sure," replied Jimmy, "this will pass soon. It is only one of life's little inconveniences."

Each of the minstrels, including Abe, tried dozing off and on. After the previous late night, they all felt totally numb. Tom dropped by with the sandwiches but just deposited some in each cabin.

"Rehearsal is scheduled for ten a.m.," remarked Scotty to Chuck. "But the weather has probably cancelled that."

"Yeah, we might as well stay in bed and enjoy this roller coaster."

Scotty was just getting into that subconscious state he called the twilight zone when the door opened with a crash. Chuck and Scotty came fully awake with this sudden noise. They focused in on the apparition before them. It was Bob, their illustrious leader, looking like the purple people eater. His eyes were bulging like organ stops.

"What the hell do you think this is?" He screamed at the not quite sober pair. "Rehearsal was called for ten o'clock and none of you assholes made an appearance! Get out of those bloody bunks and get where you are supposed to be immediately or by God, I'll turn the hoses on you!"

Chuck, startled by Bob's outburst, looked at Scotty in surprise before saying to Bob, "What the fuck are we going to rehearse? The act of trying to stand up!"

"It makes no difference," yelled Bob. "You had a rehearsal call and that means if you are a pro, you attend regardless of weather. Now I expect all of you topside in five minutes!"

Each of the cabins received the same wrath before beginning the struggle of shaking off the cobwebs and ultimately finding their way to the night club. It was a sorry looking bunch of musicians who entered the place of rehearsal to find Bob, the Cruise Director, and Jan Kelly, the singer, awaiting their presence. The comedian and magician were not in attendance. Their acts were straight forward enough. It was only Jan who required a run through as her material was different for each show. Bob was aghast to see his gallant crew dressed in brown chino pants and T-shirts. In order to meet the five-minute command, they had donned their clothes in haste.

"How dare you call yourselves professional musicians dressed like that!" Bob was on his high horse again as he stared in disbelief at his motley crew. "Get below and put on ties! You will require them when I take you to the bridge to be logged! Now get those ties on at once!"

As the lads shuffled off and left the club, they could not believe their ears at Bob's unreasonable request. And he had never threatened them with being logged. Scotty was the last one through the club door, so he did a little Stan Laurel imitation before following his buddies. They looked to each other and Chuck got an idea. "Bob said we had to get our ties on, fellas. Let's make sure to get that done straight away." Chuck then grabbed his tie and tied it around his head.

Scotty laughed at Chuck before saying to Jimmy, "Bob is going to shit a brick. This is going to help my hangover" The rest of the crew joined in and returned to the club playing their instruments with ties on their heads.

Bob's companions burst into laughter at the audacity. Bob did a couple of spins, appeared stuck for words, and finally gave in to the musicians' piece de resistance. They stood in a line with their feet together and hands at their sides. When the ship rolled to port, they leaned toward starboard as if cheating gravity. This was the same effect comedians use on stage when their boots are bolted to the floor. The lads had perfected the technique over the years and had demonstrated it to passengers on many occasions. The only one having problems was Abe, who looked like the little guy in the Harmonicats who could never find his place in the group. In addition to this routine, they began to sing the opening number from the show, "How do you do everyone! How do you doo-dily doo-dily doo..." Bob knew it would be useless to continue any form of chastisement. And their little act changed his whole mood.

"Tom," Bob shouted, "go below and fetch a couple of bottles of Scotch."

"I'm highly amused at the antics of your gang, Bob," stated Jan. "I must confess that I had some trepidations about coming on this cruise. My worst fears were that I would have to put up with inferior musicians. Men who would have difficulty playing my charts. But I couldn't be happier. I've really enjoyed having you fellows back me up!"

The accolade helped restore Bob to his good-natured self. Whatever had been bothering him blew over. Tom returned with the requested spirits, and Bob did the honors.

"Feeling rough, Abe?" Bob asked, noticing Abe looked a little out of sorts.

"Yeah. I'm not sure that I can put the sax in my mouth for rehearsal. I can't throw up, but I feel like I want to."

"Tom," called Scotty, "mission of mercy. Go below and fetch us a bottle of gin, please."

"Sure thing, Scotty," replied Tom, eager to help his buddies. Tom returned promptly with the elixir. Scotty took the bottle and half-filled an eight-ounce glass with the medicinal potion. He escorted Abe to the corridor outside the men's room.

"This," Scotty advised his seasick friend, "is an old English sailor's cure for what ails you. Now just do what I tell you."

"Sure, Scotty," replied Abe weakly as he accepted the glass of gin and they entered the men's room.

"Now I will count to three and on three you will drink the gin straight down in one gulp. Then go right into the toilet. The way you're feeling, this will bring up your whole guts, but make you feel brand new again. Okay?"

"Sure, Scotty, anything," Abe replied ready to follow whatever command would remove the ton of lead that was sitting in his bowels.

"One last caution before you start to heave," warned Scotty.

"What's that?"

"If a small brown ring comes up, swallow fast, because that's your asshole!"

"Fuck you, Scotty," snapped Abe lifting the glass to his mouth in readiness.

"One, two, three," Scotty counted off.

Abe threw back his head and chug-a-lugged the gin as instructed. At first Abe's eyes bulged in their sockets. His face went from a greenish tint to scarlet. Then his cheeks blew out all of a sudden and he charged into the cubicle. The gin had found its mark and rebounded from his stomach bringing forth everything, including his ingrown toenails.

Pleased with his handiwork, Scotty returned to the club for rehearsal. He was followed a few minutes later by the patient, who was well and smiling now.

"Say, Abe," remarked Bob, "you certainly look more chipper. Feel better?"

"I sure do," came the reply. "Give us a fucking drink and let's get going here with this rehearsal!" The band just laughed at the little monster they had helped to create while Bob merely shook his head.

They soon finished the rehearsal, had their lunch, and went off to enjoy their free afternoon. Leaving the dining room, Scotty passed Walter's table.

"Hi, Walter," he greeted his friend. "We'll be in aft library this afternoon because it's a little too cool on deck."

The weather had improved. The sea was smooth once again, which made the ship's motion acceptable to the passengers.

Jimmy, Chuck, and Scotty had settled down with their beers and copies of the ship's newspaper when Walter entered the library and joined the trio.

"Well, gentlemen," greeted Walter, seating himself in one of the large comfortable leather chairs, "I see you have obtained copies of the ship's paper and, I expect much like its counterpart ashore, it is just a compilation of negative postulates." It took a couple minutes for the group to analyze the statement and realize Walter was referring to the mayhem and sensationalism that all tabloids contain. Especially those big city daily news types.

"Yeah," remarked Scotty, "we were just discussing these terrorist acts. What the hell is the world coming to? I know we agreed it was an insane society, but now more and more innocent people are getting killed. First it was airplanes, and now even ships are being threatened.

Christ, the day might come when we have to add guns to our equipment. Can you imagine? Have drums and gun – will travel!"

"That's good," approved Chuck.

"Of course," interjected Jimmy, looking very thoughtful, "the way I see it is everything has political overtones. And that of course usually involves lots of lies. Looking at it objectively, the Arabs did get a raw deal from history. The Irish have the same problem."

"Let me tell you about the Irish," demanded Scotty. "The British displaced the Irish supporters to the North and thus created the Orange Free State. This left the South to nothing but misery and poverty. Just like they did in India by creating Pakistan. What do the authorities expect to achieve from solutions like uprooting people and transplanting them like a mere house plant?"

"It seems that whenever there is a lie, there is trouble," continued Chuck. "Now what is the truth about the Middle East? We forget how many Arabs were displaced there or, as Scotty says, "transplanted." The politician tells us that Israel was intended as a homeland for the Jew, but could this be put to the test? Don't forget that the major powers had to agree among themselves before Israel was allowed to exist. Russia was only too happy to give its endorsement in order to get British Imperialism out of the Middle East. Now, it has to contend with American Imperialism. The question really is, was the creation of Israel really to supply a homeland for the Jew or use him as cannon fodder in the war against the Arabs? Remember, there are always two opposing factions. Even among the Jews, and I believe they prefer being called Israelis, anyway, even they detest what is taking place and are beginning to realize they are pawns. The Zionist, which is a militant group as far as I'm concerned, appears to have the upper hand. Walter has told us that there will always be problems when there is a lie involved. And I think there are a lot involved in the Middle East."

"I think you're right," acknowledged Jimmy. "History also shows that it is always the good and trusting people that are killed in conflicts. Never the people who start the war or finance the war or profit from the war."

"I've sat quietly listening to your points of view, and you are each well informed both in current affairs and history. All I can say is what I've said before, we live in a truly insane society. Each one of us must start to understand the workings of the spiritual universe. If we don't, we will continue to solve insane problems with insane solutions. You have probably heard this many times, but nothing can be achieved with force because force only begets force. Remember, you cannot commit any transgression without creating your own punishment. I think I told you how people will call the police and confess to murder and things. This is because of guilt. They know that they've done something and now try to create their own punishment. As to the Middle East and who's right or wrong, let's look at it from what we have discussed so far. As you know, I am totally opposed to violence and abhor the killing of anyone whether he be Jew, Arab, Irish, or whatever."

"Me too," agreed Chuck.

"That's right," said Jimmy.

"Well maybe the Irish," snickered Scotty with that devilish look of his. "Oh, I'm only kidding. You guys must be Irish."

"Why's that?" asked Jimmy seriously.

"No sense of humor," replied Scotty, trying to lighten the conversation.

"Getting back to business," Walter called them to order after their teasing session. "These fish wrappers that we are exposed to, called newspapers, and that my fine fellows is the extent of their value, are used by the politician to vent his rage against the perpetrators who are committing terrorist attacks. This politician is saying nothing but justification, justification, justification. Look what these terrorists are doing to us. Over and over it is always the same, look what they are doing to us. Has anyone, just once, suggested taking a look at these terrorist attacks from the guilt-punishment angle? What is it we are doing to them, to cause them to do this to us?"

"Yeah," interrupted Scotty, "all you ever hear is that it's always their fault. I remember you said that no person, group or nation could engage in a disagreement without the incidence of another. We don't have to look far to see the other interfering factor. Will the people ever wake up and realize what kind of game the politician is playing? You know it would be such a nice world if it was run by musicians! Right?"

"Right!" agreed Chuck and Jimmy with a cheer.

"What we should do is bring back public hangings and hang at least ten politicians every Monday! Right?"

"Right!" they cheered again turning the conversation to a lighter side.

"And six rock and roll bands! Right?" Scotty was on a roll now.

"Right!"

"Two policewomen! Right?"

"Right!"

"Five male ballet dancers! Right?"

"Right!" they continued to cheer with hands held high for power.

"Ten newspaper reporters! Right?"

"Right!"

"And a partridge in a pear tree," sang Scotty at the top of his lungs.

They all had a good laugh. Even Walter had to smile at this crazy threesome of smart and talented musicians. They settled down to the business at hand after Albee had brought them a new round of beers and a pot of hot tea for Walter.

"What kind of beings are these whose whole profession is a lie?" asked Scotty, referring to his favorite subject, the politician. "If the public think they are concerned with solving the problems of the masses, then their heads are up their asses. Do you know where the real homes of organized crime are?" he asked, looking at the group intently. "I'll tell you. The British Houses of Parliament and Capitol Hill in Washington, D.C. These, as far as I'm concerned, are inhabited by criminals who serve no one but their benefactors. The only man who has ever entered the Houses of Parliament with honest intentions was Guy Fawkes!"

This brought a smile to Walter's face, because Guy Fawkes was involved in the Gunpowder Plot on November 5, 1605. This was a conspiracy to blow up Parliament while King James I was participating in the opening day ceremonies. The gunpowder was stored in the cellar of the House of Lords. Guy Fawkes was arrested as he entered the cellar. This uprising of English Catholics only worsened their plight.

"Any man that would condone the destruction of life or property, as in the case of the statesman, regardless of what country he belongs, is a sick man manifesting his own insanity. Furthermore, any man who would carry out the destruction of life or property, as in the case of a soldier, regardless of what country he belongs, is a sick man and manifesting his own insanity." A thoughtful silence followed Walter's statement. Each musician was absorbed in his own thoughts in relation to what he had just heard.

"Well," asked Chuck, "how would that apply to defending one's self? Do you recommend turning the other cheek?"

"Not at all, Chuck. What I am talking about is that people of all nations have to examine themselves and ask themselves why they are in a situation where they are getting themselves killed. Also, on the political side, what reason do they have to be in another man's country killing him?" What is the truth? Not what the politician tells us. Now back to your question on a more personal level. Only a sane man would know how to use anger to handle an angry person. Unfortunately, the usual Homosapien only knows anger from emotions which is a sickness in itself."

"I'm not sure I follow you on that," said Jimmy. "Could you elaborate please, Walter?"

"Certainly, my friend. If a person was in a high state of beingness, where anger was beneath him, he could knowingly descend to that level and use it to dispel the threatening individual. And believe me, a knowing being using anger has ten times the power of the man dispersed with emotion. Do you understand now, Jimmy?"

"Yes, Walter. Thank you."

"Now to finish on this subject, the sane man can easily return from the angry to his original altitude without any ill effects. But the poor soul who started it all by using emotion will go home with a headache or worse."

"Yeah," exclaimed Scotty, "and considering the odds of insane people against sane it appears that it would be more threatening and dangerous to be sane in this world."

"Christ," said Chuck, "can you imagine the loneliness? It would be like a sober man in among a bunch of drunks!"

"You could use that analogy, Chuck," said Walter laughingly. "And that's why I never visit your Inner Sanctum."

"Touché," answered Scotty.

"Walter," Chuck asked, "knowing how you feel about violence and all the stupidity that goes with it, how do you feel about gun possession?" The musicians knew what direction one would take on this subject, but waited in anticipation for his educated elaboration.

"Guns, my friends," he began sitting back in his chair, wearing a little smile and stroking his chin, "are, as we have discussed, nothing more than a product of a sick society. Guns, to use your jargon, are box office. Enormous profits are made in the manufacturing of these weapons. Every time the gun control issue hits the paper, sales boom. In other words, the rich get richer. Whether it's individual ownership, small skirmishes, or large wars. Money is being generated by this disgusting industry."

"And by creating wars," interjected Scotty, "we supply a ready market for the armaments and the big boys make more money."

"And," added Jimmy, "this serves to convince the populous of the need for more guns, armies, and such, thus more taxes."

"That's right," answered Walter, "you boys are well informed. Chuck, let's get back to your original question of turning the other cheek as it applies to our life in the home. The Constitution guarantees the American citizen, and by the way this applies only to citizens, the right to bear arms. The politician will inform you that this right was only referring to protecting yourself in time of war. Or that it only applied to the early settlers who feared the British. In fact, the politician would like nothing more than to change the Constitution and deprive you of this right and your guns while at the same time enlarging his own arsenal."

"Yeah!" exclaimed Jimmy, "He is not doing us any favors when you considered the situation ashore with all the crazies that are running around armed. And they do not hesitate in using their guns either."

"There's another side to it," interrupted Chuck. "When some nut goes berserk and commits some murderous act on innocent people, the politician immediately starts the wheels in motion to ban weapons. You never hear them ask, as Walter has told us, what is the cause of this criminal's mental problem? The politician only wants to blame the gun.

Why, most of the time the criminal gets off with a slap on the wrist."

"That's right," Scotty intervened. "The politician puts the machinery into motion to arouse public sympathy and outcry. And soon John Doe Public is voting away his own rights. When will the working man see the game?"

"Ha! Ha!" said Walter, once more in charge of his little group. "Game is the proper word. But why do you think the politician would adopt this method of retrieving your guns? Is he afraid that I might shoot you or that you might shoot me? I doubt it. Could it be that he's afraid that we might shoot him and his fellow politicians?"

"Of course," agreed Jimmy.

"What other reason would they have to confiscate our weapons?" piped Scotty in full agreement. "If the game is to control, it would be more difficult with two hundred million guns out there on the streets."

Albee appeared again to replenish their beverages.

"Scotty," Walter began after they had settled down with their fresh beers. "Two words seem to be entering our discussion and they are game and control. These two words play a very important part in our lives. A moment ago, you also mentioned creating wars. Do you have some information that you would like to share on that subject?"

"Well," replied Scotty after taking a long sip of beer and then laying the glass down on the table in an effort to sort out his thoughts. "The way I see it is that wars are not caused by some upstart who wants to conquer the world. As a matter of fact, such a feat would be damn near impossible in itself and stupid to attempt. No, I see it as a game that is well thought out and planned. Not just the conflict, but even the end result is already forecast." Only the sound of Scotty's voice could be heard as it accompanied the gentle vibrations of the ship's engines. "Many historians blame the Treaty of Versailles and its cruel reparation clauses as the cause of World War II. Also, the French marching through the Ruhr in 1926 when Germany was on her knees. But it appears to me that this was just fuel for the fire and was meant to serve a greater purpose later. As a matter of fact, going back to World War I, I was reading just recently how in 1916 Germany, much to the dismay of the parasites who were responsible for the war, was running out of money and food for the German people, and would be unable to continue the war. Paul Warburg, the head of the Federal Reserve at that time, made arrangements to issue credit to help Germany. Food was more difficult to acquire than bullets, so the Belgium Relief Fund was created. It was through this Fund that they funneled supplies to Germany via Belgium. This entitled the enemy to continue World War I for two more years, thus allowing America to enter."

"Jesus! Is that true?" asked Jimmy aghast.

"Can you believe that shit?" stated Chuck.

"And do you know something else?" continued Scotty. "The more I read on this subject, the more I realize that there's more than just money at stake. There is a terrible desire by madmen for power and control."

"Yes, Scotty, there is much to what you say," said Walter picking up the conversation. "Many writers have produced evidence of this kind of corruption, but as long as the public remains apathetic, these kinds of atrocities will continue. It's like trying to get people to understand the existence of the spiritual universe. Oh, they will discuss it. Go to their various churches and rant and rave about it. But they never seem to accept it. That's why the merchants of death get away with the game. They can always sway the attention of the masses to believe such a situation does not exist."

"That's for sure. And when the propaganda merchants bang the drum, everyone marches to the beat." Scotty expressed his ideas even further. "Young men are drafted and convinced that the cause deserves fighting for and dying for, whether it does or not. Yours is not to reason why. Yours is but to do and die. The young fellows buy it."

"Please continue," encouraged Walter. "It is not often I meet someone as well informed as you."

"Thanks, Walter," replied Scotty, eager to continue. "What I can't understand is how the politician avoids real issues and not only gets away with it but gets elected over and over again. For instance, let's take the Federal Reserve System in America. If the politician was really interested in the country, surely he would do something about an institution that is bankrupting the very country he professes to want to help. Why, most Americans do not even know that this organization is privately owned. The stock is held by six major banks. These same people have owned and manipulated the system since its inception. Joe Public will tell you that the Federal Reserve is the U.S. Government. No wonder he votes the way he does! He is uninformed! Anyway, these banks have grown and profited over the years while other banks have been failing by the hundreds. Look at the question of illegal aliens. Sure, no one would deny a hungry child or destitute person help, but it has gone beyond that. Under the pretense of a philanthropic gesture, the gates of America have been thrown open. There is no longer a quota system in America. People worry about the illegals from Mexico, that's only one problem. Thousands come in every day from Asian countries, India, Europe, and even Russia."

Scotty was interrupted by Jimmy, who decided to throw in a little humor, "Do you know who is responsible for all these Asians flooding into America?" Jimmy waited only briefly before answering his own question. "I'll tell you. It's the fucking tobacco companies! Have you ever noticed how they smoke? Jesus Christ, they must do ten packs a day. I've yet to see an oriental who does not have a cigarette stuck in his face. Here in America, we're getting away from smoking. It seems to me that the industry had to find a new market for their filth. So, what better way to go. And don't forget the medical profession also stands to gain from the abuse of tobacco."

The listeners realized that Jimmy was being more factitious than bigoted, but they did agree that smoking was more prevalent among those on the lower rungs of the socioeconomic ladder.

"You know, Scotty," said Chuck, "you have often accused me of not having any soul."

"True enough," responded Scotty, wondering where he was going with this remark.

"Well," began Chuck, looking very pensive as he put his thoughts into words, "maybe it is the smoking that kills the soul? After all, the Asians talk about their long history and culture, but what was it? One tribe killing off another! And what kind of nut sticks a sword in his own belly and rips out his guts?"

"Yeah," interrupted Jimmy, "and they can't even play jazz!"

"I see your point," added Walter, ready to add a little instruction. "Remember, we have agreed that we are each a soul or a spirit. If someone chooses to put a weed into his mouth and breathe not only the tobacco but all the added chemicals, including cyanide, this decision had to be influenced by outside sources. There is no other reason for such insanity."

"So, you fellows are really saying that I'm a screwball because I smoke," said Chuck, somewhat irritated.

"EXACTLY!!" chorused Jimmy and Scotty.

"Getting back to what we were talking about," began Scotty after the laughter had ceased, "if you can buy an airline ticket, you can come on over. This is not legal immigration; it's an invasion. There are no health exams like there was when I immigrated, consequently the public health systems in places like Los Angeles and Miami are at the breaking point. Diseases that this country hasn't had for years are commonplace again. And jobs! Let me tell you about jobs. I saw what happened in

England after the war. They opened the doors to all and sundry when the country was down and unemployment became rampant. Look at the mess in Scotland. You have three generations of Scots that have never worked. The politician must have a reason for ignoring these problems and in some cases encouraging them."

Scotty's cheeks were flush with excitement. He took another gulp from his glass. These problems were near and dear to him. His life spanned poverty, war, and success, but he could see the circle returning.

"Yes guys, as far as I'm concerned it is all planned just like I said before. Whether it is war, unemployment, or whatever."

"Scotty, what do you think is the reason these conditions are allowed to happen?" asked Walter.

"As far as I can see, it's to subjugate the American citizen and wipe out the most powerful producer there is – the American middle class. This is being done in other countries too. Look what has already taken place with all this immigration. Take the profession for example. These cruise ships are being chartered by syndicates. They immediately dump the professional seaman and replace him with minorities at less than a quarter of the salary. The poor passenger never thinks that the steward who doesn't know an omelet from porridge is the person he may have to depend on if there is an emergency. The syndicates tell you anyone can wait tables. But remember, the Merchant Marines were seamen first and waiters second. These syndicates won't deal with unions either. My brother-in-law, as an example, had thirty years at sea and he was given redundancy pay and sent home to England. A couple of years ago in Los Angeles a television station ran an exposé on the cruise ships and how the minorities were being treated. They described it as slave labor, and that's exactly what it is, fucking slave labor! The same shit I experienced on my first trip to sea. Everyone enjoyed the address from their buddy and sat silently as Scotty appeared to be getting more emotional.

"Isn't this what's happened all through industry? Syndicates take over companies, factories, or the airlines, then under the protection of the law, imposed by the dishonorable politician, implement standards to reduce the well-being of the workers. Employees lose their benefits, including retirements and pensions. The American worker is being put in a box. He has been brainwashed to accept all these negatives as necessary. His home is being foreclosed. The cars in every garage have been repossessed. What's left? He lands on the street homeless. What the fuck is going on?"

"Yes, Scotty," Walter began to explain, "as you say, there appears to be a ploy afoot, and it has been going on for a long time. Conditions have deteriorated. When you considered that America has gone from the most powerful and affluent society to the biggest debtor nation, it does look suspicious. If there is a game to subjugate the middle class and reduce them to a substandard way of life, then it would be difficult to do while there are two hundred million guns in the hands of the citizenry, as we've discussed. Remember the state Germany was in after World War I? The country was so bad off with massive unemployment and tremendous inflation, and totally disorganized as a result of the vindictive peace policy imposed by the victors. What was the result of this chaos? The German people would welcome anyone who could solve their problems. That person was Hitler, who came along at the right time, and they welcomed him with open arms. Whether or not he was evil is not the point at the moment. He proved to be a very astute politician and did begin to bring order to the country. Now you say, how could a man like this rise from total obscurity and build the most powerful war machine in the world in such a short time? All this takes money. Agree so far?"

"Sure," replied Jimmy, "and it would take lots of money which Germany did not have at that time."

"Correct," acknowledged Walter. "Then where did all the money come from? I'll tell you, from the so-called enemies. Financing was arranged by this country also. The German industries were only too happy to subscribe, because they knew Hitler was preparing for war, and they would make big profits. By the way, there is plenty of material written on the subject of Hitler's benefactors. It is up to you to locate and study them if you wish the truth. That applies to everyone. John Doe Public, as we have been calling the people of America and the world, must make the effort to investigate the truth. They have to stop accepting what they read in newspapers and hear on T.V. as the truth. Now the reason I used the example of Hitler is this. Is it possible that Hitler, himself, was a victim used by the merchants of death to further their cause? As Scotty already pointed out, wars are created and well thought out." Walter paused for a sip of his tea while the fellows concentrated carefully on all the statements he had made.

"What," asked Jimmy, looking very serious, "considering all these things to be factual, is the situation today regarding Russia? We seem to supply them constantly with money and low interest, long term loans that industries here cannot receive. We supply Russia with food while our own people are going hungry. And why would any country give the latest technology to its biggest enemy? When you look at all these daily occurrences, it certainly does appear suspicious."

"Of course it looks suspicious," stated Scotty, leaning forward to emphasize his feelings. "That is what I mean when I say wars are created. We must constantly have an enemy to keep all this shit going."

"Your politician has to keep you convinced that your economy is tied to the constant threat of perpetual war," added Walter. "Having convinced the nation of this, he now has a license to tax, rape, and exploit the hell out of you for this cause that he is creating. So, as you can see, it's all a game with only the merchants of death as the winner."

"For this game to be played," spoke Jimmy, "all the leaders of the so-called enemy countries would have to be in on it together."

"And why not?" answered Scotty. "Don't forget they are also politicians and, as we have agreed, are a pretty dishonorable breed.

Remember that old saying? You never bite the hand that feeds you."

"Yes, maybe one day the public will decide to investigate these things. I think they will be surprised to find that the so-called great leaders are all tarred with the same brush and are just a group of jolly, good pals," added Walter.

"What amazes me," continued Chuck, "is what kind of man could even condone or carry out the destruction of life and property? I know you mentioned before, Walter, how sick they are, but what gets them that way? We, for example, do not have any desire to be so cruel to our fellow man. What differentiates the politician or head of state or even the soldier from us?"

"Chuck, there are many reasons for such inhumane behavior. And believe me," continued Walter, "that subject alone would involve a serious study of the spiritual universe. But to try to explain it rather simplistic, I would say that the people you mentioned, as spiritual beings, have degraded and have been degraded for so long that such a way of life is all they know. Like a child who is born physically ill accepts his illness because he has never experienced being well. These degraded beings desire control, and that desire is so strong that they are devoid of any humanity. They only know destruction. You can see this in their way of life. Total ownership of all and sundry is their goal. Such a disposition creates the desire to accumulate as much of the physical universe as possible. This desire is occurring now in the youth of the world. You have your yuppies in America. The young Japanese fly all over the world to buy any and everything. The T.V. will tell you that the once poor Russian has lots of money to spend, but no products to buy. This drive of complete ownership becomes a trap in itself. The more solid objects such as Villas, property, castles, or Rolls Royces they add to their collection, the more solid they themselves become as a result. Try to imagine a spirit as being a light, airy, free, transparent entity. If this spirit becomes tied to all his "things" he becomes solid like his "things." The more solid a spirit or the person becomes, the less feeling he has for other persons or humanity. He only cares about his "things" not mankind. Thus, you create wars and joblessness and homelessness and poverty and all sorts of inhumanities."

There was a silence. Each musician sat with his beer and his thought. Walter had hit the nail on the head.

"It would be easier for a camel to pass through the eye of a needle than for a rich man to enter the kingdom of heaven," said Scotty, breaking the deep silence.

"Thank you, Walter," remarked Chuck. "I can now understand why there is difference in people. Those of us associated with the arts never get rich, but we are usually more caring or, as you would say, more spiritual. It is sad when you think that, like musicians, great painters actually live in poverty and are never acclaimed for their work until after death. Then what happens? The unfeeling parasite puts a value on the poor dead guy's work and they divide the spoils of a lifetime. These people have no souls of their own, so they attempt to grab life from the artist's spiritual creation. So, you see, once again the so-called philanthropist has to own everything."

"That's very well put, Chuck," Walter acknowledged the piano player. "Another analogy could be the hunter who goes out and kills for sport. You will usually discover that he is a very solid individual. He hopes that the life he destroys will somehow stick to him. Stealing a life is the only way he can feel alive. Same is true for the professional soldier."

"So, you don't believe in killing animals either," inquired Jimmy.

"Not exactly Jimmy. When one needs food, the hunter then takes responsibility for the life destroyed. This is what our forefathers did years ago. But remember, I said the killing for sport. Why not shoot at a target as there is no need at present to kill for food?"

"Okay, Walter, I got it now," replied Jimmy.

"Getting back to the proletariat and the parasite," continued Walter, "what I see of the man in the street is that the more affluent he becomes, the more stupid he becomes. Take a look at the situation ashore. It is not just a case of booze anymore, but drugs are being abused on an even larger scale. And it is not the poor derelict on the street that is using all these drugs. It is now the affluent, rich areas of society that are into these practices."

"That's right," agreed Jimmy. "The masses never seem to take advantage of the good things in life. It appears the more money they acquire, the more degraded they become. I've been to some pretty spectacular private homes to play my gigs. The owners and guests were always surprised to learn that us band members do not partake of the vast variety of drugs that were available in these homes. And they call themselves the cream of our society!"

"Yes," agreed Walter. "It is sad, because there are some wonderful things to be enjoyed in this world, and drug abuse is not one of them. Remember the parasites we were talking about? Well, they are involved with this drug culture too. When you have a society that permits the existence of parasites, then these parasites will take advantage of any situation. What came first, the drugs or the parasites? Do we have to look far for the answer? Man has always exposed himself to exploitation, but it's getting worse. Why is it happening? Because he goes blindly through life from one situation to another. He never stops to ask himself if all these problems aren't meant to control. He never attempts to find the truth behind a new law or a corporate takeover or whatever. Every time a new law is instituted, it usually means more control over us. The availability of drugs is a method of control. It is much easier to control an idiot on drugs than a sane, able person who is thinking clearly. It has to start with the individual himself. He has to become aware of who and what he is, then he may become cognizant of this global game. As we have already said, it all comes down to two words – control and game. Now let me add this. If the perpetrators of these iniquities are not aware that they are doing unethical things to their fellow man, then God help them. And if they are aware of what they are doing, then they are already doomed. I am not talking of punishment from God or fire and brimstone here. The hell these unethical people face is much worse. He will experience what his victims went through, as it will all back fire on him. One must wear his pain in penance, and believe me, he will."

"Walter, I just want to make sure that I understand what you've been telling us," declared Scotty. "What you are suggesting is that the guy with all the mansions, Rolls Royces and living high on the hog, because of his own transgressions, could after his death wake up sucking a big black tit somewhere in Africa!" Chuck and Jimmy laughed at Scotty's ever brilliant summation.

"Why do you always have to be so down to earth in your descriptions?" admonished Walter. "But you are correct."

"Well," continued Scotty, "when you consider how nutty this planet is, we must all have been a shower of rotten bastards at one time or other."

"Amen to that," acknowledged Walter.

"Hey guys!" exclaimed Tom, the steward, entering the library. "I didn't see you bums at afternoon tea. What gives? Do you want some brought up here?"

"No," answered Jimmy. "Just tell Albee to bring some more beer for us and a fresh pot of tea for Walter."

"Thank you, Jimmy. I would appreciate some tea and some scones. If you can wrangle that, Tom," added Walter.

"Sure thing, sir. You're one of the boys. I'll be right back."

"How come all these years we seem to be subjected to all this control and never get to wise it? Is there a way to stop it now?" asked Jimmy.

"Remember what we said about Germany after World War I and how Hitler offered the German people the solution of their problem? Let's apply that to the situations today. We have a society of degenerates that is based on pure greed, booze, drugs, and sex. The homeless people are all over the place, and the economy, considering the value of the dollar, is on a constant decline. Add to that unemployment, legal and illegal immigration, and the national debt. In other words, there seems to be a gradual creeping or lowering of standards throughout the nation, and we are constantly told by the economists that because of the national debt, we are heading for disaster. You must remember if you put the economy in the hands of the bankers, to whose benefit will they run it? Looking at it objectively I'd say we are being set up for something requiring a solution that will be complete control over every aspect of your life, much like Germany's Hitler. The continual outcry in this country is fight against all forms of socialism, and yet that is where you're heading. I'm sure you have heard the saying; "what you resist you get." And here it is rearing its ugly head. Yes, my friends, unless the people become interested enough to see the game, this is where they're going. No more individual thought, but under the arm of big brother, as so oft times predicted. So, realize that all the negatives that are in evidence are being implemented slowly to bring about whatever big brother decides. The losers are you."

"Sure is a nasty mess," announced Jimmy. "Walter, you said that the people responsible lack soul and are functioning from a pure physical reality, "things." What method are they using to subjugate us besides what we have talked about?"

"Have you heard of the word "cult?" asked Walter, about to explain his thoughts.

"Yeah, sure," replied Jimmy.

"Now, most people associate the word "cult" with religion such as an idolatry. Worship of one leader or some strange practice. Right?"

"Right on," agreed Chuck. "And there are some real crazies in those cults."

"Well," began Walter, "what if I told you that every aspect of life is involved with a cult?"

"I don't get that at all," stated Chuck firmly.

"All right. Let's examine cult. It can be broken down into about four steps. First, you have to realize the nature of the game. We have already agreed that life is a game. Step number one would be the creators of the game. Step two would be those who are aware of the game but choose to play it regardless of its ethics. Step three are those who suspect there is a game but are not sure. Step four includes those who have no idea at all that a game even exists. Now what you have to realize is that no matter whether you work for a large company, belong to a religious or community group, or are a member of the armed forces, you are involved in a cult. What is the purpose of a cult? To sway you from individual thought and agree to accept the thinking of the game planners. Do you understand where I'm going with this?" asked Walter.

"Yes, I think so," answered Scotty slowly. "But how does that equate to life in general?"

"Let's go back to step number one. The creator of the game, considering what is almighty on this planet, would have to be the money controllers. You may even be surprised to learn that there are only a handful of them. Step number two are those who are aware of the game but are willing to play along without any regard to ethics. This could be the tax-free foundations that were created by the banking families to protect their wealth and control the American citizen. They achieve this not only by taxing John Doe Public but also through their involvement in the executive, judicial, and legislative branches of our government. Do you understand so far?"

"Yeah," agreed Scotty.

"This brings us to step three. Those who suspect there is a game but are not sure. This could be the politician. He may start his career with good intentions but eventually doesn't much care as long as he can feather his own nest. Last but not least are the workers who, as we have already mentioned, have no idea that there is a game being played nor that they are losing."

"Wow!" shouted Chuck. "It always comes down to the poor brown bagger. He always gets his ass kicked at every turn."

"Yeah," interrupted Jimmy, "whether he has a job, pays his taxes, goes to the army, or even if he buys a car, he always gets the golden shaft."

"Now I know why we musicians run into so much trouble. Whether it's ship's officers, club owners, or whatever, we refuse to play the game," Scotty summarized.

"What you are really fighting against is the control mechanism," explained Walter. "If you involve yourself in a game that is ethical, then you will probably observe the rules. This is a must if you want to continue with the game. These club owners are trying to enforce control and, being the rebellious bunch that you are, this can only cause friction."

"Funny how all this kind of talk brings to mind past situations I have been in where I was successful but could not remain," continued Scotty. "I have done very well in each industry that I have tried ashore. But then suddenly I would become unhappy and just walk away. At first, I thought it was because I was not playing my drums and therefore putting my talent in non-existence, but now I see the game. So long as I was left alone to do my job, I was number one in the firm. One manager actually told the company I was working for to leave me alone because of my excellent production. I was having a ball until that manager was replaced by one of those industrial morons who tried to use the control mechanism. My experience has given me a good definition for these manager types – more bullshit. So, I left an excellent job even though I was making more money than I could ever hope to earn by playing drums. I see now that it was CONTROL – CONTROL – CONTROL. So, fuck 'em all. Roll on the hydrogen bomb and let's have a bash at the angels."

"I never met anyone who could go so fast from the ridiculous to the perpendicular," scolded Walter on his inability to remain serious.

"Oh, that's a good one," laughed Scotty. "Where did you get that? Have you been stealing my lines?"

The group had a good laugh at Scotty's warped sense of humor. This little diversion gave time for each musician to take another gulp of beer.

"How about all those crusades going on in the States? Like the pro and anti-abortion people with their mass demonstrations," continued Jimmy in a more serious vein. "I find that even though I may agree with their cause, I am irked at the methods they use and find myself angry at these agitators."

"This is very simple," replied Walter. "It is a classic example of the cult mechanism at work. Just locate the creator of the game and go from there. Demonstrations and riots are usually directed at the sordid part of the mind anyway. Stimuli is provided, and mass insanity is the result. Could that be why you feel uncomfortable when witnessing such scenes?"

"Yeah," replied Jimmy, brightening at the realization. "I knew it had to be something simple."

"But remember, Jimmy, you must let others be what they are and not resent them. This is for your own sanity. Anytime you resent what you consider to be bad, you are only giving power to that negative and weakening your own position. If you give enough resentment, you will actually become that which you object to."

"Christ! Does that mean our bandleader, Bob, will soon look and act like Abe?" remarked Scotty, unable to control his desire to make a joke.

"Talking about Abe," continued Jimmy, again being very serious, "there seems to be a constant hammering by the Jews of their fear of persecution. This is something you can read in any newspaper and has been going on for such a long time. How does this relate to what we just discussed?"

"Good example, Jimmy, so let's take a look at it. The Jews, like everyone else, are just spiritual entities inhabiting bodies. We know that this is a very difficult subject and totally beyond the reality of the usual Homo Sapiens. But the power of every being is very strong and is constantly involved in creative thought, whether that thought be negative or positive. When you have a mass agreement, such as you have among the Jewish people, it can become a problem for them. They, like everyone else, will have to come to the realization that we are each responsible for our own creation. As long as they put all their attention on persecution, they are only giving power to that negative. Thus, you have more persecution. You add to this the guilt-punishment cycle that exists in everyone's universe, and you soon realize that is indeed a two-way street. The next problem you encounter with this continual fear of persecution is that people tend to handle any problem with the physical universe by trying to own it. We know that the more material objects we own, the more solid we become, and less spiritual. This puts the person in need of a religious practice that will provide him with sympathy and solace. It becomes a vicious cycle all because of resentment."

"Jesus! Is there anything you don't know, Walter?" asked Chuck. "You make it all sound really simple and it makes so much sense. I think we musicians are better off than the money controllers and the rich."

"We sure are," interrupted Jimmy, "because the ones who are going to have their faces trod into the ground are the same ones who are doing it to their fellow man right now."

"The problem as I see it," began Scotty, "is the common man's ignorance of himself as a spirit. He isn't aware that he is setting his own trap for the future."

"Well said," acknowledged Walter. "But how do you know that I'm not just another nut playing a game with you and leading you on?"

"No way!" answered Chuck eagerly. "One thing about a musician, when he hears something good, he gets that little chill up the back of his neck. Shit! I've been getting plenty of them. How about you guys?"

"Better believe it!" answered Scotty.

"Cool chills, man," agreed Jimmy, who looked deep in thought.

"Well, gents, I thank you for that. Jimmy, was there something else you wanted to say?"

"Yes, actually. Getting back to the abortion issue, how do you feel about it?"

"Well, Jimmy, this is another unfortunate situation that results from the most aberrated game on the planet, sex. It's like closing the barn door after the horse has bolted. I'm not so much concerned with the rights and wrongs of abortion. I am more interested in a way to handle the insane game sex has become. This goes back to the question of destruction, and I'm opposed to that in all forms. But what is really going on here? Religious leaders, medicos, psychologists, and members of the public are voicing their own opinion on whether or not the fetus is a human being. I have found that people only argue when they don't know what the hell they are talking about. I can give you my theory, but you will not know for sure if I'm correct until you experience it. Do you want me to continue?"

"Sure," said Jimmy.

"Let's hear it," implored Scotty.

"Okay here goes," replied Walter. "Let's try a little drama. If two bodies are laying on the floor and one is dead and the other is alive, what is missing from the dead body?"

"The life force!" answered Jimmy.

"The soul!" replied Chuck.

"The spirit!" suggested Scotty.

"Good answers, fellows. We have an understanding and an agreement that something other than a physical reality does exist. Other studies," continued Walter, "refer to Karma, Elan, and other such names as we mentioned in one of our other talks. But it is pretty obvious that the dead body has ceased to function for the lack of it. Right?"

"Right!" replied Scotty, eager to learn another mystery.

"Now for the part of the scenario that causes all the problem and debate. Is that fetus alive or a dead body? If we agree that without the entity it's a dead body, then when does it attain life? It has a heartbeat. Blood and other organs are functioning with the aid of the mother's body. Remember these are all parts of the physical universe. There still requires the entrance of the spiritual entity to continue surviving. Let me caution you again that this is only a theory that you can choose to accept or not."

The three musicians agreed with nods of the heads. They were a curious trio waiting in great anticipation for what Walter would share. He had been correct with all his explanations so far.

"Now the joining of the body and the spirit is referred to as the assumption," began Walter with complete attention from his pupils, "and this usually takes place as the baby leaves the body. In some instances, it can take place in the womb just prior to birth, but mostly after. What we have been calling the spirit is simply – YOU. I know we talked about his before, and I understand a lot of the things we have discussed may sound unreal, but I am confident that one day each of you will come to know the truth. Now while we are of the subject birth, I want to tell you something else about spirits. You, the spirit, are not male or female. Spirits have no identification other than what we agree to as we got through each lifetime. Spirits are not Catholics or Protestants or Jews or Hindus or Buddhists. Spirits are inflicted with these identities when they acquire a body and become immersed in the game of living."

"So," asked Chuck, "you may be clean enough when you pick up a body, but you are then subjected to all the outside influences that shape your future."

"That's right, Chuck!"

"Like the blind leading the blind," added Scotty.

"Correct. If you are fortunate enough to have sane parents, you may survive the whole mess. Remember, you carry with you the guilt from your previous experiences. A very good example of this is found in the Dicken's classic, "The Christmas Carol," when Scrooge is confronted with the ghost of his dead partner, Jacob Marley, who was in chains and shackles. Do you remember what Marley said to Scrooge? "I forged these chains in life." Marley was condemned to wear them in infinity. That is a very good analogy of what I've been talking about this afternoon."

"So," began Scotty, eager to elaborate, "the answer would have to be live an ethical life. It sounds so easy, but how can you do that in such an insane environment? Every spirit has to put up with stupid parents, religious leaders and their crap, dumb school teachers, and all the nutty monsters you go to school with. When you are a little older, you are at the mercy of the industrialist in the work place. As though it wasn't bad enough, those madmen we call our leaders get a war going, stick a gun in your hand, and send you into their battlefields. That has to be the greatest laxative known to man. Now I ask you, what chance has a guy got with all this propaganda and brainwashing? No wonder he has all this resentment! Is there any way out?"

"Well, Scotty," Walter began in his understanding tone, "maybe, unknown to you, the wheels are already set in motion to escape the sordidness that you have described. You are one step ahead of most people in the world by your questioning and searching for the truth. But remember this, all of you, everyone has to go through what he has to go through. We are not all ready at that same time. Involvement in drugs of any kind is only a means to hide from the guilt that has been created and cannot be confronted. One day when the drug or alcohol abuser comes up to realizing that he needs help, he may be ready to take responsibility for his past. Now you know why these substances are so popular among the rich throughout the world. Until then, he'll just remain on the merry-go-round playing the same silly games over and over and over again."

"I think this man is stuck in a very precarious situation," continued Scotty. "I hope that one day he will wake up, take a good look at himself and begin to handle these problems."

"In the meantime," instructed Walter, "we each have to try not to be resentful or judgmental. This will not only help to keep you sane, but it will further your own spirituality. Also realize that salvaging YOU, the spirit, is more important than those body games. Once you have achieved the heights of spiritual awareness, you will realize that there are far better games to be played. Look at the identities that people like to have and remember that you are none of these. You are only what you agree to be. Well, gentlemen, it has been a very enjoyable afternoon, and I hope I haven't bored you too much."

"On the contrary," replied Jimmy, "I don't know when I have gotten so interested in something. I wish to thank you for an enlightening experience."

Jimmy described the feelings of Chuck and Scotty perfectly when he expressed his own thoughts. The four men stood to say good-bye. Each musician shook hands with Walter.

"See you in the dining room," said Walter as he left his friends.

The trio headed below to prepare for the cocktail session. Tonight, they would be dressed in dark tuxedos because of the cooling coastal weather. They entered Bob's cabin to find the rest of the band already celebrating with the usual splicing of the mainbrace.

"Where have you three been hiding all day?" asked Bob as he poured them the obligatory drink.

"We spent the whole afternoon in the library," stated Jimmy.

"Were you trying to read all the books before we dock tomorrow?" asked Abe.

"Actually," replied Scotty, "we were with that passenger, Walter, I was telling you about. He is a very interesting and spiritual man. He opened our eyes to how the Eastern part of the world is still involved with recognizing man as a spirit while the Western Civilization has drifted far away from this premise."

"That's all you guys need," quipped Bob, waving his hands and rolling his eyes. "That's all I need, three of my men dabbling in the occult. What's next? Are you going to hold a séance down in here in the mortuary?"

Abe floated off in his desires to have another drink while the others sat quietly during Bob's little tantrum. Scotty was not amused with Bob's criticism, but suddenly thought back to what he'd learned today.

"Bob!" Scotty said, firm but with kindness. "Do not resent!"

Bob realized he had overstepped the bounds of good taste in an attempt to belittle the person whom Scotty admired.

"You know, Bob," continued Scotty, "That's just how the uninformed usually react to any mention of the spirit. This man we spent the afternoon with really makes life so simple. There is none of the hocus pocus you get from the uninformed mental practitioners. Instead of addressing the spirit, which has all the power, and Bob, the spirit means you, all we do is direct all our attention to this hunk of meat called the body." Scotty was lecturing the whole band, not just Bob, and they were listening. "Whether it's the Hollywood star, beauty contestants, or muscle men it's always the body, the body, the body. The body has now become the symbol of worship for the entire world and provides a helluva good living for the doctors every time it belches or farts out of tune."

"Well," confided Bob, "I see your point." Bob knew he had been a little facetious with his remark and that he was also a little jealous of Walter. This mere passenger had stolen the limelight from him. He would try to remember Scotty's words about resenting.

"Hey! Less shit and more booze," demanded Abe holding forth his empty glass for a refill. He had that same silly grin on his face that reminded everyone of the first night Abe got drunk with Scotty and Chuck.

"Would you listen to that little shit?" laughed Jimmy.

"Scratch a pussy and you come up with a tiger," reminded Tex.

"And don't you assholes forget it either," responded Abe pointing to the group. "The name's Tiger. Now give us a fucking drink!" This expression had become Abe's trademark and always brought a laugh from his friends.

"No more booze for you," scolded Bob, realizing now that Abe must have been on the sauce all afternoon. "And if I need any more shit from you, I'll squeeze your head. Remember we have a show to play tonight and I don't want any repeat performance like your first show night."

"Okay then. I'll be good, but can I make up for it at the farewell party tonight?" asked Abe who was smart enough, even fortified with liquor, not to go at it with Bob.

"Yes, of course, Abe. Tom is preparing a nipple and bottle of baby formula for you tonight."

"Oh, fuck you guys," replied Abe, leaving the room sheepishly to the rounds of laughter.

Passengers attending the show were once again attired in civilian clothes as the formal wear was packed away for disembarking tomorrow. The nightclub was filled with the usual roaring drunks who were not interested in the show. These passengers have to take advantage of the last night of duty-free drinks. The sea going romancers, who had previously sworn undying love as they banged away merrily all week, were now cooling their heels. They realized that tomorrow means the real world!

Forward in the forecastle, the crew were conspiring how to get even with Captain Breathwaite. He would have to pay for interfering with tradition.

Scotty contemplated all that had happened in the past nine days as he sat behind his drums. As he thought, he realized that the only thing that is permanent is change. The crew would never be the same after the Staffy. And Walter had left a lasting impression on him. He knew that what he once considered to be fun and games was on the way out. He had often heard that smoking, drinking, and whoring were the only things worth living for, but was able now to view the source of such pronouncements.

"Ach' well," he thought feeling rather Scottish tonight, "this will be my last hurrah and I'm sure tomorrow will bring forth new adventures."

The show went off without a hitch. The little gang headed for the nightclub to meet the gals. Chuck's three broads were waiting for him eagerly. Mike had his Valerie. Bob was with Boobs and Scotty was with Lorraine. The shop girls who had gone ashore with them in Curacao were advised to meet them in the Inner Sanctum as they were not permitted in the lounges.

Everyone was half in the bag and feeling no pain as they trooped below. A few male passengers, who had underwritten the musician's alcoholic intake during the cruise, also fell in after hearing there was to be a party.

Abe tried to entice Madeline to the Inner Sanctum, but she had regained her lady-like disposition and brushed off his request and him. Abe felt like he had been patted on the head like some kind of lap dog. Here's your biscuit, now get lost.

"Fucking broads!" he muttered as he headed back to his cabin. "Now I know what they mean when they say how women chew you up and spit you out."

The Inner Sanctum was in full swing. Bob's tape player was belting out Steve and Edie. Peggy Lee could be heard from the Odd Couple's cabin. And for good measure Chuck had Big Band Jazz blasting in his room. All the cabin doors were open and couples were scurrying to and fro wherever their fancy took them. Males were chasing females up and down the corridor. The stink of tobacco and booze was everywhere. If ever there was a scene to describe the glee of insanity, this was it. The only difference between the Inner Sanctum and the funny farm was that the nut hut house has restrictions.

A couple hours later, the remnants of the party were assembled in Bob's cabin. Abe, flying as high as kite, was standing in the middle of the cabin addressing the gang like some crazy evangelist. His loyal listeners were cheering him on.

"One week and four days ago, I joined this motley group aboard this floating whorehouse," Abe began his dissertation.

"Hurrah!" came the drunken yet gleeful reply.

"I was a destitute child, innocent, and not yet de-flowered."

"Hurrah!"

"In that short span of time, I have been to the top of the mountain."

"Hallelujah!" they encouraged Abe.

"I have been to the bottom to the ocean."

"Hallelujah!"

"And somewhere in between I lost my fucking cherry!"

"Hallelujah!!"

"There's only one thing I'd like to ask," paused Abe as he looked at Bob.

"What's that, Tiger?" came the reply.

"Can I come back?"

"Sure shit you can," Bob and the band replied in unison. "You are one of the boys!"

"Hallelujah!" replied Abe, giving a toast of his glass.

"Tonight," began Scotty, taking center stage as Bob replenished the drinks, "we are going to finish the cruise with the immortal Auld Lang Syne. This song was written by one of the greatest beings ever to grace this crazy planet. A man who I have always revered and respected. A great humanitarian who left a legacy to the world in his poems. Before we get to that, I'm going to give you all a treat. I'm going to

296

recite another of his poems. It is one of my favorites and is called, "Is There for Honest Poverty.""

"Hurrah!" they shouted. "Let's hear it for Scotty!"

"But first I will have to inform you that because of your low state in life, you uncultured colonials, I will be forced to translate as best I can that you may, in your subconscious stupor, understand. Okay?" Scotty asked.

"Okay," they all cried.

"Yeah, we know when we are in the presence of greatness," added Tex.

"Hurrah!" came the cheer again. Scotty waited for them to settle down before commencing the beautiful words.

"Is there for honest poverty

That hangs his head an' a' that?

That coward slave, we pass him by-

We dare be poor for a' that!

For a' that, an' a' that,

Our toils obscure, an' a' that,

The ranks is but the guinea's stamp,

The man's the gold for a' that.

What though on common fare we dine,

Wear cheap clothes, and a' that?

Give fools their silks, and knaves their wine-

A man's a man for a' that.

For a' that, and a' that,

    Their tinsel show, an' a' that,

The Honest man, tho' e'er sae poor,

    Is King o' men for a' that.

You see yon fellow call 'a lord,'

    Who struts and stares, an' a' that?

Tho' hundreds worship at his word,

    He's still a fool for a' that.

For a' that, an' a' that,

    His ribband, star, an' a' that,

The man o' independent mind,

    He look an' laughs at a' that.

A prince can make a belted knight,

    A marquis, duke, an' a' that!

But an honest man's above his might-

    Good faith, he must not fall that!

For a' that, an' a' that,

    Their dignities, an' a' that,

The pith o' sense an' pride o' worth

Are higher rank than a' that.

Then let us pray that come it may

(As come it will for a' that)

That Sense and Worth o'er a' the earth

Shall reign supreme an' a' that!

For a' that, an' a' that,

It's comin' yet for a' that,

That man to man the world o'er

Shall brothers be for a' that."

The room was in a hush as Scotty finished. Everyone sat enthralled at his delivery of the very meaningful words. They soon burst into applause, and he took his bow.

"Okay," instructed Scotty, "let's join hands now, and let's hear it loud and clear."

The S.S. Nectar sailed into the cool night toward New York to the strains of Auld Lang Syne emanating from her stern. This simple little song seemed to join these newfound friends in spirit as it was intended by Scotland's bard, Robert Burns.

DAY 10
NEW YORK

Scotty arose from his bunk not feeling too bad considering the party the night before. His roommate was, of course, unconscious, as were the other musicians. Cleaning up, Scotty dressed and donned his favorite suburban coat with the fur collar and left the cabin. All was deathly quiet in the Inner Sanctum. Even the engines were barely turning over, indicating preparations for berthing were underway. Scotty headed for his favorite spot, forward beneath the bridge wing. He surveyed his moving kingdom as the tugs gently eased the ship round the end of the wharf where she would tie her lines. It always gave him a thrill to watch a ship docking from this vantage point. Maybe something to do with coming home. Who knows, maybe one day he might view docking in Scotland from the bridge of a ship? Dismissing his thoughts, he walked aft on the second part of his quest to find Walter before he left the ship. Entering the lounge, he found his friend looking dapper and ready to disembark.

"Morning, Walter. I was afraid I might have missed seeing you off."

"Good morning, Scotty," replied Walter who always seemed to

have an alert and pleasant disposition. "Don't worry, I would have made it a point to see you before leaving the ship. Sit down and join me in a cup of coffee." Albee was just approaching with a piping hot pot and two cups as if Walter had planned this meeting.

"You know, Walter, I still don't know what it is you do in private life. If it is not too personal? I know you are not a preacher. Are you some sort of teacher or involved in psychology or something?" asked Scotty.

"No. No, Scotty actually I make my living writing. Nothing to brag about. Just what pleases me," responded Walter.

"Really," said Scotty. "I would think that with the knowledge and awareness you have you could solve all the problems of man in your writing. Or maybe you have already produced such materials."

"Aha! But there's the rub, Scotty, to quote Mr. Shakespeare. That is where the danger lies in thinking you know too much. It's always the desire of the scholar who has achieved some knowledge of the Spiritual Universe to hasten forth and become involved in a crusade to offer solutions to all of man's problems. But that can prove dangerous and I'll tell you why. Man's only means of survival, at his present mental state, is the culmination of problems. The only way he can grow is to handle each problem and go on to the next one. The mistake many people make is offering solutions. A man could kill you for taking his problems away. So, you must never, never give him the solution."

"You've got me there, Walter. I've lost you somewhere."

"Okay, Scotty. If you understand the nature of problems then you would be able to direct the person to form his own solution. That is the optimum survival for him. As long as you do not offer him a solution. Understand?"

"I think so," replied Scotty. "In other words, if you give a man the solution to his problem, he will just give you another problem and this will never end."

"Exactly, Scotty. So, here's what I want you to do." Walter opened his briefcase and took out a book and handed it to Scotty. "My address and phone number are inside. I want you to read and study this book well. If and when you are ready, please contact me. Do I have your agreement on that?"

"You sure do, Walter," agreed Scotty as he accepted the gift.

The ship was now tied to her berth. Gangways were in position when Scotty and Walter heard some commotion and noise outside. They both left the room and walked to the port side rail to investigate. Looking over the side, they were amazed to the see at least two hundred of the crew marching down the gangway onto and through the upper dock area in Indian File with hands on the shoulders of the man in front. Their chanting grew louder and louder.

"We hate Breathwaite! We hate Breathwaite! We hate Breathwaite!"

All of a sudden hundreds of balloons with the same phrase inscribed on them were released from the forecastle area. This was a well-orchestrated plan, because there was an abundance of television cameras shooting the entire event. Someone had called ahead before the ship even entered the harbor.

Poor Staff Captain Breathwaite was looking down from the bridge wing observing the gala in his honor and feeling devastated. Whether he was right or wrong, he knew that next week he would be on a freighter heading for the China Seas.

"Well," said Scotty, dumbfounded as he looked at Walter, "can you beat that? Boy, there's no end to revenge when you try to take away a boozer's bottle."

"Ha! Ha!" laughed Walter.

"Is that the Staffy's punishment for trying to offer a solution?" asked Scotty.

"Very good! You catch on quick! But as we said, the Staffy, like everyone else, has to keep doing it until he gets it right. If I may be permitted one last parting piece of advice, Scotty," as Walter stood with both hands resting on the rail.

"What's that, Walter?" asked Scotty, waiting in anticipation. Anything his mentor had to say he regarded as another bonus in wisdom.

"Take a piece of paper and write down all names of your associates. Then write what you consider to be wrong with each of them. For example, something they do or say that you don't like. Next, write what they could do to improve. After you have done all of this apply it to yourself. That is where you are coming from. Understand?"

"Yeah," answered Scotty with an expression of gratification, "I see what you've been getting at this entire trip."

Walter extended his hand. Scotty accepted it and felt as though they had become one.

"Good-bye, my friend. I know I'll be hearing from you. You'll be okay."

"Good-bye, Walter. I feel my future is pretty safe now."

Walter left the deck and Scotty headed for the music locker.

THE END

BUT

FOR SCOTTY

THE BEGINNING

PICTURES

RMS MAURETANIA. West Indies Cruise 1961.

GETTING AWAY FROM JOE SPECK

ABOUT THE AUTHOR

Samuel Fullerton resides in sunny Clearwater, Florida. He has one daughter, Cheryl, who lives in California. He traveled around the globe six different times during his music career playing the drums. Sam even met the Beatles before they were famous during one of his trips. At 92 years young, he enjoys doing martial arts that he learned from the Grandmaster Jhoon Goo Rhee. Mr. Fullerton is working on a second book and is proof that it is never too late to start a new adventure.

www.ingramcontent.com/pod-product-compliance
Lightning Source LLC
Chambersburg PA
CBHW050922030726
47503CB00007BB/2428